AMERICAN INDIAN LITERATURE
AND CRITICAL STUDIES SERIES

GERALD VIZENOR, GENERAL EDITOR

DARK RIVER

Also by Louis Owens

FICTION

Wolfsong (Albuquerque, 1991; Norman, 1995; Paris, 1996)
The Sharpest Sight (Norman, 1992, 1995; Paris, 1994)
Bone Game (Norman, 1994, 1996; Paris, 1998)
Nightland (New York, 1996, 1997)

NONFICTION

John Steinbeck's Re-Vision of America (Athens, Ga., 1985)
(with Tom Colonnese) *American Indian Novelists: An Annotated Critical Bibliography* (New York, 1985)
The Grapes of Wrath: Trouble in the Promised Land (New York, 1989)
(editor) *American Literary Scholarship: An Annual, 1990* (Durham, N.C., 1992)
Other Destinies: Understanding the American Indian Novel (Norman, 1992, 1994)
Mixedblood Messages: Literature, Film, Family, Place (Norman, 1998)

DARK RIVER
A Novel

By Louis Owens

UNIVERSITY OF OKLAHOMA PRESS : NORMAN

This is a work of fiction. Names, characters, places, and incidents are either the product of the author's imagination or are used fictitiously, and any resemblance to actual events, locales, or persons, living or dead, is entirely coincidental.

Library of Congress Cataloging-in-Publication Data

Owens, Louis.
   Dark river : a novel / by Louis Owens.
      p.   cm. — (American Indian literature and critical studies
   series ; v. 30)
      ISBN 0-8061-3115-2 (alk. paper)
      1. Indians of North America—Arizona—Fiction.   2. Choctaw
   Indians—Fiction.   I. Title.   II. Series.
   PS3565.W567D37   1999
   813'.54—dc21   98-37695
                                                           CIP

Dark River, A Novel is Volume 30 in the American Indian Literature and Critical Studies Series.

The paper in this book meets the guidelines for permanence and durability of the Committee on Production Guidelines for Book Longevity of the Council on Library Resources, Inc.∞

2 3 4 5 6 7 8 9 10 11

DARK RIVER

1   Thunder flowed along the deep cut of the river canyon a few miles to the east and spread through the shadowed piñon and juniper forest around him, shaking tree and rock and hanging sheets of fire in the low, bunched clouds. Sparse stars shone through breaks in the thunderheads, and from a patch of opaque sky a crescent moon caught and glimmered in one glassy eye, silver curve over dark pupil doubled and engorged on the flat surface of stagnant water to his right. The odor of day-old blood hung in the charged, summer monsoon air, and he could hear but not see the buzzing insects around spilled intestines, the sound reminding him of the electrical hiss that came just before a lightning strike. And just as it did when lightning was close, the hair on his arms and neck stood up and sent a wiry tension through muscle and bone.

He unfastened the waist belt and chest strap and swung his pack to the ground, the sweat-soaked back of his shirt instantly cool in the night air. All the way up from a week on the river he'd watched the sheet lightning, seeing an occasional spindly fork touch one of the higher peaks, and wondered if he'd beat the rain to his truck near Heifer Tank. He'd gone farther downriver from his camp that morning than he'd planned, trying unsuccessfully to get a glimpse of the desert bighorn herd sometimes in that part of the canyon. The sheep hugged the cliffs, dull colored, slow, and invisible. He'd taken his time going back, fitting his rod together for a few casts in the big pools, hooking a smallmouth bass nearly every time only to reach a hand down and let each slap free into the depths, enjoying the green-gold flash of their disappearance. By the time he'd gotten back to camp and packed up, evening was coming on fast, the typical afternoon thunderstorm over, but the low sky vaguely threatening more serious rain for the night. The climb up had been slow, as he angled his way through ten trailless miles of piñon, juniper, prickly pear, and steep, rocky ground, paralleling the river canyon for three hours and hoping to hit the reservation road as close as possible to where he'd parked the tribal pickup.

The smell had stopped him a few minutes after he'd struck the road, and he'd seen it almost at once, a dark bulk right in his path. The elk's head lay a few feet from the edge of the muddy cattle pond called Heifer Tank, with antlers so enormous that they seemed to stretch toward the surrounding trees like filaments in a complex web, lengthened by the partial moon. In his exhaustion, he imagined a great spider's trap, and he stepped back for a moment to study the situation. When lightning flared, the filaments leapt even further, tendrils curling around trunk and branch momentarily before receding with the vanished light. He steeled his nerves and approached the thing. Something white hung motionless from a fork of antler.

The air stirred, and what he now understood to be a feather moved slightly. He remained still for a moment and listened, hearing a familiar vague commotion at the far end of the pond and the yammering of a pair of coyotes further off toward the canyon. In the trees not far from the water, an owl began a deep, thoughtful-sounding hooing, the call repeated at exact intervals with a questioning resonance at the end. *Ishkitini*, he thought, remembering, as he did every time, his grandmother's stories and hardening himself against them. The old woman stank, a smell of sweat, death, old age, forgetfulness, and chewing tobacco. She knew the meanings of those things that cut into the kerf of their lives two thousand miles from where he was now, knew how to answer them, and feared nothing. The grandmother was *alikchi*, he'd heard a man at the country store whisper. That meant her dreams roamed at night through the black woods, winding into lives to change and twine. It

4

meant his grandmother was feared, could not be touched, but as a child he could see nothing the old lady gained by such power if she could not save her own son, his father.

If an owl called at night and there was no answering call, it wasn't an owl but a spirit, a witch, something evil that had sought you out. He knew this was true because the owl had called for three nights before his father's death, had been there when he went to sleep and when he awoke. Nalusachito, too, stalked the swamps, had followed his father home with its woman's scream and leaped on the roof of their cabin, crying its panther anger at the missed shadow, *shilup* or *shilombish*, he could not remember which.

Each time he heard an owl call in these distant mountains so far from that Choctaw world, he tried to remind himself that it was just an old woman's stories; owls were a crucial part of the ecosystem, even protected by the federal government. It didn't help that the Black Mountain tribe, too, had stories of owls. Owl tore out hearts and flew away with them in the night.

His whole body ached as he bent and found the flashlight in the top pocket of his pack. Straightening, he shivered despite the warm summer air and swung the flashlight toward the water. When he switched the light on, the moon dove beneath the black surface of the tank, and at the far end half a dozen of the wild reservation cattle scattered and vanished in dark silhouettes with kicking feet and humped backs. "Slow elk," some people called them, but these cattle were anything but slow. Even Herefords, after a few generations in the back-country, developed lean muscles and intelligent eyes. More than once he'd seen a group of heifers circle calves and lower their horns menacingly when he stumbled upon them miles back in the remote corners of the reservation. Mountain lions and coyotes turned mush-brained domestic cattle into smart, tough survivors very quickly, sculpting deep chests and narrow hindquarters out of blocky meat producers. Those cattle ran like deer and swam the flooding river like otters. The only animal he feared in all of the so-called wilderness was a wild cow with a calf.

He moved the flashlight toward the remains, and a thousand infinitely small creatures squirmed in the light, burrowing deeper into the guts. Shutting the light off, he walked a hundred feet further up the road to where he'd hidden his pickup in the trees a week before. When he started the truck and switched on the headlights, the spindly juniper and piñon trees looked angular and crowded, and as he maneuvered out of the tangle onto the road and drove to the tank he could see a few isolated drops of rain curving in the lights. This time of year the sky could threaten terrible floods but simply scatter a handful of drops before moving on. Everything was unpredictable except the daily afternoon thunderstorm, which could be a torrent or a sprinkle that might not even touch the earth.

Out of the truck again, he bent close to study the feather in the headlights. The rounded flight feather of an owl, it had been tied to the antler with a piece of gut, a large spot of blood darkening the nearly white quill. Ishkitini. He shook his head. Owl medicine was the worst thing they could do if they wanted to scare someone. Owls meant ghosts and death. Someone was either very powerful, very brave, or very careless, or all of that.

Leaving the head, he carried his backpack to the cab of the truck, leaning it against the passenger door, and then fished a folded plastic tarp from behind the seat. In a few minutes he had the elk head wrapped in the clear tarp and levered up into the pickup bed. Sam Baca would shit his pants when he saw it, a huge trophy bull with at least six points on each side, a head worth probably ten thousand.

As he was walking around the front of the truck, a spark of color caught in the light. He moved close and crouched over an empty casing, the brass glinting dully. He picked up the cartridge casing and held it close to one headlight. "Thirty-forty," he said out loud. "Jesus Christ." The mark of the firing pin was faint and off-center. He could think of only one .30-.40

on the whole reservation, and it wouldn't be hard to match the firing-pin mark on the cartridge to the ancient gun that fired it. "Damn," he said aloud as he slipped the shell into his pants pocket and turned toward the truck.

Ordinarily this was one of his favorite places, a thirty-mile drive from the tribe's game and fish headquarters that took him up a long escarpment from the White River and across a mesa that rolled for miles into rougher hills broken by good-sized streams full of small trout. This time of summer, the grasses on the high mesas were heavy and green from the rains, and the air was sweet with pine, cedar, and damp grama. Eight miles to the southeast from Heifer Tank was a sheer edge of the Dark River canyon, the place he'd just walked out of, where the river slowed and pooled in long, deep corners, its warmer water filled with trailing moss and smallmouth bass. Twisted junipers lined cracks in the canyon walls in that part of the river, and cholla cactus and prickly pear grew amid cottonwoods close to the water's edge. From there the river curved for fifty miles through dryer and lower country until it joined the Salt River and died in barren desert reservoirs above Phoenix. He knew because he'd walked every foot of it right to the first dam and then turned around and walked back. In his first years on the reservation, he had walked the entire one hundred and twenty miles of river, several times. He had sat on a red rock outcropping and imagined using a sniper scope to kill every single one of the flaccid people on houseboats that floated above a dead river. But he wouldn't do that. Jacob Nashoba was adjusted.

If he went north from where he stood, he could cut across the great oxbow curve of the Dark and in a single day's hike arrive at the same canyon forty-five miles upstream, where the water was fast and cold and held big rainbows and spawning browns in the shadows of tall pondorosa pines. He preferred that northern stretch and liked to imagine the time, a hundred years before, when stories said that spawning steelhead trout and salmon had swum all the way up from the Sea of Cortez.

7

Maybe the stories were just somebody's fantasies, but he liked to imagine those beautiful fish slipping through desert streams toward the far mountains, silvery flashes beneath saguaro shadows drawn by memory as old as the desert and mountains themselves. Now the river no longer crossed the desert, and there was no connection to the sea, the mother water itself. He thought of dynamiting the dams, sending a wall of water through Tempe and Phoenix all the way to the gulf. He liked to imagine desert animals watching that water racing down the ancient path toward the ocean. The animals wouldn't be surprised, because the water had been stopped for such a short time. The eagle would remember when his ancestors had watched for fish in the same river that had temporarily vanished. The deer would recall coming to the water at evening to drink two hundred years before, flocks of white-winged doves startled from the stream's edge, puma and jaguar tracks in the mud causing taut muscles. Two or three human generations were not even a blink of a deer's eye.

As he climbed back into the truck, the owl called from the trees again, a single long note followed by several shorter ones like some kind of code. He started the engine and drove away, forcing the owl and the rifle cartridge out of his thoughts with images of the river canyon in its long, arcing fall toward the Arizona desert. What must it have been like to see the rivers come together and flow across those hundreds of miles of desert? Maybe someone at Black Mountain remembered stories about that time, but if so they probably wouldn't tell him, except perhaps Shorty Luke, whom he'd have to speak with pretty soon anyway.

Lightning continued to flash in layers across the clouds, leaving streams of fire for an instant before the low rumbling of thunder covered the truck's clatter. Here and there stars still shone through odd clearings, and the crescent moon played a disappearing game with each turn of the road and shift in the distant winds. He rolled his window down and breathed in the damp air heavy with cedar fragrance. It took only one such breath to know why cedar was sacred. The aroma lay over the mesa with a healing weight.

In daylight he might have seen one or two elk, a few deer, and hawks by the score, maybe a bear shambling away or a lanky coyote sitting in the tall grass watching with a tongue-hanging grin. At night his headlights would pick up disembodied eyes staring from meadows or from brush beside the road. But this night he kept his eyes fixed on the road and was already on the switchbacks heading down to the White River bridge before he knew it.

The truck moved past the tall brick shells of the old Indian school, empty now but dark and haunted by so much unhappiness, looking precisely like an abandoned prison. The school had been built on the ruins of the old cavalry fort, both institutions designed to contain and erase Indians. Dead cottonwoods hovered around the buildings, their bare branches stark and disturbing. He didn't bother to look down at the river as he crossed the bridge. Running just behind the old school grounds, the White was shallow and littered from the reservation homes and small tribal capital a couple of miles upstream. He always tried to avoid looking at the dirty and exhausted river when he crossed the bridge, even at night. Somebody should clean it up, but the garbage would be back in a few weeks. Better to let the annual high water wash it all downstream at least once a year.

At the game and fish office he drove to the rear and opened the big sliding door, removing the plastic tarp and dragging the elk head into the back room where his boss, Sam Baca, couldn't miss it. Then he locked the door, got into the pickup, and began the twenty-five-mile drive to the corner of the reservation where he lived.

That's what they say.

2   He was drinking his second cup of coffee and reading Hemingway when the phone rang. Leaning forward in

the swivel chair, he slid a pair of hackle pliers into the book, picked up the receiver, and sighed, hearing the amplified wind of his own breath.

"Yeah, Sam, I put it there. Surprised it took you so long to call. Right by Heifer Tank. No shit."

He listened to the phone for a moment with his eyes closed, his vision of Sam Baca too vivid. In the front office of the tribal game and fish headquarters, Sam would be sitting surrounded by dead, stuffed animals artistically arranged. They even had a stuffed wolf in there, a show for rich white hunters, as though they were in Africa or somewhere.

"Right. That's what I said. Heifer Tank. Yeah, large caliber; you should have ballistics run on it. Yeah, I already wrote the report. Someone heard shots at Pachita Lake? No, Sam, I've never heard of anybody poaching with an automatic weapon. Yes, Bwana."

The voice on the other end of the phone said, "Jesus Christ, Jake, this is serious business. You find any other evidence out there?"

"Nope."

There was something unusual about Sam's voice. Jake tried to imagine Sam finding the head, owl feather, and cartridge. In some ways, Sam was pretty traditional. He'd be scared. When Sam didn't reply, Jake added, "Maybe you should call in the feds. Like I said, get the ballistics boys on the case." He could feel Sam's uneasiness in the silence of the phone, and he reached a hand into his pocket and fingered the shell casing.

"We don't need the feds, Jake. We can take care of this. Xavier doesn't want the government in on it."

Jake listened, trying to fit pieces together and thinking now of Xavier Two-Bears. "Sure," he said, bringing the cartridge out and spinning it on his desktop beside the coffee cup. "You've already talked to Two-Bears about it?" He wondered what he was going to do. Everything had ramifications. Everything and everybody were related. No politics in the world were as complicated as tribal politics.

Outside the small office where he worked and lived, Jake could hear Mrs. Edwards wringing the Plymouth Rock rooster's neck, going about the business so thoroughly that he could see the whole scene right through the wall: the old woman as big and dark as a mountain in her wide blue skirt and yellow ASU sweatshirt even in the heat of summer, planted solidly on the high rubber soles of her basketball shoes with one heavy arm held out toward the east and the limp rooster twirling until centripetal force brought everything to a stop. He winced at the soft sounds, thinking of the damned dream again. Thunder, coming through a thousand layers of cotton, murmured unceasingly somewhere to the southwest.

"You still scouting the elk herds by helicopter for great white trophy hunters, Sam? You ever feel a little guilty about that?"

"Fuck you, Nashoba. That was maybe eight or ten thousand bucks you left on my floor last night, not to mention the mess. I was you, I'd be a little worried about my job."

"Well, I sure don't want to lose my high-paying job, Sam, but I guarantee I didn't shoot it. Say, did I ever tell you why I like to read Hemingway? You ever read his stuff?"

"What the fuck are you talking about?" Sam yelled. "You got blood all over my goddamned floor last night."

"It's mostly his language, Sam. It's restful, you know, and honest; it doesn't require some kind of action. His people are all fucked up, just like the rest of us, but there's this sense that he's not trying to hide anything, that nothing's going to change and it's not so great but basically okay. I tried one of those Indian novels, a best-seller supposedly written by a real Indian, but it was nothing but a bunch of stupid skins drinking and beating each other to death and being funny about it. At least the writer was trying to be funny about it."

"Fuck Hemingway and fuck Indian writers and fuck you, Jake. We have a problem here. Have you talked to anybody about this head?"

"How could I talk to anybody about it, Sam? I didn't get it to your office till around eleven last night and then I came home."

"Good. Keep your mouth shut and your ears open. You sure you didn't stumble across anything else out there?

"Like what?"

Sam was silent for a moment. "I don't know. But listen, anything you learn comes to me or Xavier, understand? Anything. If I hear you've said a single word to anybody about this poaching, I'll fire your ass, and I don't give a shit if you're married into the tribe."

"No problem," Jake said, holding the shell casing up to the morning light of his east window. "You know that nobody talks to me."

"Stop the bullshit, Jake." There was a pause, and Jake could hear Sam swallow something, undoubtedly one of the first of his many cups of coffee. "If you know anything about this, you'd sure as hell better tell me before you do anything or talk to anybody."

"Of course, Sam. You're my boss, right? By the way, I'm heading to the upper river tomorrow, and I'll check out Pachita Lake on the way." He listened for a moment, nodding his head slowly. "No, like I said, I've never heard of poachers using an automatic weapon." His eyes drifted to an electric beer sign on the wall above the gun rack, a gift from a Choctaw guy he'd met in a bar in Albuquerque. According to the guy, the sign should have shown a man in a canoe paddling endlessly through an infinity of electric ripples. "It's a symbol, Cousin," the Choctaw had said. But something had blown or burned out the first time he'd plugged it in, so now the sign was cold plastic. The white man in the canoe didn't move, the waters didn't flow, the grass on the island didn't grow.

"Forget the river," Sam said. "Two-Bears wants to talk to you. He said to tell you to meet him at the lodge about five this afternoon. They're having a council meeting and a reception or some kind of shit for a politician and some film crew. You can check out Pachita after that."

"I'm not going to forget the river. What's Xavier want?"

In the moment of silence before Sam responded, the ranger studied the beer sign, trying unsuccessfully to imagine the endless cycling of the invisible ripples. Then he thought of the stuffed wolf and felt himself getting mad again. He'd seen a white wolf on the river ten years before, but they were supposed to be extinct in the whole Southwest. The wolf had stood on a rock ledge above the river, scarcely a hundred yards away, and watched him calmly. The long legs, narrow hind-quarters, and intelligent, deliberate face had told him immediately what it was even though he'd never seen a wild wolf in his life. They'd studied each other as equals for a few moments, and then the wolf had turned casually away and walked back up the slope into the pine forest. He hadn't told anyone about what he saw, and he'd never seen another one or even a track. Nashoba, "wolf" in Choctaw, was his name, his grandfather's name, too, so maybe it meant something. Who could know?

"I don't know what Two-Bears wants, Jake. But listen, let me know what you see at Pachita. Automatic weapons fire is weird shit. And we're not getting the feds involved in this poaching, understand? Like I said, we can handle this ourselves."

There was a strain in Sam's voice he hadn't heard before. Sam was definitely holding something back.

"How's Tali?" Sam asked.

"How should I know?"

"Your wife, ain't she?"

"Ex. Your cousin. You ask her how she is."

"Cross-cousin. I think I'll come up there and see my good-looking cousin. By the way, from what I hear you'd better forget that river, permanently." The phone clicked dead, and the ranger put both large hands over his temples, brushing his graying hair back so he could massage the soft places just behind his forehead. He tried to remember the last time he'd had a haircut, thinking that it was funny he was becoming a longhair just out of absent-mindedness.

His head was beginning to throb. He didn't give a rat's ass about the poaching, but the shell casing had been an unpleasant surprise. The tribe sold trophy elk permits for thousands of dollars each, with money-back guarantees of world-class racks. Sam and his staff at headquarters located the elk herds on the mountainous reservation by helicopter and then guided great white Phoenix real estate hunters and Texas oil ranchers out to assassinate a big bull. The whole thing made him sick, but word was that business had dropped off significantly that season. The person or persons who'd killed the bull he found had taken the meat and left the trophy to rot, an attitude he could identify with, and because of the empty cartridge he knew who was doing it. And the owl feather was meant as a message.

He knew the feather wasn't aimed at him, but he was the one who'd found it. Nothing like that happened by accident. He thought of the dream he'd had that night, and a feeling of deep unease seeped through him. Why hadn't he told Sam what he'd really found? He rubbed both temples again. Nothing was ever simple except the river. The river stayed within its rock walls, moving always in the same direction, rising and falling with rain and snow, speaking one language. Whenever he left the river canyon for even a few days, he could feel it pulling at him, almost hear its song.

He knew it was the old lady outside because it was her rooster, and he knew it was the black-checked rooster because of the particularly deep-throated outrage that had emerged from the muffled sound of a cornered and caught chicken. No one else in the community would have the courage to touch one of her chickens. He thought of the great shining breast and neck of the arrogant old cock who had loved to scratch and leave black-and-white droppings in the dirt of the basketball court. The Plymouth Rock was a venerable elder in the village, and he'd taken a particular liking to Jake, racing up whenever Jake appeared from his office with crusts of bread or salami. Jake in turn had become attached to the bird, always pausing to say good morning and toss a treat to the hard-case chicken. He wondered what he might have to trade to the old woman for such hackles, perfect for tying mosquitoes or Adamses or his own special Nashoba Dispensable or a dozen other flies.

He turned away from the now-silent wall, beyond which the old, dark-skinned woman with silver braids to her waist would be starting to pluck the chicken in defiance of the whole community, a community that had admired the rooster greatly, letting the downy feathers of the legs and back fly loose across the hard-beaten but dusty ground between his wildlife office, her plastered HUD house, and the clapboard shack where Domingo Perez, the surviving twin and hairspray addict, would at that moment be staring dumbfounded and spray-brained through his dirty window at the floating feathers of death, twirling a string of his thin hair between the thumb and forefinger of his left hand. If Jake didn't act quickly, Mrs. Edwards would have already begun to strip off the hackle feathers, loosing them to the dirt and mongrel dogs and dry pine forest surrounding the knot of houses. The creases on either side of Domingo's mouth would be dark with dirt and grease. Domingo was another sore spot, like the polluted White River and the stuffed wolf. Something needed to be done about Domingo, soon, by somebody. About everything.

He imagined again the old woman sewing the sky with speckled feathers. Sam was right. Poaching could mean his job because he was an outsider to begin with. But what he'd found was screwy, and a lot more than just poaching. To begin with, a poacher with any brains used a small-caliber rifle with hollow-point bullets and discarded the remains where they weren't likely to be seen. Meat hunters went after cow elk because they were everywhere and easy, and the meat was better. Obviously somebody was making a statement, and there was no doubt in the ranger's mind who the somebody was.

In his dream, he'd held his brown hat inverted in his hands, and four tiny bears had nestled in the bowl of the hat, sleekly feathered bears speckled a softer gray and white than

15

the rooster, each curved warmly into the other. He'd gazed wonderingly at the little bears and heard something in the dream distance that sounded like an owl. That the dream had been so undisturbing was perhaps the most frightening thing of all. He had simply accepted it, feeling something approaching with a terrible force but awaiting that force with a sense of inevitability and peace. He knew he should talk to someone, but common knowledge said that the old woman was the only one on the reservation who knew about owl medicine.

The door of his office swung halfway open and a young, handsome head ducked through the doorway and hung in the bar of sunlight. The brown eyes glanced around the little room, taking in all the tribal and federal papers tacked to the painted Sheetrock, the rusted, confiscated traps hanging from nails, the antique snowshoes with their cracked gut webbing, the sleek, oiled .270 rifle in its rack opposite the high-piled desk, and the door that led to the room where the ranger lived. Finally the gaze lighted on Jake, and the face smiled. A long arm extended into the room and there was an explosion of sound as the hand at the end of the arm slammed a basketball onto the plywood floor.

The door opened all the way, and a tall, lanky body followed the head and arm into the room. A light brown young man in his midtwenties, wearing cutoffs, a sleeveless blue T-shirt, and a bone choker around his neck from some Northern Plains tribe, stood there grinning, slamming the ball down, palming it for a second, and slamming it down again as his ponytail swung back and forth. The ranger closed his eyes, the sound of the basketball reminding him of other, more terrible sounds.

"Stop that goddamned noise, Jessie."

"You've been sitting in here all morning, and now I'm ready to whip your decrepit butt," the young man said, his eyes shining and the grin widening to expose perfect and ridiculously white teeth. "Come on, I double-dog dare you, Kimo Sabe."

The ranger grimaced at the pounding in his head and the very stale joke. The people in the town had started calling him the Lone Ranger so many years before that he'd almost ceased to hear it anymore, and since the Tonto Apache were near neighbors to the west, the Tonto jokes had started at the same time. The way the joke went on the res was that the Lone Ranger called his sidekick "Tonto," which meant "stupid" in Spanish, and the Indian called his boss "El Que No Sabe," meaning basically, "He who doesn't know shit."

He lifted the cold coffee to his lips and then set it back down. The sun would be high and bright that late in the morning, and the basketball court would be inch-deep in powdery dirt from the dogs and chickens. In a little while the thunderheads would start rolling in for their regular afternoon show, sometimes real rain and sometimes just theatrics. However, there was an ominous quality about the day, beginning with the dream and growing heavier with the phone call and the old rooster's death. He'd felt days like this begin in the war, and it was always still, deep, and quiet. Something was getting ready to happen. Death was in the roiling monsoon air, a quality he'd felt all the way out from the river. The image of a crescent moon in a glassy eye appeared in his mind, reminding him that he had unpleasant obligations ahead of him.

"Hey," Jessie said, motioning toward the beer sign with his chin. "I always liked that sign. Bet I could fix it for you. Probably just a bad connection."

Jake looked at the sign. "I don't know," he said. "Maybe I like it just as it is."

"No way. Imagine how great it would be with all that simulated motion. I saw one of those in a bar in Flagstaff, and it was great. It's got these ripples going all the time, with that guy lifting and dipping his paddle. Drives you nuts trying to figure out where one of those ripples starts and another one ends and how the guy looks like he's moving but he's not. Everthing tells you this guy's going somewhere, real lifelike, but it's just illusion."

Jessie walked over and lifted the bottom of the sign, peering underneath. "Hey man, there's one hell of a spider back there," he said. "Black widow, I think. It's shiny black with one of those sticky, thick webs with no pattern to it." He lowered it to the wall and turned. "I'm good with electronics. Just give me the word. Ready to do a little one-on-one?"

"What the hell." Jake pushed the chair back and stood up. He paused to loosen the multicolored sash belt Tali had woven for him right after they were married. A pattern of yellow, blue, black, and white, the belt, he knew, was the only colorful thing about him. He enjoyed wearing it, knowing that it cut his green-brown self right in half just below his growing belly.

"All right, L.R." Jessie grinned and spun the ball magically on his index finger. "I need some real competition. There's no decent beeball on this res except Marcus, and he's still kind of shy."

L.R. was what some people called him. Over the years, a few of them even seemed to have forgotten his real name. The only one who seldom failed to use his name was the old lady. Mrs. Edwards knew more than anyone what a name meant.

When Jake stepped from behind the desk, the younger man cupped the ball against his chest and edged back into the doorway. The ranger stood half a head taller than Jessie, and when he stooped through the door his shoulders nearly touched both sides of the frame.

Outside, Jake squinted and shaded his eyes toward the unpainted plywood backboard and the incongruous new white net on the hoop.

"Well, shit." Jessie was staring down at a pile of fly-buzzing chicken guts and bloodied feathers in the soft dirt directly under the net. "Grandmother Edwards must've known you were going to shoot hoops with me. She wouldn't do that to me. I just put that new net up."

The ranger looked at the entrails with their colorful tangle of blue-black entrails, red blood, and yellow-and-white organs, with a few adhering speckled feathers, and then around him at the off-kilter and colorless square made by the dilapidated homes surrounding the basketball court. "I think the old lady probably left that stuff there just for you."

"For you, my grandfather," Jessie replied. "She left it as a reminder of your venerable friend."

A chain saw ripped at the quiet distance. From the sound of the high-tuned motor it had to be Shorty Luke, the other surviving twin and widely traveled story thief, using his Stihl 026 to buck firewood in the aspen up the hill. No one else at Black Mountain owned a saw that sounded so good. The high-tuned saw gave off a feeling of power and authority. And Shorty, the only one besides Jessie whom he could remotely consider a friend on the reservation, knew every corner and crevice of the mountains where live oak or aspen could be found. Jake imagined the muscular little man up there with his saw. He'd be talking with Shorty soon enough.

Above the log house he'd built beyond the east end of the square, Jake could see a thin column of smoke that told him Tali was getting a very early start on dinner. That would mean she was having even more relatives than usual over, and so he wouldn't have seen her even if he'd stayed home. Home, a bad joke. Even after all the intervening years—years in which he hadn't set foot inside the log house—he could see her clearly in his imagination moving gracefully about the big kitchen. The stone in his guts had worn away over time, and with each of her after-dark visits to his little shack, so that now when he imagined her or watched her walk across the square he felt only a vague sort of ache, the way his knees throbbed in cold, wet weather. The woman who came to him once or twice a month when not even the reservation dogs were barking was a different woman, not a wife. When she came silently to his door, opened it, and glided across to the room where his bed was, he invariably felt as though one of the spirits had come down from the mountain, what the people called *gaan*, and he knew it was a blasphemous thought. That shadowy woman had nothing at all to do with the dancer who had brought him home.

19

Black Mountain was a kind of little outpost on the reservation, not a real town, just a plaster-and-plywood jumble of poorly insulated, wood-heated HUD houses bulldozed through the trees and inhabited mostly by his relatives through marriage. Up the road a dozen miles was the new tribal casino, a brightly lit, shoddy affair next to a quick-stop gas station and store. He turned back to see Jessie scooping entrails with a wooden shingle blown from someone's home. Jessie flipped the guts to the space behind the basketball post, where they disappeared into the thick, powdery dirt.

"This ought to be okay," the younger man said doubtfully, scuffing his Nike hightops in the dust to cover the chicken blood. "We'll play to ten. Okay, Grandfather?"

The ranger half-smiled to acknowledge the honorific title of Grandfather, acknowledging at the same time, as he always did, the irony behind the word. He wasn't old enough to be Jessie's grandfather, at least. Father, maybe. He wasn't anybody's grandfather, not technically. "You get first outs, Grandson," he said, feeling his cracked lips open into something more like a smile with the final word. His dark green pants, ugly wool-and-synthetic blends he bought a half-dozen at a time for four bucks each from a military surplus store in Flagstaff, and his brown work shirt with the tribal badge were both tight around his heavy hips and belly, and the bulky hiking boots held his feet to the earth. He was getting fat. He could feel himself growing closer to the earth with each passing month, the hard-muscled frame of his youth giving way to long seasons of rain and deep-banked winters. The backpacking trips into the canyon were becoming a little tougher each year. Why Tali still came to him on those random nights was a mystery. Soon someone would scoop him up with a flat-nosed shovel and toss him between the outbuildings like the remains of a useless rooster. But not yet.

Jessie dribbled to the imaginary half-court line, each thump of the ball sending up a puff of powdery dust. A door opened and slammed in Tali's former house, and a scrawny little man with a peach-pit face and long, stringy hair stepped out to sit in a ragged lawn chair on his front porch. A short-haired black mongrel with white chest and feet slinked around the corner of the house, a downy feather stuck to its grizzled muzzle, and lay carefully down in the dirt close enough to touch the man's foot with its nose. Tali had given the little plywood house to one of the surviving twins when she'd moved into the log home.

"Uncle Domingo's rooting for you," Jake said. "He always favors the underdog." A trio of adolescent boys had appeared from behind a cluster of plaster houses, each with his black hair cut short and greased on the top and sides and left long and straight in the back. Their brown arms protruded from sleeveless sweatshirts, and denim shorts bagged to their calves, the asses dragging nearly to the knees. One of the boys cradled a basketball against his flat belly as the three watched Jake and Jessie with something that looked to the ranger like amusement.

"Uncle Domingo's playing a totally separate game in his head," Jessie said. "Like those boys."

Jessie glanced at the boys, and then with a too-obvious head fake to the right, he moved suddenly left, quick and deft as an acrobat, passing the ball between his legs and driving left-handed past the ranger, so that Jake stood for a fraction of a second admiring the pure grace of the action. That was why he loved basketball. Nothing else on earth allowed the mind and body to come together with such rapid beauty, except perhaps war, but in war no one had the luxury of observation, except the one who told the story afterward, and then it was either remembrance or lie. Memory in someone else's blood. Why, he wondered suddenly, did Jessie's move toward the hoop seem so fraught with danger, so portentious?

As Jake stood enthralled, the ball seemed to disappear in the flash of motion and reappear at the end of the extended left hand as Jessie soared toward the basket. But just as the ball began its roll off the outstretched fingers, the ranger moved suddenly and his great right hand came down from above, causing the ball to hang frozen for an instant before it reversed direction and smashed the shooter between the eyes.

Jake picked up the ball and dribbled deliberately away from the basket, sending up little puffs of dust.

"Remember, you have to clear everything," Jessie said in a muffled voice from where he sat in the dirt cupping his nose in one palm. "Behind the key. How'd you do that?"

"What key?"

Jessie waved vaguely as he got to his feet, dusting off his shorts with one hand. "Ten feet behind that chicken-gut spot. Man, I didn't even see you move. How'd you do that?"

Jake glanced at the boys, who were uniformly and not very successfully suppressing grins. He bounced the ball toward Jessie. "Your game," he said. "I forfeit."

"Come on. I thought we had a game." Jessie touched his nose and then examined his hand for blood. "You never finish a game."

"Got to check some things out." Jake walked away from the basket toward his office.

"That's a chicken shit excuse, no pun intended." Jessie moved slowly to where the ranger stood, each bounce of the ball creating a small dust storm.

"By the way, how's business?" Jake asked. "You got any New Yorkers or Europeans or New Age Los Angelinos wandering around in the woods?"

The young man held the ball against his hip with one hand and rubbed the bridge of his nose with the other. "You know that would've been a blocking foul if we had a ref. You didn't have position. Not even close. Could've broken my nose. VQE business is kind of down. Must be the international economy. Even the Germans seem to have less disposable income."

The boys had drifted silently close to the basket as the men stood talking and began taking turns shooting and rebounding. Two of them were Shorty Luke's grandkids, Jake noticed. The third was Marcus Baca, Sam Baca's nephew, who had been dropped off by his mom at the beginning of summer. While his mom did something in Phoenix, the boy was living with his grandmother, old Benecia Martinez. It had taken one day for

Marcus to establish himself as the preeminent basketball player at Black Mountain, except for Jessie.

Jake shook his head to clear out the image of the moon in the elk's eye, and let out a deep breath. "I'm heading down into the river again pretty soon. I don't want to run over any of your starving customers."

The ball hammered into the dust and sprang back up to the spot between hand and hip. "How would you like some company on your trip? Remember when I was a kid and you took me down there? It was great, and you said you'd take me again, but you never did."

Jake squinted against the sun that had momentarily cut past clouds. He remembered the trip. Ten-year-old Jessie had been full of wonder at the beauty and wildness of the canyon. They'd come across a small yearling black bear, which had promptly run away, and to Jake's surprise the boy had never seen a live bear before. He'd shown Jessie how to cast a fly and play the big rainbows that were everywhere in the river, and he'd sat by a fire for three nights listening to Jessie talk. He'd told the boy a story from his own grandmother, about how Choctaw people had migrated into Mississippi from the west, carrying the bones of all their ancestors, bones that formed the base of the great mound, Nanih Waya. He'd tried to imagine in half-remembered words how the sacred pole leaned each morning and how, finally, the two brothers, Chahtah and Chikasah, had been separated with their different bands by a flooding river and formed different tribes. Jessie in return had begun to tell excitedly about twin brothers in the Black Mountain creation story but had suddenly stopped. "It's summer," he'd said. "We can't tell that story now."

Instead, the boy had slowly pieced together a story about himself, about a white father who had been gone before his son's birth and a mother who had died on a Gallup sidewalk after leaving her month-old baby with Mrs. Edwards. Fragments he'd learned from the mean teasing of kids, the overheard whispers of adult conversations. Listening, Jake had tried to

23

remember the shadowy image of his own long-dead Choctaw father, and he felt the vast space that revolved around the two of them, man and boy, alone by a fire. Hold your people close, he'd wanted to tell the child. The whole world tried to take such things away in long night roads and burning jungles. But Jessie had learned that without being told.

After that trip, Jessie had hung around the office for days at a time, even after Tali had thrown Jake out. A boy without parents and a ranger without a family seemed to go together, and surprisingly Mrs. Edwards didn't object, but he'd never taken the boy with him again. The time had never felt right, or there had been something, he realized in retrospect, he'd been afraid of. Gradually, Jessie had drifted away, settling at a comfortable distance, but always there where he could be seen, as though, like Tali, he needed to keep track of Jacob Nashoba. When Jessie had come back from the university he'd moved into one of the empty cabins at Black Mountain, visiting Mrs. Edwards every day but living alone.

"I've changed my vision quest locations for the purpose of greater privacy." Jessie looked toward the southeast. "I took two new clients down into the river canyon."

"Into the canyon?"

Jessie looked back to the ranger. "Shorty Luke showed me a couple of good spots above the river where we didn't think you would run into them. I've got a French woman going on day four at the spring below Gobbler Point. She wanted the full deal. I guaranteed a complete vision if she put in a minimum of five days. You should see her. Beautiful woman, and tough as anything."

"No food?"

"Well, I picked up four pounds of jerky from the Quick-Stop. That expensive stuff. I put it in a nice simulated deerskin bag I bought at the casino shop and told her it was made by an ancient medicine woman specially for vision quests, said the peppery flavor came from chokecherry bark and sacred beaver gall. She's got water, of course, because she's right by the spring. In fact, if she wanted to cheat a little I think the wild plums and chokecherries are almost ripe. I found some grapes, too, down by the river. Just a little green. Good cathartic, maybe."

The ranger scratched his forehead with two fingers. "She wouldn't know what those things were. How much do these people pay you?"

Jessie looked serious. "Four thousand for a minimum of five days, vision guaranteed. Two for the short, three-day version, no guarantee. Have you seen those great books by Ed McGaa, Eagle Man? He's got sample prayers, something he calls a Lakota Mother Earth Relationship Word List, a sweatlodge recipe, lists of Indian names white people can give themselves, everything you need to be a spiritual Indian."

"Nobody can guarantee a vision."

Jessie spun the ball on the index finger of his right hand, keeping it spinning with touches of the left hand. "Sure I can." The chain saw started up again in the woods, and somewhere a child yelled excitedly.

"Mystical secrets of synthetics and tribal culture." The young man watched the spinning ball.

"What do you do with all the money, Jessie? I never see you spend any."

Jessie smiled at the sky before looking back at Jake. "VQE tribal scholarship fund. Haven't you heard about it? Any kid in the tribe who can make the grades gets help. Five or ten thousand doesn't go that far in college these days. Takes a lot of dinero."

Jake watched the young man with both admiration and a growing sense of uneasiness. The old sense of impending violence hovered at the edges of his thoughts for the first time in years, and he was beginning to feel less accepting than he had in his dream. Maybe it was the combination of the dream and the death of the old rooster, or maybe it was the rifle casing in his pocket and the image of spidery elk antlers, a feather, and a twice-reflected moon.

Jessie lifted the ball and rested his chin on it, looking over the arc at the ranger. "Oh, yeah. I forgot to mention that Alison's down there, too."

"Alison. What the hell?"

Jessie shrugged. "My other client. She's been after me to do it for a long time. I said no a hundred times. I told her about it not being traditional for our people and all, but she wanted to do it anyway. She said she could learn from our native brothers and sisters in other tribal cultures. No shit. She really talked that way. I kept saying no until finally she said she was going to do it on her own—to commune with the *gaan*, she said."

"You mean you took my granddaughter and left her by herself down there?"

Jessie squinted over the ball, with one slanted eye nearly closed, his nose visibly reddened. "I thought you said she wasn't really your granddaughter. She told me she wants to be a warrior, like all those famous women warriors in the past."

"How much did you charge her for that bullshit?"

Jessie rubbed the bridge of his nose again. "You think I'd take money from Alison?"

"Where the hell did you leave her?"

"She ordered me absolutely not to tell you on penalty of death. She said you'd probably try to save her or something because you're a male chauvenist outsider who doesn't understand our culture."

"Alison said that?"

Jessie nodded, the ball moving with him. "I lectured her on respect for elders."

"Is she in the canyon?"

He nodded again.

"Where?"

Lowering the ball to his stomach, Jessie cocked his head. "I'm going down there tomorrow afternoon. It's time for my French lady's vision, and I planned to check on Alison after that. I'll do it without letting her see me, and if she's not in perfect shape I'll bring her home."

Jake closed his eyes. "Where is she?"

"She's on the side of the ridge just above Elk Creek, up by the spring. You know the spot, about a quarter mile from the river. I always leave my clients by a spring. You can live a long time without food, but you have to have water. But remember, Alison isn't one of my New Age clients. This one's for real, so you can't mess with her if I don't bring her out. Even if she is sort of your granddaughter."

Jessie glanced backward and arced the ball in a high curve toward the basket, where it banked through and bounced away toward Mrs. Edwards's house. He watched the ball for a moment and then turned back. "It's the law of supply and demand. There are all those Plains Indians and white shamans selling sweats and visions up in Santa Fe and out in California, even in Europe, but nobody else has ever offered an Apache vision quest."

"Probably because, like you just said, nobody's ever heard of one."

"Well, that's what makes it exotic. Besides, white people don't have a clue, and they're crazy about Apaches even if they don't know what we are. They think everybody's Geronimo or Cochise. You heard of that English rock star who calls himself Apache Indian?

"VQE is kind of like Disney World except when my customers go away their lives are changed for the better. When are you going down to the river?"

"Tomorrow, I hope, but I've got some business to take care of. So I don't know for sure. If you promise to check on Alison."

"You should see this French lady. She's something. Told me she'd spent a long time studying some kind of weird Himalayan martial art or meditation or something like that. She's even been down the Amazon with what she called an indigenous guide. But there's a sadness about her, you know?"

Jake turned and looked at the big log house set back in the trees at the east end of the group of buildings. Smoke from the house's stone chimney rose straight for a dozen feet and then

27

bent in a curve toward the heavily forested mountains for which the community and reservation were named. Thick clouds had gathered above the higher ridges like they always did in July and August and huddled together in the hot sky, darkening from white to nearly black in the center. A shimmer of lightning flashed across the cloud front with no accompanying thunder. The people of Black Mountain had stories about beings who lived up in the peaks, but he'd deliberately shut his ears to all that from the beginning. It wasn't his culture, and it wasn't any of his business. He'd never heard of any Choctaw mountain spirits, but then there weren't too many mountains in Mississippi except the great mound his own people had made with their bones. Maybe all mountains were made of bones.

"Man, I thought you'd busted my nose that time, Grandfather. You shouldn't do that." Jessie ran a hand across his forehead and let it trail back to the ponytail before folding his arms again. "I think Grandmother Edwards and me and Shorty are the only people on this reservation who aren't afraid of you. Two-Bears acts like he isn't, but I can tell he's scared that you'll go off the deep end someday. You walk into a room and people get all tense. That's why Grandmother Tali set your stuff outside the door, isn't it? Despite all that teepee creeping that goes on, that you thought I didn't know about. It's that Vietnam experience still bottled up after all these years, I guess. Don't you ever want to talk about it, get it all out? A ceremony maybe?"

Jake stopped and looked into the eyes of the young man. He'd tried once, at Tali's insistence, but there'd only been questions without answers. Do you have dreams, the therapist asked. Do you feel moments of inexplicable rage? What do you remember? Are there gaps in your memory? Do you ever cry without knowing why? How many did you kill? Do you remember? Do you feel guilt? Are there gaps in your memory? Inexplicable rage? Dreams? The soft, pale man in Phoenix had asked questions until Jake felt rage each time merely at the sight of the therapist's office. I don't know, he'd said. I don't cry. I don't know. I don't remember. I don't know. But he'd lied, because though he never cried he did remember, and there were no gaps. That was the real problem. He wished for gaps, but it was all there, not just every minute but every second. The worst was when he recognized their faces. When at night the door opened and they stepped through and he knew them, one after another, each one looking directly at him. Sometimes they spoke, telling him it was a better world where they were now and inviting him to join them. Ghost sickness, Tali called it and recommended that he talk with Mrs. Edwards. But from the first he'd felt that the old woman was his implacable enemy, that she'd seen into his heart at first glimpse and knew his irremediable guilt.

On some nights when the door stayed closed, something moved in the dark and he naturally tried to kill it. Tali had gone to Phoenix with him twice, saying afterward, "It doesn't work if you don't tell them, Jacob. You can't lie and get well. You have to tell the whole story." But he'd known for a long time, really since the last moment in Chu Lai, when he'd thought he saw the jungle through clouds but wondered even then if he was seeing anything or just remembering—was there jungle down there, really?—that someone else would have to tell the whole story.

He breathed in slowly, feeling the pine- and lightning-teased air pass into his chest. "I didn't realize," he said to Jessie, "that you'd spent so much time studying me."

"Well, this isn't a big place, Grandfather."

"I'm not your grandfather. I'm not anybody's grandfather. What are you, the tribal counselor now?" Immediately he regretted his tone. He liked Jessie and knew he'd missed something in keeping the boy at a distance. Sometimes he felt Jessie was too smart to survive very long on a reservation. Thanks to Mrs. Edwards, Jessie had avoided the booze and drugs. Anger smoldered in so many, raising a stench like burning tires. Those empty kids hitchhiked up and down the highway, their eye sockets filled with flame and their flesh scorched.

29

"As a matter of fact, I guess I am sort of the tribal youth counselor, at least at Black Mountain. Haven't you heard about my film series? It's very educational, paid for by Vision Quest Enterprises." Jessie turned to the boys shooting hoops. "Hey guys," he said, "come over here for a second, okay?"

One of the boys caught a rebound and the three turned to look at the men for a moment before they walked slowly over.

"A little quiz for you guys to impress the ranger." Jessie winked.

"Ah no, man. This ain't school," the one with the ball said. Taller and thinner than his friends, the boy was almost a replica of Jessie at the same age.

"Just an easy question, Marcus. Who can tell me who Russell Means is?"

The boys looked at each other, and the shortest one grinned, his chubby face rippling with the effort. "That's easy, man. He's that actor that was in *Last of the Mohicans* and *Natural Born Killers*. He was supposed to be a Navajo in that one. That was funny."

"He did that chief's voice in *Pocahontas*," the other of Shorty Luke's grandsons added. "And Sitting Bull in some movie. And he was on TV the other night. He was supposed to be some kind of shaman in the Kazoo or Yazoo or Wazoo tribe in that one. I bet he's one rich Indian."

"You mean Pocahooters." One of the shorter boys nudged his brother. "Yeah, but Russell Means ain't as good as Graham Greene in *Dances with Wolves*." The boy grinned at Jake. "Kicking Bird was way cool. And old Red Crow Westerman was good, too. He was on TV this week, too. He kept appearing and disappearing in that show about the Kazoon Indians. Really weird."

"Who cares?" Marcus said. "Bunch of rich Indian actors. Who gives a shit."

"Thanks, guys," Jessie said. "We're going to see *Thunderheart* this weekend, remember. It's about a half-breed FBI agent who returns to his Lakota roots and is embraced by his relations.

Indians have always loved the FBI, especially at Pine Ridge, right? And the actor who plays the agent has a Cherokee great-grandmother."

"Right," Marcus said, rolling his eyes and spinning the ball on one finger.

Shorty Luke's grandsons grinned simultaneously and then followed Marcus back toward the hoop. Jake watched the boys return to shooting baskets and shook his head.

"Russell Means is a movie star? That's all they know? What about AIM?"

"They've got to know what's happening today, Grandfather, not ancient history. I have to say they really got into those kazoomers on Disney's Pocahontas."

"Why're you doing this, Jessie?"

"I'm just trying to make sure the kids know their roles, develop their sense of irony so they'll know how to function, how to adapt like Russell Means."

3 As he walked toward his office-home, Jake paused to look back and admire the work of his hands, perhaps his original big mistake on the reservation besides arriving in the first place. Compared to the cookie-cutter government houses and shacks in the community, the log house looked huge and substantial, which in fact it was. And he'd done every damned thing himself, with Tali, partly because much of his life he'd dreamed of building a log house and suddenly he'd found himself on a reservation surrounded by millions of perfectly straight lodgepole pines. But mostly to show up his wife's relatives, at least a dozen of whom now lived in the house he'd built. He hadn't counted on a couple of things. First, as Tali had explained, the tribe was matrilocal, which basically meant that he and Tali were expected to live with her parents, sisters, unmarried drunken brothers, and anyone else who dropped by. A lot of modern couples didn't conform in that way, but it was also considered pretty bad manners to rise above your relations, to show off materially. The only way Tali could deal with the fact of the huge house was to invite half of her family to live with them. The second thing he hadn't considered was that in the tribe the wife owned the house. The husband was a kind of guest, and in his case not even high on the bathroom waiting list since he was not just a husband but a foreigner. For two years he'd tripped over Angel and the other brothers—who tiptoed drunkenly around him after he'd thrown Angel against the living room wall—plus Tali's children, who for a long time seemed to view him as a strange tourist in the community, and an eccentric aunt who insisted on cooking but burned everything she touched until the day she died of a burned-biscuit heart attack.

The only private thing he had managed to hold on to for two years was his bedroom with Tali. She had acknowledged his strangeness by allowing him to post a No Trespassing sign on the bedroom door, and no one had ever violated the sign. Finally, however, Tali had solved his difficulties with the crowd by setting his few possessions on the porch so that he found them there when he came home one day.

As Jessie had said, it had begun in Phoenix. The thing that rose from its own ashes was him, maybe, but he wasn't sure if after twenty-five years he was risen or only learning to sit up. Phoenix in 1970 had been different, a small town really, not the smoggy bowl of destitute poor and rich, blue-haired, Mercedes-driving New Yorkers and midwesterners it had become. The red neon, sombrero-topped saguaro had flashed at him from ten blocks away, standing straight and then falling down and standing up again. The Saguaro Club had beckoned him just as the desert had, and he'd driven toward the tilting red cactus like he'd been driving toward the tilting red sun every day since being discharged in New Jersey. He'd drunk and fought his way across from Amarillo to Albuquerque and down to Las Cruces and through Silver City, Patagonia, and Tucson before turning the Chevy pickup north to Phoenix. Flagstaff was on the other side of Phoenix, and he had a Navajo buddy in that patriotic-sounding town who said it was full of beautiful women and cheap liquor. Navajo women, the buddy had said. So he'd circled like Old Buzzard heading north finally to be beckoned aside by the falling cactus and find himself sitting twelve beers later watching the most beautiful woman he'd ever seen take off her clothes on a little stage in a small barroom on a street where rags of paper hung to real cholla cactuses and dark-skinned men and women littered doorways.

Her bare, brown feet were small and high-arched, gripping the stage like talons, the smooth curve of each instep a deep invitation. He drank and imagined her a molting hawk. Her eyes looked almost black as they stared over the heads of people like him, eyes with spikes of light in each pupil, and the cords of her neck stood out between strands of long black hair. The smile was a teeth-baring threat that no one in the room seemed to understand but him, and he marveled at the way all of her flowed in a continuous, dangerous circle like the eddy of a fast river. He waited for her to rise above the stage, flap her wings, and soar.

The barroom had been jammed with men in cowboy hats and boots, and clusters of men in uniform, not just fatigue jackets and jeans like him, but guys still caught up in the gut of the government and waiting to be shit out just like he'd been.

The room seemed devoid of light, but from somewhere came beams that played across the dark skin of the woman dancing, fingers of gold tracing her long legs and flat stomach and small, taut breasts. The vee of her crotch was a moving, pulsing shadow, and the light pulled at the G-string and gathered in the angles of her rib cage and spilled down the slope of waist-length hair. He found himself lost in the swirl and was rapidly drowning in the whole drunken experience when he noticed three cowboys standing at the edge of the stage and reaching toward the dancer. He stood up then.

The second time the cop hit him behind the ear with the nightstick, he found himself able to focus. There was a tangle of white men and cowboy hats and at least one police uniform between overturned tables near the bar, and just as the cop hit him again he began to suspect that once more he was somehow responsible for a problem. That was a memory gap he'd never told the therapist about.

The judge had been lenient because he'd been back from Nam and discharged for only a month at that point. People had mumbled things about delayed stress syndrome and shaken their heads and patted him on the shoulder. And it was Tali's brothers who had bailed him out, perhaps the last decent act of their collective lives. He remembered as though it were the day before how he'd sat on the bench waiting, his head bandaged and feeling like he'd done a header on a grenade, and then looking up to see the woman standing in front of him. Her hands were on her bluejeaned hips, and her black hair hung over the pearl snaps of a sky-blue western shirt. He glanced at her feet, but her high insteps were hidden in Tony Lama boots. Behind her stood three dissipated young men, all dark-skinned and watching him as though there were bars between them, which there were.

"You're so fucking stupid you must be some kind of Indian," were the first words she said to him. Two months later they were married in the courthouse in Springerville, the three brothers and a swarm of other relatives, including her three children, crazy aunt, and the huge old woman they called Mrs. Edwards, all bearing witness that indeed here was a marvelous and strange thing in the world that they were claiming. Angel, the youngest and drunkest brother at the wedding, called him the Gray Ghost, as if it had some kind of meaning, but nobody would explain it, and he never did find out what Angel meant.

But he remembered more than anything the first night in her bed. She had undressed him with what could only be described as tenderness, removing his boots first and then unbuttoning his shirt and trailing her mouth across his chest as she pushed the shirt back over his shoulders. Then she had moved to the pants, and when they were off she had pushed him onto her small bed, her mouth and tongue touching and tasting him from his wide forehead to the tips of his toes. And after what seems hours she had stood and removed her own clothes, dropping the shirt and bra on the floor and stepping out of the jeans with the grace of a water bird. For a moment she had stood beside the bed, her body incredibly unlike that which he had seen onstage. The breasts were delicate, fragile looking, and her long legs seemed to hold to the earth with only the greatest of effort. To prevent her from rising from the earth he'd reached for her hand and drawn her down to him. She had rolled beneath him at once and he'd been surprised to find how wet she was already, flowing like the source of a river, as she guided him inside her. And as they made love she had held his shoulders to her with a grip that made him think he could never leave. When she came the first time, he was watching her face, astonished both by the beauty of her smile and by the flood that seemed to wash over him. And when she shifted to look down upon him and came again, he had joined her, but he had been the one who cried out in pleasure and an irrational fear of drowning while she held the smile. They had slept that night locked in an embrace that kept dreams a thousand miles or more away.

It had taken six months for him to convince her and then two years to build the house, just the two of them, with children always underfoot and her brothers observing and commenting, planning, cutting, peeling and pulleying logs into place, hammering and caulking after his day's work logging for the tribe and on weekends. By the first winter they'd had the shell and roof up, and while logging was shut down by snow they worked together on interior walls, cabinets, plumbing, and wiring and slept at night on a mattress on the floor while Tali's children argued, laughed, and slept in other rooms. Four years after they began the house, Tali had thrown him out. They'd spent night after night in their locked bedroom, once the children were fed and asleep, in the same passion as the first night, when they joined their bodies as tightly as possible as though each was afraid the other might escape. But almost

35

from the beginning some nights turned out differently. Sometimes he'd fall over the edge of sleep into that other world, a black, tangled place where everything conspired to destroy him, and he'd leap to protect his life. Those were the times he'd awakened to find his wife on the floor or against a far wall of the bedroom, her mouth or nose bleeding and her eyes staring in terror. Each time he'd had the realization that he was responsible for something that had gone wrong, but the how and why were locked in dreams. People in the community who had been at his wedding and had made guarded attempts to communicate saw his wife and stopped talking to him. Tali's children began to avoid him, her brothers looking at him more and more darkly. Tali herself had argued and wept until he agreed to go to Phoenix for counseling. But the therapist's questions hadn't produced answers, and he refused to explain what he knew: that it was because he was alone, locked irretrievably into another place that had little in common with the daylight world in which people ate, worked, talked, and made love.

When he'd come home from logging one day, he hadn't been suprised to find his belongings boxed neatly on the front porch and Shorty Luke sitting in a wooden chair beside the boxes to politely explain the situation. He had felt something like relief. It was divorce Indian style. He'd seen how sorry and sympathetic Shorty was, but he'd had no defense. Like always, he was guilty. He also wasn't surprised that the cowardly brothers weren't there, only surprised that, as Shorty explained it, Tali had thrown them out of the house also. All three had piled into Angel's pickup and headed for Flagstaff, never to be seen again. From that time on, the log house was a woman's house. Men entered by permission and left quickly.

Now he saw Tali pause in the doorway of the house, the summer sun only midway down its slow evening path through the clouds and shining in her long, still-dark hair. Her hands rested on the hips of her ankle-length skirt, and from across the big plaza her eyes looked nearly black. She hadn't stopped loving him, he knew, on the day she cast him out. She'd put him out, but unlike the two fathers of her children, she hadn't thrown him away. He knew she wanted him there in the game warden's little shack where she could watch him, and that she had undoubtedly used her influence with Mrs. Edwards and Xavier Two-Bears to get him his job. In the end, he had to admit that his wife operated by a system of laws he couldn't even begin to understand. Part of that was her Indianness. After all, Tali had grown up knowing exactly who she was, and who she was was a member of the Black Mountain tribe, while he had only shadowy notions of what it might mean to be Choctaw. But maybe an equal part was simply that Tali was a woman. There were profound differences between men and women, he'd come to suspect. Now he watched as she stepped off the porch, walking toward him.

"I saw what you did to Jessie," she said when she was close enough. The topless dancer had become a tribal matron, powerful and respected, someone who would probably be a member of the tribal council soon.

He shrugged. "It's a contact sport. He knows that."

"You do it because he's younger and faster. And you feel guilty."

He looked at the forested ridge. "I do it because if I didn't he'd think he could beat me. And that wouldn't be good for him."

"Jessie looks up to you, Jacob. Don't you know that? He was always a good boy. Think about what it took for a boy from this place to go to a university, and think about what it took for him to give that up and come home. He's a good man now, despite that vision quest business. I know you don't like it, but it's harmless. And you've never even known how much Jessie loves you. The world beats you, Jacob, because you want it to. If you'd ever recognize that fact maybe you could live with yourself."

She gave him an expressionless glance and for the millionth time his stomach dropped sickeningly as he fell in love with the dancer who'd brought him home. As far as he knew, neither of them had had anyone else in all the years of their separation.

"And maybe you could live with others, too, Jacob. Did Jessie talk to you about Alison?"

He nodded. "It's rough going down there. Too rough for a sixteen-year-old girl."

"Baloney." Tali turned to study the few scattered thunderheads for a moment before turning back. "Trini and I have both tried to talk with her," she said. "Alison won't listen anymore. She could go to college. She's a smart girl."

"And you think letting Mr. Vision Quest abandon her in the mountains will help her."

"Jessie wouldn't hurt Alison. And maybe it will help her. Mrs. Edwards told Alison about the women in the old days who learned to ride and fight just like the men. So Alison chose to do this even though it's not traditional. I think she's trying to invent her own traditions. Mrs. Edwards said she needs to be taught by a warrior." She looked directly into his eyes, the look so sharp he felt wounded.

He folded his arms across his chest. "Oh no. There are plenty of veterans on the reservation. Besides, I don't know anything about your culture, any culture. I don't know the stories. I don't know anything. And I'm no warrior. I went to that war because I wasn't smart enough or didn't have enough guts not to, and I tried to keep from getting killed while I was there. That's all. The whole thing was stupid and wrong, and I'm the wrong one to help anybody. Remember, you brought me here and then threw me out of the house we built. For good reason, I admit. Now I do my job and write my reports and send them down to the tribal office. What do I have to teach anybody?"

"I threw you out because I had no choice. I know you understand. Now people say you're drinking too much."

"People always say that. I hardly drink at all. Besides, didn't you see that new study that said Jewish men have a high suicide rate because they don't drink enough? I'm avoiding suicide and depression. Maybe you should talk to Avrum Goldberg. He doesn't drink enough."

"Avrum is traditional. He doesn't drink at all."

"Traditional what? As a matter of fact, Shorty told me that your tribe used to make beer from cactus or something, traditionally. So if Avrum was traditional, he'd be out getting zonked on cactus beer."

She smoothed the pleats of her skirt and closed her eyes for a moment before speaking again. "I'll try to explain. The tribe leaves you in your office and sends you down that river because they're all afraid of you. They gave you the game warden's job for that area because they figured nobody else could or would patrol that canyon and it gets you away from them. So they killed two birds with the same stone. You make everybody too nervous. Now Alison needs something nobody's been able to give her, and Mrs. Edwards had a dream. She thinks you have to go down there where Alison is, that you can help Alison or something. She wasn't very clear." She paused. "I wouldn't be talking to you about this if it wasn't for the dream. Maybe it's the other way around. Maybe Alison can help you."

He unclasped his arms and rubbed his forehead with one broad hand. In the slanting sunlight Tali appeared to be made of obsidian, the angles of her scalpel-sharp and glinting. "I know," he replied. "A dream about feathered bears."

He could see by the slight shift of intensity in her eyes that she was startled, and he was pleased that for once he'd been a step ahead of her.

"How did you know that?"

He shrugged. "Something's going on, Tali. I don't know what."

She reached out and touched his forearm with the tips of her fingers, the touch warm with the certainty that they'd never again have what they once had. "There are some people doing intertribal healing sweats up in Flagstaff," she said. "Mostly veterans. I know some of them and they'd like you to join. They've heard about you from other veterans. You should think about that, Jacob. It might help. No one can do everything by himself."

He looked at the odd combination of sun and dark clouds. The deep creases of the clouds caught the sunlight in silvery wrinkles, and graying curtains showed rain falling far to the north. Some people can only do anything alone, he thought. "I'll consider that," he replied. "What have they heard about me?"

Tali turned back toward the house, and he watched her walk, the long skirt almost motionless and the moccasined feet gripping the earth the way her bare feet had gripped the wooden stage many years before. "What have they heard about me?" he repeated, but in a voice so low no one could hear. He remembered the sweet smell of her hair when it trapped the summer sun and how her brown body seemed to burn like a furnace in deep winter. There would never really be any danger of Tali falling, he thought as he watched her. And then he thought of the brief portion of his life he'd spent in her bed, barely a tick of the clock, not much more time than he'd spent in Nam.

The thickened clouds over Black Mountain had quickly spread, and this time the rumbling of thunder was deep and menacing. Large, slow drops began to pock the powdery earth around him, and he quickened his pace.

When he entered the office, the first thing he saw was the old woman sitting stolidly behind his desk, both feet planted on the plywood floor. Her arms rested on the arms of the oak chair, and her thick braids hung down over each shoulder. A red bandanna was folded into a headband low across her forehead, and a turquoise cross hung over the university sweatshirt she still wore. Her broad face held an intense, serious expression as usual.

"This won't be easy," the old lady said.

He stood in silence for a moment, looking over Mrs. Edwards's head. The calendar on the wall beside her was two months out of date, and he realized he'd forgotten for weeks to wind the old clock on the file cabinet. From the moment he'd come to consciousness on the reservation, the old woman had positioned herself as his enemy.

"Has anything ever been easy with you?" he responded.

She looked past him at the wall. "I told them to get rid of you" had been the first words she'd spoken to him after Tali brought him home. "I didn't think you could be saved."

No one had ever told him her real name, not even Tali. Everyone called her Mrs. Edwards, or Grandmother, or sometimes, if they were impatient, the old lady. He'd finally gotten Tali to explain that her great aunt had been married once, for three weeks, to a white hell-fire-and-brimstone preacher who'd shown up one day and immediately begun to spend all his time trying to convert the old woman. Word got around that he'd been tossed out by his congregation in Prescott for scaring the children too much, so he'd apparently decided to preach to heathens. In three months he'd converted the old lady to Mrs. John Edwards, with a legal marriage certificate, and after three more weeks he'd packed his van and left. No one ever learned why he left, though gossip as usual was complex and thorough, revolving mostly around the probability that she'd worn him out in bed, but from that time on she'd kept her married name. Rumors persisted that she had begun screwing the other resident white man, an anthropologist, almost as soon as her husband was gone, and maybe even before, but no one had ever actually seen them together. It was just a community feeling, and gossip of sexual sorcery was whispered in dark corners. Domingo Perez swore he'd seen the spirit of the anthropologist flying toward her house on dark nights, but everyone knew that Domingo was subject to hallucinations. "I think the name's a kind of protection," Tali had partially explained. "It's a sort of neutral name, so nothing can get at who she really is. That's my guess."

"Why are you doing this?" he said. He shoved his hands into the pants pockets and listened to the Arizona monsoon thunder. Heavy rain began to pound the tin roof for a moment and then stopped with sudden finality. Probably, the rain had barely touched the earth. Thunder snapped above the mountain.

"Why didn't you ever tell your wife or her children about your own culture?" the old woman asked. "Did you forget everything, or don't those Choctaw people you come from have stories?"

"*Chahta*," he said. "*Chahta okla*. White people say 'Choctaw.' They have plenty of stories. Stories, in fact, that tell me who you are." He knew he was treading on thin ice. He remembered only the barest fragments—*alikchi*, sorcerors, dream-senders, *isht*-something or other. There were good ones and bad ones with different names. His granma's stories had become bits and pieces like a jigsaw puzzle dumped thoughtlessly on the ground, some pieces carried off by careless children. There were owls and foxes meaning different things at different times. Different kinds of owls. Screech owls were witches. He was supposed to be afraid of *ishkitini*, the great horned messenger owl. The panther was she, and she came for you. He yearned, suddenly, for deep, dark waters and forests forever in shadow, remembering an old, stringy-haired man whose eyes were the color of the brown river. What would his own grandmother have said to this woman, he wondered, summoning up a picture of the heavy old lady spitting brown tobacco juice into red mud. His granma had been afraid of nothing.

"Then why have you never gone home?" She looked at him keenly. "Hasn't that old man called you?"

He thought of the cabin in Mississippi, his father, whom he couldn't visualize in his memory half as well as he could the old man across the river, his granma talking about blooded earth as though sacrifice had been made, and his thin, Irish mother brushing hair back from her face in the cabin door. "Look, Grandmother, I'm no Indian. My people have stories of leprechauns, too, and something called the *sidhe*. You know about those? Besides, home is where the heart is, and I'd like you to stop messing with my dreams. I don't know what you're up to, but I don't like it."

42

She waved him off with a motion of her hand. "I didn't send that dream. It came from somewhere else, and what you call yourself isn't important. However, I think this trip is going to be difficult and dangerous. There's nothing I can do, but without the girl's help you won't make it. I doubt that you'll make it anyway. They're waiting for you down there. For years you've been going to that place and they've been watching you, studying you, but now they're waiting. I've seen all of this and waited for the story to happen. Shorty tells me things. Are you surprised that Shorty Luke knows more than an old witch?"

He stared at her, startled by the word nobody ever used. "Nothing about Shorty Luke surprises me."

"And you don't even know who they are." She brought out a piece of black cloth and unfolded it on the desk. "I saved this for you."

On the cloth were the neck and shoulder hackles of the rooster, with skin attached, beautiful and shining, long, lovely feathers of bluish black and gray beside somewhat wider and shorter gray-and-white speckled spears. He remembered the dream of feathered bears.

He looked from the hackle up to the old lady. Her broad, dark face was almost unwrinkled, though he knew she must be seventy years old or more, the teeth strong looking and white as new snow. The university sweatshirt brought back for her by Jessie several years before was threadbare, the red ASU letters and pitchforked Sundevil barely visible where the shirt was stretched across her broad shoulders and still heavy breasts. Her skirt covered the chair and touched the floor, hiding the hightop basketball shoes she always wore. He realized with a shock that the old lady was incredibly beautiful, or maybe desirable was the right word, and he wondered if he was the victim of medicine, of witchcraft.

Mrs. Edwards was the center of the Black Mountain community, an important person in politics all across the reservation and beyond, her word reaching even down to Tucson and up into Navajo and Hopi country. She was powerful, admired, and above all, feared. He'd heard that it had been the old lady who'd solved the dilemma of her sister's twin sons. In the old days, twins were a bad sign, evidence of promiscuity or worse, even witchcraft. Some said one twin always had to be killed, but others said those were old nonsense stories. Mrs. Edwards had settled the matter by giving her nephews different names pulled from nowhere, Domingo Perez and Shorty Luke, and insisting that each boy would always be referred to as "the surviving twin." That was to fool witches and evil forces that might be listening. That the boys themselves came to be somewhat confused while growing up seemed of little consequence to anyone. Each was the surviving twin and that was that.

While Domingo enlisted in the army and returned from the war in the Pacific desolate and scarred, haunted by visions he would not name, his brother had gone to Hollywood to become an extra in dozens of western films. Now Domingo lived alone, shriveled up with his black-and-white dog, his curiosity, his hairspray, and his disability checks. Shorty lived with his wife, two daughters, and eight grandchildren farther down the road where the forest thickened, spending most of his time cutting and splitting pine, aspen, and oak to sell while shouting snatches of Italian at reservation women. And telling stories again and again. Pretty soon, the ranger thought, unless something was done Shorty would legitimately be called the surviving twin.

"Domingo will survive," the old lady said. "Something is being done."

"This was generous of you, Grandmother," the ranger answered, holding the hackle in his hands. "The feathers will come in handy. But I'm nobody's grandfather."

"The feathers can remind you of your friend the rooster," the old lady said, the eyes sharpening. "You will honor him by using them, and he will remember. That's important. Being a grandfather isn't just blood. Who measures blood except the white government? When I was a child there was an old man with us. He was Apache, but they said he had been captured as

44

a child from the white invaders. Still, he was Apache. Now this girl needs to learn more about the world, about how people live out there. She should go to college." She waved vaguely toward the world outside the office. "But first she needs to learn other things. Our people used to go down into that canyon to gather plums and chokecherries. In the winter the elk could be found down there. Now no one but you goes there, except Jessie."

"And now Jessie's customers."

"But for years it was only you."

"That's because nobody here but me likes to fish."

"Our people never used to eat creatures from the water. I have trouble understanding how you might find pleasure in luring the underwater people into the air world that kills them."

"My people ate everything they could get from the water, which was a hell of a lot. My ancestors might have trouble understanding how your people could eat insect larvae. But it's too rough down there in the canyon for a young girl."

"The women of our tribe used to be trained just like the men. Did you know that?"

"Somebody told me."

"Our women could ride and fight like men, and our men could sew and cook like women because one never knew when a person would have to do both."

"How does Alison feel about this?"

"I've spoken with her." She picked up the end of one braid and admonished him with it. "I saw it from the beginning. You fell in love with that river, not Tali. I heard them calling to you from the first day. That's why you never had to learn how to live with a real woman again, or real people. You knew that the other was waiting for you down there, and it was easier. Now you spend all your time there, so much that they say the tribal council is getting suspicious." She smiled ironically. "Everyone thinks you haven't been with a woman in years. Mrs. Martinez is spreading gossip about a *gaan* down there who you go to sleep with."

A flare of pain coursed through him. He closed his eyes, envisioning the group of potbellied men and stern-faced women talking about him and spirits. Outsiders, all nonrelatives in fact, would never really be trusted by the tribe. The word "witchcraft" was seldom used, but he knew that was at the deep bottom of the distrust. As long as he, a mixedblood from some tribe most of them had never heard of, had married into their tribe, then he had to be accepted. But by making him a game warden and giving him the remote and wild river canyon, more than a hundred miles of rock, rattlesnakes, mountain lions, bears, beavers, bighorn sheep, elk, and river, they could ensure that he was isolated as much as possible from human beings. Paradoxically, their own action had made him seem more dangerous still, more of an outsider, suspected of consorting with powerful spirits.

In fact, that must be precisely Jessie's reason, the ranger realized, not the hunters. In the canyon no one from the tribe would run across the crazy white people starving in the woods and sensibly try to feed them or lead them out. The idea that somebody from Berlin or Paris, New York or Los Angeles could be on some kind of vision quest caused most of the Black Mountain people to double over in laughter. Shorty Luke had once put on an imitation at one of the drinking parties by Oak Creek. "Oh, look," Shorty had said, pointing at the stars. "I see a vision. It is so beautiful." He'd turned to the other surviving twin, Domingo Perez. "Hey, that's a nice hat you got. Where'd you get it? How much? Good boots, too." When Domingo just looked confused, Shorty glanced up at the sky. "It must be a sacred vision I see. Buffalo are flying, I think. That must be my totem." He turned to Jake. "How you feeling, my good friend? You don't look so good. Maybe now that I am a shamans I should do a sacred flying buffalo healing ceremony for you. *Ciao, forestiero.* How much money you got?" By that point, most of the people present had been rolling on the ground in helpless laughter, all but Mrs. Edwards, who had shown up just in time to hear the story before telling everyone to shut up and go home, which they did. The evening had ended, he recalled now, with him leaning against his pickup all alone except for the old lady, who stood with crossed arms glaring at him as though the drinking party had been his idea. She'd turned and walked into the woods without a word, and it was only when he was driving back that he realized the old woman had a ten-mile hike through piñon and juniper to get home on a moonless night. Maybe, he'd thought at the time, she'd just fly there.

The tribe sold hunting and fishing permits, but no one bought permits for the canyon that knifed down through the eastern edge of the reservaton. It was too rough. The canyon walls were mostly vertical, broken masses of granite and volcanic debris with only a few creeks making passable folds into the depths. If you didn't know the creeks you could be in trouble, and there were plenty of lakes and lots of hunting up on top where someone could just park his pickup and walk a few yards from the road. He didn't know a single Indian who liked putting a heavy pack on and walking through neck-breaking terrain, and white people wouldn't venture into a part of the reservation without trails.

"They still don't know who you are." Mrs. Edwards looked at him shrewdly, adding, "maybe because *you* don't know who you are."

"I've heard that, too. But the council and Sam don't care how much time I spend down there. I could live on the river for all they care."

"For all they used to care, but things change. People's feelings change. You should certainly know that."

"You're talking about Tali."

She snorted. "My niece had already thrown two no-good men away before you. Those two never had the nerve to even come back. I knew she would do the same with you the minute she brought you home." She snorted again. "Men today are all too weak. Not like the old ones. Be careful."

She stood up, the skirt catching on the chair arm and causing the chair to spin as she stepped away from it. He moved aside for her to pass, and she paused in the doorway. "Was it coyotes or owls you heard?" she asked before turning and closing the door behind her.

4   For half an hour he sat behind his desk, feeling the presence of the old woman in the room and thinking about Shorty Luke. Shorty seemed to know everything about the reservation and the tribe. He knew how to get any place anyone might want to go, and he knew every story associated with every place.

He tried to figure out what he might say to Shorty Luke. The Apaches were fighters. The U.S. cavalry hadn't been able to do a damned thing with the Apaches until Apaches signed on as scouts. It was Apaches who tracked down Apaches, because the white men could never do it, a variation on the same story all over the continent. Like the Indian police who'd killed Sitting Bull and arrested Crazy Horse. He'd read a quote from an old Apache scout who, when asked if it had been hard to get Apache warriors to scout against their own people, said quite the contrary, "It was like turning bird dogs loose in a field of quail." Where the old man had heard about bird dogs was a mystery, but the statement had always been pretty chilling. Shorty Luke was a walking history book, encyclopedia, and record player combined. And a tape recorder that spliced the character of Shorty Luke into every story it heard.

Hell, his own Choctaw ancestors had been the ones to fight the Creeks and Chickasaws for the English. You could call them dumb shits, but those were old enemies. Why would Pushmataha and the other Choctaws have sided with foreigners like the Shawnee warrior Tecumseh, when they at least knew the English and white Americans? Whites never understood that, thinking that all Indians were the same.

He studied the motionless sign of the man in the canoe. What was it about a man in a boat in constant motion that never went anywhere people found so attractive? He liked the still white man, the eternally raised paddle, the half-risen fish. And he knew he was avoiding the question of Shorty Luke.

After half an hour of pointless thought, he climbed into the cab of his official pickup, leaving his backpack in the office. There were at least four hours before dark at this time of summer, enough for him to get to the tribal lodge to meet Two-Bears, but not enough, unfortunately, to go by Pachita Lake and also get down to the river before nightfall. If Alison was where Jessie had said she was, he'd be able to find her in the dark without her knowing it and make sure she was okay. Then he could camp further down the river, where Elk Creek entered the Dark. But he'd have to push it, and making camp at night wasn't pleasant, especially if it really decided to rain, always a good possibility in August. He wondered if Jessie had left Alison and the others with tarps at least. Surely he would have. So he'd go down there in the morning. Meanwhile, he had additional concerns.

Driving out of the little community of Black Mountain and onto the asphalt road, for the thousandth time he wondered at the beauty of the place. He hadn't expected this country when Tali and her brothers brought him home from Phoenix. On his journey west, he'd passed though the mountains above Albuquerque by night, failing to understand the dark forests on either side of the freeway, and then he'd turned south and west again, crossing the seared lands of southern New Mexico and Arizona. Desert had appealed to him then as the furthest thing he could find from where he had been. And the smell of desert air just before dawn had felt like the finest dream he'd ever had. But he'd been foreign and strange in the desert. There weren't enough shadows there. At noon between Tucson and Phoenix, he'd pulled his truck over and stood on the barren shoulder of the highway while cars raced past, watching his shadow pool at his feet and the open land seemingly gutted by the killing sun.

But when he'd opened his eyes to the Black Mountain country, peering from beneath bloody bandages and a crushing pain that welled in his head, even then he couldn't believe the beauty of the land. There was water, like the place of his birth, but instead of the dark, impenetrable rivers in that distant place, here the streams were fast and clear, hiding nothing. The air was clean and cut through him like medicine, the delicate shadings of gray and green in the shorter forest rising to the green-black of lodgepole and big ponderosa pine forests higher up. As soon as he was able, he had walked out among the trees around the little town where Tali lived, reaching his hand down to dig beneath the pine needles into the black earth, and touching everything. He'd bought maps, talked with everyone who would speak to him, and learned as much as he could about this extraordinary new place. And, he realized now, it seemed that the more he learned about the land the less he knew about the people. In fact, he had unthinkingly willed himself not to learn about Tali's people, feeling every bit an outsider without the right to know such things.

Every time he pointed to a place on a map and asked·Tali, or Shorty Luke, or anyone else about it, he could tell that their replies contained only a fragment of what they knew. When he'd asked Tali about that, she'd said, "There are stories, Jacob, stories about every place and everything you see. Nobody's going to just tell such things to a stranger." And after twenty years he had remained a stranger, he knew now, not just among the people of the tribe but even to his own wife. He knew the country, the creeks and dry streambeds, the creases and secrets of the river canyon, the wide mesas, but he knew only the surface. The anthropologist, Goldberg, had been able to cross that threshold somehow, to some important extent, but he hadn't.

He'd asked his granma about the old man. "Luther Cole," was all she'd said, shaking her head and spitting the eternal tobacco juice. And then his mother had taken him away from whatever that dream had meant. He lived with a vague yearning to go home, but he couldn't locate that place on all the maps he bought and hoarded. When he'd finally found his way down into the canyon for the first time, he had felt with each downward step a kind of exultation. At the river he had sat with an astonished sense of having arrived somewhere at last. The violence that pushed at his flesh from within disappeared in the canyon. Down there he slept at night for the first time since going to Nam. He already knew the length of the river, every bend and pool, better than anyone when Sam Baca offered him the job of game warden. Before Tali had put him out.

The low sun rested between thunderheads, turning the edges of the gray clouds a fine silver. Off to the north was a scimitar curve of blue-black rain that walked across the Mogollon Rim toward the Black Mountain range—what the weather people called locally heavy showers, the kind that could drown you in a bone-dry arroyo miles from where rain fell. He turned the radio on and was blasted by a song in Navajo before tuning in a country western station from Holbrook. A woman sang about no-good, snake-belly, lower-than-a-toad-frog, good-for-nothing cowboy loves while mild thunder rolled down from the mountains and over the pickup.

5 The tribal casino blazed pink, green, and gold when he drove by, the lights like ax blades against the surrounding pines. Rivulets of people merged at the edge of the parking lot into a stream that flowed from lot to casino and back again, blue hair, baseball caps, and bald heads shining like various stars. After the dull colors of the fish and game office and houses in Black Mountain, he felt blinded by the casino. Keeping his left hand on the steering wheel, he reached into his pants pocket with the other hand and fingered the rifle casing, glad that he hadn't mentioned it to Sam Baca. Sam was up to something, and Sam wouldn't be up to anything unless Xavier Two-Bears was behind it. What he felt between thumb and forefingers was a smooth brass messenger of confusion and trouble.

He'd never driven by the casino when it wasn't blazing, day or night. He'd gone inside only once, and had been forced back by the evil of the place. Touching the rifle shell, his mind wandered. For the first time since childhood, he thought of the dead-woman tree, his granma in Mississippi gumming tobacco and pointing to black blood on the dirt. "Man trouble," she'd said. He'd known it was a straight razor that did it. Jimmy McKelroy had seen it happen. The Yazoo River slid along in his memory brown and mean looking, inviting children to tumble into its dark mouth. Then his granma had told about the land of the dead where bad Indians went, a dry, dead-tree, stinking-mud place where doomed shadows washed ashore from a river of snakes and toads. He'd been ready to ask about his own dead father when the old woman rose from her stump seat, spat a black wad onto the dirt, and dragged her feet back toward their cabin, leaving his five-year-old self alone with tree, river, and blood.

He remembered. Underneath the Ybernee Apartments that first year in California, where the trains thundered past fifty feet away every hour, he'd crawled into the dark to find stuffed up against the spiderwebbed and rich dirt-smelling corner of a far dark place a painting. He couldn't even remember what the painting showed now. But it seemed important that somebody had painted it, not reproduced but painted it, and somehow it had ended up beneath the shabby two-floor apartments where trains shook the four-by-four foundations every hour. What he really remembered about the Ybernee Apartments was an absent dead father, a painting that someone had made with his or her hands, the regular shaking of people who were going someplace he wanted to go, waiting on the stair steps of the county health clinic with other poor, snot-nosed kids, and a great, arching, chrome and black stove that looked like a wood stove but, miraculously, lit with butane. That was only a couple of miles down the tracks from the poultry co-op where they bought half-live chicks for a dime and nursed them into flaming, arrogant health in their small apartment. Then they moved first to the county housing project and finally to the wild coast range. But things go too fast. Do you know, Shorty, about the long, deep canyon that sliced into the Santa Lucia

Mountains, live oak and poison oak and mountain mahogany closing in until it choked the boy in poison oak and brush so thick he watched his black-and-white dog turn back? Bears, wild pigs, and mountain lions even there.

A river curved from south to north there in California, with dry arroyos dropping down to the sycamore and buckbrush and wide, dry riverbed. Why their rivers had to be dry he never understood, for he had been born and lived by a deep, brown river and had seen other California rivers that ran fast and deep on television, but this river was dry and brushy. Early in the morning, when the sun is just beginning to touch the hairs of the finest oat stalks, you see the sun not yet showing but firing the stalks with light that rises from the earth.

He knew what it would look like inside the casino. People would be crowding the slot machines, feeding tokens in with dexterity that belied their arthritis and bursitis and osteoporosis, smoking and breathing through clear plastic tubes out of each nostril, pulling oxygen canisters on little carts. The interior lights turned their skin a lifeless gray, and young, expressionless Indians would be circling endlessly with trays of tokens and change. Buses brought the old ones northward from places like Phoenix and Scottsdale, Paradise Valley and Mesa where they'd gone to die, caravans of buses winding ceaselessly through the northern edge of the Sonoran Desert, up cottonwood canyons over the Mogollon Rim and through the miles of pine forest to dump retirees from New York and Kansas right into the tribe's lap. From the west and north and east, from Flagstaff and Strawberry and Holbrook, Winslow, Payson, and Springerville, came small-town farmers, ranch hands, storekeepers, layed-off loggers, and Forest Service and BIA employees who also swarmed there to lose. Carved only four years before out of reservation forest, miles from any established tribal community, the casino burned like a crowned-out project fire twenty-four hours every day and night. The tribe was making a bundle, doing to the white world what that world had always done to Indians. It was like those liquor stores in Gallup that sold booze to Navajos and said it wasn't their fault if Indians liked to drink too much. It had begun a long time before, around 1492 maybe, when Europeans started to run up a big bar tab in America. Payback was slow coming, but now the tribe was plowing the profits back into medical centers, retirement care, prenatal counseling, a few college scholarships, housing, and investments that would ensure a cash flow when the feds or the state managed to squash the too-lucrative gaming. Xavier Two-Bears was as shifty and shrewd as they came, the only tribal chairman in the Southwest with a Harvard MBA degree. You could dislike and distrust him, but you couldn't deny that he was helping the tribe.

A blur caught the corner of Jake's eye as a coyote darted across the road right out of the casino clearing and stood with tongue hanging out, half-turned to watch the ranger's truck disappear. He studied the creature in his side mirror for a moment before it trotted into the pines.

Twenty minutes later, he headed south on a newly black-topped road through a pine forested valley that opened up every couple of miles to meadows where elk grazed by night. At the end of the valley the tribe's resort hotel, built from old-growth pine harvested on the reservation, stood like a big ski lodge against a wide, smooth-surfaced lake. He parked in front of the hotel and paused as he stepped out to watch men in belly boats fishing for the stocked trophy rainbows. Anything above twenty-four inches was an extra fifty bucks, and to his knowledge no one had ever complained about the price. Shaggy pine shadows rippled behind the inner-tubed fishermen as they drifted and looped their flylines in great curves. The trophy trout had been Xavier Two-Bear's idea, and Jake had to admit it was a good one. Across the lake, in a fine dark crease against the eastern horizon, was the crest of the Black Mountain range, and he imagined the long half-circle he would soon be making toward the river deep in those mountains.

The hotel lobby was jumping the way it always was in the summer, with guests checking in and out and uniformed employees, both Indian and white, pushing carts and carrying tablecloths. He wiped his boots carefully outside the front doors and then headed to the far side of the room and down a short flight of stairs to a sunken reception area where cut-glass chandeliers poured light into deep beige carpet. Brightly colored paintings by Indian artists hung on two of the rounded walls, with a pair of gray-and-brown Navajo blankets on the third. To one side of the room stood a larger-than-life granite sculpture of a woman wrapped in a blanket so that her polished stone face stared blankly from the gray depths. A podium had been set up in front of a half-circle of expensive-looking chairs and couches, and a few feet from the podium a short, very large man reclined in a leather chair, the face and hands that protruded from his pinstriped suit the same color as the dark leather.

"Come on, Wendell, get your damned skinny ass into it. You can do better than that." The man in the chair lifted a hand, heavy with turquoise and silver rings, toward a bony boy in a black suit, white shirt, and silver bolo tie who stood behind the podium fiddling with a droop-necked microphone. "You don't sound like him one damned bit." The hand dropped back to the fat arm of the chair and the boy sulked dispiritedly behind the podium, his brown eyes on the wall across the room.

"What's up, Xavier?" the ranger said from a few feet away.

The man in the chair turned his large head slowly, his long, unnaturally black hair tied in a tight ponytail and his heavy, handsome face stern. "I'm trying to get Wendell to sound like a politician. You know, 'My good friends' and all that. I was thinking about running my nephew here for the state senate in a few years, but I'm not sure he's got the stuff. He seems disgruntled. Perhaps our friend Udall could coach him a little, you think? Hey, you think being gruntled is good if disgruntled is bad? You ever thought about that? Ain't that what it means, like ungruntled? Like somebody stole your gruntles."

Jake squinted toward the boy, who had managed to make the microphone stand up and was now edging away from the podium while his uncle's attention was distracted. "Sam said you wanted to see me. I'm on my way down to the river again for a few days."

"Nobody better take my gruntles." The big man grinned, and then the grin disappeared as he looked hard at the ranger. "That river again, huh? Well, that's part of what I wanted to talk to you about, Jacob."

The ranger felt his body and mind jump at the sound of his name. He tried to remember when Two-Bears had used his first name before.

The tribal chairman gestured toward another leather chair beside his. "Want a drink? Hey!" He waved at a young blond-haired man who stood attentively nearby with a towel over his arm. "Bring us a couple of Perriers, and get somebody to drag that podium out of here."

The man nodded and left quickly, and as the ranger lowered himself into the chair Xavier Two-Bears turned and winked. "I like to keep 'em on their toes. These college boys need to learn their place, gives 'em a better start in life. That one's from U of A." He grinned again. "They really ain't worth shit at first, but they can be civilized. It's just a matter of acculturation. Kill the European to save the man, if you get my meaning." He reached back and pulled the ponytail tighter. "Wendell's graduating from Cornell next year. What do you think? Hey, what do you think about that Wildcat beeball team? Final Four prospect, I'd say. Jessie should've played for a team like that."

Two young men appeared and began to unplug the microphone and wheel the podium away. The ranger glanced in their direction as they disappeared out an open archway at the rear of the room, and then he turned to study the chairman's heavy face, the long, thin nose, broad cheekbones, and square double chin, settling finally on the opaque brown eyes. "You wanted to talk to me about the river?"

The waiter reappeared with a tray and two glasses of bubbling water, a slice of lime floating in each glass. As he held the tray out, his cheeks seemed to redden in what the ranger would have defined as a blush.

The chairman took both glasses and handed one to the ranger, and the waiter retreated quickly and silently to the edge of the room.

"Sam told me you found an elk head out by Heifer Tank last night. A big one."

The ranger nodded, drinking half the water in one breath before speaking. "Six points on each side, if I counted right."

"Damn. You know how much money that represents?"

The ranger nodded. "A lot."

"Damn straight, and they left the rack right on the ground, just taking the meat. That's wasteful. Think what one of those New York or Texas hotshots would've paid for that elk. Probably ten grand."

"You said something about the river."

"Sam said you left the head at the office, said there was a feather tied to it. What do you think?"

Jake shrugged. "Owl feather, I'd say."

"You notice anything else, any other kind of evidence?"

"It was dark. Couldn't really see much of anything."

"Nothing, huh?"

"Nothing but the head and guts."

Two-Bears nodded. "Keep this to yourself, Jacob. Me and Sam have an investigation going, don't want anything messing it up. So you don't tell anybody, and anything you hear comes straight to me, right?"

"Sure." Jake looked at the granite statue, wondering what Sam and Two-Bears were up to and feeling the weight of the cartridge shell in his pocket.

"My grandmother used to gather plums down in that river canyon," Two-Bears said. "I ever tell you that? When she was a girl. Maybe one of the last ones to do that at Black Mountain. She was down there in Mexico with the warriors for a while, too, when she was a baby. You ever hear about those times?"

The ranger shook his head.

"Shorty could tell you about all that. He knows the stories, but of course it'll be him down there in Mexico giving Geronimo advice if he tells it. Say, I'll bet there's still lots of wild plums in that canyon. You ever notice? Bears and birds eat them, I guess. Lots of bears down there, too, I bet. I think about going down there myself sometimes, breathe a little wilderness air, but you know how it is. Not too much free time these days."

The ranger nodded.

"Imagine what it was like, Jacob, before all these whites came. Just think what it must have been like when there was only our people here. Sure, you had to worry about putting enough food away for the winter. Winters get hard up here sometimes. I don't have to tell you that. And teaching your children or nieces and nephews or grandchildren. Maybe a few raids on the Navajo or Pueblos for recreation. Easy stuff like that. All winter when the snow piled up outside your wickiup you could tell stories just the way it had always been. You ever think about those things? Like trying to hold water in your hand, you know." Two-Bears sighed tragically.

The ranger thought about the river and grew increasingly alert as the chairman circled toward his subject. Over the years he had come to realize that the more Xavier Two-Bears circled the bigger the prey would be.

"Course you don't, since you don't come from here. But maybe you think those things about your own ancestors. I never studied much about the Choctaws in college, too busy with numbers, you know, but I do remember your ancestors were pretty much massacred by one of those first Spaniards. That one named after an automobile. First white man they see and he starts spearing them and letting man-eating dogs loose on them. Think about it. You know, I read where the Choctaws, Jews, and Quakers were the only ones to send money from America to Ireland during that potato famine they had. The Choctaws sent a hundred and seventy bucks, about ten grand by today's calculations. That's something. You see, your ancestors were thinking internationally way back then the way all of us ought to be doing today. They were acting as a sovereign nation. What we Indians really need is a seat in the U.N., not just those committees in Geneva that can't ever agree on anything. You must be what, a quarter or something like that?"

"Half. A lot of Choctaws had Irish relatives." Jake looked again at the granite carving, wondering how much the tribe had paid for the art.

"I see what you mean." Two-Bears took a small drink from the Perrier. "All my relations sort of thing. But you get my point anyway, right?"

The chairman pushed himself more upright in the chair with his massive hands. He pulled a white handkerchief out of an interior pocket of his suit and wiped his forehead, watching the stairs leading down into the reception area. "Well," he said, stuffing the handkerchief back. "This ain't just me, you understand, but some people been thinking that maybe you ought to spend more time up on top. They say nobody's going to shoot an elk down in that canyon. Heck, they say nobody can even get down there but you. So." He took a big drink of the water, letting the lime slide into his mouth and chewing for a moment and swallowing before he spoke again. "Matter of cost effectiveness, the council thinks. Normally this sort of thing wouldn't come through the tribal chairman, but you got most people kind of afraid of you." He grinned at the ranger. "Hey, enough mundane business. We've got some of those *National Geographic* film people and a guy from Washington here tonight. Big shot from Interior Department. You ought to stay and meet everybody. Now all we need is Shorty Luke to show up and start telling those dumb-ass stories like he does. Him and Goldberg have some kind of presentation they want to make to the tribal council tonight, after the reception. You seen Shorty? I need to have a talk with him."

When the ranger didn't reply, the chairman said, "You know, there's still people think of you as an outsider, not to mention a pretty strange cookie." He chuckled as he said the last words and then spat a seed into his cupped fist. "So they think maybe you shouldn't ought to patrol the river anymore."

"There's a lot of wildlife in that canyon," the ranger said finally. "That herd of bighorn sheep down there's on the endangered list, not to mention the Apache golden trout."

Two-bears shook his head. "How many people you see down there in a season, Jacob? One, two, none maybe? You and me both know you never see nobody down there. Nobody's going to poach those sheep or trout. Heck, those endangered species'll do better if you stay up on top. Then nobody'll be bothering them. Pretty soon they'll even be releasing some of those Mexican wolves in there, and those guys are shy. Big fella like you'd scare the hell out of them. Say, I tell you about that Albuquerque investment we're considering? Big condo complex called Vista del Vista overlooking the Big Rio Grande River. Sure thing, our advisors say. Real estate's booming over there with both Intel and America Online moving in."

There was a commotion at the top of the stairs, and the chairman turned quickly and leaned close to Jake. "You know anything about who's doing this poaching?"

When Jake shook his head, Two-Bears added, "Sam seemed to think you might know more than you told him. You sure you don't have any hunches or anything? Not protecting somebody, are you?"

Jake again felt the weight of the cartridge in his pocket. "I'm sure," he said.

A group of men and women began to descend into the reception area, dressed in a combination of suits and traditional tribal clothing. Two-Bears rose to his feet with surprising speed and grace, like an immense cat. Without looking at the ranger, he said, "You understand, Jacob? You work outside that canyon from now on; you don't set foot down there. I have to tell the council that you agreed, okay? Sam and I want you to drive around tonight, do some patrolling."

The ranger glanced at the knot of tribal council members and politicians pouring into the room. He felt conspicuous in his uniform. "Sam doesn't seem to know what he thinks. He told me to check Pachita Lake. There was some shooting over there." He paused, sensing the council members eyeing him without ever looking directly at him. "And I need to make one more trip downriver."

"You can check Pachita in a couple of days, and forget that river. No more trips down there, period. Tribe's losing a lot of money. That bull you found was worth about half your salary for a year. Can't afford that kind of expense." The chairman looked meaningfully at Jake. "Go out and sneak around. Use that Marine training."

Jake considered reminding Two-Bears that he'd been Special Forces, not a jarhead, but he said nothing. It didn't matter to Two-Bears, who'd had a college deferment.

"No more river, Jake. Understand?" Two-Bears wasn't even looking at him as he spoke. The chairman began to laugh and shake hands with the crowd like a politician, and Jake saw the tribal members flinch slightly each time the big man grasped and squeezed a hand the way he'd learned in graduate school. In some ways, Two-Bears was as foreign to the tribe as he was.

Jake moved toward the stairs through a path that opened before him. No one acknowledged his passing, but he was so used to being shunned by most people that he hardly noticed.

Jake pondered Two-Bears' tone. There was a kind of urgency he hadn't heard before in the chairman's voice, an uneasiness. And why had Sam thought he knew more than he'd said?

At the top of the stairs he ran into half a dozen casually dressed white people walking on both sides of Avrum Goldberg, the resident Black Mountain anthropologist. The small, thin man wore a traditional breechcloth and Apache leggings and moccasins, his torso covered by a cotton shirt and vest and his long, thinning gray hair held back by a blue headband. His face, skull, and hands, all that showed of his skin, were as brown as coffee, and his stolid expression suggested both wisdom and resignation.

"Chief Gold Bird," a woman with long blond hair was saying, "it's very generous of you to share traditional lore with us on film. So many native people are reluctant to do that." She turned a technological smile on the anthropologist, and the ranger caught a brilliant flash of blue eyes. She was the most beautiful white woman he'd seen in years, but the face was like a dancer's mask, showing fine lines at the corners of the eyes. Stress fractures, he thought, realizing that the woman was older than she appeared at first glance. The face wouldn't get her very far with Avrum, but he knew the tribal matrons waiting below would recognize the threat and close ranks quickly.

"I'm not a chief," Avrum began to say, but a loud, high-pitched voice cut him off.

"I opened my eyes to the darkness of winter," a man chanted from behind the group, and all but the anthropologist turned toward the voice.

Jake saw Shorty Luke, in work boots, denim overalls, and a red-plaid flannel shirt rolled up to the elbows, standing just inside the lobby door, his crewcut a gleaming silver. "As a youth I learned to love wild city canyons and quested for visions among pigeons and feral cats. Africa was my goal but my dissertation director sent me to the savage Apaches."

"Who is that?" the woman asked, staring at Shorty.

"*Ciao, Bella,*" Shorty called to her, waving a hand over the crowd. "*Che bellezza! Che splendore!*"

Turning to the anthropologist, she said, "An Italian here on a reservation? They're always so crude." She shook her head and took a step forward.

"A demented tribal storyteller," Goldberg said with a shrug, brushing strands of hair back over his shoulder. "A stealer of stories who learned fragments of pidgin Italian in Hollywood."

When the woman seemed perplexed, Goldberg shook his head disgustedly. "He used to be a Hollywood extra. He picked up his scraps of Italian from the other Indian actors. Now he steals everyone's stories, including mine."

Shorty Luke had been listening to the discussion with cocked head and bright eyes. "Sal Mineo was my best friend in Hollywood. In the end, he got shot off his horse, too," he said sadly.

The woman's look of confusion deepened as the group walked past the ranger. "What did he mean˙about pigeon visions and New York? And what did you mean about your story?"

Goldberg held both hands out, palms upward, and shrugged. "Some people think a demented tribal storyteller who babbles Italian is holy. So who knows what he means? That's a mystery for the Great Spirit."

While the men and women crowded past, Jake heard an earnest young man ask, "Gold Bird, is that a sacred name or birth name? Can a Black Mountain person tell his real name to the cameras? Are you afraid the camera will steal your soul?"

"*Che malato d'amore,*" Shorty Luke shouted after them, standing on tiptoe in his heavy work boots.

When the film crew had gone down the stairs, Jake stood face to face with the other surviving twin. Shorty Luke smiled, showing the wide gaps in his yellow teeth, and the ranger found himself grinning back despite a heavy feeling in his chest.

"Gold Bird took off his pants and soared with the eagles," Shorty said. "Anthropologists and Italians became the real Indians. Old Lady Edwards heard so many Indians say 'Fuck the anthropologists' that she decided to fuck the anthropologist."

"Don't defame the elders, Shorty, especially your aunt and your friend. How's the family?" The ranger noticed chain saw shavings on the little man's shoulders and arms. Shorty Luke was the hardest worker on the reservation, too independent to be trusted with tribal politics and also suspect because he had been contaminated by Hollywood and by association with Avrum Goldberg.

"Gold Bird wears leggings and cock-and-butt flaps to be Indian on television." Shorty's grin widened. "He forgets the stories of his people and shifts shape. I have to give him a little shit about it now and then. The family's good. Little Kimo's got one of those summer colds, but everybody's good. Lots of wood to cut. That big snow last winter took down a lot of aspen. Say, did I ever tell you about the time I watched a battle between a praying mantis and a great wasp? We were bored, with just a few mortar rounds coming in, and someone had a praying mantis in a little bamboo cage. A guy named Keller. My friend. He liked to meditate. This other guy brought in a giant wasp and put it in the cage. People began betting. The battle took days."

"Shorty, that's my story," Jake said. "I told you that. And it didn't take days. The mantis bit the wasp's head off in about a minute."

"Now it's my story. The world's story. You tell it your way and I'll tell it mine. I heard Two-Bears was kissing some important ass over here and thought I'd look in for a minute or two. I like those stuffed mushrooms he serves. Reminds me of my silver screen career."

The ranger glanced at Shorty's dark eyes for a moment and then looked away. There had always been a hard resistance within Shorty's expression, a flintlike edge that no one could miss, which was probably why Two-Bears and everyone else put up with the little man's constant taunting. Shorty always seemed to know more about everything than anyone else. "Xavier said you'd be dropping in," Jake said. "He said you and Avrum had a proposal for the council. I guess in the meantime he's going to let Avrum be the official Indian for *National Geographic*. Good joke." The ranger nodded his head in the direction from which he'd come.

"The white man's heart will soar like a beagle," Shorty said portentiously. Changing tone, he added, "The tribe likes that because it keeps white folks out of their hair. And you've got to admire Avrum's sense of humor, too, to go along with it. Avrum has this cockeyed idea he wants to float to the council tonight. Thinks we ought to become a theme tribe."

"Theme tribe?"

Shorty shrugged. "It's complex. I'll explain it later. By the way, the moccasin telegraph says the council's been talking about you. Be careful. Now I'd better get down there before those mushrooms are gone, also to make sure they know who's the real Indian around here."

"I wouldn't count on that, Shorty. Gold Bird looks more Indian than you do. He dresses right, knows all the stories, and has a more Indian-sounding name than you do. He also speaks the tribal language better."

"My tribal tongue was stolen in Phoenix, at the Indian school," Shorty Luke said. "And Hollywood. Avrum came to salvage our culture but got fucked by the Old Lady. Since when is Goldberg an Indian name? It's worse than Two-Beers."

"Don't let Xavier hear that, and it's Gold Bird, didn't you hear the beautiful lady?"

"Ah. *Quanto mi piace.*" Shorty raised his voice. *"Madonna mia. Quant' è bedda!"*

"Those white people won't believe you're Indian, Shorty. Your hair's too short, you blather Italian, and you're dressed like a white man. Face the facts. You're Sicilian to them, mafioso for the casino. You're not a very marketable Indian."

Jake looked over his shoulder and down the stairs. A flock of waiters had appeared to set up several tables with small edible things on them, a Sterno flame burning under each of the silver pans. Young white men circulated with trays. He smiled to himself at how the Indians took the college boys for granted, pretending not to even see them as they accepted drinks and small plates of food skewered with toothpicks. One council matron, Benecia Martinez, who lived in a house with no electricity or running water, held a stuffed mushroom with her pinkie finger extended, mouthing exaggerated words to a woman he remembered as her cross-cousin. He knew how much everyone enjoyed such a scene. They were playing the white man, a subtle and satirical amusement on the reservation. Two-Bears hand-picked the waiters at auditions held at the universities. The tribe paid extremely well, so there was no shortage of applicants. Two-Bears' grandmother had been rented out from Haskell Indian School in Kansas on a work program, worked nearly to death by a Swedish farmer. Two-Bears wasn't one to forget or forgive. Indian retribution was patient but inevitable.

The ranger forced himself to look into Shorty Luke's black eyes. "Did I ever tell you you're the only man I admire on this whole reservation?" he said.

Shorty's eyes narrowed further.

"Could we step outside and talk for just a minute, Shorty?"

Shorty Luke's demeanor changed. The ironic smile disappeared, and Jake was looking into a face from a nineteenth-century photograph. Shorty nodded and held the door open for Jake.

Outside, Jake glanced at the darkening water and glimmers of lightning far to the east. He reached into his pocket and pulled out the .30-.40 casing, holding it up so that it caught the lights from the lodge.

"What you got there, Jake?"

"Thirty-forty," Jake replied. "Found it next to the head of a poached elk last night. Real old gun with a worn-down firing pin."

"No kidding?"

"No kidding."

"We didn't mean for you to find that stuff, Jake. Avrum figured you'd be down on the river for three or four more days and Sam would be the one to find it. Sam found the other ones."

"Other ones?"

Shorty nodded. "Three so far. That's about thirty thousand dollars down the tubes. We left them where Sam would be the first one to see them. He was scheduled to get an anonymous phone tip about the head by Heifer Tank, but I guess you got there before he checked his answering machine."

"Why?" Jake asked. "And who's 'we'?"

"Me and Avrum."

"Avrum Goldberg? You're kidding."

Shorty drew in a deep breath. "No, Avrum Jones. It's complicated, but I'll try to make it simple. We found out that Xavier and Sam've been selling trophy elk hunts secretly and pocketing the money, ten thousand for a hunt. Sam reports a couple of hunts to the tribe and keeps the money from the rest."

"Why didn't you go to the FBI?"

"You trust the FBI, Jacob, on a reservation?"

When Jake didn't answer, Shorty said, "Avrum and I figured if we eliminated all the real trophy bulls it would put those guys out of business, and we wouldn't have those rich asshole hunters crawling all over the reservation anymore. That would leave the young bulls to keep the herds going. Also, we made sure Sam and Xavier knew we were on to them."

"Why the owl feather?"

"Sam's pretty scared of owl medicine, with good reason. We know he must've found cartridges like that one you have, because we left them in conspicuous places, but you notice he hasn't said anything about it."

"What the hell do you do with all that meat?"

"We been giving it to hungry people, Jake, Indians and whites both. Lots of people out of work now, and we got our own little food bank going. Not too many vegetarians around here, and one big elk feeds a lot of people. We drop off a quarter or some ribs here and there. But I think we'd better stop now. Sam may think that you know, since we left those .30-.40 shells at every kill. He probably figures you wouldn't miss something like that. We don't want to cause trouble for you."

"So what? I'm taking this to the feds."

Shorty shook his head. "All you can prove, Jake, is that Avrum and I killed an elk without a tribal permit. The feds won't give a damn about that, and you got no evidence against Sam and Xavier. I think maybe we better both be quiet about this and keep our eyes open for a while. I'll tell Avrum. They'll probably stop stealing those elk now, if they think you talked to me and you know, too."

"That's a lot of money they've been making. Xavier's going to be damned mad."

"But what can he do, shoot us? Xavier ain't like that. I'll tell Avrum." Shorty turned and went back through the door.

Jake walked down the steps toward his truck, watching die-hard float fishermen rippling the lake like rising trout. "Maybe," he said aloud to himself. He thought about Two-Bears' order that he look around for poachers. Either Sam hadn't told Xavier Two-Bears anything, or the chairman just wanted to keep him busy for some reason. At least Shorty and Avrum would be safe in the middle of a council meeting, or at least as safe as anybody could be in a tribal council meeting.

For the first time in many years, Jake felt violence piling high in his blood like summer thunderheads. Lightning building. He hadn't felt such a desire for monsters to slay in many years.

"Jake."

He turned toward the voice and saw Sam Baca walk out of the shadows at the end of the lodge porch.

"How's it going?"

"Great, Sam."

"Nice present you left for me."

Jake watched the short, squat man without speaking. Sam was a fullblood, dark and powerfully built. He kept his hair cut to within a quarter inch of his head. He'd been an easy man to work for.

"We need to catch those poachers, Jake." Sam had his hands in his pants pockets and was looking at the lake.

"That's what Xavier was just saying," Jake replied. "He told me to do some patrolling tonight. What do you think?"

Sam seemed to consider the question. "Good idea. Why don't you just stake out some good spot for two or three hours and then go home and get some sleep."

Jake nodded. "I'll do that, Sam. You have any suspicions?"

Sam sucked in a deep breath. "Wish I did, Jake."

6   For the first day she hadn't really heard. The spring had slipped out of the mossy rock into its small pool, gathered, and welled over the pool's lip into a stream that fell silently down the little side canyon toward the creek not far below. The spiderlike insects that skated across the pool had moved as quietly as air, their shadows refracting beneath them. The trees had stood ominously around and above her, letting their needles drift down without sound.

On the evening of the second day she had become conscious of the difference. The fragile water insects stirred the pool when they moved, sending a faint tingling music into the air even above the chiming sounds of the spring emerging and breaking like glass over the cushioned granite. Now there was a whirring in the air, and she realized it was the sound of the pine needles and tiny branches coming free and swirling toward earth.

By the third night all the mountains were whirling with sound like strange, always approaching music. What she knew must be coyotes sang and warbled and howled and barked all around her, while some other creature sent shrill, wirelike whistles echoing through the big canyon. Bats fluttered between the trees, their wings making a noise that reminded her of the down pillows of her childhood. Insects hummed and buzzed and crackled in the air and beneath the earth's surface. Huge creatures came toward her through the forest but stopped before she could see them, their enormous legs shaking the earth as they approached and retreated. She heard the air explode in and out of their nostrils and smelled their wildness. When the brief, warm rains came, she sat on the inflated ground pad Jessie had provided, huddled inside her big, hooded storm parka, and listened to the language of water on her shoulders and back until the storms moved on. The thunder that mumbled through the blue-gray clouds frightened her, but it was quickly gone.

On the afternoon of the fourth day, she was completely awake. The pores of her flesh felt open to the warm, moist air, and she had ceased having thoughts of any sort. Smells, feelings, and sounds had merged into a single sense that enveloped her. Without deciding to do so, she had begun to keep her eyes closed nearly all of the time, seeing the whole forest through the translucent veil of her lids. When her body unfolded from the sitting position she had held for hours and leaned over the spring, she was outside of the motion, observing the wonder of it and drinking the cold water the way an animal would, her mouth beneath the surface and her eyes closed. When she sat back up, she opened her eyes and looked at the leather pouch with the vision food in it, still half full.

There was a loud crashing in the brush below the spring, and she saw the face of a wolf.

7   When the *National Geographic* guests and the politician were gone, a dozen Indians were left in the sunken reception area, sitting in the big chairs or standing next to the hors d'oeuvre tables. Two-Bears sprawled in the leather chair he had inhabited for most of the evening, his bolo tie loosened and coat spread to show his rumpled white shirt. He took a drink of Perrier and waved a hand, thinking of the phone number the blonde had given him before she left. She was a hot one.

"Business," he said.

The crowd turned toward him, people chewing rapidly in case they might be expected to speak. Shorty Luke sucked a mushroom off a toothpick and elbowed Avrum Goldberg, who was scrutinizing the mangled remains of a cheese platter.

"I know it's a funny place for a council meeting, but I figured we could kill a couple of birds with one stone. A Gold Bird even." Two-Bears grinned and someone in the crowd laughed out loud. He wondered if the woman, Donna, would be pissed if she figured out they'd pawned a Jewish anthropologist off on her as a real Indian.

"That reminds me of the story of Raven Old-Man's son-in-law," Shorty said. "But it's the wrong time to tell that."

"Sure as hell is," Two-Bears said quickly. He looked at the others and thought of the phone number again. It wouldn't be too late to get up to Show Low for drinks with her if he didn't let the council do its usual four-hour song and dance. "We can make this quick. Professor Gold Bird and Shorty have an idea they want to broach. And I don't have a clue what it is. So let's hear it. By the way, Avrum, thanks for being Indian tonight. You were good, real good. I don't know what we'd do without you."

There was a smattering of soft applause as the group turned to grin at Goldberg.

Avrum stepped forward. He waited until the space was entirely quiet, then he folded his arms and spoke to the wall beside Two-Bears. "Happy to be of service. My idea is this. The tribe is making a pretty good income from the casino and lodge and other things, like hunting." He looked at Shorty and noticed that Two-Bears was also watching the little man.

There was a satisfied murmur of assent from the group.

"But there's a cultural cost involved in such enterprises."

The group fell intensely quiet, and several people folded their arms and stared hard at the anthropologist.

"Gambling attracts the wrong kind of people. People who can have a bad influence especially on the young. And some might question the morality of selling our animals to rich hunters."

He looked directly at Two-Bears this time, and the chairman returned the gaze with serenity. "Cut to the chase, Professor," Two-Bears said. "It's getting kind of late."

Everyone looked at the chairman with surprise. To interrupt a speaker in that way was unheard-of rudeness, and rushing a council meeting was a white-man way of doing things.

"My proposal," Goldberg replied, "is that the tribe give up the casino and lodge and commercial hunting and instead become a traditional tribe again, living the way everyone lived before the white men came."

The room remained silent, the heavy men and women looking at the anthropologist with curious amusement, waiting.

"Avrum thinks we can make a lot more money this way," Shorty interjected, stepping up beside Goldberg. "He's looked into it, and he thinks that if we convert our whole reservation into a traditional eighteen-hundreds tribal community we can get a lot of grants."

"That's nuts," Two-Bears said.

"I've looked into it," Avrum said evenly. "If we lived entirely traditionally in every way, we could get grants from an incredible number of sources. Costner, Fonda and Turner, Paul Newman, the MacArthur Foundation, Guggenheim, National Endowment for the Humanities as well as the National Foundation for the Arts, not to mention at least a hundred other culturally and historically sensitive organizations."

"You forgot *National Geographic* and Disney," Shorty said.

Avrum nodded. "Both have expressed deep interest and more or less promised technological and financial support."

"You mean, if we all live like our ancestors lived two hundred years ago, people will pay us for it?" someone asked.

Shorty nodded emphatically. "We're talking a lot of money here. You see, it's not just the grants but all the tourists that'll come." He looked around the room. "How many authentic Indian villages do you know about?" When no one responded, he said, "That's right, none. I mean, nobody's going to go out to Sioux country because they get depressed by the poverty, and that bunch of Cherokees in North Carolina have nothing but a little circus and they still attract millions of tourist dollars. I read up on them. Tourists'll be coming here by the hundreds of thousands, crawling all over us. We'd be bigger than Yellowstone or Yosemite, bigger than Universal Studios or Disney World."

"How much?" Two-Bears asked.

Avrum looked serious. "Millions."

A murmur buzzed through the group.

Mrs. Martinez raised her wrinkled bulk from a chair and stood with hands on hips. "What do you mean by 'traditionally'?"

Avrum began to speak, but Shorty cut him off. "You know, the old ways. We'd tear down these government shacks and build authentic wickiups, eat venison and dried chokecherries and that sort of thing, dress like Avrum, tell stories, make arrows and bows in the old way, hunt, all the things our ancestors did. Avrum's an expert; he can teach us."

A short, stocky man in a pearl-snap western shirt, new jeans, shiny black boots, and a wide black hat stepped forward with his hands in his pockets. "So we could make a lot of money living like that?"

Shorty nodded. "Yeah, Carlos. You heard Avrum."

"Only one problem then," the man said. "How we going to spend it? We got to live in wickiups and make our own clothes and eat berries and walk everywhere, what're we going to do with all that money? I mean we can't have no satelite dish or color TV and no Land Cruiser, can we?"

"We couldn't even have electricity," one of the women put in.

"That's crazy," Mrs. Martinez said as she dropped her bulk with a thud back into the chair. "Nuts. Besides, we already have that Native American village thing in June with authentic dwellings and dancers and stuff for the tourists."

"Wait a minute." A tall, angular old man with very dark skin and a long gray ponytail stepped out of the crowd, and everyone fell silent. The man folded his arms across his skinny chest and looked deeply at Avrum Goldberg. His polished brown boots, neatly creased brown slacks, and starched white shirt gave him an impressive, unyielding appearance.

"The professor may have a good idea." He looked around before going on. "I never liked that casino too much, and I get kind of mad when I see them rich fat white men come and kill our animals for money. And on top of all that, my wife and me been thinking it might be nice to get out of the cold winter now we're getting a little older."

Two-Bears shifted his hands restlessly on the arms of the chair and clenched his jaws. The old man was the former chairman of the tribe. Like everyone else, Two-Bears kept a respectful silence.

"It's true we couldn't have no satelite dishes and stuff here. But," he held up a hand. "But the professor ain't said we got to live here all the time. If we could make all that money, we could all buy condominiums down there in Scottsdale on one of them golf courses. We could live down there where it's warm and just come up for weekends during tourist season."

There was a soft laugh at the edge of the crowd, and Two-Bears looked up to see Tali near the statue of the Indian woman, arms crossed and eyes shining. He hadn't even been aware of her entrance, and from the way Jake had left he could be sure Jake hadn't noticed either. The easy laugh, he knew, had just doomed Goldberg's insane plan more effectively than any argument would have.

"We could pay some young folks to live up here when it's cold," someone added from behind the old man. "Maybe we could hire some hippies to live here. There wouldn't be no tourists to speak of in winter anyway, and hippies like to dress and live like old-time Indians."

"Heck, we could buy one of those little jets and fly back and forth," Carlos said. "Black Mountain Jetways, how's that sound? I think I'd like to learn golf."

Again, Tali's soft laugh laced the air, and several people turned to look at her respectfully.

"A theme tribe?" Two-Bears cut in. "You'd be willing to become a Disneyland theme tribe?"

"I wasn't thinking like that," Goldberg said. "I meant we could all live better, healthier lives, right here in the old ways."

"We'd have to really do it, right here," Shorty said. "We couldn't hire any hippies. Costner and those others would insist on authenticity. I know those Hollywood people. They want the real thing. One slip and funding's gone."

"No television or microwaves," someone said.

"No chain saws, Shorty," Carlos added.

"No condo, no Land Cruiser."

"No deal." Two-Bears stood up. "I'm going home and get some sleep. Shorty, you and Gold Bird go get some sense."

8   Jessie peered through the wild plum thicket. The image of the young woman was fringed by nylon wolf lashes uncomfortably close to his eyes. She sat on the ground pad next to a big pine where a spring welled from rock into a clear pool and then made a stream down the canyon side. Her legs were crossed and her hands clasped in her lap. Dirt stained her red rain parka, and he could see a couple of pine needles in her slightly matted hair. With her eyes closed, she seemed to be sleeping. Beside her the bag of beef jerky appeared to be at least half full. She must have taken the fasting part pretty seriously, he thought.

He felt a twinge of guilt, but it was what she wanted and had come all the way from Paris for. She'd remember it all the better for the minor suffering. But now it was time to give her her money's worth, and she definitely looked ready for a vision.

The wolf backed away a few paces and then moved around the thicket, stepping silently into the clearing where the young woman sat. He settled onto all fours and made a low, growling sound.

Her eyes were already open, staring at him intently without any sign. He was surprised by the absence of fear or recognition of any sort. That hadn't happened before.

He rose into a half-crouch and began to speak in a low, soft voice. "Remember the song I am going to teach you," he said. "It will be your power song." And then he felt a searing pain in his chest and felt himself hurled backward as he heard a loud explosion. All around him the air was filled with a shrill sound that he realized rather vaguely must be the sound of the woman screaming.

"Got the sonofabitch," someone shouted.

The wolf lay on his back, a blade of fire streaking through his chest and down the rope of his spine. He was aware of a spreading dampness inside the synthetic suit. The shrill sound seemed to waver in the high branches of the forest, and in the distance he could make out the rush of a river current as well as a soft wind in the tops of the pines.

"You okay, lady?"

Jessie could see two men dressed in camouflage, both holding rifles.

"You shot me," Jessie tried to say, but the croak that emerged sounded like the plaint of a dying wolf. The Frenchwoman had stopped screaming and was staring in terror from the men to him and then back to the men.

"You shot my vision," the woman said. "You killed my animal spirit helper."

Something touched his side, and the flame stabbed through his chest and down his spine again. He looked up at the man who had prodded him with the toe of a boot.

"Funniest looking coyote I've ever seen."

"Looks like a strange kind of wolf. Is it dead?"

The wolf rolled its head in the negative. "I'm not dead," it said, the voice coming out half-croak and half-whisper.

Both men stepped back, the assault rifles swinging toward Jessie. "I hate to see an animal die," the shorter man said. "Always have."

"It's not a real wolf." The young woman stared wide-eyed at the wolf, her exhausted face framed with shoulder-length brown hair and her green eyes tired and tearing.

"I'm Jessie," the wolf said through tight lips. "Jessie James."

One of the men scratched at his short-trimmed gray beard and said, "You hear that, Tom? It said it's Jessie James."

"It's a vision," the woman said, her voice climbing as with difficulty she rose to her feet. "My totem."

"Jessie James is your vision?" the bearded man said. "Jessie James the wolf?"

"Steady there." The thinner, clean-shaven man reached a hand out to hold the woman's shoulder, but she twisted away.

"You shot my vision," she said. "You have shot my animal spirit." The woman fell to her knees.

"What kind of accent is that? I hate to see anything die." The one named Tom pushed the fatigue cap back on his forehead and looked intently at the wolf. "Maybe we ought to finish it off. Put it out of its misery. I hate to see an animal suffer."

"Sorry," Jessie tried to say, still lying flat and looking up at Sandrine. "It always worked before." The words came out as a whimper.

With his right paw, Jessie waved and then reached for the baffled zipper in the belly of the wolf suit, groaning loudly with pain.

"Careful, Henry," Tom said as the bearded one stepped closer.

The woman stood, brushed twigs and pine needles off her jeans and parka, and moved so that she could look down at the wolf.

"You're not a vision." Her words came out weak with surprise, with just a trace of French accent.

"I'm Jessie," he replied, his words a whisper.

"Goddamn," Henry muttered. "Hold this." He handed his rifle to his companion and knelt beside Jessie, the man's thick, wire-rimmed glasses making his eyes look huge and watery. Very carefully he felt around the wolf's neck until he found the snaps. Working gently, he unsnapped the head and pulled the wolf's head away.

"You're Jessie," the woman said.

"What the hell's going on here? If he's Jessie, who are you?" The man with two rifles looked from Jessie to the woman.

"I'm Sandrine Le Bris."

Jessie stared up at them, his loose hair pulled out onto the pine-needled ground. "I sell vision quests," he said, but he couldn't hear his words.

"It's an Indian. Damn. Let's see how bad it is." The man with the beard removed Jessie's arms from the wolf sleeves and worked the suit down to his waist. He pulled a big knife from a scabbard on his hip and began to cut the front of the sweatshirt.

"Sorry to shoot you like this," the man said. "But, well, hell."

"I understand," Jessie tried to answer, but he couldn't feel his lips move.

"What going on here?" Tom looked from Henry and the wolf to the Frenchwoman.

"He sold me a Native American vision quest," Sandrine said, her words barely audible. She collapsed into a sitting position on the ground next to Jessie. "But I guess it was all fake."

"No shit? Explains the suit at least. How long you been out here?"

"I've been four days. I was supposed to fast and dream of my animal helper."

"How much you pay for this crap?"

"Four thousand dollars American. And it cost a lot to get here from Paris also."

"Cut a couple of poles, Tom," Henry said. "We can make a stretcher out of this dumb-fuck wolf suit. This guy needs attention back at camp." He knelt and lowered his own face close to Jessie's, then he reached a hand up to feel behind Jessie's jaw. "Wait, he's dead. He just died." The man's voice was filled with wonder.

"No, I didn't," Jessie answered, but his words sounded hollow to him.

The other man squatted and looked at Jessie. Jessie found himself standing next to the large pine by the spring, leaning his shoulder against it with his arms folded and watching the scene.

"Goddammit, Henry. Stroud won't like this one bit." Tom lifted the fatigue cap off and ran a hand over his grayish brown stubble. "We ought to just bury him right here in that damned suit and not say anything to anybody."

Henry shook his head. "We have to take the body to camp." He nodded toward Sandrine. "Besides. What about her? You want to shoot her, too, Peters?"

"I didn't shoot the Indian. You did."

The Frenchwoman had retreated to her spot by the spring. Her face was in her hands, and she was sobbing without noise.

"Hey, we didn't mean to kill this guy." Tom Peters looked irritably from Henry to the Frenchwoman, Peters's blue eyes bright with panic. "We thought it was a damned wolf about to rip your throat out. We were trying to save you. You speak English?"

"Of course she speaks English. Jesus Christ, haven't you been listening?"

"Well, she sounds foreign."

"The wolf is supposed to be extinct in this region," Jessie said, "since the twenties." Sandrine looked up, confused, and her head turned toward him.

Jessie followed the woman's gaze and, seeing his arms and legs, noticed that he seemed to still be wearing the wolf suit, but he couldn't feel the slick synthetic liner anymore. Her eyes fixed on him.

"You okay, Henry?" Peters placed a hand on the other man's shoulder. Henry was kneeling beside Jessie, his whole body seeming to shiver.

"I've never killed anyone," Henry said.

"You mean all that Vietnam stuff was a lie?"

"I was a supply clerk. I never even saw a VC."

"No shit?"

"You ever killed anybody, Peters?"

Peters was silent for a long time before he shook his head. "No," he said softly. "Hell, I had a student deferment."

"Well, you sure have now, white man," Jessie said from beside the tree.

"I sure as hell have now," Henry said.

"It could've been me, Henry," Peters said. "You were just faster, that's all. In a firefight you would have saved my ass."

"You killed him," Sandrine shrieked, her eyes still fixed on the place where Jessie leaned against the tree. She began to scream again, and in two strides Peters grabbed her, lifting her with his left arm while holding his right hand over her mouth.

"Damn, she's strong. Stroud is going to be pissed as hell." Peters stared glumly at Henry as the woman hung limp in the circle of his arm.

9 Jake pulled his truck behind a thick copse of aspens and shut off the headlights. Moon Lake lay in its meadow a hundred yards away, a flat black dish reflecting shards of moonlight as the clouds shifted. It was as good a place as any to sit for a couple of hours before going home. The lake was just a couple of miles off the highway, so poachers wouldn't be likely to pick that spot, but sorting out his thoughts, not poachers, was his concern.

The highway had been deserted the whole fifteen miles from the lodge. Casino traffic mostly came from the other direction, and people didn't drive around much at night on the mountain roads if they could help it. One vehicle had been behind him for a ways, but it had turned off on one of the forest roads, probably a teenage couple looking for privacy.

He rolled the window down and listened to the aspen leaves trembling, a sound he loved, and watched the flicker of bats out over the water. He pulled the .45 from its holster, made sure a shell was chambered, and laid the gun on the seat beside him.

For a while he pondered what Two-Bears' reaction might be when the poaching stopped. Would Two-Bears and Sam get the message and give up their illegal hunting sales, knowing somebody was on to them? It was hard to imagine the chairman giving up easy money in large quantities.

He thought back to the first time he'd seen Shorty and Avrum together. He had just been made a tribal game warden and had pulled into a Burger King in Show Low on the way back from Phoenix. Before he could get into the drive-though line he noted a disturbance in the parking lot. A large woman in a Burger King uniform was waving her hands and shouting at someone crouching on the pavement. It took a few seconds for him to recognize the crouching one as Avrum Goldberg, dressed as usual in breechcloth, high moccasins, and cotton shirt, with his long hair loose on his shoulders. The wiry little man was bludgeoning something on the blacktop with what looked like a tire iron. Then Jake had noticed Shorty Luke standing beside the big woman and gesturing mildly with his hands. A crowd had begun to gather from inside the hamburger stand and the nearby sidewalk to watch.

He'd climbed out of his truck and approached cautiously. From a few feet away, he heard Shorty Luke saying to the woman, "It's traditional. His tribe are traditional enemies of the underwater people, enemies to the death. Always like this. Very primitive, I'm afraid."

Jake had edged around Shorty and the woman to see Avrum raising the tire iron yet again to strike the head of a huge catfish.

"I'm calling the cops," the woman said. "We're not having any savage abusing animals in our parking lot."

Jake stepped forward before she could move, making sure that his new badge was conspicuous. "It's okay, ma'am," he'd said. "I'm a tribal law officer and I'll take care of this." At that point Avrum had stood up, holding the ten-pound catfish by the gills, blood dripping onto the ground. He saw Jake and nodded.

"Looks dead," Shorty commented.

"Sure as hell ought to be," Avrum replied, the only time Jake ever heard the man swear.

"We got to be going," Shorty said to Jake. "Pretty good burgers here, but the fries are sort of limp." Looking at the woman, Shorty added, "His tribe won that one, but it was close. Heap bad enemies with underwater people. Ought to check that french fry oil, I think."

It had been weeks later that Jake heard the whole story from Shorty. The two had been coming back from the Gila River with the big fish alive in a wet burlap bag in the back of their pickup when Avrum started to feel guilty about letting the animal suffer. Shorty had come out of the Burger King to find Avrum trying to put the fish out of its misery with the tire iron and the burger woman having fits. "That Avrum," Shorty had said. "First he embarrasses me by dressing like that, and then I got to bail him out of animal abuse."

Jake was still grinning at the memory when he saw an elk step halfway out of the trees on the other side of the lake, a blocky shadow that moved cautiously at first and then glided onto the grassy shore. Two more of the huge animals emerged and dropped their heads to graze. The first two were cows, but the third was a massive bull, big enough to make a lot of money in a trophy hunt. He knew that the bulls usually pushed cows into clearings ahead of them to sort of test the waters. A big bull didn't get big by being stupid.

The first time he'd seen a bull elk he'd been with Tali. She'd taken him to one of the really remote lakes, one they'd had to walk five miles up a steep, trailless mountainside to reach, and he'd enjoyed every step of the way as he walked behind her, admiring the strength of her shoulders and back, the swing of her long, black hair, and the taut buttocks and long legs that climbed seemingly without any effort at all. As she walked, she sang a song softly in a language he didn't know.

Since bringing him home, she had never once mentioned the way they'd met. Her dancing and his drunken brawl were parts of a past that no longer existed. Freed from children for a day, they climbed toward the lake as though life had begun just that morning. He'd never felt as strong or as happy as he did walking behind her and listening to her voice and the rustle of aspen leaves in the warm beginning of fall.

The small lake had sat on a shoulder of the mountain, dropping off on one side to the huge valley of the White River. The sun flashed on a metal roof miles away, a barn somewhere on the reservation that was still a mystery to him, and the same sunlight shone like silver on the still water. Without a word, Tali had stripped her clothes off and waded out into the water until her hair began to float behind her; then she began a slow, deliberate swim toward the center. He watched until she turned back toward him, treading water with small motions of her arms and hands, the hair fanning out on both sides of her shoulders.

"Don't dive," she'd shouted. "It's too shallow."

He'd felt huge and clumsy as he removed his boots, jeans, and shirt, stepping finally out of the military-issue underwear and shuffling into the water.

"You're like a bear," she called to him. "That's how a bear enters water."

He wanted to ask her when she'd seen a bear wade into a lake, but he was too self-conscious of the disturbance his bulk made as he moved toward her until he, too, felt freed from earth and was able to swim with smooth, silent motions. In the water he no longer felt the weight of himself, and when he reached her she placed her hands on his upper arms and leaned in to kiss his forehead. "I love you," she said, and he'd believed her completely.

On shore, she'd spread a blanket taken from his pack, and they'd made love slowly and soundlessly close to the lake's edge, ending with him lying cupped against her back and staring out across the water toward the bright air above the river valley. It was then that the elk had appeared from a cluster of aspen, the golden leaves parting and trailing along his sides as he moved out and raised his enormous antlers against the pale blue sky. Jake had held his breath and tried to count the points on each side, but the effect of dancing leaves, empty sky, and reflecting water made the elk's rack an uncertain, shifting thing like dark tongues of thin flame.

From that day forward he would always think of Tali and water together. She was a beautiful bird and a creature of water together, and she walked on the earth with a certainty that often left him feeling dizzy and unstable. She burned with a fire that made her skin hot no matter what time of day they came together.

"Why can't it always be like this, Jacob?" she had asked, and the question had sent his mind tumbling back to the dark uncertainties he'd carried with him always, it seemed. They had ended the day by walking back to the truck in a heavy silence.

He watched the two cows and the bull elk move cautiously to the water, the bull keeping watch while the cows drank. Finally, the bull lowered its head beside the cows, and the three silhouettes blended into one.

Jake felt his eyes begin to droop. He'd give it twenty more minutes and then go home, but in the meantime he had to take a leak. He got out, careful to make no noise, and walked toward the front of the truck. He was unzipping his fly just as both side windows of the pickup exploded and the crash of a rifle slammed into the clearing.

He dove to the ground and squirmed around the front of the truck, getting to his knees and scrambling to the passenger door. He jerked the door open, reaching for the pistol on the seat. Calculating that the driver's window had imploded first, he decided that the shot had come from that side, traveling through the cab and the second window, and through his head if he'd still been sitting there. Following an old rule, he rose abruptly behind the bed of the truck and fired off four rounds in the direction of the trees on the north side of the lake and then shifted the gun to fire four more into the woods on the east side.

He dropped to a squatting position and felt for the extra clip on his belt. Assured it was there, he rose and emptied the pistol at the trees, immediately ejecting the spent clip and jamming the full one in. A theory he'd tested more than once was that no one liked to hang around when a lot of indiscriminate firepower was in the air, so he rose and fired once more.

He duck-walked to the rear of the pickup and watched the trees in that direction, listening. In the distance he heard a motor turn over and then the revving of an engine being taken up through gears. Somebody was leaving Moon Lake in a hurry, and he decided at once not to interfere with the exit.

Keeping low to the ground, he slipped into the aspens a dozen yards from the truck where for ten minutes he crouched in the trees, listening and watching the margins of the lake.

From the sound of the vehicle leaving, he figured that whoever had shot at him had followed, watched him settle in, and waited for him to let his guard down. Or maybe it had taken them that long to get the courage up to shoot.

He zipped up his fly, used his bandanna to brush glass off the seat, and then drove around the aspens to the lake road, accelerating into second even before he hit the road and clutching into third by the time the pickup tires struck the familiar ruts leading out to the asphalt. The truck jumped and crashed onto the road, and he drove with his left hand on the wheel and the .45 in one hand atop the floor shift. He felt an odd exhilaration, a feeling that had been missing for nearly three decades. He was worth killing, and he had survived again.

In minutes he was on blacktop and into fourth gear with the accelerator pressed to the floor. The speedometer pushed sixty and seventy and eighty, but no taillights appeared in front of him.

When he reached Shorty Luke's house, no lights were on, so he drove past the house with its maze of lean-to, add-on bedrooms until he came to the trail that led to Avrum Goldberg's home. He left the truck on the road and quickly walked the hundred yards back to the wickiup.

Seeing a light frame around the blanket door, he paused and said loudly, "Avrum, you in there?"

"Who's asking?" came the nasal voice.

Jake lifted the blanket and stooped into the dome of woven sticks covered with deer and elk hides. Avrum sat toward the back of the circular room, the red coals of a small fire between him and Jake. Avrum was running a long, thin branch through rounded notches in a stone and then holding the wood over the coals before doing it again.

"Making arrows?" Jake said.

Avrum nodded. "I'll refrain from any sarcastic rejoinder," he said.

"Where's Shorty?" Jake glanced around the surprisingly large room, amazed that after so many years of curiosity he had just walked into Avrum's home. As far as he knew, only Shorty had been there before, and probably Mrs. Edwards.

"Home asleep would be my guess," Avrum replied. "What happened to you? Your face is bleeding."

Jake reached up and felt crusted blood on his right cheek. Gingerly, he pulled a sliver of glass out of his skin and tossed it into the coals.

"Somebody tried to shoot me."

Avrum set the stone and arrow shaft on the floor to one side and looked carefully at Jake. "You seem almost joyful about it. They didn't hit you?"

Jake shook his head. "They shot out the windows of my pickup."

"How'd they miss you?"

"I happened to be outside the truck for a moment."

"Think it was a warning shot?"

"I don't know. I thought Shorty might have an idea."

"I don't think Shorty explained things to you correctly," Avrum said. "We've been giving the elk meat to people who don't have enough food. Traditionally a man hunted for his family and the community. People shared what they had. But today people have forgotten. Even Indians are putting their old people in retirement homes the way white people do. Shorty and I have been trying to rectify a situation of cultural imbalance and feed people at the same time. Not just Indians. There are a lot of white people around here that are pretty badly off. Little kids hungry all the time. Hunger knows no color."

"It's okay. Shorty and I worked that out," Jake said.

"It was Sam," Avrum said.

"Sam Baca? Who shot at me?"

Avrum nodded. "Sam wasn't at the meeting, and Sam probably knows you found one of those .30-.40 shells and talked to Shorty. So he most likely figures you know about him and Xavier. It makes sense. They won't want to give up an extra fifty thousand dollars a year, which means they need to silence all three of us. Sam probably thought that he could scare you and make you think poachers did it."

"Sam wouldn't shoot anybody."

Avrum looked steadily at Jake. "I said scare, not shoot."

"Sam would be afraid to take a shot at me," Jake added.

"Sam is afraid of Two-Bears, and Sam doesn't have much imagination." Avrum picked up the arrow shaft and sighted down it toward the coals. "Sit down. You look absurd hunched over like that. Sorry I didn't build this for basketball players. Jessie always used to bump his head till he got used to it."

Jake sat beside the fire, cross-legged on a deer hide, wondering when Jessie had been in the anthropologist's home. "This is pretty nice," he said.

"Thanks. But what are you going to do about Sam? And maybe you could put that gun down, too."

Jake looked in surprise at the pistol still gripped in his right hand. "Oh," he said. "Sorry."

They sat in silence for a moment. "I have to find Alison," Jake said finally. "Jessie took her down into the canyon, and I have a feeling I need to find her before I do anything else. Sam and Xavier won't go anywhere."

"Mrs. Edwards told me." Avrum began filling a stone-bowled pipe with something from a pouch hanging on the wall beside him. "Smoke?" he said.

Jake shook his head. "Never liked to. Will you tell Shorty what I've told you? It's too late to get there tonight, but I'll head down in the morning and be back late tomorrow. In the meantime you and Shorty watch out for yourselves. We'll decide together what to do about Sam and Xavier when I get back."

Avrum picked up a coal from the fire and held it between his thumb and forefinger at the bowl of the pipe, puffing small clouds of smoke out the corner of his mouth.

"You sure?" he said, holding the pipe toward Jake. "You know what this is?"

Jake reached for the .45 and stood up, realizing for the first time that he had to stoop even in the center of the wickiup.

"Never acquired the habit," he said. "I'll be back tomorrow night."

"You should see Mrs. Edwards about the owl, Jake."

Jake nodded at Avrum and went back out through the blanketed doorway and was halfway to the pickup when he realized that Avrum Goldberg had acted neither surprised nor even disturbed by what he'd said. Maybe Avrum was in on it. Maybe he was going to tell Sam or Xavier as fast as he could. After all, Goldberg was not part of the community.

Jake drove the windowless truck to his office, hearing coyotes celebrating not too far up the ridge. He knew the pack was separating for a hunt. If he waited until just about daylight, he'd hear them come back together for another celebration. For such quirky animals, coyotes were pretty predictable.

In minutes he had the backpack ready and leaning in a corner of his room with a new box of .45 cartridges stuffed into an outside pocket of the pack. He looked at his watch. Midnight. He could get four hours of sleep and still be gone by daylight. An owl called through the thin walls of his shack, and when he lifted the dingy curtain on his small window he saw the moon break in half and flutter like cusped leaves from the cloudy sky. A slash of lightning stabbed at the broken moon and refracted in the side of an amber bottle on the windowsill.

10   Jake lay on his narrow bed, his head pounding while the coyotes celebrated another night of survival and a dawn that would come in two hours. He thought of grabbing the deer rifle and blasting the hillside to shut up the shrill-voiced things, but the very idea made his head hurt even more. Thunder muttered in the corners of his little room, and then he realized what had really awakened him. He heard the outside door to his office pushed shut and then soft steps. The door to his bedroom moved, and then she was standing beside his bed, a tall shadow.

He lay without speaking, feeling through the pounding in his brain the difference her presence made in the room. Her hair hung loose over her shoulders, and when she released the thin robe and let it drop to the floor, the hair shadowed the darker shadows of her breasts.

He shifted back toward the wall and clumsily raised the sheet so she could lower herself to the bed and lay her body parallel to his own. At once, her lips brushed his forehead and her hand moved across his chest.

He kissed her temple and breathed in the fragrance of her warm hair and then parted the hair to taste her neck, letting his mouth continue down across her shoulder and upper arm.

She pulled herself closer so that he could feel her breasts hardening against his chest and the heat of her body. Her mouth touched his eyes and cheeks and lips and her head moved so that her face lay against his chest.

He slipped one arm beneath her and the other around her waist and drew her as tightly as possible to him, and they lay together for several minutes in that locked embrace, his face buried in the fragrance of her hair and her pulse echoing through his body. The thunder had grown more muted and now whispered across the low ceiling of the room, misty clouds gathering in the corners like gray webs, and the song of the coyotes had subsided to a faint note that came from inside his own chest. He held her more tightly until she pushed against him.

Tali reached down and guided him inside and then turned so that he was above her. And then again they lay together in motionless silence. When she began to move, he responded. When her tongue traced the line of his jaw and her teeth found his earlobe and sent a fine, pleasant pain through him he began to drive more deeply into her, soft and insistent and then harder as she rose to meet him, her teeth finding his neck and shoulder and her hands tight against his buttocks.

"I hate you, Jacob," she said. "I love you."

He felt as though she had woven herself around and through him, as though strands of her had entered his muscle, tendons, and bone and bound him in a single, undulating force until she dug her sharp nails deeper into him and cried with deep breaths.

"Too long," he said, knowing that they had both wanted the embrace to last till daylight. "It's been too long."

She touched a finger to his lips. "Don't say you're sorry, Jacob. It is wonderful. Always."

"Maybe we—" he began, but her finger pressed harder on his lips.

"No, Jacob." She kissed his forehead and rose from the bed.

He watched her pull the robe back over her head and lift the long hair free so that again it spilled across her shoulders. He looked toward the floor, but the robe obscured even the outlines of her feet in the dim light.

"We still love each other, don't we, Jacob?" she said.

He nodded faintly, so imperceptibly that he thought she probably couldn't see him. She turned and went through the door, and as she pulled it closed he whispered, "Don't come back, Tali. Don't ever come back."

As he heard the outer door open and close, he realized that the light in the room had changed. The beginnings of dawn were framed in the eastern window, and the awful silence of coming light reminded him of the rooster who had crowed every morning but was making soup for an old woman now. He felt a terrible loneliness. Fucking women. They lived their lives totally separate, using men when they needed them, sometimes one man for an entire lifetime, sometimes who knew how many. But they kept that distance always, like those missiles everybody was talking about in the '70s. What had they called them? "Self-contained mobile units." White men never understood that, never grasped the reality, but a lot of Indian tribes knew. So the tribes gave all property to the women, children to the women, everything to the women. Men married into the woman's family, were expected to bring home the bacon, herd the sheep and cattle, keep the fires burning, service the women when the women wanted it, fight the wars, and if they got fucked up in the wars to then just stay out of the way. And when a woman got tired of a man, she just set his belongings outside the door of her house, *her* house even if he built it, which he always did. Fuck them all. In Nam it had been a beautiful little mamasan who screwed him and then, on her way out of the compound, dropped a grenade into the gas tank of his Jeep, the pin pulled and the tape that held it together designed to dissolve in gasoline. For some damned reason he'd slept in, been late for duty, and the grenade had blown his empty Jeep to tiny pieces. He'd found himself laughing when he walked out and saw it, knowing that he'd deserved it, earned it, even wanted it. But again it missed him, like the piece of lead that had shattered his pickup windows.

He rolled to a sitting position on his cot, swinging his feet to the floor and immediately desiring coffee more than he'd ever desired anything in his life. He felt empty, and brown stars like coffee crystals danced in his painful head. A clanging sound startled him, and he looked down to see the .30-.40 cartridge spinning on the linoleum. It had been somewhere in the sheets the whole time. He pieced together events of the recent past. Owl feathers. Owl woman. Evil incarnate. Baby eater. Had Sam Baca really tried to kill him? Impossible. Were Xavier Two-Bears and Avrum Goldberg part of it? Had Tali really appeared in his room? A dampness told him that she had, and he got to his feet and went toward the little bathroom in the southwest corner of the room.

When he appeared again, he headed to the stove, moving slowly to dump the old grounds in a sodden grocery bag, rinse and fill the blackened pot. Avrum wouldn't do anything evil; he was suddenly sure of that. He dropped two fistfuls of coffee from a big can into the pot, lit a burner on the stove, and set the pot on the burner. Outside, a flicker began drumming on the plywood of his office, the sound riveting his head. He slammed a fist into the wall to scare the bird, and his fist sank an inch into the Sheetrock.

"Damn," he said. There were many other holes and depressions in the walls of the small room. Fortunately, no one ever came into the room except Tali, and then it was always dark. He pulled on a pair of gray boxer shorts and baggy green pants and reached for the brown shirt hanging on a nail, his head pealing with outrage. Was Mrs. Edwards sleeping with Goldberg or not, using the anthropologist to get her ancient rocks off whenever she felt like it? Had a moment come when the anthropologist became more Indian than the tribe he had started off studying and ended up becoming? Maybe anthropologists were the real Indians, anyway. If the whole idea of Indian was just an invention, then it made sense that an actor hired to play Indians, even if he was a fullblood like Shorty, would have a lot in common with an anthropologist who studied what his own kind had invented. Was everybody just playing some kind of role written for them by somebody else? With sudden clarity he thought that Xavier must understand all of it. That was why he stuffed the lodge full of Indian art and insisted on traditional dances and feasts to entertain visiting politicians. Two-Bears had even imported some Plains fancy dancers with their pink and green feathers and a Cherokee hoop dancer when a bunch of East Coast politicians had descended on the reservation. Black Mountain tradition was too dull. "These bozos won't believe we're real Indians," he'd said. "Do I look like Geronimo to you? Look at those boys spin." Xavier was a modern Indian. He knew exactly what he wanted.

So what was Jacob Nashoba doing in these cold mountains alone, married but not, visited in confusing nights by his beautiful wife, patrolling such a remote part of an Indian wilderness that in almost twenty years he'd never seen an Indian there? Never a single Indian in twenty years. Patrolling for what, his own reflection in a still pool? In a corner of the room his backpack stood upright, loaded and waiting, the self-inflating ground pad tied neatly to the outside and the metal fly rod case that doubled as a walking stick leaning next to it. Obviously, he had come home from being shot at and seeing Avrum and packed his pack. Why didn't he remember all of it? Had Tali's visit erased other things?

His lapse became clear when he saw the empty pint of Jack Daniels on the floor. He remembered now returning to his preposterous home and seeing the emergency bottle on the windowsill. He remembered thinking that he was forty-eight years old and nothing in his life had made any sense, even the fact that people repeatedly tried and failed to kill him. People he knew, had known for a long time. Maybe. He remembered slumping in a strange blend of self-pity and the adrenalin joy of survival, thinking of his wife in the log house and himself here in this shell of a building, thinking in his drunkenness that he was as much in love as he'd been that first night or first week or first year. But no one could live with him and no one could kill him, though many had tried the latter. He was the world's enemy. "I will kill the world," he'd said as he rolled to his side and fell into a sickened sleep in which he battled a brother he'd never had, circling in the dark and hearing the clatter of metal as his brother stalked him. In the background a train whistle sounded like the repeated cries of owls, or owls cried like a distant train.

The coffee boiled over, sputtering in the fire, and he jumped up to turn off the burner. He lifted the lid, splashed a tablespoon of cold water into the pot to settle the grounds, and remembered the can of sweetened condensed milk in the refrigerator.

When he opened the door to the other room, something was wrong. He jumped back and grabbed the .45 on its crate beside the bed and then pushed the door slowly open again. He stood for an instant with one hand on the knob and the other holding the raised pistol, surveying the room, and then it literally flashed at him. The beer sign was brilliantly lighted, the man in the canoe once again paddling his endless circles, each ripple the same with each electric stroke, beginning and ending simultaneously, never going anywhere. A trout broke the surface of the lake just behind the moving motionless canoe, broke the sparkling blue surface again and again. Action without effect, motion removed from time, a man in unceasing movement going nowhere beautifully. Even alive, the grass didn't grow, the water didn't flow.

He watched the sign for a moment and then grabbed a can from the refrigerator and returned to his bedroom. Setting the gun back on its apple crate, he poured a large mug full of coffee and spooned in two thick mounds of the hard cream. He stirred the coffee and let it cool as he looked around for his wool socks. Outside, the flicker began knocking loudly on the building once more.

"Come in, goddammit," he shouted, grabbing the thick socks from the floor. He sat heavily on the edge of the bed, the image of the lighted sign rippling in his brain. "I'm nuts," he said to himself. "My wife comes like a goddamned burglar, fucks me, and disappears. I'm living in some kind of insane asylum, and I'm the craziest bastard of all." The flicker pounded harder on the plywood wall, the sound beating on Jake's temple so that he held one of the smelly wool socks to the side of his head and grabbed for the coffee cup, spilling the near-boiling liquid on his left foot.

"Ouch shit," he yelled, spilling more coffee as he jerked his foot off the floor. "Shut the fuck up," he screamed, hurling the half-full cup at the wall, where the cup shattered and left one end of his room splashed brown.

He stood up, holding the soiled sock to his forehead. "To hell with all of it. Fake grandkids, fake wife, fake bullshit river. Fake fucking Indians. Fake bullets." He pulled another cup from a peg above the stove and poured the rest of the coffee from the pot, watching the stream of black grounds that flowed out of the spout. It came to him that he could throw everything he owned into the back of his Chevy pickup and just leave. Right then.

He looked around the room and almost laughed. After twenty years he didn't own a damned thing. A rifle, a pistol, a few boxes of ammo, enough clothes to fill a duffle bag, assorted worn-out backpacking and fishing equipment, fly-tying supplies and tools, a beer sign. It wouldn't even take up half the bed of his truck. He could go home. He thought of California and then Mississippi. No one came with the thoughts. No one he remembered was in either place. Then the face of the old man across the river appeared to him, the stringy old Choctaw man who'd invaded his dreams. He felt sure the old man would still be there even after so many years; if he could find that exact spot again the old man would be waiting. There had been some kind of unspoken promise. To hell with Black Mountain and all of them; they were as strange to him and he to them as any people could be. There wasn't any such thing as an Indian. He'd pack up and be gone in an hour. The thought of a long, long drive all alone soothed him like medicine. Outside, a scrawny young rooster crowed, the imposter's sound hanging in the air without resonance before vanishing.

11   Domingo swirled the two pink inches in the bottom of the plastic milk jug and lifted it to his lips, letting half the liquid pour like sweet flame down his raw throat. Behind him he heard the wood stove crackle as if a fire were roaring, but the stove was dead and still in summer. The hanging lamp Tali had left in the living room swayed slowly, balancing cartoon shadows on first one wall and then the other. A mosquito zinged around one of his ears, and he cocked his head to understand the little song until there was a scratch on the door. He slapped at the mosquito with his free hand and the hand fluttered helplessly in the air.

Domingo looked at the door for a long moment and then turned and marched to the sink, setting the plastic jug down with precision, spinning stiffly on one heel, and marching to the front door.

When he opened the door, the black-and-white dog smiled up at him from where it sat, a proud expression on its graying face and its cataract-dulled eyes. At its feet, laid precisely across the cement step, was a once-beautiful, long-haired, silver-gray Persian cat, the thick fur matted and plastered slick with mud and dog slime and the eyes dead to all worlds but the tenth.

Domingo looked down at the cat, noting the depression left in slimed fur by a nearly toothless dog mouth and the teeth-baring death grin of the Persian. He raised his eyes to the dog, who had tried to catch Shorty's cat many times but never even come close. The cat had always been younger, faster, smarter, and meaner than the ancient dog. It had never even been a contest. He looked back down at the cat, not just a cat but Shorty Luke's prized Persian cat, the other twin's beloved, expensive, Hollywood-born and -bred cat. Domingo felt a combination of pride in his arthritic dog and panic in what the future held.

"Why Shorty's cat?" Domingo asked, but the dog responded with its happy expression.

"Lots of cats," Domingo said. "To kill. Not Shorty Luke's." The reservation was crawling with starving, half-wild cats no one would miss.

The dog wagged its tail while Domingo studied the dead cat. Shorty Luke had been given the cat, which he called Mingo, by a famous Hollywood actor named Iron Eyes Cody when he'd gone back for a stunt man's big party only three or four years earlier. Shorty said the cat was more valuable than all of Black Mountain. "You could sell this damn town," Shorty had said when he'd first returned with the kitten sitting in the palm of his hand, "and you wouldn't raise enough money to buy this cat. *Che bellezza*, no?" He'd shown everyone a photograph of the very old Indian actor holding the kitten. Domingo had thought the actor's black hair was floating half an inch above his white scalp and very wrinkled face. The man looked like he had makeup on. He'd said as much, but Shorty had glared. "That man's rich and famous," he'd said. "He's been in three hundred movies."

"That's a lot of times to fall off a horse," Jessie had inter-jected. "That could definitely raise your hair."

"Me and him and Sal Mineo used to eat lunch together," Shorty insisted, glaring at his twin before turning to Jessie. "Sal didn't speak good Italian like some of the other actors, but before lunch he always used to say '*Non esco mai con la pioggia che non mi pigli un raffreddore.*' I remember that because Sal was delicate. I think he was self-conscious about not speaking Italian as well as most of the other Indians. You know how it is."

Domingo looked around. No one was in sight. Quickly, he bent and scooped up the cat and carried it inside, closing the door after the dog.

He laid the cat across the cold wood stove and studied the situation. Shorty would be angry. Shorty would be more than angry. Shorty had a sharp chain saw and a bad temper, and the old dog's life might be in jeopardy if Shorty found out. Domingo turned and walked carefully to the sink, lifted the jug to his mouth, and drained the last of the pink Montana gin. He walked back to the stove, where the dog sat eyeing the stretched-out cat with obvious pride.

"Don't touch that dead cat, sir," Domingo said. "That's an order. Do not slime the cat again, please." He heard his own words as though through thick cotton. Everything had a pleasantly blurred outline, but in the middle of everything was the potential catastrophe represented by the object on the stove.

He nodded to himself decisively, squared his shoulders, and opened the door. He paused in the doorway as Jake Nashoba's tribal pickup went past, and then he stepped out. Keeping his back straight, and hearing thunder softened by the thick sky, he walked across the square and up the steps to Tali's house, where he opened the door without knocking and entered.

Tali was peeling potatoes at the kitchen sink. The rest of the house seemed deserted. She looked around and stopped. "Uncle Domingo," she said. "Welcome."

"I would like to borrow your hair thing, Niece," he stated clearly. "For only a little while."

Tali set the potato and peeler down on the counter and, wiping her hands on her apron, came closer. "Which hair thing would you like to borrow, Uncle?"

Domingo looked pained. He reached up and fingered strands of his greasy hair. "The wind thing."

"The hair dryer?" Tali cocked her head, studying Domingo's hair. "Would you like to borrow some shampoo, too, to wash with?"

Domingo considered the offer and finally nodded.

Tali left the room and reappeared in a moment. She held out a hair dryer in her right hand. "You just plug it in and push this switch," she said, indicating the switch with her thumb.

In her other hand she held two bottles. She pointed to one bottle with the muzzle of the hair dryer. "This is shampoo," she said. "See. It says 'Shampoo.' And this is conditioner. After you wash your hair with shampoo, you rinse all of the shampoo out and then put the conditioner in. It makes hair soft and managable. After three minutes you rinse all of the conditioner out. Then you dry it with the hair dryer. Maybe you'd like to do it here. I could help you."

Domingo looked into his niece's face with a confused expression, grappling with thoughts. Finally, he held out his arms, cradling the bottles and dryer to his chest when she gave them.

"Is there a special occasion, Uncle?" she asked.

"Thank you," he said before turning and going back out the door.

When he entered his own house again, the first thing he saw was the cat sprawled atop the cold stove, with the old dog watching alertly as if it might try to get away.

Domingo deposited the hair things on the kitchen counter and went back for the cat. Laying the stiffened cat in the sink, he turned on the hot water and let it pour over the animal, turning the cat over several times. When all of the thick hair seemed wet and free of mud, he squirted shampoo from the cat's ears to the tip of its tail and began to massage until a thick lather had formed. He lifted the cat and did the same thing to the other side and then rinsed all of the soap away. When the conditioner came out of its bottle in a very fine thread, he unscrewed the cap and poured the contents first on one side and then the other until the bottle was empty, working the thick stuff deeply into the fur.

He stepped away from the sink and sat in a wooden chair, remembering the three minutes Tali had insisted upon. After counting to ten thirty times, he returned to the sink and rinsed the conditioner out of the fur. Leaving the cat in the sink, he went into the bathroom and came out with a threadbare towel, which he wrapped around the corpse and squeezed. When the towel was soaked, he took the hair dryer to the place where Tali had once kept a television and plugged the dryer in before going back and picking up the dripping cat by the tip of its tail.

Holding the cat by the tail, he switched the dryer on and began to blow the thick hair, moving the dryer around and around and around the cat and up and down the stiff body until the beautiful silver hair was rippling like high grass before a wind. He kept the wind blowing on the cat until the fur stood out thick and straight, reminding him of a squirrel he'd once seen electrocuted on a high-voltage wire.

He pushed his nose close to the cat and sniffed. The fragrance of roses came back at him. He turned the cat, giving the belly and tail one more blast of hot air before he was satisfied. Then he went out the door, holding the cat by its tail and leaving the dog inside the house.

12

A young rooster crowed, and the cawing bark of a raven answered. Domingo Perez sat in the single wooden chair in the one room of his plywood home, preparing his early morning cocktail with care. At his feet the black-and-white dog lay dejectedly.

"You could not keep that cat, mister," Domingo said. "Don't feel so bad."

Behind Domingo, the wood stove stood cold and gray, a faded picture of a scrawny, crucified Jesus on the brown wall beside the stovepipe, with half a dozen badly tarnished war medals stuck to the bottom of the picture frame, the ribbons darkened with soot. Beside Jesus a framed color photograph hung on the Sheetrock, showing Domingo carrying the American flag during a big intertribal ceremony in Gallup one year. He'd just returned from the war and was the most decorated veteran, so he got to carry the flag. His back was straight and his shoulders square as he proudly walked at the head of all the veterans. Behind his image, the stands were filled with Indians in all kinds of traditional dress, and elaborately costumed dancers lined the edges of the room, waiting to join the flag procession. The glass in the frame was cracked, the fracture running right up through the middle of Domingo's chest and the drooping flag. A tiny spider had woven a web in an upper corner of the picture, running fine, dust-thickened filaments all the way across to the lower edge of the frame. On the potbellied stove a skillet held fragments of scrambled eggs, and a plastic bowl sat on the floor between chair and stove, licked clean. Domingo was worried because the cat had visited him in a dream, walking up his body from his feet to his chest and staring him directly in the eyes. The cat smelled like roses, and its fur stuck straight out like the quills on an angry porcupine. It hadn't said anything but just pushed its red tongue out between those sharp teeth. That was when he saw that the cat's eyes were red, too, and he'd awakened to find the dog sleeping stretched across both of his legs at the foot of the bed. He couldn't feel his feet and had been forced to get up and march several times around the stove before returning to bed.

Now, the bad dream still hanging heavy over him and his long hair drooping on both sides of his thin face, Domingo held a nail to the top of the Aqua Net hairspray can and tapped delicately with a piece of two-by-four. Air began to hiss softly from the hole, and Domingo nodded, his eyes fixed with purpose. He was proud of his skill. Such a thing had to be done just right. If you hit the nail too hard, all the liquid inside the can would shoot out with the air and be wasted. "You look like a medicine man," one of his drinking friends had said once, watching his hunched precision. That was when he'd been living in the abandoned train car in Gallup with all his friends. Every day they'd scrounge aluminum cans or maybe a little temporary work for enough to buy a dozen containers of Aqua Net, then retire to the tracks. They came from all over, but the guys he hung out with were mostly Navajos. The Zunis and others all had their own places. Most of them, like Domingo, had been in jail more than once for things like vagrancy, shoplifting, or fighting. A lot of them stole things, whatever they could find, and they'd wait for somebody to be drunk enough to fall down and then roll them. More than once Domingo woke to find his disability money gone from his pockets the morning after he'd cashed the check. Food had come from the soup kitchens or the backs of grocery stores and restaurants. About once every week or two somebody would fail to turn up and they'd know he'd been found stiff somewhere, or somebody wouldn't wake up and they'd have to carry the body out to where it would be found without getting them in trouble. It was while in the Gallup jail that Domingo had heard of what they called "diesel therapy." Every day, every time a person could look up at the sky, the government had huge jets flying back and forth across the country full of prisoners. Hundreds of men flew, shackled in their seats, back and forth all day and night. The thought was a terror to men in prison, and often Domingo looked up at a jet that might be only a speck of reflected sunlight far away and thought of men like him chained in those planes. Nothing could be worse than to be forever in motion, far above the earth.

They talked about the jet prisons and counted passing trains during the night to tell time because a watch seldom lasted more than a day before being sold or traded, and sometimes they would look at the newspapers in the sidewalk machines to find out what day it was. Most of the time they'd pass the plastic gallon jugs and tell war stories. Between them, they'd been at Normandy, Pearl Harbor, Iwo Jima, Corregidor. One, an Osage halfbreed, had been captured on Bataan, knocked his guard in the head, and swum to Corregidor, he said, only to be captured again and spend three years in a Manchurian prison camp. One was a Navajo code talker who'd been captured and tortured by U.S. Marines who thought he was a Jap. He showed the scars. They all laughed about that, but it was hard laughter. Over and over they told the old stories, counting coup with their words, making the stories more and more elaborate each time so that everyone understood what was happening. Domingo had been happy that Shorty Luke was never there to steal those stories, because everyone respected everyone else's stories as the only valuable property anyone possessed.

It had changed quickly when the younger ones began showing up, the ones who'd been in the new war. Their stories were different and disturbing to the old vets. They talked of killing children and women, laughing about burning what they called "hooches" with whole families in them, fire raining out of the sky to leave black corpses on the roads. They didn't seem to care about anything, including elders. They laughed about losing the war, about knowing it was lost all the time they were killing, and the good drugs they could get. They laughed about the sores on their mouths and arms that frightened the older men. They didn't have any of the drunken warrior's pride the old vets had, just that ugly laughter that was like the laughter of ghosts. When the younger guys told their stories, the old vets fell silent and shifted further back against the train walls. And then one day Mrs. Edwards and Tali had appeared in the big door of the rail car, framed against the just-risen sun and frightening the men who were awake. Without a word, the women had picked him up by the arms and dragged him outside while other men sprawled inside the car watched silently. That was how he'd come home to Black Mountain and Tali's old house. Sometimes he missed his Gallup friends, but most of them were dead now anyway and replaced by the ghosts from the new war.

Beside the chair, the black-and-white dog whined and pushed closer to the old man's foot until its muzzle touched the two toes that protruded, sockless, from the tennis shoe. Domingo reached a hand down and massaged the dog's ear and then concentrated again on the can of hairspray. After the hissing had stopped, he lifted an empty plastic milk jug from the floor and inverted the can to let the liquid from the can drip into the jug. When nothing more would come out, he tossed the can toward a corner of the room, got up, and went to the rusting sink, where he filled three-fourths of the container with tap water.

Smiling to himself and trying unsuccessfully to hum the tune to a traditional song he'd once known, he pulled a package of sweetened Kool-Ade from the pocket of his flannel shirt, tore the corner of the package, and poured the red powder into the jug. Some people liked the taste of what they called Montana gin or ocean straight, but he preferred it with Kool-Ade. He moved the jug in half-circles, careful not to spill any of the uncapped liquid as he mixed, and then walked back to the chair and sat down with a contented sigh. That was when the room went dark.

One moment he was looking happily at the pink jug, and the next instant he could see nothing at all. He felt the jug slip from his fingers, heard it spill, and began to wail what he imagined was his death song. He knew it was the cat that had sat on his chest. It hadn't been a real cat the dog brought home at all. So this was what all the others had experienced, he thought. Death was sudden darkness in which your brain kept working for a while. He heard the dog growl weakly at death, and he realized the dog had not known about the witch cat. He forgave his old dog and wished, for the first time, that he had given the dog a name.

"Keep that bag on him," Shorty Luke said. "I'll hold his arms."

Avrum Goldberg held the burlap bag tightly to Domingo's thin shoulders. "Let's just take the chair and all."

"Good idea." Deftly, Shorty wrapped a hemp rope around Domingo's legs, pinning them to the chair, and continued to wrap upward so that Domingo's arms were also strapped down. Domingo's wail rose to a howl, and in the corner of the room the dog began to howl in exactly the same timbre.

"Can you make him stop that?" Avrum said.

"Stop what?"

They lifted the chair with its shriveled occupant and backed toward the door, Shorty kicking the door open with a foot as they carried Domingo out. The dog stopped howling and followed.

A pair of ravens with the sun behind them sat in a big pine at the side of Domingo's shack and barked at the sight of two men carrying a third in a wooden chair with a bag over his head. On the other side of the basketball court, several young children kicked out of a house at daylight stopped beating the ground with sticks to watch, and further away a group of four drowsing men sat on the porch of Tali's log home balancing cups of coffee and observing with mild interest. Shorty glanced at the men, knowing they had been handed coffee through the doorway because Tali did not allow men into the house.

Domingo's dog stumbled behind them, mixing whining growls with barely audible barks. Gathering its stiff legs, the dog shuffled to catch up with the men and succeeded in fastening its few remaining teeth in the leg of Avrum Goldberg's high, elkskin moccasin. The anthropologist stopped and shook his leg, but the dog held on.

"Careful. He ain't got but three teeth left," Shorty said as they carried and dragged the wailing Domingo and growling dog toward Mrs. Edwards's house.

The cluster of children had crossed the basketball court to stand close to the pickup with broken windows and watch, their sticks held like spears, but when the old lady appeared suddenly at the gate of her yard the children scattered.

"The dog can come, too," Mrs. Edwards said as she held the gate open.

"Well, that's a relief." Avrum swung his right foot slowly, dragging the dog in a gentle arc.

Mrs. Edwards held the door to her house open, and men and dog disappeared inside. Across the square, the four on Tali's porch looked on without expression and continued sitting with chairs tilted back against the log wall. Thunderheads that had been piling up all morning began to rumble, and a few lethargic drops pocked the dry earth and then ceased. The young rooster crowed again behind Mrs. Edwards's house and the ravens jolted upward to join a flock of seven that flapped off toward the mountains. Tentatively, the children drifted back onto the basketball court, dragging their sticks across the seed markings of rain.

13 Jake finished dressing and, out of habit, scrambled fried potatoes and eggs together. Outside, Domingo Perez's dog was barking strangely, but he didn't feel well enough to open his door and look. At least the flicker had gone away. He ate and then carefully washed the dishes, placing them beside the sink and looking at the new stain on his wall and the litter of his life in the little room before he picked up the full backpack. There would be time to leave when he got back. To hell with whoever shot at him. He'd let Shorty and Avrum work out their own problems. It wasn't even his tribe, anyway. But first he'd find Alison and say good-bye. He had held her and sung to her when she was a baby and then moved to the margins of her life, so he would have to tell her at least that he was going. She could tell Tali and the others.

He glanced at the electric sign again as he left the office, wondering how in hell Jessie had found time to break into the office and fix the thing. He glanced at the windowless tribal truck and then threw the pack into his old Chevy pickup and drove straight to Pachita Lake, not because Sam had told him to, but because the talk of assault weapons had aroused his curiosity. At the lake, he found that four-wheel-drive tracks had

105

torn up the fragile shore, and shell casings littered the ground near the shot-up hulk of a refrigerator. The doorless and gutless refrigerator had been dumped there since the last time he'd been by the lake, a month before, undoubtedly by someone from a local town who didn't want to spend the three bucks the county dump charged. The .223 casings by the refrigerator looked to be no more than a couple of days old. It seemed somebody or -bodies had brought out their AR-15s and blazed away, odd behavior for poachers, to say the least. It looked like they'd illegally converted the semis to fully automatic.

He walked back to his pickup, thinking for the hundredth time that they ought to fence lakes like this one, maybe fence the whole boundary between the National Forest and reservation, just to keep such assholes out. White people didn't seem to care what they did to the world. Probably most Indians weren't any better—the trash-filled White River testified to that—but at least Indians didn't have the technology to destroy at the magnitude of white people. And if they listened to the old stories, and believed them, Indians wouldn't destroy the earth anyway. The simple point was that Indians weren't going anywhere. If they cut down all the trees on the reservation and polluted the water and killed all the wildlife, they'd still have to live there, right in the middle of the mess, because it was all they had left. Whites always came from someplace else and figured they could just keep moving because they owned everything and could leave any mess behind. So they dumped refrigerators and then shot the shit out of them for fun. Especially if it was on Indian land. So maybe, he thought, there was such a thing as an Indian, something that cut across the lines of Choctaw and Cherokee and Black Mountain and Lakota to make some kind of connection.

In Nam they'd called VC-controlled areas Indian Country, the same way they'd done in the so-called Gulf War. Indian Country was always out there somewhere, beyond law, and whatever somebody did out there didn't come home with them. He'd seen the photos of charred bodies lining charred roads in Iraq, and he'd seen the smooth sand where U.S. tanks had buried thousands of men alive during that phony war. The twisted bodies beside the road, welded by heat, had reminded him of the gray photos of Bigfoot's band massacred and frozen at Wounded Knee. Sure, it was all different. Iraq was doing bad things and maybe had to be stopped, while those Indians had just been trying to save their children and elders, but what the pictures showed him were the rigid remains of dark-skinned human beings left from a massacre by the U.S. military once again, blackened with ice and frost or blackened by fire, but human beings indisputably.

It occurred to him that he, himself, had come from someplace else, had headed west just like white America. And he'd made a mess, too. And now he was about to leave again, but maybe he'd go back where he'd come from. Back to that other river.

He tried to imagine the ones who'd been at the lake with the AR-15s. They were in fatigues, and they kept their finger welded to the back of the trigger guard until it was over. Maybe they even had that familiar thousand-yard stare, but probably not. The kind who came out to shoot up old appliances were most likely the ones who wore their beer bellies like Purple Hearts. Probably half of them had ponytails and beards and most had undoubtedly never really been in combat or maybe even in Nam at all because they were too young. That kind learned the words and body language from the real vets. And now the enemy was even more invisible, rising up occasionally as a rusting appliance or ponderosa snag. Or sometimes a federal building filled with children and people coming for government help. White people were insane. More than half of him was thus insane. No wonder I'm a goddamned mess, he said to himself. He thought about the person or persons who'd perhaps tried to kill him, and he couldn't even find anger there. It was just another fact. Someone had shot at him and missed. It didn't matter if it was Sam Baca or anyone else. He didn't belong there.

Returning to the truck, he opened the door and paused for a moment to stare out across the lake. The still water curled around shadows of straight, black pines. Stipples all over the surface showed rising trout, stocked rainbows to lure the tourists, the kind of fish that came excitedly toward a shadow because shadows tossed food upon the water. Stupid, flaccid, diseased fish that were ruining all the rivers in America so that fat men with expensive equipment could catch them. Real, wild trout raced away from any shadow, hid and lived by swiftness and cunning.

He glanced around to see what kind of hatch was bringing the fish up. Caddis, he decided. Down on the river, he'd use an Adams, the universal catch-all, for one last time. Maybe a blue dun, too. The river fish were wild and strong; any stockers that got down that far were snacks for the big rainbows and the browns that came upriver in late summer. After he found Alison.

Around the lake the dark mountains rose in high, swelling pine forests toward the sky. The thunderheads of midday had drifted off to the northeast, and the sky was an endless pale blue, marked briefly by a flight of crows like pencil marks over the highest ridge. There was no sky in the world like that above the Black Mountain range. His memories of Mississippi were all shadows and tendrils of night that rose from dark earth to wrap around trees and climb toward a sky he couldn't remember, only to fall back to the decaying ground in curtains of thick vine. There had been the river that he recalled as barely moving, like a lighter brown portion of the earth itself set into reluctant motion. Creatures burrowed into the river as they did into the wet earth. A man didn't cast a delicate, transluscent fly onto such water; men wrapped and tied the entrails of large animals onto great treble hooks and weighted the mess to the bottom of that water, hoping for a gut-tightening struggle with whatever huge thing sucked such carrion into itself. As a very young boy, he'd hidden in the woods once and watched the stringy old Choctaw man haul a mudcat out of the river, the ugly fish longer than the man's arm. The old grandfather had clubbed the fish with a piece of oak and then, unexpectedly, raised his eyes to look directly at where he hid, the eyes so taut that he could feel them go over him like smooth hands. He'd run from the old man then, Luther Cole, the one he'd heard the grown-ups say was friends with the witch woman in her trailer, and he'd never gone back to that place. Not because he was afraid of the old man, but because of a feeling so much like love that he feared he would be drawn into that world forever, on the other side of the river. His father's father had died before he was born, and so he had no Indian grampa like other kids had, but in dreams the old man pulling the fish from the river had become his grandfather, had stood beside his bed singing so softly there were no words, smooth hands brushing the hair back from his forehead the same way the eyes had touched him by the river. As a child, he dreamed he was swimming the river, his hands grasping at the brown water like fistfulls of earth in a grave. And then his father had died too, and somehow the events seemed connected, and he had never been able to shake a sense that he was to blame, that in some way he had betrayed his father by dreaming of the old man. He'd wondered if his father had been sucked down that awful death river his granma had described. He had nightmares of watching his father trying desperately to balance on a black, slimy log over a river of snakes, and he always awoke with his father still struggling.

But his father had died of something simple, the kind of thing Indians and black people around them died of every day, and his mother had taken him away during a night of his fifth year, leaving the tobacco-spitting granma, the sharecropping farm, and everything Choctaw behind. A hallucinatory, two-day train ride had tumbled him into the sunlight of California, and there he had stayed with his waitress mother, receiving visits once or twice a year from his white grandmother, who was always with a different man.

He grew up remembering ever more vaguely that he was half of something called Choctaw, something having to do with the old man across the river, remembering for the most part only when schoolmates pointed out a difference in skin tone, breadth of nose, black hair. Dreaming at night when he lay half-asleep and waiting for his mother to come home from her shift.

Watching the edge of a small, new cloud sneak onto the smooth water, he thought of knocking Jessie down the day before and then of the days when he had really played basketball. At six-five and over two hundred pounds he had dominated in high school without really trying, and he remembered punishing opponents in games and even teammates during practice, using every weapon he had. That was why he had refused to play football. In basketball you had to pretend to a poise and indifference that belied the bloodshed you desired, every elbow or shoulder a casual encounter, almost like what he'd read about counting coup for the Plains tribes. In basketball his team flew like a raiding party into enemy territory and, invariably, fed the ball to him so he could bring his coup stick down on the enemy, and then they'd explode whooping toward the other end, their own camp, and punish each transgression. Football was too much a white man's war in which the armies faced each other and stupidly hurled line against line. He'd started getting calls from college coaches as a junior in high school, but he didn't call back. When they watched his games during his last year and sought him out with whispered promises afterward, he shrugged them off. There was a war going on somewhere a long way from home. Basketball was a child's game.

Vietnam, he discovered, wasn't a white man's war at all. The small brown people they were trying to kill dictated the kind of war it would be, and those people had dreamed of nightmares and ghosts white people couldn't even imagine. That was why so many went crazy and brought that craziness home with them; they didn't have any groove in their genetic memories for the horrors they were seeing, feeling, acting out, and becoming. Ironically, it was a kind of war more familiar to Indians than to anyone else, but it was without honor or meaning. Even more ironically for Indians, the problems really began when they had to come home. He'd seen those casualties at the center in Phoenix, and he'd looked at the Navajo and Pueblo and Zuni and Pima veterans in the interminable waiting rooms and realized he wasn't like them. He wasn't really an Indian, he knew, or really anything else. His mother had died during his first tour of duty, and so he was tied to nothing in the whole world except a childhood vision of an old man he never knew. Luther Cole. *Alikchi* was the word his granma had used, an easy word to remember even if you didn't know what it meant.

He started the truck and drove away from the lake, catching out of the corner of his eye a small flock of wild turkeys skulking into the woods, their sleek, blue-black forms surprisingly like thinner versions of Thanksgiving dinner. Glancing at his watch, he pushed the accelerator as he hit the main road. The rear wheels spun and fishtailed, and he punched the gas harder. That was an advantage of a tribal vehicle. He could take the rough reservation roads as fast as he wanted. New struts and shocks weren't his problem. Motor mounts were replaced every year, and oil leaks were taken for granted. But his old pickup rattled and shimmied, and he felt its pain. He'd begun reading about the Choctaw nation finally, after too many people had asked him what kind of Indian he was. And how was he to know, now, that he was racing toward death along the narrow rutted road through thick pine forest?

14   In the growing dimness of evening at the canyon's bottom, Stroud stood like a rock among the shadows at the edge of the camp, watching the six men move about with a strange combination of clumsy awkwardness and military precision as they set up tents, gathered wood, and dug a fire pit. Several of the men looked like they'd never been more than a mile from a golf course before, but four of the others obviously knew what they were doing. The smell of pine was

strong on the damp air, and the purling river soothed his taught nerves. So far this project was going to hell, and they'd barely gotten started. If they aborted, it meant forty thousand bucks down the tubes, but something about this particular session was making him increasingly uneasy.

Ravens or crows, some kind of big, black birds, chortled nearby, the sound like a fighter's laughter, the kind that preceded violence. Somewhere up the ridge an elk had whistled just a few minutes earlier, the call strange and chilling. He'd never heard an elk before, and the man named Jensen had had to explain it. The sound reminded him of ghost stories they'd told in Boy Scouts when he was a kid. He'd read that elk would be rutting this time of year, or soon at least, the bulls dazed and apeshit from the pressure of their own balls. But overlaying the whole scene was the smooth sound of the river breaking softly against rocks and sliding through its shallow channels. A small river, not even a hundred feet wide in most places and pooling deeply in the frequent sharp corners of the stone canyon, the Dark was as perfect as a river could be. And the canyon was the perfect training ground. Nine times out of ten, the kinds of enrollees they attracted could shoot off their own nuts and nobody would be any the wiser. Especially their wives. But again he watched Jensen expertly tie off a guyline and another of the men rigging the food cache bag, and the ease of their actions was disturbing.

That there was a hitch already had taken him by surprise. He'd scouted the place several times, finding the faint path down from the top of the canyon with no signs of anyone having camped anywhere in years. The tribal official he'd made his deal with had assured him they'd be uninterrupted as long as they stayed on the reservation—for 20 percent of gross, cash that naturally wouldn't be reported to anyone. Despite the unfortunate blowup during a break at the lake, when Jensen had gotten trigger happy with the fancy rifle he'd brought, Stroud was positive no one had seen them come in, and they'd hidden their vehicles well off the old logging spur road up on top.

He turned to a tall, heavy man beside him. "Remember, Walter," he said in a voice held even with apparent will, "no pine. Use oak kindling to start it and split oak for the fire. If I see smoke from that fire, I'll have your considerable ass."

"Yes, sir." The man, a camouflaged car salesman from Tucson, grunted as he drove a huge machete-like thing called a Woodman's Pal into an upright round of oak, splitting the hard wood. Like a kid, he glanced up to see if Stroud had noticed how well he'd split the oak.

Amused by the big man's need for assurance, Stroud looked again at the men busy with the camp. The green nylon tents were up quickly and taut looking, and a drab green tarp had been rigged efficiently over the cooking fire. The rifles, sheltered by another tarp, were leaning in an even line against a rope tied between trees, so that a man could grab his weapon and react in seconds, a charade he liked to maintain. That had been his own idea and innovation, and as he explained it he could see how much it appealed to his students. Like most of the gung ho types who ended up in his camps, this assortment of assholes had watched too many John Wayne and Rambo movies, or worse. He liked to order rich men around. Usually they were soft, the kind of soft that came from live-in cooks and golf cart athletics. And every one, car salesmen, lawyers, and real estate tycoons, wanted to be Rambo or that muscle-bound cartoon in the movie *Predator*, saving Western civilization from alien invasion. They wanted to live the warrior life they'd missed as clerks in Nam or, even more often, had only seen in movies. Thank God for Nguyen, he thought.

"Awake, Captain Stroud?"

A man stood before him with an AR-15 cradled toward the earth and a quizzical smile on his face.

Lee Jensen and the three men who'd come with him were the damned exceptions, the one thing that didn't make sense. The rolled up sleeves of Jensen's camouflage shirt showed corded forearms, and the expensive gun lay across a stomach with no trace of fat. His shoulders were broad, his jawline muscled, his neck thick as a telephone pole, and his blond hair cut within a quarter inch of his scalp. How the hell did I let those sonsofbitches in, Stroud asked himself. His own silent answer was, of course, money. The course hadn't been filled and four men meant twenty thousand bucks gross.

"You looked like you were dreaming of the good old days, Captain." Jensen shifted the rifle to the side and leaned it out upright from his hip. "Slicing up a few VC, maybe?"

"Just planning tomorrow." Stroud noted the hard line of Jensen's mouth. The man was too young to have been in any war, and he hadn't even bothered to lie about the so-called Desert Storm bullshit the way so many others did. The business was chock full of fake war heroes attracted by Stroud's ad in magazines like *American Survival*, but Jensen cheerfully admitted that he'd never been in combat or even in the military. He seemed to be a war hobbyist. There was little doubt, however, that he clearly knew a hell of a lot about it, and there wasn't much doubt that the three older men with Jensen had seen a lot of shit. They hadn't said diddly squat, but instead let Jensen do all the talking and, Stroud had noticed, they were careful not to embarrass the ones who really were rookies. A real Nam combat vet stood out, probably because it was only the frauds who wanted to talk about their so-called Nam experience. The ones who'd been there were usually quiet, and they recognized each other pretty fast in their silence. Those three were the real thing.

"Mind if I take a closer look at that?" Stroud said, nodding toward Jensen's rifle.

Jensen looked down at the spotless, gleaming black-and-chrome rifle and grinned. "Not at all. I was wondering when you'd ask."

"I was curious about what you had in that case on your pack. Not too many men take a match rifle out on maneuver," Stroud said as Jensen handed him the gun. "Doesn't seem real practical." Stroud regretted the note of contempt that had crept into his voice. That was a weakness.

"AR-15 A-4NM."

"No shit."

Ignoring Stroud's comment, Jensen looked at the gun proudly. "The most accurate .223 military configuration in the world. Chrome bolt carrier, rear sight base with quarter- and half-inch adjustments for wind and elevation, front sight post machined to twenty thousandths, four sixteen stainless steel ultra-rifled SGW barrel blank, and taper-reamed flash hider."

"Kind of delicate for a firefight, isn't it?" Stroud sighted up the rifle toward the sky. "What're you firing?"

"Federal sixty-nine-grain hollow-point match, mean velocity of two thousand seven hundred and eighty-seven feet per second."

"I'll take an M-14 any day," Stroud said.

"This little jewel is light, fast, and doesn't miss, ever." Jensen lifted the rifle out of Stoud's hands. "Of course a lot of the old vets still prefer the M14, especially over those HBAR AR-15s you provided for the rest of the guys."

Stroud noted with a touch of amusement the way the younger man had gotten back at him. He knew he could break Jensen in half any time he felt like it. A show-off body and a tournament rifle were signs of weakness. It didn't take a body-builder to crush a windpipe or take a man's ear off with the edge of a hand so that the man bled to death at your feet. Knowledge and experience killed the enemy, and he had an increasingly odd feeling that Lee Jensen was some kind of enemy.

Jensen nodded toward one of the tents. "Was that a .308 I noticed in there with the night scope?"

Stroud nodded. "Part of the standard training. You familiar with it?"

"A little. You know, I heard about you—" Jensen began, but Stroud cut him off.

"What are you doing here, Jensen?" he said quietly. "What are you and those other three doing in my camp?" He watched the big, triple-chinned car dealer, Walter, carefully building a kindling pyramid with oak slivers, the man's nearly bald head damp with sweat and his face showing heavy stubble after just a day out. Like so many men who signed up for his training, Walter was actually a timid person, probably a man who lived in fear of his wife's displeasure or a sign of disrespect from his employees. Stroud felt sympathy for such men.

Stroud turned his eyes fully on Lee Jensen. "Your application said you'd been in a TRS camp in California, but not much else. Those other three said they were vets who wanted to brush up. Frankly I didn't ask too many questions because I wanted your money, but now I'm starting to get curious. Why pay five thousand bucks for a course you or any one of those three could probably teach? And where do guys like those get an extra five grand?"

Jensen shrugged. "You're familiar with Tactical Response Solutions." He looked straight at Stroud. "They're familiar with you. You're kind of a legend among those SEAL and Delta Force vets, you know. Word gets around."

"Bullshit. Which TRS camp was it?"

"DSTC. Delta/SEAL Training Camp. What else?"

"Nitske's operation?"

"Right. Every instructor was a real-deal SpecOps. SEAL Six and Delta grunts, UDT guys. SEAL Unarmed Combat System. You know all that."

"How much you pay for that?"

"Six thousand per four-day camp."

"You did more than one course?"

Jensen smiled. "I liked it. Thought I could use more polish. And they liked my money."

"I know the guys you're talking about, and they don't tell stories. You didn't hear all that shit about me in a TRS camp, especially Nitske's. So what are you and your buddies doing here with me and these car salesmen and real estate barons? I don't have anything to teach you."

Jensen continued to smile. "I guess those TRS fellows are getting old and romantic, like a lot of Nam vets, but after a couple of beers they really did talk about you. No kidding. Especially some of that CIA PsycOps stuff in Africa and Central America." Jensen's smile became a grin and his eyes sharpened. "Like the time you told those villagers you'd turn their water to blood and then dropped dye in the reservoir. Or better yet, when you spread those stories about vampires and then hung a few Africans up by their feet and made two little incisions in their throats so the blood would drain out before you left the bodies in the middle of villages. That was especially good."

Stroud watched Jensen without speaking. Where the hell was Nguyen, he wondered?

Jensen looked hard at Stroud's eyes. "I'll tell you the simple truth. We've organized a little group here in Arizona, what you might call an elite cadre to prepare and train others for when all the shit comes down. No wackos or racists or Christian Identity lunatics, just competent men who can make others follow them and establish order when necessary. Everyone said you were the best, so I came looking for you. We'd like you and your Vietnamese partner to join us. As for the money, let's just say that I inherited a little and put my colleagues there on scholarship just for this mission."

Stroud looked away to watch Walter labor at the fire. Walter was pretty typical, a middle-aged man who'd avoided Vietnam but was now convinced the New World Order wanted to take away the guns he didn't know how to use. Crossing his arms over his broad chest, Stroud looked up at Jensen. "I'm not interested in joining anything, and Nguyen won't be either. I also have to tell you that this encampment is already a bust. We're going out in the morning, and I'm returning everyone's money. You and your SEAL friends can go fight the New World Order on your own, if you can find it. You need to understand that Nguyen and I are in this for the money. Period. No ideals, no revolutions. I hope that doesn't disenchant you."

Jensen smiled. "Did I tell you that the barrel on this baby is finish chambered, with a head space of one point four six four five inches, the tightest chamber you've ever seen? Tight is good, don't you think? We've got all night to talk, Captain Stroud, and tomorrow is another day, as they say. I'll try to convince you to change your mind. We want you because you're the best. Or used to be."

"You poor deluded bastard." Stroud looked toward a man siphoning water from the river through a purifier. "Goddamned river's bound to be full of giardia," Stroud muttered. "And now we have an unwanted guest."

"More guests are arriving by the minute, too." Jensen nodded toward the creek north of the camp.

Two of the men were approaching with a stretcher, an exhausted-looking woman stumbling along behind them.

"Mother of God," Stroud said.

The group arrived, and the men lowered the stretcher onto the ground a few feet from the small fire.

"Henry shot him," Tom Peters said, sounding like one child telling on another.

"We thought he was a damned wolf," Henry added. "He was wearing a wolf suit."

"He was wearing a fucking wolf suit." Peters pointed to the lower half of the suit still covering Jessie's legs and the wolf head and remaining wolf skin piled on his crotch.

"He's an Indian." Jensen had walked over to look down at the body. "Dead as hell, too. The only good one . . ."

Stroud knelt over the stretcher. "I guess we have an even bigger problem." He stood up and looked at Sandrine. "Do you know who this is?"

While Peters explained, Stroud noted Jensen's eyes fixed intently on the woman. She was probably in her mid or late twenties and uncommonly pretty, with a dark complexion, brown eyes, and chestnut hair. What was most impressive about her, however, was the look of pure hostility on her face combined with the absence of fear.

"So this French woman says the Indian sold her a fake vision, and Henry and me just happened along when he was playing wolf," Peters was saying.

"Henry and I," Jensen remarked. "Peters and the wolf."

"What?"

"Never mind," Stroud said. "Jesus fucking Christ on a cross."

Jensen had begun to grin openly, and Stroud struggled to control a growing rage. He hadn't faced this kind of death in nearly thirty years. He was supposed to be playing virtual reality games in the woods with a bunch of helpless wannabes. Now a young man was dead, killed by a gun he had supplied to a goddamned dentist. And the dead man was very likely a member of the tribe on whose land they were camped. Another member of the same tribe was currently imprisoned in a tent. A French national had witnessed the killing. And there was Jensen.

Stroud's thoughts wandered to his youngest daughter's gymnastics competition that weekend. He'd hated to miss it. He knew she felt bad about his not being there. She had his body, short and powerful, stong-muscled and well balanced. Maybe too squat for the kind of pubescence the Olympics slavered over, but someone who would never fall off this earth. However, the combat survival course had been planned long before he'd known about the gymnastics meet, so his wife would have to cheer for both of them. And the money was too good to pass up. Even with the pay-off and Nguyen's cut, he would have still had more than twenty thousand for the week. After expenses it was quite a profit.

He looked around at the semidark canyon. At this point, where the creek entered the river, there was a nice flat in the pine and scrub oak for camping, yet he could throw a stone and hit the cliffs on the other side of the river. The setting sun had left a layering of warm light in the moist air, and the trees thickened into a solid mass of shadow rising up the hillside. He'd picked the spot for precise reasons. Scaling the volcanic cliffs opposite the campsite would be a good exercise, requiring wading with weapons held high before the actual ascent and then rappelling down. He considered each of the eight men, gauging who would have had the hardest time of it, who might actually have made it, and then he breathed in the faint fragrance of the oak kindling and noticed with satisfaction that virtually no smoke rose from the growing fire. Most of the ones who signed up for his courses were pretty decent men, actually, with only a few wackos, which he usually managed to screen out. His ads specifically said no racists, and Nguyen would have made short work of any of those who slipped through. A good proportion of the applicants had simply missed out on the hopeless glory of Vietnam, and they had a hard time living with the fact. They usually had pretty bizarre ideas, and he'd learned to foster their paranoia a little so they'd feel they'd gotten their money's worth. Most of the fake recon rangers and Special Forces guys were a hell of a lot bloodthirstier than the real ones, but he'd never had one who was actually nuts. Not like the group of antiwar vets he'd tied in with in Santa Barbara after discharge. Like a lot of them, he'd come back from the war knowing who the real enemy was, and he knew they weren't little people with brown skins. On G.I. Bill, he'd enrolled at the University of California in Santa Barbara, and almost immediately he'd hooked up with a bunch of brain-warped vets who knew who to fight and had the weapons necessary. It was the government, the fat-assed motherfuckers who'd sent boys to die in a war that meant nothing more than votes back home. So they'd organized and waited for the right moment. They had everything: M-16s, plastic, radios, grenades, the whole shitload. And when the stupid-fuck LAPD tac squad came into the student community and started beating the hell out of everyone, the vets were organized and ready to blow the cops' asses all the way to Honolulu. But they didn't. Their nerve had failed.

The vets had watched students and street people beaten and shot. They watched the Bank of America burned by a bunch of dumb amateurs and the cops driven out of the student community by a band of ex-frat kids throwing Molotov cocktails. They watched a boy get shot through the heart by a deputy sheriff sharpshooter with an infrared scope, a cop the vets could have taken out without anyone even knowing. They watched a bunch of pigs do the kind of shit they'd seen their friends die for in Nam, but they wouldn't agree to act. Everybody, it seemed, had really had enough of fighting.

That was when he'd become cynical and turned away from it all, determined to form his own army. He knew it would take time, years, but that eventually he'd find enough like him to make it worthwhile. One day they'd come together, and they'd take down the same bunch of fat-assed rich bastards who'd killed fifty thousand boys in Nam just to get elected to a bloody path of money. Eventually he'd have an army that could gut the bastards. And he'd be the first to slip the tip of the knife in, but this time it wouldn't be a little brown man who was fighting for justice but a rich sonofabitch who needed killing. Yet somewhere along the way it had all become business.

"I need a little privacy to think," he said. "Watch the woman."

He walked into the growing darkness of the trees along the river. The oak tannin and rising pine sap lay heavy in the summer air, and the river seemed to carry the whole canyon with it in its southwestward arc toward the distant Gulf of California, so that he had a wonderful feeling of swimming easily against a fine current of both time and space. It was an old feeling, one he'd had in Nam when the shit would come in heavy and all sense of time and space would be altered. His most vivid memory was of standing in a small clearing, where the elephant grass had been beaten down by choppers and his squad was diving and rolling and crabbing to escape incoming fire from the entire perimeter, a place where they had been dropped like fish in hot grease while the copters banked and rolled far away into the sky. It was then that two things happened. The first was that he had realized one can stand in the path of death with indifference because every infinitesimal thing in the universe has already occurred, including one's own death, and there isn't anything to do about it. And then the second thing happened: the Indian had taken him down, coming horizontally out of somewhere to strike him chest-high and send him sprawling to the padded stalks. He'd tried to fight, gathering the power of his massed muscle, but the Indian was huge, holding him to the earth by the weight of all time and history, until the firing stopped and the perimeter had been secured. The Indian thought he'd saved his life and that he was a fool, and for six months more, until the half-savage was rotated out, he'd seen it in the Indian's eyes. And he'd often dreamed of killing the bastard who'd taken him out of the air of gods and fate. Other times he'd dream of that embrace when he lay on the hot earth and the feeling then was different.

He'd sent the Indian out on point time and again. He'd put him out on loan for several of the long-range reconnaisance patrols that seldom came back. But the Indian had always came back even when other Lerps didn't, until the last time. And the big sonofabitch wouldn't admit to being Indian. He held his ground in-between, neither Indian nor white. Every Indian in Nam was called "chief," except that one. There'd been a pretty funny discussion about it among the blacks in the platoon. One of them, a fresh fish from somewhere in the South, had called the half-breed "chief" and been convinced to retract the title seconds later. Then another soul brother had started in. "Now, what I want to know, motherfucker," the man, a skinny guy named Atkinson, had said, "is how come Jackson there got to be a brother when he's whiter than your butt? I mean, the brother got just a drop of black down there somewheres, but he ain't got a choice. Ain't no honky motherfuckers gonna let the brother be white if he's got that piddly-ass bit of Afro in there. Thing is, he got to be a soul brother even if he don't want to be. But you don't got to be no real Injun even if anybody can see you got that bitchin' all-year tan. All these white motherfuckers back home go round bragging they're Injun and then other Injuns and white folks say they can't be Injun cause they ain't Injun enough. You don't see white motherfuckers bragging they black and people saying you can't be black cause you ain't black enough. Any motherfucker dumb-ass enough to say he's black is black, period. Now anybody look at you and they see an Injun, but

you say you ain't neither Injun or a honky white motherfucker."
Atkinson had turned to Stroud then. "This don't make no sense.
How come this motherfucker ain't got to be nothing? He got to
be something. You the man, so you tell the brother he got to be
Injun or white, he got to choose. He can't be no in-between."
But Stroud had just laughed with the rest of them, both black
and white, while the non-Indian had grinned and walked away,
and now he was dead, like Atkinson and a lot of others.

Stroud headed back toward the camp, trying to pinpoint
the time when his feelings had all changed. He'd begun by
imagining an army of trained killers, like himself, men dedi-
cated to destroying the rich elite who sat at expensive dinners
and decided who and how many little people would die in
distant places for profit. Nguyen had been his first recruit,
brought out of Nam to Phoenix under Stroud's sponsorship
when Stroud found out the little man was still alive. Soon,
however, he and Nguyen had become businessmen, teachers
whose students graduated with nothing but a little thrill and a
swagger. Gradually, they were both becoming rich, living the
good life in Scottsdale while the little town of Phoenix, where
Stroud had been born, turned into a smog bowl like Los
Angeles, and Scottsdale became filled with art galleries and
coffee shops. Everywhere you looked there was Indian art, but
you never saw any Indians in Scottsdale.

Everything had gone to hell this time, however. It had been
his job once to make life-and-death decisions in an instant, but
now he wasn't sure what to do. The only thing he could think
of was packing up in the morning and taking the body in to the
cops in Springerville. The women would be witnesses, as
would everyone with him. He hadn't pulled the trigger, but he
might as well have. But hell, the guy had been wearing a wolf
suit in the middle of a wilderness. And he was an Indian. As
fucked up as it was, the lousy attitude toward Indians in these
parts would help a lot, even in this era of supposed political
correctness. The law would go easy on Henry, a respectable
dentist who'd probably never even had a speeding ticket. They'd

found the women lost in the woods and thought they were helping them; how in the hell could they know this bullshit about vision quests was true, since they'd found both women without food or shelter in the middle of nofuckingwhere? They could hammer out a story about a bunch of ex-military buddies on a campout. He'd have to give the money back and face a significant financial loss. But a young man was dead who shouldn't be. Stroud felt very tired.

15 Jake parked his truck in the same clearing he always used, close to the end of the Forest Service logging road but back in the trees where even hunters would not be likely to see it. He'd noticed an unusual amount of signs of vehicle activity on the road, so the woods were probably crawling with elk hunters, the kind who didn't even sight their guns in and mostly road-hunted, gut-shooting half the animals they saw. One deer or elk was worth a hundred of those assholes.

He'd spent a lot more time than he'd planned having a leisurely breakfast, drinking two cups of coffee, and later walking around Pachita Lake. Now the sun had already vanished, leaving the ten-thousand-foot mountain crest in a nice half-light, the pines vertical tangles of shadow on both sides of the rutted road. On the way in he'd spotted half a dozen elk in a single meadow, all cows, of course. Somehow the cows always knew when they couldn't be legally shot. He'd also noticed the single coyote sitting in a locust thicket beside the road to watch his truck pass, like one of those trick pictures where you try to find the animal hidden in the scribblings of other things. To an Apache or Navajo the coyote might have been disturbing. If they knew what his last name, Nashoba, meant they'd be even more disturbed by him, too. For him the coyote was just nice to see, a reminder of some things still at least somewhat beyond man's reach. They could be trapped, shot, poisoned, run over on the roads, but they were never afraid, always back there on the edges watching and learning.

One time he'd come across something rare and horribly beautiful on a long, grassy bench near the river. A deer was defending her newborn fawn from a big male coyote. The July day held midmorning warmth and bright sunlight, and he was hiking out after ten days on the river, sweating and tired. A warm wind blew down the slope into his face, bringing the fine smell of heated grasses and pine sap, and his feet were still pleasantly cool from wading the river minutes before. Caught up in the struggle, neither animal had seen him approach and stop a hundred yards away. Poised on her hind feet, the doe lashed out with her front hooves like black-tipped spears, the tiny, spotted bundle of fawn lying in the creased shadow of a log behind her. The coyote lunged forward and then leaped backward or to the side, always a fraction of an inch out of range of the hooves, drawing the mother away until he could flash past her and rip at the baby with his sharp canines. The doe would wheel and drive him away again, and then they'd begin the fatal dance once more, the grinning, confident coyote luring her inch by inch until he could lunge past and again rip a bloody slash in the fawn.

He had been transfixed by the immaculate grace of the doe poised on two delicate hind legs, and the smug, wide grin of the coyote, who knew he couldn't lose the game, a game the coyote had undoubtedly played many times. Jake regretted what he had done then, denting his metal fly rod case loudly against a rock and shouting so that doe and coyote both heard and saw at once and fled simultaneously in opposite directions.

He had walked up to the fawn with slow, fatalistic steps, knowing how stupid he'd been. Never interfere with nature had always been his law. You don't kill rattlesnakes just because they might bite, you don't "save" the fish that get stranded by dropping river levels, and you leave the nestling on the ground when the wind takes it out of a nest. That's the way the world had always worked. Rattlesnakes bore powerful medicine; things that could kill also had the power to heal. And racoons and other creatures would feed on the stranded fish and fallen nestlings. The big heron tracks around stagnant pools, plus the perfectly cleaned skeleton of a heron that lay at the bottom of one pool like a white, two-dimensional pterodactyl, testified, as did the osprey descending into its nest with a fish or writhing water snake in its talons. It was his prime directive, do not interfere. He'd seen enough interference in his life.

"Situational ethics," someone in Vietnam had once said, referring that time to a young girl, maybe sixteen, a "gook," dying in a spreading puddle of blood on a muddy road with an undetonated bomb strapped to her back. The captain, a man named Stroud, had shot the girl through the guts from a hundred yards away because of the bulge on her back. It might have been a bag of rice or a baby sister bundled tightly, but Stroud had been right. The girl had been walking directly toward the platoon with enough C-4 to take them all out. He thought then of a new guy who'd stepped on a claymore mine one week into his tour. Charlie frequently found the claymores and moved them, turning them around, so that what was supposed to guard a perimeter was instead aimed right at their nuts. The medics had tried to save the guy's legs, but everybody had walked past without looking, knowing it was just make-work. The guy, whose name he couldn't remember even learning, was dead a long time before he stopped breathing.

The fawn was already in shock when he reached it, with deep rips in its neck and sides and blood covering the tiny flanks. He knew it would be dead in minutes, and he knew he'd frightened the doe off permanently, so that even if by some miracle the fawn could have survived the trauma it would be abandoned. The coyote would double back, unafraid of man smell, for its meal. It was probably watching him right then, as a matter of fact, waiting patiently. There'd been an unusually big crop of fawns that year, probably owing to plenty of moisture and feed, and the coyotes he'd seen had all looked sleek and fat. Staring down at the fragile, brown-and-white baby, he swore to himself then that he would never interfere again. Never play God again. He knew it had been the hopeless courage of the mother that had made him act, not the annoying arrogance of the coyote and not the seeming tragedy of the good-as-dead fawn, but the extraordinary beauty of the mother's instinct that existed independent of everything else in the world.

Always the coyotes were there, singing somewhere close enough to be heard but not seen. That's why there were all the cute coyotes with handkerchiefs around their necks in Scottsdale and Santa Fe stores; people wanted to pacify old Coyote, domesticate him, make him cute, make him what they'd made Indians in their imaginations. But Coyote was still out there, waiting and watching, untouched and untouchable. You could shoot him and hang him on a fence, and she'd be back the next night, still watching. He loved the wild song of coyotes, the mixed-up mess of cry and lullaby and angry shriek all in a single garbled note. Owls were a different story, and not good. He didn't like to think about owls.

He opened up the back of the pickup and dragged the heavy pack out. When the pack was adjusted on his shoulders, the waist belt and chest straps tight, he pulled his aluminum fly rod case out of the truck, looked at it, and replaced it before locking the camper shell. He checked to be sure the front doors were locked and then started downhill across a thinning unit where the Forest Service had dropped small trees in a random mess between the larger pines. He picked his way slowly through the tangled slash and timber and vanished into the old-growth forest on the other side of the unit. In a few minutes he was stepping across the rusting barbed wire fence that lay on the ground to mark the boundary between National Forest and reservation. And then he plunged straight down a nearly invisible path toward the creek that would lead him to the river.

16   Alison lay in the tent thinking back over the last twenty-four hours. Everything seemed crazy. She couldn't believe she was a prisoner, like Lozen and the others who'd been tricked into exile and prison by lying whites.

She had sat where Jessie had indicated she should sit, her legs folded on the ground pad he'd given her and her shoulders hunched inside the parka. Cramps spread from the base of her neck into both shoulders, and she rolled her head and rubbed alternately one shoulder and then the other with her hands. She had managed to stay awake all of the first day and night and through the next day as well, hearing wings in the trees above her and the movements of animals around her but seeing nothing except moving clouds, tiny, floating insects, and fluttering gray birds. Despite all her will she had fallen asleep on the second night, lying on the inflated pad with her head on her arm, trying to stay awake and listen to the words of the forest until sleep overtook her and dreams came drifting down the mountain flanks to surround her. In a succession of dreams, animals came to stand over her and discuss her. A spotted and beaded lizard told her she was too weak, and a turtle said, "When trouble starts, cousin, just climb inside my shell." But the turtle looked like a man with no shell. Birds came and hopped from foot to foot beside her. Raven and Piñon Jay and Red-Tailed Hawk stood side by side and discussed her plight. "Dreamer," said Raven. "What a lovely girl," Jay answered. "Hunter," said Hawk. Then a black wind swept like a river down from the mountain, carrying an enormous, broad-winged owl in its rush, the nearly white bird as silent as one of the clouds and casting a shadow even in the night. The birds tumbled off into the air of the canyon pursued by the owl, leaving a turtle who looked at Alison with blinking eyes before pulling its head into its shell and sinking back into the pool of the spring. She woke cold and shaking in a hard downslope wind and got to her feet to drink from the spring and then move about to warm her body. Even in summer the canyon could get cold.

Near morning she had fallen asleep once more and had been awakened at dawn by a strangely warm sensation on the back of her neck. In a half-sleep she heard a snuffling and smelled a sweet, musty fragrance. She lay unmoving for a few moments before finding the courage to sit up.

Nothing was there, but as she looked around she found the large pad prints of a bear in the earth beside her, the unmistakable plump-human tracks no other animal could make—small heel, narrow instep, broad ball of foot and fat toes. But how had it disappeared so quickly, she wondered. And when was she going to have her vision? She had dreamed of strange animals, things she had heard about in stories, and now there was the bear that wasn't there. But there had to be more. Her stomach twisted in pain, and she thought of the bag of jerky she had resisted for three days now. Suddenly she was starving for the dried meat. But the bag was gone. It had been beside her head when she slept, and now it was gone.

She laughed weakly. The bear must have come for that.

"You looking for this, Miss?"

She jumped to her feet and then doubled over with a sharp pain in her stomach.

"Careful. You don't look too well."

A large, soft-looking man in a military uniform stood just a few feet from her. She had thought he was one of the tree trunks, but now he stood holding her bag of jerky in one hand and a rifle in the other. And around him were several other men.

"You need some help, miss? You lost?" the man with the bag said. He was a pleasant-faced, middle-aged man, but the gun in his hand was the kind that had a magazine clip in it, the kind she'd seen in war movies. The other men were dressed the same and held the same kind of guns.

"I'm not lost," she said. "This is my reservation."

"Well, you should probably come with us," the man said politely. "We have a camp real close, where you can get out of the weather and get some decent food."

"I'm not going anywhere," Alison said. "It's you who have to leave. You're not supposed to be hunting down here anyway. So just go away."

A thin, darker man stepped forward. "You really don't have a choice," he said. "Walter, grab that pad of hers and let's

129

go. Stroud's going to have to figure this one out. Cute one for an Indian, ain't she?"

"You can't make me go with you," Alison said.

The thin man lifted his rifle toward her. "We can shoot you," he said simply. "Nobody will hear the shot and nobody will find you. So take your choice."

"Jesus Christ, Vasello," the man who'd spoken first said.

"Vasello's right, Walter." A third man stepped past both of the others and came very close to Alison. "She's just a kid. She shouldn't be out here alone like this. Here." He handed his rifle to Vasello and pulled a bandanna out of his back pocket and tore it into three strips, which he knotted together.

"Put your arms behind your back, little girl," he said. When she made no motion, he added, "Vasello will actually shoot you. I've heard that he's done it before, in Vietnam, and word is that some of them were brown young girls a lot like you, even younger."

"Fuck you, Jensen," the man said. "You never heard shit about me."

Jensen looked over his shoulder. "On the contrary, Vasello, if I hadn't heard a lot more than that about you, you wouldn't be here right now. And one other thing. If you ever even suggest an insult to me again, I'll break your neck." He turned back to Alison. "I won't make it too tight, but I think it's necessary. Don't worry about him."

Vasello stepped back, his rifle half-raised. "Whenever you think you can do that, Jensen."

Jensen waved a hand toward the other man without even looking. "What's your name?" he said to Alison, who glared back.

She pushed her arms behind her and felt her wrists bound loosely with the bandanna. "I'm not worried about any of you," she said. "When my cousin and grandfather find out what you've done, you'll all be sorry."

Jensen cocked his head and smiled at her. "Your cousin and grandfather wouldn't be somewhere around here right now, would they?"

130

Alison shook her head quickly. "They don't know where I am. But my grandfather will be looking for me, and you'll be sorry if he finds you."

"My goodness, an Indian war." Jensen continued smiling. "I'd like to meet your grandfather. Must be a great warrior, I guess. But don't worry. Nobody will hurt a single hair on your lovely head." He half-turned toward the others. "If anyone harms this girl in any way, even insults her, I'll kill him. Understood?"

"Who made you God?" Vasello replied.

Jensen looked coldly at the other man. "I did. God of war. Any objections?"

Out of the shadows a small man stepped, making absolutely no sound. He walked to within three paces of Alison and the man who had bound her, and he looked with a faint smile into the man's face.

"Well done, Jensen," the man said in an unusual, nasal voice. "You are clearly a natural leader, if not quite a god. Though we must have other means of enforcing discipline than killing. We might run out of personnel too quickly that way."

For the first time, Jensen looked slightly nervous. "I didn't know you were there," he said. "Or I would've—"

"Okay, no problem. You number one."

Jensen's look of confusion deepened, as though he suspected that he was being ridiculed but wasn't sure.

To Alison the little man looked like one of her uncles, the one named Angel who was always drunk. But this man was clearly not drunk. In fact, she had never seen anyone so sober in her life.

"So what do you think, Lieutenant?" Jensen pushed the camouflage cap back on his forehead and kept his eyes on Alison.

"I think you are right, Jensen," the dark-skinned little man said. "But there is something strange here in this place. If you'll forgive what you would call superstition, I have to say my sixth sense tells me, plus those." He pointed toward the distinct bear tracks beside the spring.

131

"Holy shit," the plump man said. "That's got to be bear, a big one."

"Real bear or spirit bear?" Nguyen asked, a slight smile on his thin lips. "Are you familiar with spirit bears, Lee?"

Alison saw a brief flash of anger cross Jensen's face before he looked at Nguyen blankly. "I'm familiar with dead bears."

"Lee, you take the girl to Captain Stroud and I'll wait here with Walter and Vasello. I want to look around a little. Maybe that grandfather of hers is trying to find her."

Jensen took Alison by the upper arm and gently guided her before him down toward the river.

17   The stream, narrow enough to jump across in most places, wound and dropped from one small pool to another, the water nearly black. When there was enough light, Jake liked to count the Apache golden trout, mere fingerlings, in each pool. The feds had come in a few years earlier and poisoned out the big rainbows in the creek and restocked with the endangered native goldens, but the little trout didn't appear to be taking hold very well. There never seemed to be more, and they never seemed to grow. Maybe the big ones made their way down to the river to serve as endangered entrees for the bigger trout there. It was a mystery he kept hoping to solve, since he'd never seen a golden in the river.

He ignored the stream and moved along the flat bottom of the feeder canyon, wading through high grasses and willow thickets. Beavers had dropped more small trees alongside the stream, and he kept having to detour about their slash piles. In half an hour he struck the rivulet where the spring came down to the creek, and he began to climb. Even in the half-light, he could see two sets of tracks, obviously Jessie's and Alison's from several days before. It took only a few minutes to reach the spring, and he stopped in the trees for a moment before approaching.

In the vague light of the ponderosa forest the spring was a dark motion as it rose from the rock, formed a small pool, and began to fall in irregular shelves toward the creek a quarter mile below. A nickle-sized frog swam tentatively out from the pool's edge, sending black ripples a couple of inches before both ripples and frog were gone. Where a granite ledge made a backrest beside the spring, the imprint of a sitting person could be seen even in the graying light. Beside that mark was the imprint of an unusually large bear track, and beyond that more bear tracks leading uphill. Jake was paying scant attention to the sign of the girl's recent presence, or the bear's, however, because he had realized seconds after reaching the spring that there were enemies around him.

Even after almost three decades, the awareness had come the same way, beginning with the tingling he always got up the back of his neck and then the coldness in his ears and temples. They were close, and he felt as if he'd walked into a firefight half a second before the first trigger was pulled.

"Put your hands behind your head," a voice said from the trees.

He raised both arms and clasped his hands awkwardly over the top of the backpack, causing the waist belt to cut into his belly as he did so. Gas rumbled in his abdomen and he shifted uncomfortably.

"Don't move." The slight shadow of a man entered the clearing, stepping around the rock behind the spring. Two other shadows, one very large, emerged on either side of the ranger, each holding an automatic rifle pointed toward him. An atavistic habit surfaced, and like a distant observer he became aware that his brain had begun analyzing the odds even as the rest of him prepared to surrender. The three parts of him seemed to have little to do with one another, one part resigned to whatever destiny the voice represented, one readying messages of mayhem for nerve endings and muscles, and one sitting back and watching with interest as if curious as to which of the other two options would win out. If they fired, he'd be dead, but at least one of them might be caught in the crossfire. They felt too professional for that. So they would hesitate and that would give him an instant to act. He might take out one or two of the three, but not all three. The watching part of him smiled at the absurdity, and he remained motionless, his shoulders and neck beginning to really ache and a cramp working its way up abdomen. I ought to start jogging again, he thought. I'm not in shape for this.

"You must be the grandfather." The high-pitched voice was oddly familiar, and he roamed quick memories to try and place it.

"You mind if I lower my arms and adjust this pack? This is killing me. I've got a bad shoulder." Jake looked at the little man, trying to make out features in the angled shadows of the face. Even in the near-dark he could tell the man was wearing camouflage fatigues. The situation was starting to feel disturbingly familiar, and he sensed the detached part of himself almost laughing at his obtuseness. It was like a word on the tip of his tongue that wouldn't quite form. "I won't be stupid enough to try to get my gun out of my pack, by the way," he added, "but I'd like to adjust the pack."

"Okay. No problem. Who are you and what are you doing here?"

He dropped his arms and loosened the waist belt of the pack, then released the catch on the chest strap. He looked closely at the speaker, making out the delicate thinness of the slanting cheekbones, the shadowy sunken cheeks and broad forehead beneath the bill of a cap. The mouth was small and barely moved with the words it formed.

"That's what I'm supposed to ask you. I'm a Black Mountain tribal game warden and this is Black Mountain reservation land. I belong here. Who the hell are you?"

"I'm the one with the gun." The man was silent for a moment and then shifted the rifle to his left hand, a casual gesture that told Jake there must be other guns aimed at him. The man's right hand reached into a pocket, and when it rose a tiny flashlight suddenly blinded the ranger.

"Holy cow. You're Jake Nashoba, aren't you?" the man said, lowering and clicking off the light. "Nobody else could be so big and dumb sounding. Is that really you? It's me, Nguyen."

"Nguyen? Nguyen Phuong?"

"Phuong Nguyen now. Hey, it really is you. Keep your hands in front of you, where I can see them, Jake."

"I thought you'd bought it in Laos on one of those bullshit Oplan recons. That's what the report said."

"That's what the SOG told everybody, Jake, so they wouldn't have to pay my family. God bless America. But here I am. I heard you'd been blown to shit with a Yard patrol that never came home."

"Just halfway to shit. Your English has improved, Nguyen. Hell, you don't even have an accent. What's going on? Where's the girl who was here?"

"Anybody else with you, Jake?"

The ranger shook his head. "Just me. I'm looking for the girl who was here. She's related to me."

"Your granddaughter?"

"You know this turkey, Lieutenant?" The smaller of the other men stepped out of the shadows to look at the ranger's face, the rifle leveled at his midsection.

"Lieutenant? You get promoted in peacetime, Nguyen?"

"A lot has changed, Jake. You'll find that out. This is Jake Nashoba. Jake and I worked together at home. Jake, this is Tony Vasello."

"This guy was SpecOps?"

Jake turned toward the speaker, a dark, wiry man about his own age and dressed like Nguyen. A blue-black scar ran from the top of one cheekbone down below the man's mouth to the center of his chin, pulling his lips slightly crooked.

"One of the best, Vasello. A real hero," Nguyen replied, and Jake noted that Nguyen's voice rose faintly on the word *hero*. He wondered if he'd done something to piss off his old friend.

"You can call me a lot of things, Nguyen, but not hero."

"The captain will probably tell you stories about the famous Nashoba when we get back to camp," Nguyen said to the other man.

"What captain?" Jake asked, but Nguyen just extended his hand.

"It's good to see you again, Jake. What a surprise."

Jake took the minuscule hand in his own, startled even after all the years at how powerful the hand felt. It was like squeezing a small chunk of granite. Nguyen had been the one who usually went down the tunnels when they were doing that sort of thing. The whole platoon took turns, but Nguyen could slither through a snake's den and so got most of the duty. Jake had always tried to hide his terror of the tunnels and had thanked his ancestors again and again that he was too big to fit most of them. Nguyen, on the contrary, had never seemed afraid.

"Where's the girl who was here, Nguyen? Anything happens to her and you're all dead."

He saw the flash of white teeth. "Just the same, huh, Jake? Good to see that. But don't worry. The girl is fine. I sent her back to camp so she could get some food and warm up. Boy, you can imagine my surprise at finding you here."

"What camp? What the hell's going on here?"

"Come on. We'll show you. You have another big surprise waiting for you. Very big." Nguyen motioned with his rifle. "Follow Walter there."

When Jake turned around, he found himself looking at the back of the larger man, who had already begun to walk away through the trees. Before moving, Jake took a deep breath and held it for a moment. Nothing violent had happened at the spring. He'd always been able to smell the residue of human violence. An elk bugled on their side of the river, the sound barely audible through the timber, a high, wavering call that lingered for a long time.

"What's going on, Nguyen?" he said, feeling his way amid the forest debris. "How in the hell—"

"No more information now, Jake." The ranger felt the rifle touch the small of his back. "Hey, it's great to see you again. Tell me what you're doing here, Jake. People here call you Chief?"

"People here have real chiefs, Nguyen. And it's great to see you, too, pal." Jake could hear the sarcasm in his own voice and hoped it didn't sound quite as sharp to Nguyen. It really was good to see his former friend, even under such bizarre circumstances. "Like I told you, I work here. For the Black Mountain tribe."

"I thought you were some other kind of Indian, Jake, one of those southern kinds."

"Choctaw, just half. We get around. Choctaws everywhere you look these days."

"We were always sorry about what happened to you, Jake. What we thought happened. Stroud and I used to talk about you, you know."

"Stroud? You still in touch with Stroud?"

"You could say that." The gun barrel touched Jake's back again.

18

"I left my husband with a rock in his hand," Sandrine said. "A really big granite rock. This big." She cradled her arms in front of her.

Alison sat awkwardly on the inflated ground pad, her ankles and wrists bound with duct tape. There had been a big commotion outside when they brought the woman in and bound her just like Alison. Now they each sat on opposite sides of the A-frame tent, the lantern near the front of the tent throwing odd shadows on the walls behind them. The men had left them alone, and she could hear them arguing outside the tent without being able to make out the words.

She and the woman had watched one another for a long time before the woman said, "They killed someone."

Alison stared. The hunger pangs had returned to her stomach and were radiating up into her chest, and she could smell something cooking outside.

"A young Indian man," the woman said with a slightly strange accent. "He was helping me on my vision quest, and they shot him."

Alison caught her breath. "Jessie?"

The woman nodded. "Yes, Jessie. Do you know him? He was dressed like a *loup*, a wolf."

"They killed Jessie? Dressed like a wolf?" Alison heard herself begin to wail, as though she were listening to someone else. The wail turned to the kind of scream she'd heard hawks make as they called to one another in the sky.

The tent flap flew open and Jensen burst in. Without speaking, he grabbed the role of duct tape, tore off a piece, and grasping Alison's head in one powerful arm to hold her mouth closed, stretched the tape across her lips.

When he released her, she fell onto her side on the mat, her eyes closed and chest heaving.

"We can't have the noise." Jensen looked at the Frenchwoman. "Do you understand?"

"I understand that you are killers, and you are brutalizing that little girl. But I won't scream, so you can leave the tape off."

"Good. You might try to explain the sense of that to this girl."

When the man left, dropping the flap closed behind him, Sandrine shuffled across the space between herself and Alison. "It must be hard to breathe, but you have to keep quiet," she said. "I'm very sorry about the man they killed. I liked him very much."

Alison rolled her head so she could see the woman. In the light of the gas lantern, the woman seemed to glow.

"My name is Sandrine Le Bris. I think I can get the tape off your mouth, but you can't scream like that, or make any noise. I don't know what those men might do next. Okay? No more screaming?"

Alison looked at the woman's eyes. There was unusual strength there, something that reminded her of her grandmother. She nodded and struggled to sit up.

"This is going to be somewhat strange," Sandrine said. "And it might hurt, so you have to be quiet."

Alison nodded, sitting fully upright now.

Sandrine bent toward the girl, so close that Alison could smell the musk of the woman's thick dark hair and feel the lips grazing her cheek. Then the woman's lips were pressing against the corners of Alison's mouth, and she felt teeth against her skin, a nibbling sensation. Alison could smell the woman's breath and feel its warmth against her face, and she closed her eyes. The tape began to pull away from one corner of her mouth and gradually tear painfully across the width of her lips until her mouth was free again. When she opened her eyes, the Frenchwoman was kneeling before her, a strip of duct tape dangling from her mouth and an expression like a laugh on her face.

"You would make a good fighter," Sandrine said after she spat the tape onto the floor. "That must have hurt like crazy."

"It did," Alison replied in a near-whisper, her lips still sticky and burning. "Thank you. But I'm not a little girl."

"Of course. Now we have to be quiet or they'll come back and do it again."

"Jessie was my cousin," Alison said. "I'm not even supposed to say his name now."

"The men thought he was a wolf attacking me, so it wasn't really murder."

"Poor Jessie. He should have known about wolves. Wolves bring bad luck, or worse. Bears, too, because they're so powerful. I saw bear tracks." Alison pushed her face toward her shoulder in an attempt to wipe tears from her face. "Jessie was trying to help me."

"Maybe he was trying to help me, too. I'm not sure," Sandrine replied. "The wolf suit was strange. Why can't you say his name?"

"It's just bad. My grandmother said that if you say the name of the dead you may attract them to you. Why were you telling me about your husband and the rock?"

139

"I guess I was talking to myself, really, maybe trying to understand how I ended up in a tent with you and both of us like this."

"Why was he holding a rock?"

"He was using it to rebuild our stone house."

"You live in a rock house?"

"Not any longer. But I used to live in a stone house, a really old farmhouse in Brittany. It was his dream, his fantasy, not mine. I remember that he had a bottle of black wine at his feet that day, and every time he'd put a stone on the wall he'd take a drink. I could see his muscles through the undershirt when he lifted the rocks. He was very strong. And I remember that there was a herd of fat white cattle watching him stupidly, with empty eyes. For some reason that bothered me. And pigeons. The barn pigeons were flying in big circles above the farm."

"Was that why you left him, because he drank? Everybody drinks, almost."

Sandrine shook her head, her brown hair swinging. "No. It was many things, I guess, but mostly a girl, finally." She smiled at Alison. "A college girl not much older than you. He writes books, novels. And we were living in just two rooms of the old stone house while he rebuilt the rest of it himself, tearing down the old walls and putting them up again. Twice a week he'd leave me there, inside those stone walls, and go to Rennes to meet his agent, but he wasn't meeting his agent. He was fucking the college girl."

"How did you know that? Did you follow him?"

"No. I'm rich. My family is rich. So I hired someone to follow him and take pictures. With a telescopic lens, the man captured everything. The girl was beautiful, with short blond hair, a lovely face, breasts that were perfect, a small waist. The photographs showed them fucking in many positions. I think my detective was disturbed that I found the photographs attractive." She smiled at Alison's shocked expression. "The girl before that one was twenty-five, so my husband was either regressing or progressing, I'm not sure."

"Seems kind of gross to me. Why didn't you leave him before?"

"I did. The stones didn't keep me in. I went everywhere, thinking I could escape from him. In the beginning I explored Brittany by myself, when we first went there from Paris. There are megaliths, huge sacred stones stuck vertically in the ground by people called Druids more than ten thousand years ago. I even went to the magical forest of Broceliande, where the Druids lived. I saw the tomb of Merlin, who was supposed to be the son of a demon and a nun, and I went to the haunted fountain where Merlin had met Vivian. Do you know that story?"

When Alison shook her head, Sandrine said, "I'll tell you sometime. You'd like it. Vivian learned all the sorcerer Merlin could teach her and then she imprisoned him for eternity inside a tree. I like that story; she was a smart woman. But it turned out to be a very little forest and a very little spring. Then I went trekking in Nepal and studied meditation and martial art for a whole year in Tibet. I even climbed Nanda Devi, a beautiful peak where a young girl is buried in the ice, taken back by the mountain spirits. Her American father, who was a famous mountain climber, took her up the mountain he had named her for, to celebrate her twenty-first birthday, and she died up there."

"We have mountain spirits, too." Alison shivered. "But that story's creepy. How come you're here? How did you hear about my cousin's business?"

"No, Alison, it's a beautiful story. The native people there hold the girl's spirit sacred with the peak now. They say she was called home by the mountain. I even went down to South America and the Amazon River one winter." Sandrine's smile flitted across her face. "I made love to my Quechua guide in a little hut on the river. He was very young and afraid of me, but I thought maybe it would erase my husband and those stones. But when he was inside me, moving up and down without even breathing because he was so frightened, the strangest thing happened. A thin, red snake slid down from a crossbeam on the ceiling of the hut, watching me the whole time, and then disappeared beneath the door. When he was finished with me the young man got up, clothed himself, and vanished through the doorway just like the snake, without saying a word. That was my last night in Peru."

"Snakes are bad luck, my grandmother told me. Not terrible like owls, but they can make you sick. How come you're telling me these things? We don't know each other." Alison glanced toward the front of the tent and shifted uncomfortably. White people talked too much and wanted to be friends too quickly.

"He was lifting that rock when I backed the car around and left, and he was standing, holding the rock to his chest and watching, when I looked in the mirror. Now, only two months later, here I am held prisoner with you because I saw an advertisement in the window of a bookstore called Mille Page in Paris. I needed something to erase five years of lies, because I realized that I never loved the stone man. When I tried to understand why we were married, I couldn't. I must have driven him to those other women because I didn't care. I enjoyed looking at the photographs, the expressions on their faces when he was fucking them. I used to wonder if my face looked like that when he was inside me."

Alison shifted awkwardly again and looked at the closed tent flap.

"The women were beautiful, and they didn't know me or even about me, I'm sure. Now he's much better off because he doesn't have to feel guilty anymore. And when I saw the poster advertising American Indian vision quests, I was fascinated. I've never had a vision, not my own. I realized that I always followed other people's visions, the way water runs down a hill without any meaning. I liked the sound of 'vision quest,' and I thought that the American Indians are survivors, like me. I thought I could learn to have my own vision."

"So really you're still married to that man."

"Yes, legally."

"That's like my grandfather and grandmother. In our tribe a woman only has to set a man's belongings outside the house to divorce him, but white law says they're still married. Water has meaning when it runs downhill or anywhere, and Jessie got killed because of you."

"Not because of her."

Both women jerked away from Jessie, who had suddenly appeared, sitting cross-legged, on the floor of the tent near the door.

"Sorry about the abrupt transition," Jessie said. "It was the acrylic wolf suit. Real stupid idea. I think the *gaan* were upset with me, perhaps." He shrugged and held both palms out sideways. "That's just speculation, of course. Maybe it was just bad luck."

"Jessie?" Alison stared.

"You said my name, you know. Big mistake, maybe. I'm not sure." He cocked his head at Alison. "Now you're stuck with me."

Sandrine looked from Alison to Jessie. "Is it really him?" she asked.

"I don't know," Alison replied. "Is it you, Cousin?"

"I realize we're supposed to be afraid of the dead," he said. "But it's okay, Alison. I'm sort of not really dead or something. If I was, I'd be an owl, I guess, and I probably wouldn't feel like such a nice guy." He looked at Sandrine and made a wry expression. "Pretty risqué talk there a minute ago. I haven't figured my status out yet." Abruptly Jessie was replaced by a wolf sitting on its haunches and staring at them with burning yellow eyes. The wolf's fur had the sheen of synthetic material in the lamplight.

"It just happens, not like I can control it or anything." The wolf became Jessie again. "Maybe I'll get the hang of it. Must be like that cat in *Alice in Wonderland*." He grinned.

"You're a ghost," Sandrine said.

"I don't think so. How'd you learn such good English? I meant to ask you that before, but somehow it didn't seem polite."

"I received my bachelor's degree at Berkeley," she responded. "In American literature."

"Did you meet Ishi there? He was a famous Indian who lived in their museum. The perfect Indian artifact. I heard they named a courtyard for him because of some trouble-making Indian professor called Saint Plumero."

"No, I did not even hear of Ishi or this Plumero. I think he wasn't there yet."

"You see, Alison." Jessie turned from Sandrine to his cousin. "A college degree is important. You can travel the world with one." He looked back and forth from one to the other. "I'm not a ghost, exactly. Kind of hard to define, but don't worry about ghost sickness. What are these guys planning to do?"

"We don't know," Alison said.

"You're pale, Cousin," Jessie replied. "Don't be scared. Think of me as Sandrine's animal helper. I'm here to help."

The tent flap opened and a short, powerfully built man entered, stepping through the place where Jessie had been.

"You two sure are talkers," the man said in a friendly voice with steel behind it. "Couldn't make out what you were saying, but it sounded like nonstop chatter in here. I could have sworn that Jensen said he taped up somebody's mouth." He grinned at Alison and then at Sandrine. "Nice bit of work."

"Could you loosen the tape a little bit?" Sandrine asked. She nodded toward Alison. "Look at her hands. They're turning purple. I think mine are, too."

Stroud looked closely at Alison's hands, and a concerned expression crossed his face. He pulled a big knife from a sheath on his hip and carefully cut through the tape. "That Jensen's a bit gung ho, I'm afraid, and an ass to boot. Now, I'm going to leave you untaped, but don't do anything silly like trying to escape. You wouldn't succeed, and in the confusion one of those morons out there might start shooting. Okay?" When both women nodded, he added, "It's so hard to get good help these days." He paused as he was turning to leave. "We're not going to hurt you. I'm terribly sorry about the boy, but we'll

144

take his body into town tomorrow and we'll take you both wherever you want to go. No one else will get hurt."

As soon as he had closed the tent flap behind him, Jessie said, "Quick. It's time to escape."

"Didn't you hear that man?" Alison stared at Jessie, who had flashed into wolf form and back to human again.

"Sure, but if they don't have you as prisoners, Jake won't have to stay around. We can all escape."

"We promised him. Who's Jake?" Sandrine said.

Alison spoke up. "My grandfather, sort of, but he's not here. And that kind of promise doesn't count. Not to these people."

"Not here quite yet," Jessie said.

Sandrine began to ask another question but seemed to change her mind. "I don't see how we can escape without a knife to cut the tent," she said. "I believe we cannot go through the door."

Jessie pondered the statement for a moment. "I don't think my wolf claws are sharp enough."

Alison said very quietly, "I know how to do it."

They both looked at her as she pulled a bandanna out of her parka pocket and crawled on her knees to the lantern. Using the folded bandanna, she removed the glass mantle from the lamp and went quickly to the back of the tent, where she held the glass to the nylon. Instantly a hole appeared and the tent was filled with the smell of burning plastic.

She handed the mantle with the bandanna to Sandrine and then began to quietly tear a rip down from the burned hole.

Sandrine placed the mantle back on the lantern and moved close to Alison. "That was brilliant," she whispered. "I hope they don't smell it. Let me help."

Alison sat back and allowed Sandrine to pull the nylon apart noiselessly.

Jessie said from near the lamp, "If they hear you, you'll both have to run like crazy up the slope. I think you can outrun most of these fat white men, but the Vietnamese guy and some of the others look pretty tough. Maybe a wolf will have to tear their throats out."

Alison turned and put her finger to her lips, whispering, "You know you can't do that. You can't even help tear this."

"Sadly true, but don't worry. They can't hear me, though I'm working on that part."

"You go first," Alison said.

"No. You should go first, and I'll follow."

Alison shook her head. "Please just do it. It's important to me."

Sandrine held the long tear in the back of the tent open and stuck her head out. Seeing nothing and hearing the men talking on the opposite side of the tent near the fire, she squeezed her shoulders and then the rest of her body through. Outside, she squatted behind the tent and waited as Alison emerged.

"They're escaping!" someone shouted. A tall, thin figure came from the tree shadows at the south edge of camp, holding a roll of toilet paper, and both women began to run awkwardly up the slope.

Sandrine heard a crashing noise and turned back. The man had his arms wrapped around Alison's legs, and Alison was striking at his head with her fists. Sandrine ran back the half-dozen yards and kicked the man in the temple with the heel of her hiking boot. He rolled limply off of the girl, but other shadows were coming from the camp.

"Run, Alison," Sandrine shouted. "You can find your grandfather and tell him."

"She's right," Jessie said from further up the slope. "You know the woods better. Run for it, but go upriver now." Suddenly the night was filled with a head-splitting wolf howl, and the half-dozen men paused and looked around in the dark. Alison struggled to her feet and began to run upward toward Jessie, while Sandrine turned and sprinted to her left.

A roar of gunfire erupted and someone shouted, "Stop or you're dead."

"Run, Alison," Jessie said. "They have Sandrine."

Sandrine fell to her knees, and almost instantly she was jerked to her feet and spun to face Stroud, whose face was a block of lighter darkness in the thin moonlight.

"Where's the girl?" he said. "And don't try any of that kindergarten kung fu on me."

Sandrine looked at him, saying nothing.

"Scully, you go south," Stroud said. "Jensen, go straight up this goddamned hill. Henry, check downstream. Find that girl, but whatever you do, don't hurt her. Goddammit, I wish to hell Nguyen was here." He looked at the unconscious, bleeding man, one of the three who'd come with Jensen. "Nice work," he said. "Dave, you and Peters drag Nelson to one of the tents and see if you can revive him. He probably needs medical attention, so one of you stay with him. We might have to get him out to a hospital tonight."

"Let me question the French woman, Captain," Jensen said.

"Shut the fuck up and go up that hill," Stroud said. "Find the Indian girl. And remember, not a bruise or a scratch. We're helping them, not kidnapping them, got it?"

He turned Sandrine down the hill, pushing her ahead of him toward camp with his hand gripping her arm like steel. The wolf howl sounded again higher up on the side of the canyon, and Stroud stopped to listen.

"There aren't any goddamned wolves left in these mountains," he said. "Must be one of the girl's relatives." As he spoke, he shoved her before him into the small circle of light made by the campfire, then pushed her into a sitting position on the log and sat down across the fire on one of the upended log rounds.

"Look, I'm sorry about the gunfire. I knew I wouldn't hit you. Now, I also know that you won't be stupid enough to try to escape again, and I wish to hell your friend hadn't. It complicates everything unnecessarily." He lifted his cap off his head and ran his heavily scarred hand across the stubble of his hair. "I should have explained things to both of you. I have no intention of letting either one of you be injured in any way, and

147

I don't want any more accidents. I just need time to figure the situation out. This whole thing stinks."

"I don't believe you," Sandrine said.

He settled the cap securely back onto his head. "Listen. My daughter is only a couple of years younger than that girl. I promise you that I won't let either of you get hurt. Tomorrow morning we'll pack up and go find the local officials and explain things as much as possible. Nobody wanted to kill the boy in the wolf suit, for Christ's sake."

19 The first thing Jake saw through the trees was a fire, tidy-looking and half-shielded by rocks. Then he noticed the darker blocks of what must be tents. They'd chosen one of his favorite camping spots, a nice flat just a few yards from the river with Elk Creek on the north flank. The spot was protected from weather by a rock face and steep slope on the south where the river bent in an oxbow.

All the way down the creek he'd been wondering if Walter, the man in front of him, was going to trip and break his neck. Obviously the man wasn't used to navigating anything rougher than a sidewalk. At his back he'd heard the smooth, almost soundless motion of Nguyen accompanied by the louder movements of the one named Vasello. All three were dressed identically in surplus camouflage uniforms, and each carried an AR-15. Jake felt as though he were in a ridiculous dream, with Vietnam rice paddies and jungles turned into a dry pine forest and his old platoon composed of middle-aged morons. And him the enemy. Charlie in Indian Country, just like they always said. Except for Nguyen. Nguyen was neither a bumbler nor a moron. He'd never served with anyone as lethal as the little Vietnamese ranger.

Someone picked up a gas lantern from the ground as they approached the fire.

"Surprise, Captain," Nguyen said as the three of them moved into the circle of light.

Around the fire, some sitting on logs and others standing, was a cluster of men. Jake's first quick survey of the group left him confused. There was a military sense about it, but none of it felt right. These weren't all military men, despite the props. About half of the group of seven or eight had the feel of nervous beef cattle in a feedlot. The others had a more familiar feel. They were professionals.

"Jesus Christ. What now?"

The man with the lantern stepped out of the group, and Jake stiffened as the lantern was held toward his face. The voice, like Nguyen's, was too familiar.

"Stroud," Jake said, finally putting together the broad, pale face, blocky body, and voice. "Captain Steve Stroud."

"Jake?"

"Jake Nashoba," Nguyen said like a child who'd found something special, and Jake noticed that the rifle was still discretely angled toward his side, pointed so a bullet would pass through him and beyond without hitting anyone else. Nothing personal, he knew.

"Holy sweet Mother of Jesus God," Stroud said. He grabbed Jake's shoulder with his right hand. "Jake Nashoba. Man, we thought—"

"I was dead. You mind if I take this pack off?"

"Dave. Help him get that pack off." Stroud held the lantern closer and studied the ranger's face while Jake unfastened the pack and swung it to the ground, shrugging off the other man's attempts to help.

Stroud turned to Nguyen. "Where in the world did you dig up Jake Nashoba?"

"Jake says he's the game warden for the tribe." Nguyen went to lean his rifle against the rope with the rest of the guns.

"Game warden? Goddammit. Nobody told me about that." He stared at the ranger. "You're old, Chief," Stroud said. "That long hair's got a lot of gray. How the hell did you disappear like you did?"

"I can't wait to have a chat," Jake replied. "But first tell me where my granddaughter is."

"Man, it's good to see you, Jake." Stroud gripped Jake's hand. "Everybody thought you'd bought it."

"Maybe you should give us that gun in the pack, Jake," Nguyen said.

Jake cocked his head and looked at Nguyen for a moment before removing the pistol from the pack's top zippered compartment and handing it over, handle first, to the Vietnamese.

"Thanks," Nguyen said as he handed the gun to Vasello, adding, "Put this away somewhere."

"Where's Alison?" Jake focused on Stroud.

"So you're the deadly grandfather she warned us about. She didn't tell us her name." He looked a little embarrassed and rubbed a stubby finger alongside his nose. "Not too long ago she was in that first tent over there. But she sort of ran away. There's a French woman in that tent right now." Stroud beckoned with his head. "Don't make a lot of noise. Poor woman's exhausted and starving. You can see her in a minute, if you want to."

"'She sort of ran away.' What's that mean, Captain?"

"Exactly that. Your granddaughter escaped. She's in the woods somewhere and we couldn't find her."

Jake imagined Alison out in the forest at night. She'd be pretty weak by now if she'd been fasting, but he knew she wouldn't panic about being alone in the woods.

"You must have Jessie's other client," Jake replied. "Jessie said he had a Frenchwoman on a vision quest down here."

"Nguyen found your granddaughter sitting by a spring, hungry and tired. She said she was fasting. Wouldn't even eat when Nguyen brought her here. Still hasn't. She's really your granddaughter?"

"Nobody touched her?" Jake looked down at Stroud, noting that the captain's shoulders were as wide and heavy muscled as they'd been almost thirty years earlier, but the face was that of a man past middle age, the waist had expanded a little, and there was a faint hesitation in Stroud's movement that had never been there before. He could tell Stroud was worried about something. "What do you mean, 'escaped'? You were holding Alison and this woman against their wills?"

"It's complicated, Jake. They were both found during standard recon, and both said they were on vision quests. Neither one had a finger laid on her, but my men didn't know what to do except bring them here. No harm intended or done. Now, how about some coffee?" Without waiting, Stroud lifted the enamel pot from a flat rock by the fire and filled a big tin cup. "Like old times, huh?"

"You kidnap my granddaughter and another woman and say it's like old times? What the hell's wrong with you?"

"Not kidnap, Jake. My men brought them back here because they didn't know what else to do. Your granddaughter and the French woman both looked like they were starving, and these men don't know shit from Shinola about vision quests. And there was another problem I'll tell you about in a minute. A bit more serious, I'm afraid."

"Militia? Is that what this is?" Jake raised the coffee to his lips and delicately tested the boiling liquid before lowering it again. "What are you and Nguyen doing, Stroud, out here playing army with these guys? I always thought you were crazy, but not stupid."

Stroud laughed softly but uneasily, the firelight catching in lines around his mouth and eyes. He looked at the cluster of men. "As you must have figued out by now, this is Jake Nashoba," he said to the group. "Jake was . . . Well, how would you put it, Nguyen?"

As Nguyen walked back toward the fire, Jake saw that the Vietnamese commando hadn't aged at all. At fifty, though his face was lined, he looked and walked almost exactly as he had at twenty-two, lithe and delicately balanced.

"Nashoba was the second toughest sonofabitch you Americans ever sent to my country." He smiled and looked at Stroud. "The Captain here was the toughest."

151

Stroud patted Nguyen on the shoulder. "There were a lot of good men there you never met, Nguyen, but Jake and I thank you for the compliments. Don't we Jake?" He motioned toward the big windfall log near the fire. "Sit down," he said.

"Not till I see the French girl at least."

Stroud shrugged and stepped closer. "Okay, but if I let you take a little peek to see she's okay, you promise you won't let her know you're here until later? Just be a little patient with me on this one?"

"Okay."

Stroud gripped Jake's forearm and walked softly toward the nearest tent. At the entrance, he parted the door flap a fraction of an inch and nodded his head toward Jake.

When Jake put his eye to the crack, he saw a dark-haired young woman lying in a fetal position on an air pad, her face turned away from the door.

Stroud pulled slightly on Jake's arm and nodded back toward the fire. "She hasn't eaten yet, so in a little while I'll ask you to try to persuade her to do so. We really don't want to hurt anyone. That's not why we're here. Now, let's have some coffee."

Near the fire, Jake looked at the log, one he had sat on many times before when there was no one else in the entire canyon. He battled a growing sense of rage and eased himself down.

"Jake saved my life," Stroud said to the group, and his voice had a touch of strain in it. "Let me introduce you to some of my men, Jake." He nodded toward the two who'd been with Nguyen at the spring. "I believe you've met Tony Vasello and Walter Fleming already. Over here are Chris Martin, Henry Jamison, Lee Jensen, Tom Peters, and Dave Scully. A guy named Nelson is in a tent over there with a pretty good-sized headache thanks to the French lady. All here supposedly to learn a little bit about paramilitary combat."

Jake covertly examined each of the men in turn. The one called Jensen stood out, younger and better conditioned than

152

the rest, arrogant looking, a quality Jake knew would be the man's weakness. On both sides of Jensen were older men he recognized at once as vets, probably SEAL or Special Forces. The pale one named Scully was of average height and weight, going a little to fat, and had an expression of permanent hostility combined with eyes that refused to focus on any one thing. A thousand-yard stare, they called it. Some vets took that expression to their graves. Vasello, with a dark complection and thick black hair showing a buzz cut beneath his cap, didn't look quite as tough as Scully, despite the scar. He reminded Jake of the guys who got off on being recon rangers or some other kind of bad shit but were only marginally good at the game and knew it. That kind was dangerous because they always had to prove something. Vasello looked like he'd never proven whatever it was. The other men, two of whom were probably six-feet-two or -three and heavy, were the kind you could have gathered from any suburban shopping mall with a five-minute random pick. Bored husbands.

Stroud lifted a cup and poured himself some coffee. Looking into the cup, he added, "We have another surprise in store for you, but that can wait."

"This old man is the famous Jake Nashoba? The big chief himself? You're kidding me." Jensen stepped forward and looked incredulously at Jake. "Hell, Nitske even talked about Jake Nashoba."

"This is Lee Jensen," Stroud said to Jake, "a frat boy who did a couple of TRS camps with Nitske. The DSTC stuff." He leveled his gaze at Jensen. "Now he thinks he's hot shit. Right, Lee?" When Jensen merely smiled in return, Stroud added, "This old man could feed you your own asshole any day of the week, Jensen."

"So I've heard." Jensen held out his hand. "I didn't mean any disrespect, sir."

Jake looked at the hand and then at Jensen. Raising his cup to his mouth, he sipped the scalding coffee and glanced toward the river.

"Nashoba never did take things too lightly, did you Jake?" Stroud said. "I'm afraid you've insulted him."

Jensen folded his arms across his chest and stared at Jake as though he were in a museum.

"A bunch of paramilitary freaks," Jake said, still watching the river. There was a nice hole not far downstream, where the river divided, running down one side in a short riffle that curved into a deep cutbank, ran fast over a short stretch of rocks, and met up with the larger part of the stream in a long, deep pool. The trout were big there.

"I can't believe you and Nguyen are doing this," he added. "You believe in this stuff?"

"You mean do I believe that the feds have two hundred thousand Chinese troops in salt mines beneath Detroit just waiting to jump out and get us? Or the U.N. is flying black helicopters around the woods preparing to liquidate armed resistance?"

Stroud picked up the pot and poured still more of the black coffee into first Jake's cup and then his own. "You know, I miss the days when I used to add a little coffee to my whiskey, but those times are long gone. I haven't had a drink in ten years, Jake." He lifted the cup toward Jake. "Here's to sober responsibility."

"That's good, Stroud. I'm proud of you. I haven't had a beer in four or five hours. Here's to red wine and sunny afternoons."

"I have a family, Jake. Would you believe it? A great wife and a fourteen-year-old daughter who's in a gymnastics competition right now."

"You should be a grampa, not a father. Your family know what you're doing out here?"

"Fishing trip. One of the basic rules is family doesn't know, unless they're active in the movement."

"So you're one of those guys who blew up women and children in Oklahoma." Jake shook his head. "I never would have imagined that. I figured you might be dead by now or in maximum security somewhere like everybody else, but I never would have figured you for a paramilitary fruitcake."

154

"That Oklahoma bombing was a disgrace. Brain-dead, paranoid amateurs did that."

"Sounds familiar."

Nguyen stepped around Jake and stood at Stroud's elbow, bareheaded and relaxed, with his hands behind his back. "Is Captain Stroud giving you his five-dollar lecture, Jake?" Nguyen asked. "He usually saves it for VIPs."

"So it's Lieutenant Nguyen and Captain Stroud, huh? The captain give you a field promotion, Nguyen?"

Stroud shrugged. "I'm afraid hierarchy is necessary in any good organization, as much as we'd like a real democracy. You'll have to pardon me if I lecture you a little, Jake. I'm afraid as Nguyen says I've gotten sort of used to doing it." He walked to the other side of the fire and looked hard at the low flame and red coals. "You're right about Oklahoma City. That was a damned monstrosity. Did you hear about that Vietnam hero, Bo Gritz, the leader of something he calls the Christian Covenant Community in Idaho, calling that bombing a Rembrandt? A lot of those militia cowboys are both stupid and nuts, just like the rest of humanity. A bunch of PTSD guys trying to relive their glory days and a bunch of fakes who never saw Vietnam or anything else out there playing in the woods babbling about the New World Order, Hong Kong cops, concentration camps, microchips under your skin, and all that Disneyland, Looney Tunes nonsense. Killing kids in Oklahoma City."

He paced back to the ranger's side of the fire. "There's a guy going around talking about a 'fuel-air bomb' that vaporizes everybody. That's what they say was done to those poor Iraqi bastards they buried and what the government is going to do to all those backwoods patriots. That bunch up in Montana even took a map off a box of damned Kix cereal and claimed it was George Bush's New World Order map of America.

"That's not what we're about, Jake. You know me and Nguyen. This doesn't have anything to do with all that tiny-brained Cosmotheism and shit like the Mark of the Beast or Wackenhut building prisons for American patriots or bar-code

155

stickers on road signs or any of the rest of that lunatic fringe paranoia. And we don't buy into the racism of those aryan supremacists talking about Mud People and Fourteenth Amendment Citizens and that bullshit."

"So this is kind of a grown-up Eagle Scout meeting, and you're all working on a merit badge." Jake sipped the coffee. "What are you doing in this mess, Nguyen?" he asked. "I thought you were smart. How does a former South Vietnamese commando end up in a wacked-out American militia movement?"

The uneven light played across the wiry little man's smile and caught on the angles of his face. Jake could see that his hair was still black and thick, cut stylishly to just below his collar.

Stroud interrupted. "Nguyen's an American now, Jake. This isn't games in the woods. This is real. You know me and you know Nguyen. We don't play games."

Jake flung the remains of his coffee into the brush behind them and adjusted his position on the log. "You're trespassing, Stroud," he said. "It doesn't matter what your reasons are; you don't have any right to be here. This is sovereign tribal land."

"That's just it, Jake." Stroud set his cup on an upended log round beside him. Folding his arms across his chest, he went on. "Don't you think it's appropriate that we train on the lands of the disenfranchised original Americans? Hell, nobody's been treated as bad in this country as Indians. You used to say that yourself. This isn't about paranoid hallucinations, this is about what's really going on in America." He glanced up at the others and then back to Jake. "Democracy is gone, bagged and buried like most of your old friends. Have you looked at that black wall in D.C.? They've got a directory as big as the New York City phone book so you can find a name on the wall. That blew me away, Jake, a book full of over fifty thousand names. A lot of guys we knew. And now it's like the whole thing never happened."

"You're getting his hundred-dollar lecture, Jake. That makes you important. I need some of that coffee." Nguyen went off in search of a cup, and Stroud continued. "You know about the Tenth Amendment, Jake?"

The ranger looked at him blankly for a moment and then said, "It's been almost thirty years, Steve."

Stroud held the cup in both hands and blew on it. "What are you doing here, Jake? Let me guess. You're single, you probably live in a cheap trailer, and you drink like a fish. Am I wrong?" He paused. "Do you think the three of us ended up together again in this place by accident, Jake? Events have purpose."

Jake shook his head. "I'm married, I own a house I built with my own hands, I have grandkids, and coincidence happens every day."

"You're marriage is fake, you don't live in your own house, and your grandchildren aren't really yours."

Jake turned toward a young woman who was stepping out of one of the tents as she spoke. Her tangled brown hair shone in the lantern and firelight and the set of her narrow eyes gave her a drawn and exhausted look. Her tight mouth and full lips made him think she might either curse or cry at any moment, reminding him of Tali.

Jake rose to his feet.

She glared at him. "You know these men? They kidnapped me and your granddaughter, Alison. She's the one who told me about you and your so-called family."

"So one of the lost girls appears," Stroud said. "Nice to see you feeling better, though I wish you wouldn't insult my old friend. Jake, this is Miss Sandrine Le Bris, from Paris, France. Miss Le Bris, I guess you already know that this is Alison's grandfather, Jake Nashoba."

The Frenchwoman wore baggy black wool pants, probably provided by Jessie from the thrift store in Springerville, and a thick and probably too-warm sweater that showed at the open neck of her rain parka. Her hands were shoved into the parka's pockets, and he saw that she wore the same kind of heavy hiking boots he'd given Alison for her sixteenth birthday a month before.

157

"I used to know these guys," Jake said.

She came and sat beside him on the log, saying, "I'd like some coffee now."

Sandrine looked sideways at Jake. "I was in the third day of my fast." A coyote began crying on the far side of the river, and she glanced up for an instant before burying her face in her hands.

Stroud spoke up. "The Tenth Amendment says, 'Powers not delegated to the United States by the Constitution, nor prohibited by it to the States, are reserved to the States or to the people.' *Or to the people*." He looked at Sandrine. "You should eat something before having coffee. She hasn't eaten since they brought her in."

"She was on a fast," the ranger said, "a vision quest."

"So I heard. But that's over now. No more visions."

She shook her head, still not looking at him. "Maybe you're part of my vision. Maybe all of this is a dream."

"That's an interesting perspective. Maybe you're just dreaming me. I've always suspected I was part of somebody's dream, that all of the insanities of this life couldn't possibly be real. It would make everything so much more reasonable. But I'm afraid this is no dream."

He handed Sandrine a cup of black coffee, saying, "I wish I could convince her to eat first" as he turned toward Jake. "I can see now why it took thirty thousand U.S. soldiers to bring in a few dozen of your granddaughter's ancestors, and even then to succeed only through lying and treachery. When I knew we were going to train here, I read up on this tribe and this area. You know that Apaches fought their way off the reservation just twenty miles south of here, fought all the way to Mexico and then back again a couple of times? Two thousand miles, tens of thousands of soldiers and hundreds of Indian scouts, and nobody could capture or defeat them. The best fighting force the world's ever seen, Jake. If I had twenty men, or women, like Geronimo's or Chihuahua's bunch, nothing could stop me. I read that the Sendero Luminoso down in Peru have a lot of

women in their movement. Some of their most efficient and ruth-
less fighters are women. Everybody's scared shitless of them."

Stroud held a hand out, palm up, and looked around. "Jake
Nashoba saved my life in Vietnam. He's a real hero." He
gestured toward Sandrine. "Now, it would make us all feel
better if you ate. I could have some eggs scrambled up for you.
They're powdered, but pretty good with onions and the right
seasoning."

The girl stared at the fire, saying nothing.

"You should eat, Granddaughter," Jake said. "You can do
another vision quest later."

She looked at him in surprise, and then looked down at her
feet for a moment. "Okay," she said simply.

"Granddaughter?" Stroud said.

"It's a term of respect," Jake replied. "That's all."

Stroud shrugged and rose to his feet. "It's all a mystery to
me." Behind him Dave Scully set the refilled coffeepot on a grill
over the coals.

"Your poor young granddaughter is wandering around in
the wilderness right now, undoubtedly lost. I'm a little concerned. I had some men looking for her, but they gave up. Do
you know the Second Amendment, Jake?" Stroud spoke as if
reciting. "'A well-regulated militia being necessary to the security of a free State, the right of the people to keep and bear arms
shall not be infringed.' That's what it says. So when they try to
disarm the populace, they're violating the Constitution of the
United States. But they don't care. It's all about money, and the
Constitution means nothing, just like all those treaties they
signed with Indians meant shit."

"You can't kidnap people, Stroud. That's crazy, even for
you." Jake glanced up at the men standing and sitting around
the fire. Most were watching Stroud intently. Scully's face was
turned toward the river, and Jensen, who stood back a little
from the others, seemed to be studying the whole scene with
amusement. Knowing the area around the camp better than he
knew the town of Black Mountain, Jake made a mental map of

where the sentries would probably be, imagining one by Elk Creek, above the camp, maybe one down near the river ford, depending on how paranoid they were.

"I'd like to talk with this young woman in private," he said.

Stroud shook his head and laughed softly. "No, I'm afraid that's out of the question. We still have one big problem I need to discuss with you."

"They killed Jessie," Sandrine said.

"What?"

"They killed Jessie. He was dressed in a wolf suit, and they shot him. They killed him."

"Where's Jessie?" he said to Stroud. "Where do you have him, you sonofabitch?"

Stroud nodded. "I'm sorry, Jake. It was an accident. That was the unfortunate surprise I mentioned a minute ago. The body's in that far tent."

"He came to see us—me and Alison—a little while ago," Sandrine said.

"Jessie came to see you?"

"I'm sorry to interrupt this metaphysical discussion, Jake, but I'm afraid we're running a little short of time. Let's go for a walk up the river a little ways." Stroud motioned with his head. "Nguyen will take care of our guest. You and I need to talk."

Stroud gestured northward with his head and began to walk up a deer and elk path beside the river. Jake followed a few feet behind.

In a hundred yards they came to the junction of creek and river, and Jake was surprised to find no sentry. Stroud wasn't as military as he pretended to be.

They crossed the shallow creek on large gray stones and continued along the faint path for another two hundred yards before Stroud turned and sat down on a big fallen log. Jake sat beside Stroud and folded his arms across his chest.

"I'll bet there's some big trout in this river," Stroud said. "I wouldn't mind casting a few flies in there. What do they take this time of year?"

"Just about any damned thing you throw at them. Depends a little on the hatch. I always carry Adamses, Adams Irresistibles, stonefly nymphs, flying ants, hoppers, mosquitoes, usual suspects."

"You spend a lot of time down here?"

Jake closed his eyes and tried to hear the water. Instead, he felt it smoothing the boulders as it passed, brushing the trailing grasses and small branches at the edges, moving the air of the canyon like a river itself.

"Every minute I can. Usually five or six months out of the year I'm down here most of the time. Till the snow gets too deep. Snowshoed in one time on six feet of snow, so cold that my leaders froze and stuck straight out from the rod, and the flies were just balls of ice when I took 'em out. Didn't catch a damned thing, but it was the quietest world I've ever seen. I camped for a week right where your bunch is camped. Winter's nice. Everything's asleep except the ones who hunt in the winter and the ones who have to stay awake to be hunted.

"Must have been pretty damned nice, all right. You remember when it would get quiet during the war?"

"Yeah. It would scare the piss out of us every time. Me at least."

Stroud laughed softly. "Scared the piss out of me every time. This is a beautiful place you've found. Shame to screw it up with a bunch of wannabe Rambos, isn't it? You used to talk about fishing over in Nam, about all the fishing you were going to do when you got back."

Jake stared down toward the river, seeing the black outlines of rocks with even darker water slicing around them. In the tailwaters of those rocks, he knew, big rainbows would be waiting right at that moment. Upstream a few hundred yards the river curved in under volcanic cliffs and ran straight and deep for a short stretch. In that water the trout were even bigger and wilder. He wondered if Nguyen was scrambling eggs for Sandrine and where Alison was at that moment. Alison didn't know the drainage, and she could get into trouble.

"What happened to Jessie?"

Stroud shook his head. "He was dressed in a wolf costume, a very convincing one. Two men stumbled across him and the French woman, and they thought they were saving her from a wolf. They shot him."

"There aren't any wolves in the Southwest."

"Would a dentist and a plumber know that? I feel bad about this, Jake."

"You feel bad?"

"What'd you think about that song and dance back there, Jake?"

"A crock of paranoid garbage." Jake kept his eyes focused on the water as he spoke, thinking of Jessie in a wolf costume. The guaranteed vision.

"Not a bad lecture, though? And that's just a fraction of my whole spiel. I've got lots of stuff about implanted transponders, all that shit. That's why Jensen and his bunch are here. They thought they could recruit me and Nguyen into their little militia troop." Stroud rubbed both hands across his cheeks and mouth and shook his head. He sounded tired. "The speech wasn't for you or Jensen but for those others. They have to think they're out here for some other reason than playing in the woods, since I might want their business again in the future. Took a long time to work it all out, to memorize all that conspiracy craziness. Of course you pick a lot of it up just being around the kinds of people I'm around. And I'll admit there was a while when I really believed a portion of it, or maybe I should say when I cared about it."

"You sounded like you believed it. Christ, I believed half of it."

Stroud laughed a short, cynical laugh. "More than half of it's true, but that doesn't change anything. It's part of the sell, what these right-wing morons want to hear. It makes them think they're out here for some reason more important than playing with their own dicks, which most of them probably couldn't even find. Revolutionary car salesmen and real estate

162

agents. My God. You ought to see all the frauds I meet. I had some asshole show up once claiming that he'd been a SEAL deep in the Phoenix program. You know there never was a SEAL assigned to Phoenix. Another guy claimed to be a SEAL who jumped in Nam, and there never was a SEAL combat jump in the whole war. I don't show the jerks up—as long as they pay—but I have a friend in NSWC, the Naval Special Warfare Center in Coronado, who checks out these phony assholes for me so I'll know what I'm dealing with."

Stroud looked up, his face wearing an expression that struck Jake as one of hopelessness. "You know how much these stupid fucks pay me and Nguyen for five days of this? Eight guys at a thousand a day each on this trip. Forty thousand gross for five days. And most of them don't even notice the cost. Blue-collar rich boys. It's like fifty cents to these guys, they're so fucking rich. I take them out in the woods and play war with them for a few days, scare them a little, put them through some minor pain, put their fingers on an AR-15 converted to auto, show them some plastic and a claymore or two, haul out an RPG for demo, and we all go back happy. It's all I know how to do, Jake, but I'm damned tired of it." He ran a hand over his nearly bald head. "Nobody is supposed to get hurt. Nobody ever has, before."

"You killed Jessie."

"God knows I feel bad, Jake. This is the first course I've run on your reservation. Nguyen and I have been working this little scam for a few years now, mostly out in the desert, and nobody's gotten anything worse than a scratch or a bruise before. You ought to see my house in Paradise Valley. You ought to see Nguyen's. From a bamboo hut to a half-million-dollar Scottsdale golf course townhouse. He has a whole new family now, blonde wife and three kids.

"I even retired from the company right out in the open, nothing covert. I didn't want the bastards coming after me for freelance operations. Pissed those CIA bastards off plenty, I can tell you that, when I wouldn't retire covert. I was looking over my shoulder for a couple of years." He was quiet for a moment. "I guess you realize how bollixed up this one is. Christ. A stupid accident. One of these assholes sees something looks like a wolf and naturally he's going to shoot it like all good dumbfuck Americans. And now we've got your young grand-daughter wandering around lost somewhere out there. God help us all. And I still owe somebody some bucks for this course. Kind of silent money, you could say. If I have to give these boys their cash back, I'll have to front that loss myself."

"I guess your choice is to kill me plus a French tourist and my sixteen-year-old granddaughter, if you can find her, plus Jessie, who's already dead, or lose some of your bank account, huh? I have to admit that's a tough choice. You might even have to knock off some of your students to make sure nobody talks."

Stroud looked down toward the river. "Did the French-woman tell you that the kid was running a scam on her, that he was dressed up like an animal to make her believe he was a spirit vision? Pretty damned clever if it hadn't been for these morons of mine being there."

"He shouldn't have been out here being idiotic, but he shouldn't be dead."

"You and me've both seen a lot of people die who shouldn't have, Jake. At least not so soon."

"I guess I am old, Stroud, like that punk back there said. All I want is for us to just take Jessie's body back up the mountain tomorrow so he can be treated with respect, and then we can tell this story to the cops and let them sort it out."

Stroud nodded again. "I guess I'm old, too, Jake. I think this is the end of my war games business. I can't see bringing assholes, myself included, down here. It's too damned nice. But you wouldn't believe how much this business is booming. Everybody out there with or without disposable income wants to play war. It's those Waco and Ruby Ridge fiascos pulled by the ATF and FBI. Best recruiting devices the right wing could've ever come up with. Take Waco, for example. They were after one guy who had too many guns. Mind you, the guy hadn't shot anybody or done anything violent. His crime was having guns. But to get him they burned seventy-two people alive, including twenty-four children. And Ruby Ridge. A guy sold some guns they said he shouldn't have sold, so they killed his fourteen-year-old son and shot his wife dead while she was holding her baby in her arms. Now a few million idiots short a few million brain cells think the government is going to take their precious guns away, guns most of them don't even know how to use. And then there's the professional paramilitary types like Jensen and his friends back there. That rich sonofabitch could be out climbing Himalayan peaks or skiing in the Alps, but he gets his rocks off preparing for New World Order Armageddon. That's the dangerous kind."

"Like Ranton."

Stroud nodded slowly, "Yeah, like Ranton."

"I always figured you shot him. With all that incoming, who could tell?"

"Ranton was going to get us all killed. You would've done it if I hadn't."

They sat in silence for a moment until Jake shook his head. "I guess not. They were all trying to get us killed. Lieutenant Ranton was just like the rest, and we couldn't kill all of them. But maybe you felt more responsibility. That was before your promotion, wasn't it?"

"Hell of a note, isn't it, Jake, meeting like this after all these years? Looks like you finally decided to be an Indian."

"I never decided to be anything."

"We'll take the boy's body in first thing tomorrow and get a search going for your granddaughter. They'll go easy on Henry, and we'll concoct some kind of story of a bunch of buddies going camping. None of these guys'll want bad publicity, and I'm sure nobody on this reservation wants any, at least not that chief of yours. I'll stash all the illegal ordnance and just show them the legitimate stuff." He put a hand on Jake's shoulder. "I'm sorry as hell about the boy, Jake. You know, when I was with the company, doing all that bad shit, I used to lie awake at night once in a while and think about you. I wanted to tear your guts out for what you did. I figured I was supposed to die there in that LZ and you screwed it all up. It took me twenty years to realize that you saved my damned life. I guess it took getting married and having a kid to get my head even a little straight."

Jake listened to a sound from across the river. A pair of owls, great horned owls from the tone, were calling back and forth. *Ishkitini.*

"Thanks for saving my life, Jake. Okay?"

"Don't mention it." Jake reached an enormous hand out and patted the top of Stroud's fatigue cap. "I just didn't have time to think, that's all, or I would've left you standing there. How do you know my chief, as you call him?"

"Man, you were one heavy sonofabitch. You don't look like you've lost any pounds either. How about you, Jake? You ever still have those dreams where you wake up sweating and scared shitless? I mean literally shitless, a big mess? Did you get over that a long time ago?"

Jake shook his head. "I dream," he said. "What about my question?"

Stroud clenched his fingers on Jake's shoulder, and Jake was surprised at how much strength was still there. "You know, I think Nguyen's the only one of us that didn't get permanently fucked up. He's like my brother now. Would you believe me and him go golfing a couple times a week? He lives on a posh fucking golf course by Camelback Mountain. We wear those funny checkered pants and drive around in a golf cart with little holes for drinks and the entire nine yards. Both of us suck at the game, but that's not the point. He's got one of those little American flags on the back of the cart. Nguyen's more American than anybody else now. He's found his place."

"No," Jake said. "Nguyen's got more hate in him than a thousand of us. That's why he's never gotten any older, Steve. All that hate keeps him in one time and one place."

Stroud lifted his hand back onto his own lap. "Funny way of looking at it. I don't think you ever used my first name before, Jake, not once that I can think of."

"People who are going to die become close," Jake said. He stood up. "I'm concerned about my granddaughter."

Stroud walked behind him back toward the campfire they could see through the trees. "I don't know about you, buddy, but my life's really just started," he said. "You ever golf? You're close enough to drive down for the weekend."

Jake stopped and turned around, causing Stroud to come to an abrupt halt to keep from colliding with his bulk. "How many men—no, how many people do you think you've killed, Captain Stroud?"

Stroud stood unmoving for a moment. Finally he drew in a deep breath. "That was another time and another world, Jake. Another person."

Jake shook his head. "There aren't any other times or worlds. That's how everything gets messed up, thinking like that. Only one time, one world, Steve. Nguyen knows that. Every ghost you ever made is still with you. You think they're just dreams, but they're not."

Stroud brushed past Jake and walked toward the camp. "I see you've got a long way to go, Jake. I'm beyond all that. They made us what they wanted us to be, but now we can remake ourselves and say fuck them. We don't have to stay where they put us. Now, let's be sure Miss Le Bris is fed and everything's ready for tomorrow. We can spread out and look for your grandaughter, too. By the way, that French woman gave one of Jensen's commandos a bad concussion. She swings a mean leg."

20 Alison crouched behind the slab of granite, leaning into the soft moss on the rock and listening to the two men, trying to make out the words. A trail of tiny, barely visible black ants climbed the cornice of the gray stone, winding its

way in the dark from the humus at her feet upward past the place where her hands touched rock, and over the top. Idly, she wondered what uniform purpose moved the ants, and she tried for a fraction of a moment to recall a story about ants that Shorty Luke had told her. They had power, like coyotes, that could make you sick, but there was medicine to prevent it. There was a difference between red ones and black ones, and some kind of ceremony for them. "Never piss on an anthill," Shorty Luke had said solemnly, and she hadn't been able to tell if he was serious or not, though she never had urinated on an anthill and never intended to anyway.

The big man talking, she realized, was her grandfather, and from the tone the other one, to her surprise, talked like her grandfather's friend and perhaps a decent man. How could her grandfather know the man, she wondered, straining unsuccessfully to understand what they were saying. If they were friends, then the man, one of those who had held her, couldn't be evil. But something strange was happening.

When the two stood up to walk back to camp, she let them get far ahead and then followed, approaching the camp in complete silence. The owls that had been calling back and forth caused her to shiver, and she wondered what had become of Jessie. After his howl had helped her to escape, she had seen or heard nothing of him. Some people said that seeing an Indian ghost could kill you, especially if you didn't have some kind of ceremony quickly. The ghosts of white people weren't as deadly, but pretty bad. Most people didn't seem to believe that stuff anymore, or if they did they sure didn't talk about it. Jessie had said he wasn't a ghost, but what was he?

Around the fire, the cluster of men looked like a stage production, but she was relieved to see Sandrine seated on a log and eating something from a plate. The sight made her painfully hungry, and a wave of dizzy nausea washed through her. Her grandfather went and sat beside Sandrine and said some words that Alison couldn't make out, but the French-woman appeared to ignore him. The one called Stroud went to talk to a man who seemed angry in the minimal light. On two sides of that man were the dark, mean one with the twisted mouth and the other, pale one who never looked at anything out of his empty gray eyes.

21 Domingo retched, choked, and retched again, staining his already stained red flannel shirt. The smell of frying Spam had seeped into the room through the open doorway and hung torturously under his nose. The knot in his stomach twisted more tightly, as though his insides had been sewn with barbed wire. He turned his head from where it hung over the pot beside the chair and saw the black and white dog lying several feet away with its head on its paws, wisely keeping distance between them. The combined smells reminded him of the boxcar in Gallup where he'd lived for what seemed like years but may have been months or days. He couldn't remember. But Gallup had been where he'd carried the flag as the most honored veteran. There had been one good day in Gallup right after the war, but now the strip of bars and pawnshops along the highway was a ghost city where dead and dying Indians wandered invisibly among the white moneymakers and lay invisibly in locked doorways and cold alleys. The whole city had ghost sickness, he realized, from all the Indians it had killed. White people had no ceremonies against such things.

When Mrs. Edwards entered the room with a plate, Domingo leaned and retched again, heaving against the ropes that bound him to the overstuffed chair.

"Good grief," the old lady said. "When I named you for the holy day, I never thought you'd be such a pig." She set the plate down on a darkened television set and left the room, returning quickly with a wet cloth.

When she had wiped Domingo's face and chest and discarded the rag, she brought the plate from the television. "I didn't want to start you off with too strange a diet," she said, "so I've got some traditional Spam and boiled potatoes."

Domingo rolled his eyes at Mrs. Edwards and belched acidly. The old woman frowned and brought a small leather pouch from a pocket in her dress. She held the plate in front of him and maneuvered the pouch open, reaching in to take out a liberal pinch of brownish-green powder that she sprinkled on the food. "Now you eat."

"I need a drink," Domingo said, looking at the evil black television that seemed to suck the light from the room. He heard a whine and glanced over the side of the chair to see his dog lying with its head on its paws in a posture of defeat. "You feed my dog?"

"That dog's ate better than you. Here is some water."

He shook his head and closed his eyes against the woman, water, and television. His head felt ready to explode, and his stomach was squeezed now into a tiny, barbed knot that pulled at his heart. The knot had been put there almost half a century earlier, when a Japanese soldier rose like mist from a foxhole and pointed a bayonette at him. He'd squeezed the trigger of his rifle at the same moment the blade entered his guts, and then he'd walked away holding his intestines in his hands. He'd known he'd be sick long before that happened, however, because the dead were everywhere. It wasn't possible to pray enough, to ask the dead's forgiveness, and he had no pollen to make a line between him and each of the dead ones. He knew they would follow him no matter where he went, and they had. When the army doctors had sewn him up, they'd made the knot too tight, and it had pulled at his heart ever since. Only alcohol, or something even stronger than alcohol, could loosen the knot. That was one reason he'd gone to Gallup to live with the lost ones. The other reason was that by going he thought he could lead the ghosts away from his family and community. All of the sick ones in Gallup saw ghosts, and many became ghosts. The boxcar and the camps in the big arroyo had long before become crowded with the dead who couldn't leave. All of the men were used to the spirits and used to the terrible sickness that ate them from the inside. After they'd brought him home, he'd sat in the little house Tali gave him night after night trying to keep the ghosts away, so many of them now.

"I need a drink," he said.

Mrs. Edwards held the water glass to his mouth and tipped it. A trickle made it down his throat, and it was cool and pleasant. "You never told me about the knot," Mrs. Edwards said. "Or else I would have helped you a long time ago. I was waiting to see if you could do it by yourself. It would have been better that way. When you're stronger we'll go see a friend of mine in Cibecue who can help you more."

He stared at the huge woman. The powder glowed on the Spam and potatoes, and he felt his chest warming.

"Here," she said, lifting a forkful of fried meat by-products toward him.

He held his mouth closed for a moment but felt his muscles weakening and his jaws unclenching. When the Spam touched his tongue, his heart began to melt and run down though his gut in long rivulets. "All this time," he thought, "I been trying to keep it from melting."

His body became soft around him, and he heard the old woman's singing for the first time. He imagined it was his voice singing his death song. "I'm dying," he thought, and an upwelling of gratitude surged in him. "Finally."

"You're not dying, fool," Mrs. Edwards said. "You're eating. Quite the opposite." She shoved potatoes into his mouth, and he chewed and swallowed, feeling the butter flow through the empty drum of his chest and flood his stomach. Instinctively he tried to reach to hold himself together, but his arms were tied to the sides of the chair. That was it. When they'd sewn him up there in the Philippines, they'd tied him in half. He'd been trying to undo that knot for most of his life, so the two parts of him could be back together, and now the old lady had done it so easily. "How come," he started to say, but she cut him off.

"I kept hoping you'd find out for yourself," Mrs. Edwards said. "After all, you are the surviving twin."

Outside, an owl called three times and a dog began to bark.

171

22   Inside his wickiup, Avrum Goldberg built a fire of aspen and cedar to ward off the monsoon moisture of summer. He set a clay bowl close to the fire and ladeled venison from a larger bowl into the smaller one. The floor of the wickiup was covered with woven mats, and clusters of drying plants hung from the bent staves overhead. Smoke from the fire rose in a straight line to the hole at the center of the structure.

The old lady was pulling at him, but he steeled himself to hold out. He was hungry and tired, worried about what would happen next. His skin felt good from the bath and sage, however, and relief at the end of the poaching had spread throughout his bones. He had never liked killing the animals, although he understood Shorty Luke's point. If enough of the biggest bulls were gone, the tribe wouldn't be able to keep up the hunting business, which was a betrayal of the animals, and Sam and Xavier couldn't keep cheating the tribe. His body felt very light. Maybe I'm dying, he thought, surprised by the idea. Death then opened a doorway, and while the deer meat heated he stepped through to bear witness.

An ancient couple sat on two sides of a table in a small, gray kitchen, singing together by candlelight. The plump, shriveled woman had tied a light scarf over her head, and wisps of fine, white hair protruded from beneath the old man's yarmulke. The song was the kiddush, the prayer over sabbath wine, something Avrum had not heard in many, many years, its nasal tones mingling with the sounds of Bronx traffic outside the room. Beneath a cloth on the table was the challah, the three-strand, braided bread over which they would pray next. Then a piece would be passed around, and there should have been a family there to share it.

Avrum stood fixed in the doorway, seeing his parent's withered faces in the flickering light, astonished that they were still alive, and more astonished yet at the emptiness his going had left behind. For the first time in his life he understood his parents' pain at his abandonment not just of them but of everything in their world. There was a great loneliness in the little apartment. What had led him so far away from that life? In the rhythmic chant of song, the ritual of drink and bread, the ceremony of sabbath, he recognized much that was familiar to the world he now inhabited. But how had he slipped so thoroughly away from his parents' world, so much so that he had never gone home in all those years? It had happened gradually. First a fascination with the painful history that had produced his own people, then a scholar's obsession with other cultures that lead to anthropology. But it had been the people of Black Mountain, the qualities of light, air, freedom, deep relatedness with everything surrounding them, and Mrs. Edwards that had seduced him finally. His letters had brought increasingly troubled responses from home until all letters ceased. He had become so accustomed to silence between himself and that other world, and so increasingly absorbed in his reconstruction of this new old world, that he had forgotten.

It had been such a long road, and he'd walked nearly every step of it by himself, learning something essential before each foot touched the earth, reading, watching, listening, questioning, deciding, becoming. He'd moved toward the people at first, cautiously and with respect, but one day he'd realized that the people had been moving toward him at the same time and that they'd somehow crossed and gone beyond one another. In making the shift, he realized, he had, of course, become something the Indians never were and that he was, in important ways, more alone than he'd ever been. And that was when Mrs. Edwards first called him to her bed.

He felt the song surrounding him, and he shrugged it off, but found himself back in his life nonetheless. The first time it had happened, he'd been lying in his newly constructed wickiup, proud of the perfect authenticity of it and remembering the ridicule of the young people, their hoots of derision as he constructed it. Self-doubt had gripped him, and his thoughts traveled back to his childhood in New York, to the days when he'd begun to wonder who he was.

That was the first time that he'd felt himself lifted and carried through the night, arriving at the woman's house in confusion. And in confusion he'd found himself enveloped within her, his old self sliding away like a snake's skin until he was completely one with her. He'd experienced sex before, the rhythmic motions of coupling and desire, but he'd never felt himself lost until that moment. What he'd learned to call orgasm had become, that night, a giving up of everything he'd learned to call himself, an outflowing of a rigid core of resistance. And when it was over, Mrs. Edwards had been sitting beside him, her long, silver hair loose and shrouding both of them and her smile holding him motionless in the night. Her breasts were red and swollen, as though she had suckled him, and her eyes shone with a nearly black fire. Where their skin touched he felt a warm fusion, unable to tell where one stopped and the other began. Beyond it all was her smile, kind and understanding and still desiring. The aroma of sex lay over the room like the moisture of summer clouds, and he'd felt with complete astonishment the renewed hardening of desire. Mrs. Edwards had straddled him then, taking him inside and bending so that their merger vanished within the shadow of her flowing hair. He had forced her over, tumbling so that he was now on top and driving against her, his hands on top of hers and his hips holding her to the bed, aware all the time of a great storm outside, one of the summer monsoons that crashed down from the southwest and shouted and hurled fire at the earth. He'd come the second time with a sudden rising and feeling of racing wind that left him alone again in his own bed. Fucked by magic, he said to himself now as he pulled the venison stew from beside the fire and speared a piece with his knife. Over the years he'd learned to assert his own will against the woman, and it had become a kind of teasing foreplay. When finally he surrendered to the summons, he felt himself swept through the night with something like triumph. Their coming together had become as forceful as rivers, as mountains, as thunderclouds. He smiled, contented now to be the eternal outsider, and knowing his value thereof. The vision of his parents disappeared, and he was once again inside the curve of his home, shadowed by the tall range of mountains opening to a vast sky.

23   Jake and Stroud had walked back to camp side by side. The moon had widened to a fat crescent, drawing shadows out of the brush and tree trunks and touching the stream with small lights. Something splashed in the river, and Jake imagined the big spawning brown trout that had risen. He always released the browns, and he kept only a few of the smallest rainbows to eat. With barbless hooks he could slide a fly from the fish's mouth without removing it from the stream, so that being caught was undoubtedly traumatic but not physically damaging. So he told himself.

"We'll look for your granddaughter tonight and then get packed up by dawn," Stroud said. "If we don't find her, we can get a search party out right away. Another thing, though. I'll check on Nelson, the guy kicked by the French woman. If he's not conscious, we should evacuate him tonight. Poor Henry. He's a decent guy and feels pretty damned bad about shooting the kid."

"Not as bad as Jessie felt, I suppose."

"Yeah."

The fire had been built up so that it flared and illuminated a wide circle, throwing shadows everywhere. The men were clustered around it.

"What the hell?" Stroud said. "I told you to keep that fire small."

"You two figure it all out, Captain? Like in Nam?" Jensen stood on the opposite side of the fire, in the center of the half-circle of men. "What we're going to do, I mean?"

Jake saw what was wrong. Jensen held the fancy rifle in his right hand, his finger inside the trigger guard, and the men beside him were also armed and looking nervous. Sandrine sat on the log tentatively eating scrambled eggs and ignoring the men.

"Not much choice," Stroud said. "If Nelson isn't too bad off, we'll look for the girl tonight and then pack up in the morning to bring the boy's body to the authorities. It won't be hard for anybody to see it was an accident. Henry thought he was saving a woman from a wild animal. The charges will be dismissed. But we'll all have to testify, I imagine. I'll return your payments, of course. Peters, go check on Nelson. We might have to evac him tonight."

"Don't you think somebody might wonder what a dozen guys were doing without a permit on a reservation with illegally automated assault rifles?" Jensen replied, looking down at the gun.

"That's my responsibility," Stroud said. "We'll switch to the semis and hide the rest of the illegal ordnance. We'll just be a bunch of guys on a hike. There's no law against playing in the woods. Jake will take care of the reservation permit problem, and we'll get a search started for his granddaughter if she doesn't turn up tonight."

"So the federal authorities will just wink at the rest of us, right?"

"That's right, Jensen. They've got bigger fish to fry."

"Like Henry." Jensen looked at the dentist. "Killing that boy is kind of fishy. You want to fry, Henry?"

"It was an accident," Henry said.

"You killed an Indian on a reservation with a fully automatic AR-15, Henry. You were out in the woods with a bunch of men who possessed camouflage uniforms, Kevlar helmets and vests, radios, plastic explosives, and all kinds of bad shit, and you killed a young man who was unarmed. And I do believe I saw, not just a .308 with a night scope on it, but one of those Russian M2 Starlight scopes in Captain Stroud's tent." He nodded toward Jake and Stroud. "Now, most of that's not technically illegal, but several of the men you were keeping company with have pretty extensive military records, including some spook shop stuff the government doesn't like to make public. And, sorry to tattle on you boys"—he looked from

Vasello to Dave Scully—"two of those men are actually wanted for what we call patriotism but the government calls terrorist activity."

Jensen smiled at Henry and shrugged. "In addition to killing an Indian, this bunch took two women hostage, one of whom is a foreign national and neither of whom were too happy about it. One imagines that these women wouldn't make the best character witnesses. It's starting to look kind of grim, isn't it, Henry? But don't worry, every federal prison has need of qualified dentists with nice soft asses."

"You're way out of line, Jensen." Stroud's voice grew hard.

Jake took a half-step to the side for a better view of the group. Nguyen wasn't anywhere to be seen, so he'd probably gone off to take a leak or something.

"I don't think so, Captain." Jensen raised the rifle an inch so that it still pointed toward the ground but in Stroud's direction. "You've put us in a rather bad situation here. We paid you a lot of money, and it's your responsibility to take care of things properly. That's an officer's job, isn't it, Captain? Isn't it, Nashoba? Didn't you men have a way of dealing with officers who failed their jobs in Nam? Seems like I've heard of something called fragging." Jensen looked at the other men. "You see, Tony and Dave and I signed up for this course in order to recruit Captain Stroud and maybe Nguyen, but the captain has made it quite clear that he isn't interested. So we have to change our plans." He looked hard at Stroud. "Unless the captain has changed his."

"Recruit my ass, Jensen. I don't play with paranoid children and washed-up Vietnam vets who couldn't get jobs at a Seven-Eleven. But now tell me what you suggest we do. You have my permission to speak freely." Stroud folded his arms across his chest and glanced around at the group before returning his gaze to Jensen.

Jensen laughed out loud. "Permission gratefully accepted, Captain. Isn't the solution obvious? Vasello and Scully and I talked it over privately while you and Jake were gone, and I'm sure Henry and the others will agree. The best course of action is usually the simplest. And simply put, nobody will ever find four graves in this canyon. No one knows we're down here, anyway."

"So you'd shoot those girls and Jake, too, providing you can find the one that got away? And what about Nelson? You're just going to let him die?"

Jensen shrugged. "It's unpleasant, but we didn't sign up with a Boy Scout troop. And yes, I think we'll find her. After all, it's maybe thirty miles to the nearest town, nearly as far to the closest paved road."

"I don't want to go to jail," Henry said, pushing his glasses up on his nose, "but I'm not going along with any more killing." He looked at Stroud. "I don't agree with these guys, Captain."

"You won't have to kill anyone else, Henry." Jensen had raised the rifle so that it was aimed casually between Stroud and Jake. "In the face of a clear failure of command, I'm taking over." Jensen smiled. "You're removed from duty, Captain. Oh, and don't look for your Vietnamese buddy to save your ass." He gestured to Vasello. "Bring Mr. Nguyen up."

Vasello tapped the big man, Walter, on the shoulder. "Give me a hand, lard ass," he said. Looking both offended and confused, Walter followed Vasello around one of the tents. In a few seconds the two returned carrying Nguyen between them, each holding one of his bound arms. Duct tape sealed his mouth and held his ankles tightly together. The little man's black eyes were bright with hatred as he watched Jensen.

"We anticipated things a little," Jensen said. "Duct tape certainly is the all-purpose camping aid, isn't it?"

Walter held Nguyen carefully and directed an apologetic look at Stroud. "We didn't know about this, Captain. Vasello and Scully must have done it when Nguyen went off to piss."

"Stop whining, Walter. It's unbecoming in a military man," Jensen said. "I'm sure Mr. Nguyen understands. If my sources are right, Mr. Nguyen Phuong here was a crack assassin for the USA during the war. He'll comprehend the necessity of our actions, extreme though they may be, right, Nguyen?" He glanced at the Vietnamese man and then back to Stroud.

Tom Peters stepped into the firelight, looking with surprise at the men holding Nguyen. "Chris says Nelson hasn't regained consciousness. He's been with him the whole time. That bitch has a hell of a kick."

Jake looked at each of the half-dozen men. Henry, Walter, and Peters wore expressions ranging from bewilderment to utter fear, Henry's owl eyes wide and Walter's chins almost seeming to tremble. Tony Vasello smirked as he held Nguyen, and Dave Scully stared stonily at Jensen, the expression on his pale face impossible to interpret.

"In the absence of real leadership," Jensen said, "I've devised a plan." He glanced at the men and then back to Jake and Stroud. "I've discussed it only with Tony and Dave so far, but I hope it meets with everyone's approval.

"Collectively the eight of us paid you about forty thousand bucks to learn combat technique, low-intensity guerilla tactics, escape and evasion, and so on. I think I can speak for all of us when I say we are serious about this and we want our money's worth. And I have devised what I think is a fairly satisfactory strategy for achieving our goal."

He glanced around. "Stroud and his old buddy Jake Nashoba were Special Forces in Nam. From what I was told these two were as good as they came. They're both a little long in the tooth, but you can bet they haven't forgotten everything." He grinned, the firelight cutting angles beneath his sharp cheekbones and holding beneath the brim of his fatigue cap.

"Now, I'm sure that some of us wouldn't be much of a match for either one of these two under equal conditions. Captain Stroud, especially, would pose a problem, I fear." He looked Stroud up and down. "I have to admit you're in pretty good shape, Captain. You've kept yourself up." He looked at the men beside him. "I imagine Captain Stroud has also kept up his skills pretty well with courses like this. How many of you would like to match wits and muscle with the captain?"

"I wouldn't mind that too much," Vasello said. "Not too much at all."

"Me either," Scully added.

"Well, I believe you should both mind it a great deal." Jensen looked from Vasello to Scully. "How about you, Henry, or you, Walter? Would either of you like a little hand-to-hand combat with the captain? Mr. Peters, how about you?"

When no one responded, Jensen said, "My thoughts exactly. However, luckily that still leaves us with a half-breed game warden and former Special Forces officer." He nodded toward Jake and his white smile flashed. "Who is completely expendable."

Jensen studied Jake, looking him up and down. "I also heard a little about Jake Nashoba over there in California. It seems he served with Captain Stroud in Vietnam and became somewhat of a legend himself. Point man, long-range recon, all kinds of impressive things. Supposed to be able to see in the dark, use extrasensory perception." He laughed out loud again. "But." Jensen rubbed his chin with the knuckles of his free hand.

"But frankly, Nashoba, you don't look so good. While Captain Stroud has evidently been working out pretty consistently, you really don't look to be in top form, I'm afraid. Kicking back a few beers, I imagine." Keeping the gun aimed in the general direction of Jake and Stroud, he looked around at the men once more. "Doesn't it appear to you that Mr. Nashoba has been doing most of his exercise with a bottle? I imagine a mile run would just about clean you out, right, Jake?"

Stroud turned to Jake. "Don't let this jerk screw with you, Jake. He's just full of shit." He stared at Jensen. "Don't tell me that you're afraid to deal with me instead of Nashoba. It's been almost thirty years since Nam, and you don't think a half-dozen men with automatic weapons are a match for me? Hell, Jake wouldn't even give you a contest, but I definitely would. Look at him. He's in rotten shape, just like you said. No offense, Jake."

Jake glanced up at Stroud and then turned his attention back to Jensen. "No offense taken, of course. Besides, Jensen's right. They're no match for you."

180

"I admire your attitude, Captain, but I'm afraid there's also the fact that this whole group holds you in a little bit of awe. I don't think they would be at their best hunting you."

"What the hell are you talking about, Jensen?" Walter let go of one of Nguyen's arms and stepped closer to the fire. Without the additional support, Vasello let Nguyen sink to the ground, where he lay on his side with his eyes moving from Stroud to Jensen.

"It's not complicated, Walter. I'm talking about a little search-and-destroy practice here. We give Nashoba a slight head start and then we hunt him down. Of course, we'll have weapons and he won't, which might seem a little one-sided. But if you think that's not sporting, remember that in his prime Nashoba was a finely trained hand-to-hand killer. Or so I've heard. And some of you"—he glanced at the three men—"if I remember correctly, are more accustomed to selling real estate, fixing dentures, and such."

"That's ridiculous," Peters said, his pinched face showing open disbelief. "We didn't come down here to kill anyone. We're not killers. Besides, Nashoba would head straight for the cops. You think he'd just hang around until we shot him? And he knows this country. We don't." Peters shoved his hands in his pockets and glared at Jensen.

Jensen smiled again. "That's part of the perfection of my plan. I can't believe I worked it out so beautifully in so little time. You see, right in front of us we have this young lady, who is, to put it bluntly, a hostage. And out there in the woods we have Jake's pubescent granddaughter."

Jake focused all of his attention on Jensen.

"Here's how it will work," Jensen went on. "We keep Captain Stroud and this young lady tied up and under guard in camp, and we let our hero here run for it. However"—he paused and swung the rifle back and forth between the two men, his smile still broad—"here's the real beauty of it. The stipulation is that if Nashoba doesn't check in with us at least once every two hours, we kill Stroud and the girl, plus Jake's little granddaughter when we find her. Now we all know Jake Nashoba won't abandon this young lady to certain unpleasantness and death, and I doubt he'd do that to Captain Stroud either."

"What do you mean, 'check in'?" Henry asked. "This is insane."

"Not insane, Henry, though it may seem a bit extreme to a guy whose big thrills come from drilling teeth. It's more like virtual reality war, except the reality bleeds. All you have to do, Jake, is let us know you're around every two hours. Nothing spectacular, just give a couple of shouts from hiding, kill one of us, something minor like that." He looked at the men. "You see, two hours wouldn't possibly be enough time for him to contact anyone and get back to save this lovely tourist or his old friend."

"Nobody's going along with this insanity," Peters said.

"Quite the contrary," Jensen replied. "I believe everyone will. Walter, I wouldn't be easing discreetly toward the guns if I were you. Tony and Dave understand our limited options and agree with me totally, right?"

"Right," Vasello said, standing with his legs spread and the rifle leveled. Scully just nodded, his gray crewcut shimmering in the light from the fire, and the hard lines of his cheeks giving him a mechanical appearance.

"Now, I want everyone to remain right here until we're all clear on the scenario. And just to make a point about how clear we should all be, I've figured out what to do with Mr. Nguyen." Jensen swung the rifle and fired twice into the little man's chest, jerking the gun back toward Stroud and Jake before they could move. The men around Nguyen had leaped away, Walter tripping and flopping on the ground like a walrus.

Sandrine dropped the plate on the rocks around the fire and stared in frozen silence.

"Jesus Christ!" Walter yelled, scrambling backward from the body.

"You bastard," Stroud said. "You're dead now."

A head appeared from the nearest tent. "What's going on?" the man shouted.

"Nothing, Chris. Just a demonstration. Get back inside and keep an eye on Nelson," Jensen replied.

Nguyen moved spasmodically for a moment and then lay still, blood pumping from his chest and running out of his mouth. "Now Henry and I are even," Jensen said. "We both know what it's like to kill somebody. Our instructor and his friend, like Tony and Dave, know what it's like to kill people, don't you? And they were probably all people who looked just like that man there. Ironic, isn't it, that this courageous Vietnamese man fought and survived a whole war and traveled halfway around the globe just to be shot by an American who has admittedly never been in actual combat?"

His voice became businesslike. "Okay, listen carefully. We don't want this to turn into one of those predictable Stallone-type chase sequences, where the good guy runs, struggles, lots of camera close-ups, seems about to succumb, and then somehow, someway manages to not just elude but destroy his pursuers. We've all watched that tired old scenario on television too many times, or read it in a novel. Like that 'Chato' movie with what's-his-name, Charles Bronson, playing an Apache breed. Anybody see that? You know it's a foregone conclusion because the outnumbered hero is part Indian and so he has all kinds of supernatural powers, moves without making noise, can see in the dark, or whatever. The usual. The white men are just no match for him. Naturally they panic and do everything exactly wrong and the stealthy Indian picks them off one by one or something like that. It's been a long time since I saw it. But anybody who expects that kind of Hollywood plot here might as well pack up—although that's just a metaphor, since I can't allow anyone to leave. So first we'll have both of you toss your knives onto the ground by the fire. And no sneaky throws. You do have a knife, don't you, Nashoba?"

Stroud took his knife out of its scabbard and pitched it onto the dirt by the campfire.

"It's in my pocket," Jake said.

Jensen nodded, and Jake pulled out a black-handled Buck pocketknife, dropping it beside Stroud's big survival blade.

"Now, Peters, you and Henry search them. Make sure they don't have anything—no matches, no nothing. I want them with nothing but the clothes they have on. It may seem one-sided to you men, but I happen to know that Nashoba here has had very extensive SEAL Team Unarmed Combat training, even though he wasn't technically a SEAL. In his prime he wouldn't have needed a weapon to take us all out, would you, Jake?"

"You're already a cliché, Jensen," Stroud said. "A dead one. This is a bullshit fantasy, some kind of movie running through your stunted brain. Fed by these two over-the-hill Rambos you brought along."

"I'm not part of this," Peters said. "I didn't sign on to murder people."

Jake looked at Peters with interest. A man of medium height and average build, graying hair parted low on one side and combed over his balding head, Tom Peters would have blended into any crowd. He looked like the perfect ordinary American, but there was a strength in his expression that surprised Jake. If he were recruiting revolutionaries, Peters would be the kind he looked for, the kind that no one would notice. Now Peters stood indecisively looking from Jensen to Stroud.

"First of all, Tom, you must admit that murder is just a concept. Is it murder to shoot a man who's tied up and help-less, but not murder to send a cruise missile into a civilian town as our own government has done? The purpose of war is to effect and maintain control, and the most effect way to control a person is to terminate that person. Consider Nguyen. Alive he was quite an intimidating individual, a potentially disruptive element to say the least. But dead he is potential compost, nothing more. He's out of the equation now and we don't even have to think of him. Just like that poor wolf-boy in the tent."

"You're crazy," Henry interjected, taking off his fatigue cap and wiping his brow with it. The stubble on his chin quivered as he spoke, and his brown eyes looked like those of a school-boy confronting a bully.

"No. It would be easier if I were crazy, but I'm sane. And let me make one thing perfectly clear, as our old friend Nixon liked to say. You are all very much part of this, Mr. Peters. You, Henry, and Peters, and Walter, and even Chris back there with Nelson in the tent. Consider poor Nguyen's condition."

Slowly, the two men moved, neither looking at Jake or Stroud. They finished the search quickly, Peters's jaw set angrily during the process. "What about fingernail clippers?" Henry asked.

"Nothing. No fingernail clippers, no matches or lighter. No nothing, got it?"

When the search was completed, Jensen motioned to Walter. "Get the duct tape and secure Captain Stroud. Be sure not to cut off circulation, but you'd be wise to also ensure that he can't escape." When Walter stood unmoving, Jensen let out a long breath. "You are highly expendable, Walter."

While Walter was taping Stroud's hands behind his back, Jake took a step closer to the fire, so that he felt its heat on his legs as he looked directly across at Jensen.

"Hurt my granddaughter and I'll remove your skin an inch at a time."

"Good attitude," Jensen answered. "Exactly what I would have scripted. But good grief, man, I'm not depraved. I promise I won't hurt either of these two a bit, unless you fail to report in as ordered. One failure to report and they're dead. And your little granddaughter, too, because we *will* find her. And Toto, too." Jensen grinned.

"This is insane," Henry said. The big man looked at Peters for support and then met Jensen's eyes. "We can't just murder people."

"You already have, Henry. Don't forget that. Let me put this into perspective for you one last time. You're a dentist on an Indian reservation without permission, carrying illegal weaponry, part of a paramilitary operation run by men with extensive military and CIA files. You've killed a young man who was involved in a sacred Indian ceremony. It's not cool to kill Indians any longer as far as the media are concerned, and you're not going to have O. J. Simpson's lawyers working for you." Jensen took two steps backward.

"Now, I realize that none of you except Tony and Dave are really with me on this. I know that you'll just run your asses right out of here given half a chance, but field officers have always had to deal with recalcitrant troops, throughout the history of warfare. So I've got to somehow assure your loyal participation in this little paramilitary adventure. How can I do that? Any suggestions other than the usual deserters-will-be-shot argument?"

The men stared at him, and he surveyed the entire bunch, including Jake and Sandrine. Finally he snapped his fingers. "I think I've got it. Vasello will stay in camp with Captain Stroud, Miss Le Bris, and poor unconscious Nelson. Walter, Peters, Dave, Chris, and Henry will take the Russian Starlight scope and form the first search-and-destroy team, led by Dave. I, meanwhile, will constitute my own one-man long-range recon patrol carrying that rifle with the night scope on it as well as my little beauty here." He patted the AR-15 match rifle. "Now, none of you will know where I am, and if I see anyone attempting to abandon the mission he'll suffer the same fate as our poor late Vietnamese comrade. In short, I'll kill anyone who craps out, and if I fire three times in quick succession, a kind of universal signal, Tony will have my standing order to shoot everyone in camp. Thus, anyone who decides to run for help may be the cause of several deaths, including most likely his own. Nothing personal."

Jensen smiled at each of the men in turn. "I can't begin to tell you how satisfying this is. I've wanted to do a real night mission for a long time, and we trained extensively for those in the TRS camps. Thanks to Captain Stroud's desire for veri-similitude, we have some excellent equipment, giving us both firepower and night vision. Our target is an Indian, or at least

186

half an Indian, so we can assume that he can halfway see in the dark, halfway move with stealth, and all of that. Shall we get started?" Jensen's blue eyes caught the firelight and seemed to dance with excitement.

"You're really going to do this?" Henry asked.

"No, Henry. *We're* really going to do this."

Walter stepped up beside Henry, the two big men of almost exact height and weight forming an impressive-looking pair. The light from the fire flickered on Henry's thick glasses and turned Walter's mustache and heavy stubble a deep red. Both men held their arms folded and resting on the shelf of their bellies.

"This is insane bullshit," Walter said, the red of his face deepening to gray and black. Around the campsite, the forest had become darkness broken by the darker, straight lines of pines and curling scrub oaks. The river had grown louder, its sweeping sound carving at the cliff faces and breaking in rhythmic mutterings against boulders.

"We don't have any reason to believe you. What's going to stop you from killing all of us if you have the chance, just like you shot Nguyen? If we help you kill the ranger, you'll shoot the rest of us so there'll be no witnesses. We'd have to be pretty stupid not to figure that out."

"You're not stupid, Walter, just afraid of your own great big shadow." Jensen's face was now darkened almost completely, the light of the fire offering only sketched outlines of brow, cheeks, and nose.

Jake calculated his chances of taking out Jensen, Vasello and Scully. He knew he could neutralize Jensen before Jensen could fire the fancy rifle; he could even visualize the motion that would take him across the fire and send the blade of his hand into Jensen's thorax. But there wasn't much chance that he could get the other two before at least one had a chance to fire. He couldn't count on the others to help. Hell, if they'd known how to do such things they wouldn't be paying Stroud to teach them.

"Isn't that why you're out here, Walter, trying to make yourself brave?" Jensen said. "Isn't that the case with all of you? Now, I'm tired of all this talk, but I'll try to explain one more time. If my plan works out, we'll all have the excitement of a real combat mission. No light-and-magic show. Some of us may not survive. But for anyone to make it we'll have to work together. Soldiers don't have to like each other, or even believe in the task at hand. They just have to follow orders and watch each other's backs. I know that none of you has anything against Jake Nashoba, but that's entirely beside the point. Do you think your fathers had anything personal against the Japanese or Germans they killed in World War Two or that Nashoba or Stroud or any American had a personal grievance against Nguyen's relatives in Nam? Nashoba is now your enemy, and once you start hunting him he will kill you if he has the chance because he understands what I'm telling you. For him it won't be personal either, although"—he looked across the fire at Jake—"I'm sure he feels it to be quite personal between the two of us by now, and Captain Stroud would undoubtedly agree."

Jensen swept the rifle barrel across the group of men. "We're wasting a lot of time talking, but let me make one more point. When this is over, every one of us will be deeply compromised. I mean, is any one of you going to go to the FBI, since this is Indian land, and say, Jensen made me hunt down the ranger and kill him. Jensen made me shoot the boy in the wolf suit?" Jensen looked pointedly at Henry. "I think we can count on Captain Stroud to keep quiet. His business makes him vulnerable, and he's got a family he's proud of and a lot to lose. I'm sure he'll help us explain how an accidental discharge did in poor Nguyen, and Nelson fell and bumped his head. As for the ranger, no one will ever know we met."

Vasello spoke from behind the group. "What about that Frenchwoman and Nashoba's granddaughter? They'll blow the whole thing."

"We'll worry about such things later," Jensen answered. "Now I'm really, really tired of talking. You see, we're completely in this together, bonded for life, gentlemen. Like *Deliverance*, remember that film? They had to even lie about their own friend's death. Or *Apocalypse Now*. Great stuff, right, Henry?"

"What about dinner?" Walter said.

"Oh, that's really good, Walter," Jensen shook his head. "Does a war stop for dinner? How about hors d'ouevres? One minute you're having moral qualms and the next you're worried about your stomach. Let's synchronize our watches, especially you, Nashoba. Everyone should have twenty-one hundred precisely. Okay? Dave, get me that sniper rifle with the night scope." He motioned at Jake with his AR-15. "You've got twenty whole minutes before we come after you. Enough time for these boys to tie shoes and lock and load weapons. It's nine o'clock right now, so we'll expect to hear from you no later than eleven p.m. Better use every second."

Jake looked at Stroud for an instant and then at Sandrine. "Don't worry, Granddaughter," he said. "I'll be back for you."

He began running along the faint trail to the south of camp, hearing the awful thudding of his heavy boots and imagining the terrain for miles around. He knew every crevice and rock, every pool and shallow ford in the river, but he didn't know what to do except run. At the river he splashed across the black, knee-deep water, struggling to stay upright on the algae-covered rocks.

On the other side, he sprinted up a wide draw away from the water, and as the draw narrowed, he angled to his right across a steepening slope until he struck a maze of rough volcanic cliffs.

At the edge of the cliff face, he stopped and listened, fighting to control his breath and thanking his time on the river over the years for keeping him in better physical shape than they suspected. "They have night vision," he said to himself. Therefore, they might be able to track him to the rock. But after that they'd have to guess.

He stepped behind a jagged column and squeezed through a shadowy fissure onto a vertical section of the sharply pocked black rock. The ledge disappeared, and he moved carefully, feeling for hand- and toeholds while hearing the invisible water rippling below him. He could see the rock face and the river perfectly in his mind. The Dark swept down a straight stretch and collided with the volcanic cliff face, boiling into a deep green pool about seventy feet below him and then tailing wide around the bend made by the rock. If Jensen's men knew where he was, they could train a night scope on him and he'd be dead. But they'd never guess that he'd double back across the cliff immediately facing their camp. And if he was lucky, by the time they tracked him there he'd be somewhere else.

He edged cautiously another ten feet, feeling for foot- and handholds he couldn't see, until he found the fracture he remembered. He'd first seen it years before when a great horned owl had alighted on the rock and then disappeared into the crack. Now he was relieved to discover that it was large enough for him to squeeze through into a kind of black chamber. Spiderwebs caught on his hands and swung across his face, and something glowed at him.

"Goddammit," he said, sliding his luminous wristwatch off and into his pocket. Looking upward he saw a few stars between big clouds. Weak moonlight silvered the edges of thunderheads. The fissure made a shoulders-width chimney all the way to the top of the cliff face. Near the top of the chimney, a circular web stretched pale, shimmering strands across the space, and in the center of the web a great dark spider sat looking down at him, a bright star in the sky on either side of the wide legs.

Below and downstream he heard splashing and then boots slipping on the muddy riverbank. He shrank back into his hiding place and listened. At first there was silence. Then once more he heard the river curling against and twisting around the rock face. He heard the water piling into the deep hole with a slow, heavy sigh and then became aware of another faint sound, a barely perceptible keening, songlike and delicate. It seemed to come from directly overhead. He turned his face upward and saw the web of the spider vibrating slightly, the large arachnid plucking the strands of her web.

The sound of rock falling tore his attention away from the spider. Using the night scope, the men had evidently followed him to the cliffs even more efficiently than he'd thought they would, and now it sounded as though at least one of them was trying to make his way across the face, probably exploring possible routes.

He braced himself close to the front of the fissure, looking out over the river so he could see the campfire on the other side and the darker blocks of the tents. A black figure by the fire was probably Stroud taped motionless on one of the log rounds. There was no sign of anyone else, so Sandrine Le Bris was most likely inside a tent.

Muscles taut, he braced himself more securely, hearing the scrabbling noise coming closer. Suddenly a hand appeared inches from his eyes, the fingers grasping the sharp edge of the crevice, and then the startled face of Peters appeared, staring straight into his own.

Clutching rock with his left hand, Jake reached with his right and grasped the man's shirt just below the neck. He jerked the body toward him and then thrust it away. Peters screamed as he felt himself shoved into air, and there was another scream and the sound of Peters's body striking rock just before a final splash. Jake felt a moment of regret. Peters had not wanted to be part of it all, but Jensen had been right. Everyone hunting him was now an enemy.

As he listened for signs of someone following behind Peters, there was the crack of a rifle and fragments of rock stung his face. Before he had begun to think, he already knew that the shot could only have come from across the river. Jensen had obviously waited there, followed Peters's course across the cliff face, and seen the man pushed into space. The rifle cracked again and he felt a sliver of rock slash his left shoulder as he squeezed himself as far back into the fissure as he could go.

In the loud silence after the second shot, he heard the delicate, shrill singing again. When he looked up, the spider was no longer at the center of the web. It was dancing at the edge of its woven threads, still plucking the strands with its feet. Then it began to climb up the broken rock of the chimney until, poised against the starred clouds, it paused for an instant before disappearing over the lip of the crack.

Another shot ripped into the rock, the bullet ricocheting off the back, fragments of stone stinging his neck. He climbed, bracing his feet and hands between the walls. In a moment he felt the web collapse against his face and in another moment he was mantling over the top of the chimney onto a boulder-strewn shelf of the canyon. He ran and dove behind a big downed pine as another shot slammed into the crack where he had been hiding. Jensen would be the one with the sniper rifle and scope, and obviously Jensen thought he was still in the crack.

He crawled the length of the log, keeping below its horizon, and when he reached the huge root wad, twice as high as his head, he stood up, only then daring to look back toward the lip of the canyon and the other side of the river. His shoulder stung, and when he reached to rub it his hand came away wet. He felt again and realized that more than rock had touched him. Clearly one of the bullets had cut through the outside of his upper arm, releasing a significant amount of blood. When he flexed his fist and forearm, the shoulder burned with pain, but he felt no lessening of strength.

Crouching behind the root wad, he pulled his watch out of his pocket. To his astonishment, an hour had passed. Could he assume that Peters's fall from the cliff face would be taken as his checking in, as Jensen had put it? Or might they think that the clumsy Peters had just slipped? The shots must mean that Peters's death was his first check-in and that he had a fresh two hours.

He moved silently back along the shelf in the direction from which he'd come until he reached the edge of the slope above the cliff face. He dropped to his stomach and looked over. Three men stood directly below him at the base of the cliff where it turned and angled uphill, more a diminishing break in the slope at that point than a cliff. He could not make out their words. Perhaps they were discussing whether someone else should go where Peters had met his doom, or who should be the one to do so. But there ought to be a fourth one. Jensen had ordered the big man named Walter, Henry the dentist, Peters, and Chris to go after him, led by Dave Scully. One was missing. Maybe he was already following Peters, though that seemed doubtful. Another rifle crack from across the river told him that Jensen was still stupidly shooting at the fissure, probably figuring the ricochets would get him eventually if he was there. That was how the great hero Kit Carson's men had slaughtered the Navajo, he remembered, shooting at the roof of the cliffside cave where they hid until the people began to throw children to their deaths and leap after them. But only Peters had leaped anywhere so far.

He looked straight down on the three men, the tops of their Kevlar helmets glinting dully. The fattest one was probably Walter, the big one with the heavy shoulders Henry, and the smaller one Chris. Dave Scully was missing. The three below weren't bad men, but because of circumstances they were trying to kill him. Only Scully was someone to worry about. Scully had been a Seal, and in the ranger's experience Seals liked killing and were good at it.

Jake's elbow scraped against a rough chunk of rock, and he turned his head carefully to look at it. It was the size of a basketball, probably fifty pounds worth of jagged black lava.

He squeezed his fist and felt the strength in his injured arm and then gathered his feet beneath him. Once he was squatting, he cupped both hands beneath the rock and prepared to stand, but something hard gouged the middle of his back.

"Stay right there," a voice said. "I'd shoot you right now just to get this mess over with, but Jensen wants to kill you himself."

193

"You're Dave Scully, right?" Jake said without looking around.

"Very good. Listen, before we go down there, let me tell you how fucked up I think this is. Jensen and Vasello are gung ho, but if there was any other way, I wouldn't do this. I happen to admire both you and Captain Stroud, and Nguyen for that matter. But the shit is going down anyway, as they say."

"There is another way. Listen. I'll testify that Jessie's death was an accident, and so will the French woman. You and I together can take care of Jensen and Vasello, and we can go back and let Stroud and the woman go. You can all leave while I find my granddaughter."

"I'm sorry, Nashoba. But you're not as convincing as Jensen. I'm afraid I have to take you back over there. Besides, now Peters is dead, too."

"I didn't have any choice," Jake said.

"None of us has any choice, right? Better get up now."

Jake stood up slowly, but before he reached full height he heard a strange sound and then the clatter of the rifle striking the rock. He spun around to see Alison standing over Scully's body, a heavy oak branch held like a baseball bat.

The sound of the sliding rifle caught his attention, and he dove onto his belly, grabbing for the rifle stock. The gun slipped over the lip of the cliff and rattled off the rock as it fell.

Jake got to his feet and picked up the big lava stone, raising it past his chest and over his head. He stepped to the edge of the rock face and looked down to see the three men staring after the noise of the falling rifle. He let the rock go and watched it smash with a muted sound in the center of one of the helmets and then continue at an angled glance onto the shoulder of the next man.

The first man fell as though his nerves had been severed, collapsing facedown and unmoving, but the second one was hurled sideways to end up screaming and flopping like a newly caught trout, while the third dove onto the ground and began firing bursts into the air. Mixed in with the screams and rifle fire was the squawk of a raven high up in the pines. Jake held back for a moment, watching the men. The first one, the smallest of the three, lay on the bed of gray pine needles, a pool of darkness moving out from where his face rested on something that was either a rock or a pine cone. The helmet looked to be an odd shape and appeared to be partially embedded in the paleness of skull that showed at the helmet's edge. The second man, from his size probably Walter, rolled back and forth in shadowy, now silent agony. The third man had stopped firing and had scooted behind a tree, with the rifle barrel protruding. The sound of the raven was displaced by the kree of a kingfisher that darted past the cliffs, obviously angry at the intruders. The sound of running feet came from the direction of the river.

"This man's dead. We should go," Alison said behind him, and Jake scuttled back from the rocks and began a crouching scramble up the slope, following the bent form of his granddaughter. He knew that the canyon rose gently at this point until it became the gradually sloping forest high above the river. Now that they were above the cliffs, it would be simple to get out at this spot and cut cross-country to the town of Black Mountain, but it would take at least four hours even if he were in perfect shape. Ahead of him, Alison ran smoothly along the cliff top toward a cluster of stone outcroppings. He wanted to yell at her and tell her that that was where they'd expect them to go, but he didn't dare shout.

Instead, Jake followed the girl into the vertically fractured rock, slipping behind a blade of smooth gray granite marked by symmetrical moss patterns.

He squeezed into a kind of corridor and moved forward until he found her. He could smell and feel the presence of his wife's granddaughter, and hear her soft breathing, before he saw her. He held his hands in front of his face to fend off the spidery darkness. The crescent moon, growing fatter, had risen enough to send vague light into the canyon between thin clouds.

"They were holding both of us prisoner, taped up. Sandrine, the French girl, escaped, but they caught me. She came back to save me and then they caught her and I got away. Maybe this is all part of my vision. Maybe you're not really here and they aren't. Perhaps I'm being tested."

He drew a deep breath. "Was she hurt?"

Alison shook her head. "I don't think so. But she hurt one of the men who tried to catch me. She told me to find you."

"This isn't a vision, Alison. And I don't care what Jessie told you. Your ancestors didn't do vision quests."

"That doesn't matter," she said, her voice almost a whisper. "I know."

"Your ancestors were warriors," he replied. "And you were a warrior back there. I'm proud of you."

She remained silent for several minutes. He heard her breathing become more rapid and then subside. "I'm very tired, and I'm hungry. I don't feel strong. What did that man Stroud mean when he said you saved his life?"

"I'll explain later. Just remember that these men are the enemy, mine and yours because you're related to me."

"I hadn't had any dreams anyway, though a bear sniffed me the first night."

"A bear?"

He felt her hand reach to touch his arm. "I was sitting by the spring and a bear walked up behind me and smelled my hair. I don't know how I knew it was a bear, because I didn't look, but I just knew. I felt his breath against my neck, and it was like he was breathing into me. It was really strange. I could smell him, and he smelled like all the life of the mountains smashed into one thing. And then he left and I never saw him. But I saw his tracks later. I didn't have pollen to put in the tracks."

"Did you cross his tracks, Granddaughter?"

"I don't think so. I said a prayer Mrs. Edwards taught me."

"You've had your vision, Alison," the ranger said. "Bears aren't always bad; they're powerful. When you get home Mrs. Edwards can explain it."

"I dreamed about spiders, too," she said. "I fell asleep for a little while, and I dreamed a giant spider was walking in circles around me, spinning a web or something."

He felt his skin prickle. "I never did understand dreams," he replied. "Now we'd better go. They'll come straight to these rocks to find us. And Granddaughter, remember that these men will kill you. Even the ones who seem good will kill you because they are weaker than Jensen and the others, and they're afraid."

He moved cautiously into a side crack and climbed up and out of the rock jumble, Alison following him easily.

"We have to know the odds," he whispered as they crouched in the shadow. "Four are out of commission now, but that leaves four, including the one Sandrine injured, so maybe only three. Vasello is guarding Stroud and Sandrine, so three may still be hunting us, including Jensen. If one's detailed to get the one injured by the rock back to camp, that leaves maybe only two men looking for us. Jensen has a sniper rifle with an infrared scope. Scully's the one you stopped with that club, poor bastard. I think Tom Peters and Chris Martin are dead, and the big guy, Walter, is badly hurt. That leaves the man Sandrine kicked, and Henry, who wouldn't hurt a fly if he wasn't more afraid of Jensen than us, plus Jensen and Vasello. So there are probably three of them hunting us. Now listen. At the speed with which things are happening, we won't have time to set deadfalls or snares. So we just have to stay out of their sights until we have some kind of advantage. I think we should get down closer to the river and head upstream and then maybe double back toward camp."

Alison nodded and began to scramble down the rock slope toward the river's edge. Jake's right arm was becoming numb, and he was wondering about that when a bullet smashed into the center of his back. As he was falling, he tried to shout "Run!" and heard the sound of the rifle. Of course, he realized, feeling like a fool, Jensen would have anticipated the direction of his evasion and crossed the river to come down from above while he was dealing with the others. A half-assed ambush. That would be Nitske's training. And Jensen would have the night scope on the rifle. There was a time when he would have thought all of that out in a few seconds before it happened and therefore survived, but that time was finished years ago. As he fell, he felt a second impact strike his back and wondered if his granddaughter had gotten away. There had been only the two shots, so maybe she had escaped.

The absence of pain intrigued him as he began to roll down the slope, feeling his arms and legs tangling and swinging like rubber with each turn, but no pain. He was aware, however, of the brittle live oak twigs that stabbed into him and the small, sharp rocks that gouged his hands and face, and the awareness made him happy. As long as he could feel, he was alive. He had a moment's sense of absurdity at the anticlimax of it all, his great escape ending so quickly and easily. The sky, in its turning, showed a curve of blurred cloud, star, and moon splinter, and he caught a leisurely, far-off murmur of thunder. He imagined lightning. The familiar sweet smell of moldering leaves and grasses filled his senses, and he felt himself flooded with delight at this world he had inhabited, with something like love. There was an abrupt feeling of being dropped, and when he stopped moving, he found that he could see nothing but blackness and that he heard two unfamiliar sounds.

The first was the crash of a two-legged thing as it plunged down the slope above him, driving itself into the earth heavily with each plunge. It was an alien, metallic, unfamiliar disturbance, and it rushed upon him with the utmost evil. The second was a comforting, high-pitched song that, as he listened, became words.

"Come," the voice sang. The music of the words penetrated, and his mind surged, trying to locate the song. Hands touched him everywhere at once, busy, delightfully soft hands that seemed to lift and move him. "Come," the voice sang, the word spinning deliciously in his mind, weaving through his flesh and the stems of his bones. The darkness around him warmed, was filled with a fine, musty smell like Tali's hair and the sounds of high, electrical singing from many voices. His body floated easily, suspended between sky and earth.

24 Alison heard the shots and saw her grandfather tumble and fall into darkness shrouded by the tangled roots of a great, downed tree. She realized that he must have rolled into the hole left by the massive root wad of the pine. On the slope above, far from where her grandfather had fallen, a man with a rifle was running downhill, his shadow huge and angular with the rifle before him. She crouched within a chokecherry thicket and watched the man draw close to where her grandfather had disappeared, and then the man began to walk back and forth as though confused. Carrying one rifle in his hands and wearing another on a strap over his shoulder, the man walked slowly a hundred yards in one direction and then a hundred in the other, studying the ground, stopping each time to look into the hole. For half an hour she watched the man move back and forth as though searching, and then he began to walk determinedly southward along the cliff above the river. A second figure came out of the trees to join him.

When the men were out of sight, Alison began crawling to where her grandfather had fallen, stopping every few seconds to listen. When she reached the spot where he had disappeared, she slid to the edge of the hole and looked down. She could see nothing but shadows delineated by the twisting and tangled lines of ancient pine roots. He might have fallen further and been partially lodged beneath the roots, for she could see a still deeper recession just under the beginning of the enormous tree stump, perhaps a den dug by a bear the winter before. She was about to lower herself into the pit when she heard steps approaching.

She slithered away from the fallen tree, slipping backward over the rocks until she could crouch again within the granite jumble. The man with the telescoped rifle appeared, along with another man, walked past the root wad, and then turned and walked up the slope.

Alison climbed down to the river's edge and found a deep, swirling pool, impossible to cross. She fought her way upstream through the spiny wild plum brush until she could tell that the river had spread out in a fast, shallow riffle, and she sat and studied the other side for several minutes before she began to wade. She would find Sandrine and come back with her to save her grandfather.

25 Sandrine lay on an inflated ground pad, trying to regulate her breathing and willing her heart to beat slowly. Since the bursts of rifle fire from across the river, and then the two single shots from this side, her heart had been pounding. Her fingers had been numb for some time because of the duct tape that held them together in front of her waist, and the tape on her ankles, though less tight, had long before created a tingling that was working its way up her legs. She had tried without success to get the guard's attention for the last thirty minutes, wriggling and making what sounds she could through the tape on her mouth. But the guard, his dark, rectangular face illuminated by the Coleman lantern near the door, had focused all of his attention on sounds from outside the tent.

Time, she knew, was running out. Without bothering to disguise her motions, she wriggled her body down the length of the pad until her feet were beneath the folding camp chair the man sat in with the rifle across his lap. Then she swung her taped feet as hard as she could into the canvas bottom of the chair.

The man leapt up, exclaiming, "What the—" When he looked down and saw her, he appeared confused for a moment.

She made as much noise through the tape as she could, repeating the same sound over and over. Finally the man leaned the rifle against the chair and knelt beside her, the curving scar on his face turning a deep purple in the lantern light.

"I guess you're trying to say something." He caught a corner of the tape between his nails and began to tear it away from her lips. Pain shrilled through her as the tape ripped away, but she made no sound until her mouth was free.

She drew in several deep breaths and tried to say, "Thank you," but the words came out a garbled whisper. She gathered more strength, willing her heartbeat to slow again. "Thank you," she said more clearly.

"That must've hurt," the man said. A small, wiry man of about middle age, he had a hard, cruel-looking face with thick brows and dark eyes. His mouth was no more than a narrow slash that hardly seemed to move when he spoke. "Good," he added with a slight opening of the slash.

"Please," she said. "I cannot feel my hands or feet."

"Oh." He reached for the tape around her wrists and then stopped. "This better not be a trick," he said. "Because I will shoot you." He looked at her. "Though it would be a shame to shoot as hot a piece as you." He grinned now, and where she expected the whiteness of teeth was only a greater darkness. "Too soon, that is."

"It's no trick. I cannot feel anything. There is no blood in my feet or hands."

He tried to peel back the tape but couldn't grasp the edge, so he pulled the sheath knife off his hip and inserted the point between her wrists. He cut until she could separate her wrists; then he shifted to her ankles.

"You think he shot Alison's grandfather," Sandrine said as she ripped the tape from her wrists and ankles, grimacing at the searing pain, and began massaging them, trying to keep her palms from sticking to the tape residue. "But you're wrong. They can't catch him."

The man retrieved the rifle and returned to his chair. "I doubt that. I'm afraid that old half-breed's no match for Jensen or Scully. Jensen would probably shit if he knew I untaped you. But maybe you and me could enjoy ourselves a little while those fools are out there killing each other."

201

"What is your name?" Sandrine asked.

"Tony Vasello. I thought we were just going to try to recruit some big hero for our militia unit. I didn't sign on to kill women. Jensen's nuts."

"Tony, why do you go along with this man?" Sandrine's green eyes bored into him and he self-consciously looked down at the rifle.

"Because he may be nuts, but he's right. We got in too deep, and somebody's got to fix it. But you and me'll just let them do that." He looked at her parka. "Aren't you a little too warm in that raincoat and sweater? Why don't you take some of that stuff off?"

"You could just let me go. You didn't kill anyone, and I'll tell the police that. You've done nothing wrong. If the others are gone, we could go out together with Captain Stroud and tell the police. You haven't committed any crime."

A sudden wind seemed to whip the side of the tent, and Vasello stood and moved his rifle toward the disturbance. Jessie leaned against the inner wall of the nylon tent, his arms folded across his chest and his long tail curled behind him. He looked at Sandrine and nodded toward Vasello. "This is a bad one," Jessie said. "I wouldn't trust him."

Sandrine stared at the apparition for a moment and then shifted her eyes to Vasello, but he had already forgotten the noise and was watching her.

"I can't do that," he said. "But I'll show you what I can do. I'll bet you've got one hell of a body under all that stuff. And I hear you French women are hot."

"The man named Jensen is going to murder everyone, Tony. We all heard what he said. You know he's going to kill Captain Stroud and me and Alison and her grandfather. But you probably don't realize that he may kill you, too. He'll be afraid that you won't lie for him, that you'll tell the truth." She shook her hands and rubbed at her wrists. "He has too much to lose. And I wonder why a man with your experience follows such a young person like that."

Vasello stroked the handle of the rifle and shifted the gun slightly so that it aimed at Sandrine. "Lee Jensen may be young, but he's damned good, and what he says makes sense. Besides, he wouldn't underestimate me like that," he said. "And I hope you don't either. Why don't you take that raincoat off?"

"You know he'll kill us," Sandrine said, rising to her knees from her sitting position.

The man gestured with the gun. "Stand up," he said.

Sandrine rose to her feet, and he reached one hand over and unzipped the storm parka.

"Let's see what's under there. Now," he said.

The side of the tent bellowed again, and Vasello swung the rifle barrel toward the movement. Jessie turned his wolf head and grinned, and Vasello froze in terror.

Sandrine pivoted in a fluid line as the heel of her right foot struck Vasello in the jaw. He crashed onto the chair, smashing it and sprawling on the tent floor. Sandrine kicked him in the stomach and then again in the face, causing blood to explode from his crushed nose. She looked at him for a second and then leaped over him and out of the tent to find Stroud sitting on the log with his arms, legs, and mouth taped.

Sandrine picked up Stroud's big knife from the ground and cut through the tape around his legs and hands. She was attempting to pull the tape from his mouth when he grabbed her by the shoulders with both arms and threw her behind him. She struck the log and fell headlong onto the packed dirt.

"Fucking bitch." Vasello stood in front of the tent door, his thin face and chest covered with blood that looked black in the dim firelight. He seemed not to see Stroud standing in front of him and was swinging the rifle toward her when Stroud sprang, catching the rifle blast in his chest. The shots knocked Stroud backward, and for an instant he and Vasello both stared in wonder at the hole, blossoming with dark blood, in the middle of his chest. Then Stroud reached a hand out and grasped the rifle barrel. With his right hand, he ripped the gun from Vasello's grip and tossed it across the fire. In the same motion, his left hand grasped Vasello's chin while the right came back and cupped the smaller man's forehead. The two huge arms moved together, and Vasello's head jerked to one side with a popping sound. Grabbing the belt and shirt, Stroud picked up the body and lifted it over his head, throwing it in the same direction as the rifle.

Sandrine had scrambled to her feet, watching in amazement. "You're hurt," she said as Stroud turned around to face her.

He looked down at his chest, where blood pumped out in dark welts, and then he walked to the log and sat down. For a moment he watched her with an intense, curious expression, his mouth still sealed with the gray duct tape, and then placed one hand on his chest and lifted the fingers up to his gaze. Slowly, he slipped from the log into a kneeling position, and then he fell to one side and lay still.

Sandrine knelt beside him and felt his neck, cradling his head for a moment in her hand before she lowered the head to the earth.

"Get the rifle," Jessie said. "These guys killed each other."

Sandrine walked around the fire and bent slowly to pick up the assault rifle.

"You really shouldn't touch the belongings of the dead, but do you know how to shoot that thing?" Jessie asked.

Sandrine shook her head, looking at the gun in bewilderment.

"Quick. Let's see. This must be the safety. Every rifle has a safety of some kind." Jessie pointed a finger. "Push that thing forward, and be careful. I think the gun will shoot now. I hope so."

She looked at Jessie. "Something strange is going on. I can feel it."

"Something truly strange. You're talking to a dead person." Jessie was bending over Stroud. "Captain Stroud is totally dead," he said.

"He saved my life," Sandrine replied. "Now he's dead."

"Everybody's dead," Jessie said. "Including the one in the tent over there that you kicked. Remember him? He died too, but no one was there to notice. If you were a white man or a Mexican a hundred years ago, you could take their scalps. Apaches never did such barbaric things, though maybe your French ancestors did back east. And across the river more ghosts have been made, though not Alison or Jake yet. I feel their lives still." Jessie pulled a pouch out of his pocket and drew a line of corn pollen on the ground between them and the bodies, the pollen looking white in the light from the dying fire and disappearing seconds after it touched the earth. Abruptly Jessie became the wolf again, crouching on the big log with his tail curled beneath his hind quarters, his yellow eyes glittering menacingly. Just as suddenly he rose to his feet and was the human Jessie. "But then again," he said, "nobody is dead. I wish I could control that changing business. I've never heard of anything like this, have you?"

Sandrine took the rifle and held it close to the firelight. "Of course not. Maybe it's because of what you were doing, the pretend vision quest. We can't help Captain Stroud, but maybe we can help Mr. Nashoba. We should disappear before the others come back. They will have heard those shots."

"How am I doing now?"

Sandrine looked curiously at him. "What do you mean?"

"As an animal helper?"

"I think you need to study."

26 Shorty Luke lounged in Avrum Goldberg's wickiup. A small juniper fire in the center filled the lodge with the sweet aroma of cedar, and Shorty watched the faint white smoke curling toward a hole in the roof. Lying back on the elk skin, he luxuriated in comfortable warmth, the dry grass underneath the skin thick and soft. "You were mostly right, Avrum," Shorty said. "For maybe the first time since I met you I got to say you were mostly right. They should've listened to you. Boy, those dried plums hit the spot, don't they?"

Avrum sat cross-legged on a bear skin on the opposite side of the fire. He reached to place a willow basket closer to Shorty. "I'm glad you like my plums. Everybody would be eating those if the council had listened. Instead of lard and fried bread and all of that artery-clogging white man's food."

Shorty dropped a handful of dried plums into his mouth and chewed for a moment, his eyes wandering around the portion of the wickiup he could see without turning his head too much. "You really make that bow and those arrows?" He nodded toward a dozen arrows lying by a deerskin quiver and a bow standing upright beside them. "They look just like some I saw in the tribal museum. You do that flint knapping with an antler like the old ones used to?"

"Yes, Shorty, of course I did it traditionally, and don't think I don't know when you're mocking me. Those points are all white flint. The foreshafts are mulberry, and the arrows cane. Like they're supposed to be. It may not mean anything to you, but the bow is a highly reflexed forty-three-inch double-curved with corded sinew backing, made out of mountain mulberry and liberally rubbed with bear fat."

"Bear fat? Jeez, you're serious about this stuff. What kind of feathers are those? They look like different kinds."

Avrum looked closely at his friend to see if he was being taunted again. "Each arrow has buzzard, turkey, and red-tailed hawk feathers, one of each. In the beginning the animals gave those feathers to your ancestors."

Shorty nodded, still studying the hunting tools. "Yeah. I think I remember. Grandmother told us she was going to make bows and arrows for us, and she went out to gather mulberry shafts and cane and flint. I remember being a little suspicious, but she taught us well, didn't she? She made a groove in a rock and heated the wood until she could straighten in it the groove. She made the points out of white flint like you, and she glued and tied them to the arrow foreshafts with creosote gum and sinew. She used creosote gum and sinew on the feathers, too. The bow she made out of mulberry and sinew, and when she sat two finished arrows down they magically became eight arrows. She taught us how to shoot them. 'Never, ever hold more than two arrows in your hand, she said.' She was very old, and still she taught us how to make the tools for hunting and how to dress the deer and cure the hide and everything. She taught us everything. I remember it was cold then, and there was just the beginning of winter snows on the ground. We wouldn't have survived. My moccasins were hard with ice in the morning when I started my first hunt. The frozen pine needles broke beneath my feet, and I thought the animals were probably laughing at all the noise I made. But when I shot an arrow, it went right to the mark."

"Shorty the story thief," Avrum said. "Pretty soon you'll be the hero of every origin story."

"Stories belong to all of us," Shorty replied. "The one who tells the story is the hero, but so is the one who hears. Stories are honored in the telling and hearing. Nice work on those things, Avrum; you'll be an Injun yet. You ever hunted with them?"

Avrum shook his head. "I didn't make them for hunting."

"Then why did you make them?"

Avrum looked at the fire, remaining silent.

"I wonder why we never gave you an Indian name," Shorty said musingly. "Most white men around Indians this long would have an Indian name. There was that preacher we used to call 'Takes-It-In-The-Ass,' though he couldn't understand Indian. There must be something special about you, Avrum."

"Thank the Creator for sparing me that."

"When we get back, I'm going to have a naming ceremony for you. A real one. I think you're almost grown up now. About to go on your first war party."

"What?"

"There's something else I've been wondering about," Shorty added. "You wear those loincloths and high moccasins and sometimes that nice buckskin shirt, and in the winter you put on those deerskin pants, but I've been curous about something. Don't your balls get cold in the summer with just those loincloths? Our grandmothers never told us about how our grandfathers handled that."

Avrum looked from the fire to Shorty.

"I mean, I think my balls would freeze right up." Shorty poked the fire with a cedar splinter.

"Don't you know any stories about that?" Avrum asked.

"Sensitive question, huh? Probably afraid you'll get that kind of name, something like Winter Balls Froze." Shorty tossed the cedar stick into the fire. "We both should've known the council would think of those problems about being a theme tribe. There's no getting around reality sometimes."

"Good change of subjects, Shorty, several in fact. But I think I had most of the council sold on a traditional life for a while there. Everybody but Two-Bears." Avrum sighed. "The Black Mountain people could have been world famous and lived correctly at the same time. We could have revived the families and clan structures, eaten healthy foods, and avoided the path that's killing everybody. But people had to worry about the fact that traditional Indians don't have microwaves or televisions or dirt bikes. Dirt bikes?"

"Kids love those things, Avrum. I know, I hate the damned noisy things, but kids, who can understand kids? I don't know about kids these days. They don't respect their elders or want to hear stories."

"Dirt bikes make about the same noise as a chain saw."

"Avrum, I didn't bring up the chain saw. Carlos brought that up. He's the one didn't like the idea of whittling away on a tree for a week or cutting a ring around it till it fell. It didn't take people long to understand that having more money wouldn't mean anything if they couldn't spend it. That's not a difficult concept, even for an Indian. Although that idea about Scottsdale condos almost sold them."

"There wouldn't be any need to cut trees down if we lived traditionally." Avrum shook his head. "And not in condos. Everybody's priorities got confused."

"You're Jewish," Shorty said.

"Now you're anti-Semitic all of a sudden?"

"No. But those council people are all old enough to remember when you came here the same time as that other white guy, that preacher. They remember you're a Jewish anthropologist from New York who sometimes wore a funny little hat and wouldn't eat the things they ate. Now you're like one of us, but those old people never forget. And people are suspicious of the funny way you dress, not to mention those rumors about Mrs. Edwards."

"*I* dress funny? What rumors?"

"I don't have to tell you about rumors. But don't worry; nobody's going to talk out in the open about that old woman. No one has the guts."

"Mrs. Edwards isn't so old."

Shorty rolled onto one elbow and glanced across the fire at Goldberg, a slight smile playing on his lips, and then he collapsed onto his back again, dropped several dried plums in his mouth, closed his eyes, and chewed slowly. He took a deep breath. "I like my chain saw, Avrum. Mrs. Edwards likes her satellite dish. All the kids like those new basketball shoes. Tali just got that microwave oven after all these years. She says she's going to try to cook a Thanksgiving turkey in it, says she read that if the aluminum foil doesn't touch the edge of the microwave you can even use aluminum foil on the turkey. It's just the way it is. You need to start living in the present. This ain't no disco, this ain't no theme park." Shorty was nodding rhythmically.

Avrum let his head fall onto his knees and stared at the fire.

Shorty rose onto one elbow again to look at his friend sympathetically. "But it was really a great idea, Avrum. A brilliant idea. Just ahead of its time, that's all."

"Turning the clock back two hundred years is ahead of its time?"

"Throwing the clock out. That was the white man's idea in the first place for Indians. It's still the white man's goal, you know. I have to admit I was impressed by your argument at first, but I thought about it. I agree with what people said. People ain't going to agree to live without down vests, televisions, cellular phones, four-wheel drives. But I got to say this wickiup is pretty comfortable. Gets cold in the winter though, hey?"

"No."

"Where's the insulation? I put R-19 in my house, with moisture barriers, floor and attic, too. And we still get a little cold now and then. Takes three cords of wood at least for a winter, and most people use more. Must get freezing in here. Where'd you get the bearskin, anyway?"

"Roadkill. I found it and skinned it out after a white man with a pickup hit it and left it beside the road. Snow makes insulation, Shorty. Your people lived for countless generations in wickiups, and lived very well."

Shorty looked into the empty basket. "Ah, so that's where you got the bear fat for the bow. Not a good idea to mess around with bears, Avrum. I'll have to tell you those stories; surprised Mrs. Edwards didn't tell you. Maybe I should get the grandkids and pick plums like these, dry them this way. They ought to be ripe pretty soon, don't you think?"

"Already are down in the canyon."

"Nobody goes down there."

"Where you think I got those? Chokecherries, too."

"You went down there?"

Avrum nodded. "Not too far. Just about ten miles."

"I thought only L.R. went down there anymore. Say, what if just you and me took a walk down there? We could bring back a lot of plums and chokecherries, and you could take that bow and those arrows for any kind of emergency that might come up. What you doing tomorrow?"

Avrum watched Shorty for a moment, as if assessing his friend's seriousness. "War party, huh? Why do you mock me in front of people?" he asked. "And why are you mocking me now, as if I didn't know what you were really talking about?"

Shorty pushed the empty basket to one side and sat up. "It's my job, Avrum. I thought you always understood that. You know it's not personal. We're friends. It's a friend's job." Shorty seemed to ponder for a moment. "I think it helps keep you safe, and sort of gives us both a role, you know. It's kind of like making up the story as we go."

Avrum looked at the bow and the arrows and quiver lying on a skin beside it. "Okay," he said. "As you say, I think we need to go down there tomorrow, but it's too far to go and come back in one day. We'll have to camp out one night."

"No problem."

"Be here an hour before daylight. You know the way down there?"

Shorty rose to his feet, plunging his hands into his pants pockets. "Sure. I'll bring a bag for all that fruit. It may be just what Domingo needs, perhaps. Did I tell you about my cat?"

"Yes, Shorty, you've told me about Mingo many times. You know that's a Choctaw word, don't you?"

"No kidding? Well, the funniest thing happened. Mingo died. I don't know why, but the other morning he was just dead in that basket Bernice made for him."

"Cats do that, Shorty. Especially old cats."

"Well, that's not the funny part. Me and Bernice had a funeral ceremony for Mingo. He was a good cat. Bernice cried, and I tell you I came pretty close. Did I tell you where I got Mingo?"

"Yes. Several times."

"We buried him in the backyard, a couple feet down in the ground, the way everybody does. In the dirt, you know, no box or anything, and packed it down good. Bernice put a little cross up. She's a real Christian. Now, you won't believe it, but the next day that darned cat was laying across the front porch as clean and beautiful as the day we got him."

"Still dead?"

"Sure. You ever seen a dead cat come back to life? Stiff as a board."

"Somebody was playing a trick on you, Shorty."

"I don't know. I mean he was so clean he smelled like roses. You know what I think?"

"Yes."

"Witches."

The two men stared at the fire in silence for a long time until Shorty spoke again. "If I learned one thing in Hollywoood," he said, "it's that you got to avoid cleeshayed plots. I never had no big roles, you know, just that fall-off-your-horse-white-man-speaks-with-forked-tongue stuff, but I kept track, and it was always the same old thing. You'd think the guys who write those scripts would worry about it. They should've had the white man scalping Indians the way it really was, and falling off his horse, since Indians didn't fall off horses too much and half those cavalry boys were Irish from New York. The truth would've been original and more interesting."

Avrum sighed. "Shorty," he said, "it was the clichés that made the movies popular. The problem with you Indians is that you don't understand that. I try and try to convince you that you should live the way your ancestors did two hundred years ago, but nobody listens. I could teach you all how to do that, but nobody cares, just like tonight. You all think I'm eccentric. If the Black Mountain tribe started living traditionally again, the way your ancestors really did, you could all forget the casino, forget selling your sacred animals for profit, forget selling anything, because you'd be rolling in grant money, endowment money, and tourist money. We could get a pile of grant money just to convert everything back to the way it used to be. And everybody in the Western world would come here to see real Indians. There would be Germans and Frenchmen and Italians crawling all over this reservation with fistfuls of money. Tourists would be annoying, but you'd all be rich and at the same time you'd have much better lives. No more junk food or alcohol, except what you made yourselves from mescal. No more exposure to chemicals. No more sending your children off to schools in foreign places."

"What do those tourists buy with fistfuls of dollars? Heck, you don't have to convince me, Avrum, just those council members and the rest of the whole reservation. And you saw that it ain't going to work. Nobody said this tonight, but face it. You think elders like Mrs. John Edwards are going to let you teach them how to live traditionally? You're forgetting that change is traditional, too. We were running around on foot until those Spanish brought up horses, and then everything we did was on horseback. Everybody forgot we didn't use to have horses. Look at those old pictures of the warriors. Those were proud men and women, Avrum, and you notice nobody's dressed like you. Every one of them is wearing cotton clothes and holding rifles. That's tradition, too. We all know you mean well, but this theme thing just ain't practical. Now, not to change the subject, but what I'm worried about is what's happening right now, in this story." He stirred the coals with a splinter of cedar, and the smell rose up toward the smoke hole. "I want your honest opinion."

"I'm an anthropologist, Shorty, what the heck do I know about stories?"

"I guess I should say I rest my case," Shorty said, "but I'm thinking maybe Spider and the Twins can save it. We don't want the usual violence and retribution stuff, but imagine Jake in buckskin and that other guy in metal, like the story says. It could work that way."

"Scientists don't invent stories, Shorty. We record them."

"I rest my case, Doctor Dances with Endowments." Shorty grinned. "That's good."

"Doctor Grantheart," Avrum replied.

"Last of the Mo-Traditionals."

"A Man Called Cash."

"Money Highway."

"Plenty Yo."

"PocoHondas."

"Pocahonkers."

"Enough already."

27 Jake felt his skin melting. The soft hands had gone away, and he was being cooked by a black sun. Four times he had thought he was awake, each time hearing what seemed a different song in the same voice. In his dream he sought his grandmother, drawing her face close from when he was small, but though she smiled she faded quickly. His body was soft, like melting plastic, and he remembered the old Choctaw man across the river. *Chahta*, they said. *Chahta*. With the memory, the old man approached, his broad hat drawn down low over his thin, dark face. "We don't send this dream, Grandson," the old man said. "But the Grandmother and I are watching your shadows."

Hands seemed to be probing his flesh, molding his bones. He lay next to a pool and rose on an elbow to look at himself in the reflecting water. His head was a ball of mud, without hair, nose, or mouth. He thought of the mud along the Yazoo River in Mississippi, a thick, black mud that smelled of decay and seemed prepared to suck you to endless depths. Along the banks it cracked in deep chasms and flakes. In the watery reflection, his arms ended in clubs without hands or fingers, and he felt his legs as rolled clay, without feet or toes. The heat struck him again, and his body was probed and bent, changed, pulled and pinched. Two hands appeared in the air before him, the left one holding a rifle and the right a bow and quiver of arrows. He reached upward for the bow and mountain lion quiver, and a steel splinter of pain shot from his feet through his groin, chest, and head.

Jake awoke on the ground, the warm summer dampness rising through the earth's humus into his body. Thunder was smashing and rattling in all directions, and lightning cracked so hard that he felt its hissing blades. He'd come to a stop in a deep hole left where a pine had fallen during winter, and the long, twisting roots of the great tree hung all about him, shrouding him so that he looked up at the night as if through a mass of spidery arms.

He became aware of a measured tread close by, and the silhouette of a man crossed the slope above him near the lip of the hole. The outline of the man was angular and sharp, and Jake had the impression that the one who hunted him was made of metal. The hard line of a rifle cut the man's shadow.

Jake breathed carefully, his body still burning and soft, knowing that he could not move regardless of what his enemy chose to do. But the shadow disappeared, and he listened as the footsteps continued beyond hearing.

He had been shot once in Vietnam, a sniper's bullet slicing at an angle through his hip. But he had never lost consciousness and never doubted that he'd be healed quickly. This was different. His body seemed to have been dismembered in some way and then thrown hastily back together so that the pieces didn't match. Pain had begun to gather and flower inside his head until he could hear the crackling flame.

The woman appeared at the edge of the hole he lay in. Her black hair was extraordinarily long, falling straight from its middle part all the way to her feet and hanging partially over her shoulders to shroud the edges of her breasts and thighs. She glistened darkly everywhere as though wet, and when lightning flashed he could see her black eyes narrow and shining, her smile tentative.

There was something familiar about the woman, a feeling as though he had known her for much of his life, and as he realized this the flame shifted from his head to the center of his chest. Lightning coursed through the clouds again, and he saw that she was streaming water, as though she had stepped at that instant from the river. Her hair was a dark waterfall, and at her feet rivulets of water poured over the lip of the hole.

The woman held out both hands toward him, and a storm of yellow, black, blue, and white butterflies erupted into the air, scattering in four directions. For the first time she smiled so that he saw her teeth and the sunken shadows of her cheeks. He tried to move one of his own arms to reach in her direction, but found no response. Thunder cracked right overhead, and the angry snap of the explosion became a burst of what he knew were rifle shots. The woman was gone, and once again he felt himself thrown into an oven, his skin seeming to melt from his bones.

He knew then the clean bones of his body, and he thought of the bone pickers of his Choctaw ancestors. If he died here in this alien place, his relatives would never know where his bones were. His bones would never be clean. His shadows would drift. Souleater would find him.

28 Mrs. Edwards lowered Domingo into the enamel bathtub, where the sliver of his body seemed to float in the deep water. Struck by the heat, he cringed and raised his eyes in supplication, making no sound. In response, the old lady dipped an aluminum pot into the water and poured it over his head. When she had repeated the action twice, she unscrewed the cap on a plastic bottle and squirted blue liquid onto the top of his head.

"Dish detergent," she said, starting to massage the top of his head and continuing down through the thin gray hair. After a moment she dipped the pot again and poured until no more soap came from Domingo's hair. Then she lathered up a washcloth and began to scrub his body.

Domingo tried to summon the strength to protest such invasion of his modesty, but he found that his tongue lay in his mouth like a smooth rock. Bereft of voice, he surrendered to the cloth and hands that sought out the crevices of his body with hard administrations very much, he thought, the way he had washed Shorty's cat.

Finally the old woman splashed more water over his body for several moments before she dipped her arms into the tub and lifted him out with one hand beneath his buttocks and the other behind his shoulders.

Standing him on his feet with an arm around his back, she toweled him until he was mostly dry and then lifted and carried him to her wide bed. He observed the process as though it were someone else's body that was being treated like a newborn, feeling detached and increasingly at peace.

When he lay with clean-smelling sheets tucked up to his chin, his hair damp upon the pillow, Domingo felt his body begin to tingle like a foot awakening from sleep. His flesh hovered around the bones of his body, muscle riding upon his cheeks and the skin unattached to the smooth bowl of his skull. He wondered if he had felt that way for a long time without knowing it or if this was a new thing caused by Mrs. Edwards. The knot in his chest was entirely gone, and there seemed to be a warm fluid pulsing from the bottom of his thin belly to the uppermost corners of his equally thin torso.

"Don't worry," the old woman said. She stood beside the bed braiding one half of her long, silver hair. "The pieces will come together, but first each part has to recognize itself. More important things are happening." She finished the braid and tied the end with red yarn before starting on the other side. "They're all going down to that place," Mrs. Edwards said. "I dreamed about her last night—she was with Jacob—and about all the rest of them. Jessie and Jacob first, and now Avrum and Shorty Luke are going there, too. I dreamed of spiders and the granddaughter. Others I could not recognize."

"I'm hungry," Domingo replied. Outside a rooster crowed and a gang of shrieking children ran past the house. The front door of the house opened, and from the other room a voice said, "Grandmother?"

Mrs. Edwards patted Domingo on the head and went into the front of the house, where Tali stood in the middle of the floor. She wore turquoise earrings and a white shell necklace, with a blue denim shirt tucked into a long blue skirt, and the tips of moccasins just showing beneath the skirt. Her black hair was woven into a single long braid down the middle of her back. A sash of the same colors as Jake's belt was tied around the middle.

"You are the most beautiful woman in North America," Mrs. Edwards said. "Why don't you get rid of that husband legally and find a good man you can live with? Sit down."

Tali sat on a deep couch covered with Navajo blankets, and the old woman disappeared into the kitchen. A moment later she returned with two cups, handing one to Tali without speaking.

"I'm worried," Tali said.

"Bear and owl dreams. I know," Mrs. Edward replied. "Everything is coming together now. I thought this would happen. I saw a wolf, too. And Jessie."

"Jacob is in trouble." Tali smoothed her skirt and sipped the coffee.

"You always have been in love with that guy."

"And you've always opposed Jacob. Why, besides the obvious?"

Mrs. Edwards stopped blowing on the coffee and raised her head. "Because Jacob Nashoba always opposed me. From the first day he came, when he could barely talk, I felt it and saw it in his eyes. He wanted you for himself, and he wasn't one of us."

"I married him, Grandmother. He was supposed to want me for himself."

"But not to take you away."

"Jacob didn't want to take me away. He loves this place, these mountains."

"He loves that river. He built that house to take you away from us. Look at your home, Granddaughter. It looks like those forts the army used to build to fight Indians. It's not proper."

"Why didn't you ever tell me this before?"

Mrs. Edwards stared past Tali. "Because you've always done the opposite of what I said. If I said I didn't like your new house, you would have loved it the more. I hoped you'd tire of it and leave it for him to live in, but instead you threw him out and invited your daughters' families to move in. I saw it was no use, but at least he was alone then."

"I made Jacob leave because he hurt me," Tali said. "He couldn't help himself, and he wouldn't let anybody else help him. I made him to go to Phoenix, to the Indian center, but he wouldn't really talk to anyone about it. Not even to me. So I made him leave, but I never hated him."

"You love that man."

Tali nodded. "Jacob is a fine man. He's good, he cares about other people. More than himself."

"But he didn't care enough about you to find medicine for his anger."

Tali set the coffee on a little table by the couch. "You were angry because he didn't come to you, Grandmother. I never understood that before. You wanted to help him and he wouldn't let you. That's it, isn't it?"

The old lady lowered her eyes to the floor. "I felt Jacob Nashoba's strength and illness both the first time I saw him. I knew it was too late to help him, and that's why I told you to throw him away at once. But I wanted to try to help him because of you, and because, because of other things I could see coming a long time ago."

"Will Jacob be okay? He's gone down to the river after Jessie and Alison."

"I don't know. What does 'okay' mean? My grandson Jessie is not okay. Maybe Alison will be strong enough to help your husband. I can't see enough."

There was a loud groan from the back room, and the old lady got to her feet. "Come and visit Domingo," she said.

Tali followed Mrs. Edwards into the back room, where Domingo Perez lay in bed, his hair spread on a white pillow, a sheet pulled up to his chin, and his large eyes staring at them.

"I can't feel my heart," he said. "It isn't beating."

"It's nothing to worry about," Mrs. Edwards replied.

Tali walked to the side of the bed. "Hello, Uncle Domingo," she said. "You look better. Let me feel your wrist."

Domingo snaked a scrawny arm out from beneath the sheets and held it out to her. "My chest is empty," he said. "She put a powder on my food." He pointed a twig of a finger at Mrs. Edwards.

Tali took his wrist in her hand and held it. After a moment she looked puzzled. She laid the wrist on the sheet and moved her two fingers to a spot on Domingo's neck. Finally she turned to Mrs. Edwards with a strange expression.

"He's right," she said. "I can't find any pulse."

"Just temporary," the old lady answered. She approached and laid her palm across Domingo's forehead. "The knot that held everything together has dissolved, so now it will take time for all those things to join with one another again the way it should be, without the knot. You will be fine, Domingo Perez. Don't be such a baby."

"How do you feel, Uncle?" Tali asked.

He rolled his eyes toward her. "I need something, but I don't know what it is. Where's my brother? I need to see Shorty Luke."

"Shorty Luke is on a trip. He'll be back soon," Mrs. Edwards responded from beside Tali.

"I'm going to die," Domingo whispered. "Maybe I'm already dead, like Mingo."

"Mingo?" Tali looked at the old lady.

"No," Mrs. Edwards said. "Domingo Perez is the surviving twin, remember? Now sleep."

Domingo closed his eyes and began to breathe regularly.

Back in the other room, Tali stood by the front door for a moment. "Did you put powder on Uncle Domingo's food?"

Mrs. Edward nodded. "Brown granulated sugar and a couple spoonfuls of ground-up *teonanacatl*. Nothing too special."

"What is that last thing? I've never heard of it."

The old woman smiled thinly. "Just something I learned from one of those who lived in the Mexican mountains a long time ago. It's very effective."

"Maybe when Jacob comes back he'll let you help him. I'll talk with him."

"Yes, maybe. When he comes back." Seeing Tali's face, the old woman strengthened her voice. "Perhaps together we can convince him."

"Xavier asked me to be a candidate for tribal council," Tali said.

"Xavier is a fool, then," Mrs. Edward replied. Seeing her granddaughter's dismay, she added, "You are too strong for Two-Bears, and too smart. He thinks he can use you because you are smart and beautiful and that he can control you because you're younger and related to him. But you'll be tribal chairman soon if you get on the council so people can hear you. I like that idea. Xavier's days as chairman are over. He has his hands full right now anyway."

29   Alison arose from behind a log and said very quietly, "Sandrine."

The Frenchwoman flinched and swung the rifle. "Alison," she whispered. "You are alive. Why didn't you run away?"

"We have to help my grandfather. I can't run away."

"I was looking for both of you," Sandrine said. "I thought I would go up this side of the river before I crossed, because that one named Jensen crossed below."

"How did you get free?"

"There's no time to tell you now. Where's your grandfather?"

"That way," Alison jerked her head upstream. "I'll show you. But we have to be careful because Jensen's looking for him and for me, too."

"I'll go first. I don't mind at all." As he spoke, Jessie stepped from behind a tree. "Being a fullblooded Indian, I have the uncanny ability to move through sylvan settings without breaking twigs. My four-legged brothers and sisters and the winged people tell me everything that happens. I have mystical connections with Mother Earth that white people will never fathom. I can see in the dark."

"Give me a break," Sandrine said.

"What?" Alison looked at the Frenchwoman curiously.

"I was talking to him." Sandrine pointed toward Jessie.

Jessie grinned. Now he had become a wolf again, still standing on two legs and leaning against the tree, his erect penis pink and swollen.

"You're disgusting," Sandrine said.

"What? Talking to him who? Who's disgusting?"

"Jessie. We have to go."

"Why can't I see my cousin?" Alison scoured the slope with her eyes.

"I don't know, Alison. Perhaps one of Jessie's jokes."

Jessie had dropped to all fours and was watching over his shoulder. When the women began to move, he ran a few yards up river and stopped, scratched a front shoulder with a hind leg, and looked back again. He gestured toward the higher ridge with his head and trotted away from the trail.

"I think maybe we should get higher," Sandrine said, "away from the trail in case any of them come back on this side. They'll probably be on the trail."

"Good idea." Alison was looking at the Frenchwoman strangely. "You seem to be watching something up there."

Sandrine glanced back up the slope to where Jessie stood, the lower half of his body human but the top half wolf. "Jessie says we should go higher," she answered.

Jessie lifted a paw to his lips and grinned before he began walking rapidly northward along the steep sidehill. Holding the AR-15 at her side, Sandrine followed, with Alison behind her.

"I don't mean to be rude, but this isn't going to be one of those stories," Alison said between breaths to Sandrine's back, "where the white person comes in and saves the Indians. There's too many of those already."

Sandrine spoke without pausing. "If anybody saves anybody here, it will be Mr. Nashoba and Jessie and you. And you're all Indians, I think."

"Jessie got you and me into this."

"Don't give up on Jessie," Sandrine said breathlessly. "Or yourself."

"I think my grandfather's dead, too. I think they killed him."

Sandrine saw Jessie stop and shake his head vigorously. He was all human now. She looked back at Alison. "I wish you would stop saying that. I don't think Jake Nashoba is dead."

"We have to try to find him."

"We will, Alison. Maybe we'll move a mile or so on this side and then wade across the river. I believe they're all on the other side."

"How do you know so much? Maybe we should go back to camp and shoot them when they return."

Sandrine stopped and turned around. "Do you want to shoot those men, or do you want to find your grandfather?"

When Alison didn't respond, Sandrine said, "Maybe I have a vision, and maybe we can find your grandfather without shooting anyone."

"You have a vision?"

Jessie waited a few yards away in the shadows, his tail curled around him and his yellow eyes intent upon the women. "After that," Jessie said, half-aloud, "the boy with the bow and arrows came down to the earth and slew all the monsters there. Ha ha ha ha."

30   Jensen walked the ridge and slope for an hour, looking for sign with his flashlight. In place of the sniper rifle he now carried his modified AR-15. The two men he'd sent back to check out the shots at camp had returned with the news. Peters, Nelson, Scully, Chris Martin, Stroud, and Vasello were now all dead, and the Frenchwoman was gone.

"Maybe we should just cut our losses and get out." Walter looked warily around them, probing the forest. "She's probably headed out to call the cops." His left shoulder was taped tightly to his chest, and his face was haggard.

"I don't think so," Jensen replied, studying Walter's bandaged arm with skepticism. "She's a tough one, and I doubt she'd abandon the Indian girl or the ranger. And if she did, it would take her at least a whole day to walk out even if she didn't get lost. The most important thing to remember here is that we're in a war." He ran a hand along the barrel of the AR-15. "Now there are three of us, or maybe I should say two and a half, since only Henry and I have two good arms. Five of our men are dead, KIA, not to mention our two unfortunate instructors. Our goal now is to find not just Jake Nashoba but also the two women. The reason for urgency should be rather clear. Each of us is implicated in, if not directly responsible for, eight deaths so far. It seems we just keep getting in deeper and deeper, doesn't it?" Jensen smiled at both of the very nervous men.

"Now, I have to admit that I don't have a lot of faith in either of you. If Jake Nashoba were at full strength and armed, I'd give us collectively a quite poor chance against him. If Stroud was alive, I'd give us zip. However."

Jensen held up the palm of his left hand. "Nashoba is not armed. We know that. Furthermore, I saw very clearly that I hit him with at least one of those sniper rounds. In the upper back and close to the dorsal spine, I think. My belief, therefore, is that Jake Nashoba is lying dead somewhere around here and that our chief worry—no pun intended—is now the two women, mere witnesses. I have faith in the probability that they won't abandon the girl's grandfather, that they are, in fact, searching for Jake Nashoba right now just as we shall soon be.

"Any comment?

"Good. Now, as I just said, ordinarily I would believe the women were headed back to the top as fast as they could go. But I'm sure Jake's granddaughter won't leave him like that, and I think the French woman will hang around to take care of the girl. Those women have a lot of guts, is my guess. More guts than brains, sadly.

"I may be very wrong, and if I am we are all fucked, but my plan is to keep searching for Nashoba's body, making all the noise we need to, until the women come to us."

"At least one of those women has a gun." Henry's round face looked very sad as he spoke.

"True, Henry, but how often do you think either of those girls has fired an assault rifle? In fact, we don't have any evidence that they even know how to fire a weapon, though the possibility does make our task more exciting."

"I don't like it." Walter held a rifle in his right hand and continued to look nervously about at the dim light of the forest. Below them the river slid with a fine, smooth sigh through the canyon. The tall pines leaned in black lines out over the lower gorge, backed by the dark wall of rock on the far side. In the nearly complete silence an elk's whistle came from far down the canyon, ending in a vague series of coughing sounds. A big raven made repeated circles above the tops of the trees over them.

Jensen ignored the comment. "There is a chance that they can fire that rifle and they might get one or two of us. Which one or two we have no way of knowing. Could be you, Walter, or me, or Henry. But isn't that what you paid your money for? Survival experience? It's going to be daylight in half an hour or so, and that will make everything much easier. We'll find poor Jake Nashoba, undoubtedly stiff as the proverbial board, and the women will find us. Then we'll have to start digging some deep holes before we leave. Understood? Excellent."

31

Shorty pulled his pickup into a clearing on the canyon rim a few minutes after the sun rose. Avrum Goldberg was out of the truck before it had completely stopped, and by the time Shorty reached the tailgate, Avrum had his small pack out and was swinging it onto his back.

"Let's go," the anthropologist said. "I know this creek. It'll take us to the bottom in forty minutes if we don't screw around."

Shorty dragged his own pack out of the open pickup bed and slipped his arms through the straps. "I know this creek, too, Avrum, but I don't feel plums. I don't see visions of ripe chokecherries."

"What do you see, then?" Avrum impatiently adjusted his waist belt. He carried the bow and two arrows in one hand, with his quiver of mountain lion skin with more arrows strapped to the side of the pack.

"I see the dreams I had last night. I see a story, but I don't know how it ends."

"You always see a story, but I don't know what you're talking about. Did you lock the truck?"

"Did you notice I'm wearing deerskin, Avrum?"

The anthropologist looked hard at his friend. "How could I have noticed? It was dark and you had that jacket on. Now I see you're wearing deerskin, and if you think I don't know why, you're crazy. Remember who the expert on tradition is here."

"You still out-traditional me, Dr. Goldberg."

"I'm the one with the arrows. Let's go." The anthropologist started down a draw below the truck, saying over his shoulder, "What dreams?"

"A metal man, the one whose clothes make noise and who carries a rifle. A dream of a dark metal shield and spear. Of one eye like the moon. In part of the dream, sun and water were fighting."

"Where's your rifle? You always carry that rifle, Shorty."

"A rifle is useless today, my friend. Useless for me, anyway. As you say, you're the one with the arrows."

The anthropologist stopped and turned to look at Shorty Luke. That was the second time Shorty had called him friend. The Black Mountain people did not use such words lightly, and they ridiculed white men for doing so.

"So you know why we're going down there?"

Shorty nodded. "Of course. The old lady told me, sort of. A dream, I guess you'd call it. I'm not sure who I'll eventually tell the story to."

"Eventually?"

Shorty gestured down the draw with the back of his hand. "The problem is that since we know all of the old stories we know how they will always end, but all kinds of little things and even big things can change between the beginning and end. And it depends on who's telling and who's listening, right? I think we'd better hurry, though, because I don't know all of this one."

"I find it interesting to hear the biggest story thief in the world say such things, Shorty. Since when was any story not your property?"

The cool dawn was pierced by a bugling elk, the call as thin and fine as the air itself, followed by celebratory coyote barking. A raven swooped onto a pine branch above the men's heads and croaked a shrill, twisted word at them.

"The world is a big place. We'd better hurry," Shorty repeated. "It's happening now. Do you miss your parents often?"

32   At nine-thirty in the morning Xavier leaped out of sleep. He lunged across the blonde in the bed beside him and grabbed the phone. The woman stirred and turned into him, and as he heard Sam Baca's voice he was aware of her breasts pressed into his chest.

"This better be goddamned important, Sam," he said into the phone. "Elk Creek? Oh God, Donna."

"Yeah, Elk Creek. What?" Sam's voice had an irritated pitch to it.

"Nothing." Xavier shifted the phone to his other hand and ran his fingers along the woman's bare shoulder as she slid further down in the bed.

"Oh God," Xavier moaned.

"What the hell, Xavier?" Sam said. "You need to get over here."

Two-Bears laid the phone down on the bedside table and put both hands on the woman's head. "Sweet Jesus," he said. "I have to go, Sweetheart. Emergency."

From the phone, Sam Baca's voice said faintly, "What the fuck's going on?"

Two-Bears reached across and hung up the phone.

The woman's head slid back up to the pillow, her mouth moving across his fleshy chest and nibbling on the soft line of his jaw. "Now?" she replied.

"I'm afraid so, Donna. Tribal emergency." Xavier Two-Bears looked at his suit hanging over the back of a chair and then at the film producer's bra dangling from the top of a cowboy boot by the television.

The woman rose up on one elbow so that her breast pushed against his cheek. "Are you sure?"

He nodded, causing her nipple to move up and down. "I'm afraid so."

She changed positions so that her breasts framed his face. "Are you coming right back?"

When he tried to reply, his word were muffled and unclear. She slid back down and traced his mouth with her tongue. "I'm sorry, dear, but I didn't quite understand," she said, moving her mouth down to the swelling of his belly.

"Got to go," Two-Bears said almost pleadingly. He moved one foot beneath the sheet toward the edge of the bed.

"Didn't your people traditionally have several wives?" the woman said, her head disappearing beneath the sheet. From out of sight, she added, "I'll bet you could satisfy several."

Two-Bears closed his eyes and held his breath. Finally he said, "Holy shit, Donna, I really have to go. Emergency."

She appeared again, smiling up at him. "You're a big man, Xavier Two-Bears."

He patted her shoulder and slid a foot out onto the floor, carefully moving his other leg after the first. When he was sitting on the side of the bed, he felt her breasts against his back and her sharp teeth on the lobe of his ear. "Go take care of your tribal emergency," she said. "I'll be back from L.A. in five days, if I go."

"Wonderful," he replied. "Ouch. I really mean it. That's wonderful. If you go?"

"Be ready to have your brains fucked out, Chief."

He turned and stared at her. "I'll be ready, but I'm not a chief. Don't you have to go to L.A.?"

She pushed her arms around his chest from behind and slid her hands all the way down.

An hour later, Xavier Two-Bears stood in the lobby of the tribal game and fish office, surrounded by dead animals. He wore the same suit he'd had on the night before, the pants and coat wrinkled, and the white shirt open at the neck. His hair was pulled back and tied hastily with yarn so that strands of hair stuck out on the top and sides.

Two-Bears looked with revulsion at the antlered heads and stuffed four-legged creatures that crowded the room. Sam had built a low wooden stage that took up half of the room, leaving just a narrow space in front of the desk where the staff sold permits and answered questions. Expensive brochures in bright colors touted the hunting and fishing on the reservation, mostly elk hunting. The stage had different levels, so that wolf stood snarling twelve inches higher than bobcat, who crept stealthily toward porcupine lower still. Eagle and red-tailed hawk rested on dead cedar branches bolted to the wall, looking down on the dead gathering of four-legged people. Great horned owl perched stiffly on a mortared niche slightly lower than the other birds. A large-antlered mule deer posed with dead dignity close to a sinewy mountain lion silhouetted by the large front window.

Looking at the wolf, Xavier shivered. The animal seemed to wink at him, and he glanced quickly away. He hated to come to the office and usually did everything he could to avoid it. Each time he entered the room, the stuffed creatures brought back a swarm of his grandmother's stories like the ones about Big Owl killing babies, the horrible monster called Broad Horns, even the hideous thing she'd called Vulva Woman who had teeth between her legs. The memory caused him to shudder.

There was a story for every animal, usually about how they had been people and how they had helped his own ancestors or, most often, how dangerous they were. There were so many rules to follow it made you dizzy. Remembering his grandmother's stories, he shook his head at the old lady's thoughtlessness in telling a story like Vulva Woman to a boy. If he hadn't been as strong as he was, it could have scarred him for life. He could have become an Indian monk and never had a day or night like the ones that had just passed. He'd been surprised when the *National Geographic* producer had invited him to dinner, more surprised when she suggested they go back to his house for drinks, and shocked almost out of his senses by what followed. He'd never known a woman who didn't try to feign innocence of some kind. Donna Green had been laughing and unzipping his pants almost before the front door had closed. They'd been awake until dawn, slept several hours, ate scrambled eggs, and went back to bed. The past day and night were a blur of extreme feelings, including pain. What if she didn't really go to L.A.? What if she just stayed in his house and was there when he got back? The story of Vulva Woman returned, and he shook his head to clear it. She was so beautiful, maybe the only woman he'd ever known who was more beautiful without clothes than with them. And she was insatiable.

More images and words rose out of his memory of his mother's mother. Black Thunder, Black Water, Eagle catching up humans in his great claws and smashing them against rocks to feed to his young.

"Chief Two-Bears?" a voice said, and Xavier jumped. He looked away from the animals to a young man behind the desk. It was the new kid they'd just hired out of college. He wasn't from the Black Mountain tribe, but he was some kind of Indian at least, a Lakota or something like that, and he was a wildlife behavioralist.

"Oh, hello. I let myself in, and I'm not a chief. Just tribal chairman. I told you that last time."

"Sorry, sir. Did you hear about the sheep?"

"Sheep?"

"Yeah, we located a herd of about fifteen endangered desert bighorn in the upper canyon. Big find, and they look good."

Xavier nodded. "Great, excellent. Sam wanted me to meet him here. Woke me up on my day off, so it better be more than sheep."

"Oh, yeah. He's in back now waiting for you."

"Keep up the good work, like those sheep and . . . things." Xavier pushed past the swinging gate between the desks and disappeared through a door. The office on the other side of the door was empty, so he crossed the room and opened a further door.

Sam Baca sat in a folding chair in the bare, concrete-floored room. He was staring at an elk head, a really big one with several points on each side of the rack. Dried blood appeared to have been painted on the concrete where the head had been dragged from the wide garage-type door at the rear of the room. Sam's face was sweaty and exhausted looking.

"This better be damned important, Sam," Xavier said. "What's this about Elk Creek?"

Sam raised his eyes reluctantly, without getting up from the chair. His hands were folded over his knees, and his shoulders curved. "I waited as long as I thought I could this morning before I called. Must have been some night. I tried to find you yesterday, but you weren't answering your phone."

Two-Bears shrugged. "Had to go to Show Low. I forgot the damned phone."

"Funny. I thought I saw your truck in your driveway yesterday."

"What the hell did you wake me up for?" Two-Bears looked around the room.

"I think Jake knows everything," Sam said.

Xavier stepped forward unsteadily. "What the hell do you mean? What's he know?"

Sam straightened. "Shorty told Jake. I saw them having a big conversation in front of the lodge when that meeting was going on two nights ago. I couldn't make out the words, but I saw Jake pull out one of these and show it to Shorty." Sam dug a rifle casing from his pocket.

231

"Where's Nashoba now?"

"He headed down toward the river yesterday, like I told you. I watched him go. That's why I was trying to reach you."

"After I told him not to?"

"Mrs. Edwards told me his granddaughter, Alison, was down there, at Elk Creek, so I guess he went after her."

"Nobody's supposed to be in that canyon."

"What's the big deal about the canyon? At least he's not calling the FBI while he's down there."

Two-Bears started to speak and then stopped. After a moment he said, "I gave him orders."

"Well, he's not alone."

Two-Bears looked up, clearly startled.

"Jessie took Jake's granddaughter, Alison, down there for a vision quest, and Jessie went down ahead of Jake to check on her."

"For a what? That bullshit business of Jessie's?"

Sam shrugged. "Mrs. Edwards said Jessie has a French woman down there, too."

"Holy shit," Two-Bears said. "Who else is down there? The Springerville Boy Scouts, maybe?"

"Not that I heard, but I saw Shorty and Avrum going toward the river just after daylight. They had packs in the back of Shorty's pickup."

Two-Bears stood up, shaking his head and beginning to pace back and forth past the dead elk. "How the heck do you see so much and hear so much, Sam?"

Sam shrugged. "I went to see Mrs. Edwards to ask her advice about the owl stuff. She wouldn't talk to me about owls, but I passed Shorty and Goldberg when I was leaving."

"So Jessie and Alison and some foreign woman are in the canyon. And Jake's headed down there. And now Shorty and Goldberg are probably going there, too. It's a damned party." He turned to glare at Sam, his voice rising. "I thought nobody even knew how to get down to that river anymore. Where did that head come from?" Two-Bears seemed to see the elk head for the first time.

Sam watched the glazed eyes of the elk. "Jake left it while I was gone. That's how he figured out about Shorty, I guess. By the way, Mrs. Edwards told me she's holding Domingo Perez prisoner until he dries out."

Two-Bears stared at Sam, his mouth working for a moment before he spoke. "Domingo Perez? I wouldn't care if the god-damned Iraqis were holding Domingo prisoner. You know how to get down to Elk Creek?"

Sam thought for a moment and then nodded. "There's some kind of secret short trail on this side of the river, but I only know the long way down this side. If you go up to the bridge and drive across you can catch a Forest Service spur road that takes you to a spot right above Elk Creek. Only about a forty-minute drive. Hard darned walking, just about straight down, but it's quick."

"Let's go. I need a gun. What do you have here?"

Sam looked at his boss curiously and then went to a metal cabinet at the side of the room. He unlocked the cabinet and came back with a lever-action rifle in one hand and a semiautomatic pistol in the other.

"Which one? This is a .30-.30, good rifle for quick shots. The pistol's a .40-caliber, ten-round clip."

"I know what a .30-.30 is. You take this." He pushed the pistol back at Sam.

"Me? I've been awake for twenty-four hours, and now you want me to hike into hell?"

"I've been fucking awake, too," Xavier said. "Or awake fucking." He grinned weakly. "Get some ammunition for these things."

Sam went to the cabinet and returned with two small boxes. "Want me to show you how to load?"

Two-Bears looked sharply at the game officer to see if there was a note of derision in the man's voice. "Okay," he replied irritably. "You load. I'm in a hurry."

Sam dumped half the box of .40-caliber shells into his hand. "Nashoba won't be too happy to see me, I think."

"Why's that, though I really don't care."

"Because he probably thinks it was me who shot at him the other night, since he must figure it was one of us and he knows you were in that meeting."

Two-Bears was working the lever on the .30-.30. He stopped and stared at Sam. "You shot at Jake?"

Sam nodded. "Missed, too."

"Thank God, you dumb sonofabitch."

"I missed on purpose, Xavier. You think I'd shoot Jake? I waited till he got out to drain his lizard and just put a slug through his windows. I thought it would discourage him. So what's your plan, if you don't want these guns to kill Nashoba?"

"Money," Two-Bears said. "We'll offer Jake an even split, one third. Now that we know who the poachers are, we can stop them easily enough. With Jake's help we can add a couple of more elk hunts per season. Let's say we only do six a year, that's ten thousand clear each for three of us. Jake isn't stupid, but he is always broke."

"So why the guns?" Sam thumbed shells into the pistol magazine.

Two-Bears watched Sam punch the magazine into the pistol and then start to fill a second one. "Let's just say there may be unforeseen complications down there. I'll explain when the time comes. Need-to-know basis. But"—he jacked the chamber of the rifle open—"you don't shoot at anybody. We're not killers, Sam. At least you're damned lucky you're not one already."

"Well, when the time comes you'd better have a good explanation."

33

Jake was no longer beneath the pine roots but walking through thick, black grama grass that rose almost to his waist. His toe caught and he stumbled. When he recovered his balance, he went back to see what he had tripped over. There was only a small black hole in the ground between the clumps of grass. He began to walk away, but a voice said, "What are you looking for?"

He stopped and tried to find the speaker, but no one was there. "I'm looking for my own people," he said. "I've been gone a long time, and I have a long way to go."

"Don't you realize that no one can go to that place?" the voice said.

Jake looked down to see a black spider at the top of the hole. "Come into my house, Grandson," the spider said. "Don't be frightened."

How can I go into such a tiny hole, Jake thought, but he closed his eyes and when he opened them he was in a warm, lighted room much like Avrum Goldberg's wickiup. An old woman stood smiling at him, and around the room lay beautiful young women, all naked with dark, shining hair and smooth, sleek-looking bodies. Their breasts were small and taut, and as the girls rested on backs and elbows watching him he could see that they were smiling. He thought of his wife.

"Let's see that nice belt you have," the old lady said to him. Her silver gray hair hung over her shoulders like strands of a web, and her eyes sparkled. Her skin, like that of the girls, was remarkably smooth and glossy, almost black. "I mean, take it off," she added, her thin lips curving at each corner in what he thought must be a grin. "Don't worry. Your pants won't fall down."

There was a murmur of laughter in the room as he removed the belt and handed it to the thin old woman, who looked at it delightedly.

"Now you can rest. You're very tired, poor boy."

Jake looked down at the soft dirt of the cave. The girls were lounging bare in the same dirt, but they appeared to be immaculately clean and shining. He sank to his knees and then stretched out on the warm earth and fell into a dreamless sleep.

235

34
Xavier Two-Bears leaned the rifle upright between himself and Sam.

Sam grabbed the rifle as the truck fishtailed out of the parking lot, squealed tires on the asphalt, and roared through the little tribal capital, awakening Irvin Garcia in his patrol utility vehicle at the north edge of town.

"Take it easy," Sam said, bracing himself against the door and glove compartment.

"Take it easy, hell. Just hold on." Two-Bears gunned the truck even harder.

Garcia sat up and recognized the truck as it vanished northward. He shook his head and sank back down in the comfortable Blazer seat. Xavier Two-Bears always had some kind of shady deal going on, either with somebody else's wife or with somebody else's money, or both. He'd seen the chairman drive into town the day before with the blonde woman from the film crew. Since his divorce quite a few years before, no woman had been safe from Two-Bears' smooth attentions, and women seemed to find the big man damned attractive. Whatever was going on, it was best to stay out of the chairman's way if you wanted to keep a job.

Two-Bears hit the crossroad just as Sam said, "Turn right here."

The pickup slid halfway around on the pavement before it swiveled and righted itself on the east-running gravel road. He pushed the accelerator hard and the V-8 responded, spinning tires and leaping over depressions in the earth. A much-dented guard rail followed the sharp turn and a hundred feet of the gravel road, and along its smashed and scarred surface someone had spray-painted "I Love You Linda Dawn" in a deep red.

"You see that?" Xavier shouted above the roar of the truck. "I love you, Linda Dawn. That's love, poetic as hell. Wouldn't you like to feel that again, Sam?" He hammered the truck through a fast switchback, and Sam Baca reached to pull the seat belt across his body and click it into place.

236

"Who the hell's Linda Dawn?" Sam asked, staring at a big pine that appeared to be hurtling toward them.

"How should I know? It's the abstract feeling, goddammit," Xavier yelled back. He was silent as they completed the second half of the switchback and he shoved the accelerator down again on a long flat stretch of mesa aiming toward the pass that would take them down to the Dark.

"You ever hear of Vulva Woman?" Two-Bears asked abruptly, shifting into fifth and pushing the pickup toward sixty.

Sam stared wildly at the road that seemed to drop off into an abyss not far ahead. "The one with teeth in her pussy," he shouted, his voice trailing off as he tried to judge where the road went.

"Yeah. She went around killing everybody she fucked," Two-Bears said. "Biting their dicks off. Where you think a story like that comes from?" The road suddenly dropped off the side of the mesa, and for an instant they were airborne before slamming into the mouth of a widening canyon. The truck slid sideways and then straightened toward the river bridge a quarter mile away.

Sam was about to say truthfully, "Your grandmother," when he clenched his jaws. The Dark River was black where it passed beneath the bridge, the only portion of the river visible for many miles. "Mythology," Sam replied finally, his stomach beginning to settle.

"It must mean something, though. I mean, it has to come from somewhere, some kind of profound human truth." Xavier Two-Bears allowed the truck to slow to fifty as they rushed toward the bridge.

"Look," Sam managed to say just before a potbellied white man sprang up in the middle of the road and gunned a small dirt bike out of their way down the steep embankment. Sam glanced back to see the man and the skinny motorcycle in a pile below the road. When he looked up, they were already across the bridge and climbing a switchback out of the canyon.

"It comes from the fact that you're afraid that blonde's going to cut your nuts off," Sam finally said, adding under his breath, "fuck it."

The chairman turned to glare at Sam, and the truck began to fishtail on the gravel. He looked back at the road and accelerated out of the slide.

"About a mile up ahead, take the first logging road on the right," Sam added before Two-Bears could speak again. "Watch out. It's a sharp fishhook turn, and you could roll this thing."

"Where the hell would people come up with an idea like that?" Xavier said, as though speaking to himself. "Vulva Woman. Why would somebody's grandmother tell him a story like that?"

"Well, it wasn't because of Linda Dawn, whoever she is," Sam answered.

A half hour later they skidded to a stop at the end of the spur road. The spot had been easy to find because Jake Nashoba's battered pickup was already parked there.

Two-Bears jumped out onto the soft earth and stood for a moment looking down at his new ostrich-skin boots. Only then did he realize he was headed down into the canyon in new boots and one of his best suits. "Heck with it," he said aloud, grabbing the .30-.30 from the pickup.

"Heck with what?" Sam stood beside him, the pistol tucked into his belt near the buckle.

Two-Bears noticed that Sam Baca was wearing hiking boots and loose-fitting pants. Sam was always prepared to walk.

"Nashoba went this way," Sam said, pointing with his chin toward a steep draw. "Yesterday, I guess."

"How do you know it was yesterday?"

"There's a day-old deer track right on top of that heel mark," Sam replied, pointing with his lips. "See?"

"How long's it take to get down there?"

"This way, just a couple of hours. We can get there easy enough, but doing anything and getting back out before dark'll be a good trick. We should've brought camping stuff. What you plan to do anyway?"

"You'll see, and don't worry about camping equipment. That's the least of our worries."

"You say so. As long as it don't rain." Sam looked up at the sky, where clouds seemed to be drifting in from the southwest with no deliberate goal. "He sure didn't try to hide his tracks, did he?"

"Why would he?" Two-Bears replied. "Christ, that's not a trail. It's a dry waterfall."

"A lot safer than your driving."

The route was straight down, and Sam began the climb as though descending stairs. Two-Bears waited until the other man was a few yards ahead and started after him, catching a heel between rocks and beginning to fall with the first step. He reached out for a branch and cursed with pain as a half-inch thorn ripped his palm. What passed for a trail was simply the beginning of a rocky draw, steep as a ladder, that sucked water off the ridge during summer rains, funneling it to the creek and river far below. The draw was lined with locusts, which in turn were lined with thorns like cat's claws.

Two-Bears fell forward, the rifle clattering down the rocks so that Sam Baca jumped to the side to keep from being smashed by the careening .30-.30. "Fuck!" Sam yelled as simultaneously the pistol stabbed into his groin and his hand closed on a locust thorn.

Sam wiped the bleeding hand on his loose jeans and looked up at Two-Bears. The chairman was using his teeth and left hand to tie a white handkerchief around the palm of his right hand. Sam pulled the pistol out of his belt and stared at it with hatred, then looked down to where the rifle had lodged a dozen yards below him.

"Those .30-.30 sights ought to be in real good shape now," Sam said. "I'll bet a guy could maybe hit that mountain over there with that rifle now."

"Go to hell," Two-Bears said. "I just tore the shit out of my hand. You call this a trail?"

"No, I don't think I exactly called it a trail. And I feel like I just had prostate surgery with a jack handle." He held the pistol out for Two-Bears to see. "This thing just about disemboweled me."

"Keep going," Two-Bears said. "We have to get down to Elk Creek as fast as possible."

"You know something I don't?"

"I know a lot of things you don't, Sam. A whole lot."

"Hotshit college graduate."

"What?"

Sam began climbing down the rocks. "I didn't say nothing. Not a damned thing." Under his breath he whispered, "Mr. Vulva Woman."

"Fuck it," Two-Bears said at Sam's back. "Goddamned Choctaw outsider, goddamned vision quest salesman, goddamned woman warrior bullshit, goddamned Shorty and his anthropologist sidekick, goddamn them all." His coat sleeve caught on a branch and he jerked it free, enjoying the ripping sound as though the coat had become an enemy. Again he wondered if Donna would be waiting when he returned, fearful both that she would and that she wouldn't. He'd heard of a judge up in Holbrook who'd died with a prostitute, fucked to death they said, though it was a coronary that had done it.

35 Tali left Mrs. Edwards's house and walked slowly back toward her own. As always, several kids were passing a basketball around and shooting lazy arcs toward the backboard. Shorty Luke's youngest granddaughter was bouncing a red rubber ball off the side of Jake's shack, each collision with the plywood sounding hollow and reckless, testifying to Jake's absence.

She turned abruptly and went to the door of the green-painted building and entered without knocking, the first time in several years that she had gone there in daylight. The echo of the ball stopped as soon as she was inside, and she realized it was the little girl's thoughtfulness to which she owed the silence.

In the light of day, the office was startling. What were only shadows by night stood out in hard angles now. Even the edges of papers on the desk look razor-sharp and deadly. The beer sign rippled with light, and she paused for a moment surprised by the endless motion.

There was a stillness about the room that caught her and crept like deep cold under her skin. In the middle of the desk a novel lay with small pliers protruding from its pages. It struck her as odd to see a novel about the sun in such a cold room. She pushed the other door open and entered Jake's one-room home.

The bed was made, and a dish, cup, spoon, and fork were washed and lying beside the small sink. Everything was in order except for a large brown stain that covered the far end of the room. Below the stain lay shards of a coffee cup. Like the office, the room held an unnatural stillness and a cold that should not have been there on an August day. A rhythmic sound dug into her consciousness, and she turned toward the sink to find the faucet dripping heavily.

He's not coming back, she thought as she shut the faucet firmly. That's what felt different about both rooms. Jake's home had given up on him.

Tali walked quickly from the cabin and climbed into her pickup, spinning both tires as she drove out of Black Mountain and headed west on the blacktop road, accelerating until she neared the casino. At the four-way stop, she turned left and took the pickup rapidly into fourth gear, the transmission whining in protest.

Halfway to the tribal headquarters she passed Irvin Garcia parked in trees beside the road and aiming a radar gun at the blur of her truck. In her mirror she saw the tribal policeman pull out and begin to speed up with flashing lights. Abruptly, however, the lights on the patrol car went dead and the Blazer swerved to the side of the road and stopped. She smiled a thin, hard smile to herself. Irvin must have recognized her truck and realized discretion would be valuable. He wouldn't want to explain a ticket to Mrs. Edwards.

She drove past the large, brown stucco tribal headquarters building and turned up a side road. At Xavier Two-Bears's small HUD house she pulled the pickup in beside a new white Camry in the driveway, noting the nice red and yellow roses the chairman cultivated in his front yard. Two-Bears was a strange man, with the only roses on the reservation.

Banging on the door with her left hand, Tali pushed the doorbell with her right. When the door opened, instead of Xavier Two-Bears a blonde woman wearing only a man's large blue flannel checked shirt stared back at her.

"Can I help you?" the woman said, looking directly into her eyes.

Tali looked away for a moment and then realized the woman was part of the film crew she'd seen at the lodge. She looked back, making fleeting eye contact with the friendly but entirely self-confident-looking woman.

"I need to talk with Xavier," Tali said.

"Come in." The woman stepped to the side, holding the door open, and Tali smelled the fragrance of strong coffee.

"Xavier isn't here, I'm afraid," the woman said after she'd closed the door. "Would you like some coffee? I just made a pot."

"No thanks. Do you know where he is?"

The woman went into the kitchen, calling over her shoulder, "You look like you need some coffee. " In a moment she was back with two cups, pushing one toward Tali. "You also look like the black coffee type, like me."

Tali accepted the cup automatically, seeing for the first time how beautiful the woman was. The flannel shirt was held closed by only three buttons, opening at the top to expose the curve of full white breasts and at the bottom to show a tiny vee of red panties. From her days as a dancer, Tali was used to naked or semi-clothed women lounging unselfconsciously with cups of coffee, but the woman's ease in Two-Bears' house in the middle of the Black Mountain reservation struck her as astonishing. Unthinkingly, Tali lifted the coffee to her mouth and sipped.

"Are you Xavier's, um, ex-wife maybe?"

Tali felt the woman examining her body as she asked the question. She shook her head. "My name's Tali," she said softly.

"I'm Donna Green, with the *National Geographic* crew." The woman held out her hand and Tali shook it carefully with the fingers of her own hand. Donna Green smiled. "I'm always surprised by Indian handshakes. I mean, they're different from white people's." She looked a little off balance for the first time. "You know, that hard, macho kind of handshake?" The woman pushed hair back over her shoulder and laughed lightly, again in control. "And I'm relieved that you're not the ex, because frankly you'd be tough competition."

"His ex-wife moved to L.A. a long time ago," Tali said. "Do you know where he is?"

The woman shook her head, causing the blond hair to sway. She sipped the coffee and went to sit on a big leather couch, tucking her feet beneath her. "He got a phone call this morning and went storming out without saying much at all. It must have been an emergency because he left in the same suit he wore on our date last night."

Date? Tali looked around the room. Two-Bears was an immaculate housekeeper, much tidier than his wife had been. He'd brought her back from college, an eastern white girl who'd never made a bed or set foot on a reservation before, and the marriage had lasted a violent five years, surprising everyone by its endurance. The wife had been the opposite of this self-possessed woman.

"I need to ask him where my husband is," Tali said, feeling the strength go out of her words as she uttered them.

"Why don't you sit down, honey?" Donna waved a hand toward an overstuffed leather chair that faced the couch across a clean glass coffee table. "It's easy to lose husbands, isn't it? I lost three without any effort at all."

"No. It's not like that," Tali replied. Donna Green looked radiant, like a woman who had made love all night and felt wonderful about it. Tali imagined Xavier Two-Bears naked, and she grimaced inwardly. She'd learned before she'd even grown up that women's tastes were totally unpredictable.

"All I can tell you is that I heard him say the name Sam. I think it was somebody named Sam who called him."

"Sam Baca?"

Donna shrugged. "All Xavier said was Sam, and I think I heard something about Elk Creek. But I'll be staying here until Xavier gets back, and I'll tell him to call you. I was supposed to take a meeting in L.A., but I called in sick. So who should I tell him you're looking for?"

Tali set the cup on the glass table. "Does Two-Bears know you're waiting for him?" she asked.

The woman smiled. "I plan to surprise his superb ass right off."

"I have to go," Tali said, getting up and heading for the door.

"Nice to meet you," Donna called. "Let me know if I can help in any way. I'm good at finding men."

Tali stopped with her hand on the doorknob and looked back. The woman was smiling, with a friendly expression. This one would probably go over worse on the reservation than the first one. As she headed back to her truck, Tali thought it would be amusing to see the huge Two-Bears bossed around by this self-possessed white woman.

36 Above and below Jensen, Henry and Walter walked fifty feet apart, shining lights on the ground and moving reluctantly northward on the west side of the river. When daylight began to filter strongly through the pines, Jensen waved for the men to gather. Scarcely two hundred yards across, close to the river, the canyon held the darkness grudgingly, while the lighter sky struggled to descend.

"Okay," he said. "We don't know where the hell any of them are. It's ninety-nine to one that Nashoba's dead in the brush somewhere, or he fell into the river. It was too dark for me to see well. He could be carp bait half a mile downstream for all we know. And maybe I was wrong about the women. Henry, you backtrack, go to camp, cross the river there, and head up the east side, upstream. That means against the flow of the water, understand?"

"I know what 'upstream' means." Henry looked sullenly back toward the direction they'd come from. The camp wasn't very far away, so it wouldn't take him long to get there, but the thought of all those bodies made him queasy.

"Good, Henry. One-arm Walter and I will go up about a mile, cross, and head down. Keep your eyes on both sides, and we'll do the same. We can be pretty sure they're not on this side, however, so maybe we'll catch the women between us. And don't even think about crapping out on us, Henry. You shot the kid, and you're in real deep shit. Remember that. Besides, you try to run and I'll hang you with your own guts."

"Voltaire," Henry responded. "And it was priests, I think. Go to hell, Jensen, and I'll see you there."

Jensen grinned. "Well, even dentists get some education these days, and you're toughening up, aren't you, Henry? Good man."

The two men stood looking at him, their faces beyond exhaustion. "Nobody's eaten anything in a hell of a long time, Captain," Walter said.

"You're hallucinating, Walter. I'm no captain. An officer earns his rank. I just happen to be the one in charge here." Jensen looked at Walter's bandaged arm in disgust. "Because I'm the one who'll kill anybody who craps out. Now, let's consider our situation. We are up against a probable corpse and two young women who have been fasting for several days and, though one of them has quite a kick, are probably on their last legs, so to speak. You, who have been fed pretty regularly up until the last twenty-four hours, are wasting away. And let me make sure I've got the rest of this straight, Walter. Nashoba killed Chris and dislocated your shoulder with a rock. He threw a rock—one rock, right?—at the two of you, plus Henry here, all of you armed with automatic weapons, took out two men, and got away. Am I correct?"

Walter looked at the ground morosely. "One big god-damned rock," he said. "And he was right above us. More like he dropped it."

"Oh, yes. I forgot to mention that he also knocked Dave Scully's head off with a stick just before dropping a rock on you. And you, Henry, popped a dozen rounds off into the sky but didn't hit anything. Sometimes I forget little details like that, so I just wanted to be sure. Okay, let's go."

Alison and Sandrine lay behind a windfall log and watched the three men divide, with one of the men walking directly toward their log.

"Do you know how to shoot that?" Alison whispered.

Sandrine nodded. "Do you think we have to shoot them?"

Alison sank down lower behind the log. "They want to kill us. We know what the one named Jensen will do, and maybe they've killed my grandfather already. But perhaps we could just tie this one up."

"Tie him with what?" Sandrine noticed Jessie sitting on the log, leaning against the first big branch. He shook his head at her and drew a finger across his throat.

"He says we have to shoot them."

"Who says?"

Sandrine watched the man come closer while the others disappeared upstream around a fold in the canyon. She took a deep breath. "Jessie," she whispered. "Jessie is with us again."

Alison looked frantically around, keeping low behind the log.

"You can't see him," Sandrine said.

"Why should a French woman see my cousin's spirit, but not me?" Alison replied. "I don't believe you. Besides, it's really bad to see a dead person. A ghost. Almost nothing's worse."

"Remember what Jessie said in the tent, Alison. Jessie must be my animal helper," Sandrine whispered back. "Sort of. He's a wolf, some of the time. Fulfilling his contract with me, I think."

"Half paid in advance," Jessie said.

"Where are you, Jessie?" Alison kept looking around. She turned to Sandrine. "Where is he?"

"That man is close," Sandrine whispered. "We have to do it now."

Alison peered over the top of the log and saw that the man was only a hundred feet away. She sank quickly down. "Okay," she said. "Let's count to five and then you shoot."

"All right. You count."

Alison nodded. "One."

"That poor man," Sandrine whispered, looking over the log again. "He's exhausted."

"Do you want to shoot him or not?" Alison whispered back.

"Probably not, I'd guess." Jessie was sitting cross-legged on the log a few feet away from the women.

Sandrine jumped. "Stop doing that," she said.

"Doing what?" Alison whispered.

"We can't shoot him," Sandrine replied. "Look at him."

Alison raised her head enough to see over the top of the log. The man was walking toward them dispiritedly, the assault rifle hanging limply by the top handle, the man's eyes on the ground.

A shout from the river caused the man to look up and then down toward the water. Xavier Two-Bears was waist deep in the water, gesturing with the .30-.30 like a brave on horseback. Behind him was another man, whom Alison recognized as her grandmother's cross-cousin, Sam Baca.

"Who the hell are you?" Henry raised his A-15. "You look like Wayne Newton with a gun. And a sidekick."

Two-Bears reached the near bank and clambered up by grabbing exposed roots with one hand and heaving himself into the brush. Sam followed easily, and in a moment both appeared side by side, Two-Bears holding the rifle by its barrel like a walking stick, the white handkerchief around his hand dark with blood and dirt. His cowboy boots and his slacks from the knees down were caked with mud, and there was a big tear in one arm of his suit coat.

When the men were ten feet away, Henry said, "Close enough, friends. Who are you?" He kept the A-15 leveled at Two-Bears, not seeming to notice when Sam eased the pistol out from his belt.

"Xavier Two-Bears, chairman of the Black Mountain tribe," Two-Bears said breathlessly. "I have to see Stroud immediately. This is Sam Baca, head of tribal fish and game."

"Stroud is dead, Chief," Henry said. "Why'd you want to see him?"

"Dead? How did . . . I arranged for Stroud to use the reservation. He was supposed to pay me."

"Well, you may wait a long time for your money, Chief. You could say that things went kind of nuts. Stroud isn't the only dead one by a long shot. There's about eight other corpses scattered around. Why don't you drop that rifle on the ground so we can both relax a little bit."

"Why don't you drop that thing?" Sam said, leveling the pistol at Henry.

"Oh, Jesus," Henry said.

Two-Bears let the .30-.30 fall at the same instant that Henry gently lowered the AR-15 to the pine needles. Two-Bears shoved hair away from his face. "What's going on?" he asked.

Henry put his hands in the air, seeming relieved to be free of the rifle. "Tell your associate not to shoot me, please. I don't actually know the answer to your question. This was supposed to be a militia course, but both instructors and most of the so-called students are dead, along with some kid. Now I'm supposed to be looking for a dead ranger and two live women. Anybody ever tell you you look like Wayne Newton?"

"Ranger? You mean Jake Nashoba is dead, too?" Sam Baca asked.

"Yeah, I think that was his name, though we don't really know if he's dead because we haven't found a body. Jensen says he killed him, but all we have is Jensen's word. The women are an Indian girl and somebody from France. We're supposed to kill them."

"That's crazy," Two-Bears said. "One of those women is related to me, and the other one is a foreign national. Who's Jensen?"

"With Stroud dead, Jensen sort of took over. He's a psychopath. He'll kill everybody before he's through, I think." Henry looked at Sam. "How about aiming that gun somewhere else? As you can see, I'm not armed."

Behind the log, Alison stared in astonishment. "That's the chairman of our tribe," she whispered, "and that's Sam Baca with him. Are they part of those men?"

"Not part of them," Jessie said. Alison whirled to see her cousin sitting cross-legged on the ground behind them, leaning back against a tree trunk.

"Jessie? How come you've been hiding from me?"

Sandrine touched Alison's shoulder. "Jessie's been helping us all the time. As I said, I think he's sort of my animal helper, my totem.

"Is Two-Bears one of these killers?" Sandrine asked Jessie.

Jessie shook his human head. "Uncle Xavier, like Sam, is only greedy. Neither is one of the monsters. Actually, there is only one monster among these men. That dentist didn't mean to kill me; he thought he was protecting you from a big, bad wolf. It was my fault, not his. Want my advice?"

Sandrine nodded and Alison stared.

"I was wrong a minute ago. This isn't a bad man. Just capture him. Capture all three of them."

"You were wrong? My animal helper tells me to kill one minute and a minute later says he was wrong?"

Jessie shrugged. "Practice makes perfect."

"Capture them?" Alison said. "How?"

"First surprise them. They don't know we're here. Make Sam put his weapon down and then tie them up like you did the other one. It will be easy. Look at the dentist. He wants to be captured by somebody. And Sam and Two-Bears aren't killers, I think."

"You hope," Sandrine said.

Sandrine and Alison looked at each other and then stood up at the same time.

"Please put your gun on the ground," Sandrine said.

"Or we'll kill you," Alison added. "She will."

"Alison," Two-Bears said, staring past the man to where the two women had arisen from the log. "Granddaughter. Tell her not to shoot."

"Hi, Grandfather Two-Bears." Alison spoke quietly, exhaustion dulling her words.

Sam stood rigidly, raising his pistol toward the women.

"Mr. Two-Bears," Sandrine said. "Maybe you should tell that man that our gun is more powerful than his."

Two-Bears looked at Sam. "Don't be a total dumb shit," he said. "That must be the French woman, and she has an assault rifle aimed at us." He shifted his attention to the women. "Be careful. If you shoot him you might hit me."

"That would be a shame," Sandrine replied.

"Oh, what the hell. I give up." Sam dropped the gun and raised his hands.

Henry looked at the women. "I assume you want me to raise my hands, too?"

"Okay," Sandrine said. "Raise your hands."

Henry put both hands over his head, an expression of relief on his face. "You wouldn't have any food, would you? I'm starving. But we'd better get out of here in case Jensen comes back. He'll shoot all of us when he finds out we surrendered to you."

"They killed Jessie," Alison said.

"Killed Jessie? Is that the kid he meant?" The tribal chairman stared at the girl stupidly.

"Raise your hands, Mr. Two-Bears." Sandrine gestured with her rifle. "You, too, Sam Baca. Keep your hands raised."

"Uncle Two-Bears is okay," Jessie said. "You don't have to fear him. He's just a corrupt tribal official, nothing out of the ordinary. But you better watch Sam. Sam lacks imagination."

"Jessie?" Two-Bears stared in astonishment. "They said you were dead. We shouldn't even be saying your name."

"Whose name?" Sam asked. "Jessie who? Where?"

"He *is* dead," Henry answered. "I shot him by accident. You must be hallucinating from that hike."

"I am dead," Jessie said. "The fat dentist shot me by accident."

"Wait a minute." Sandrine gestured with her rifle once more. "Pick up your gun, Chief Two-Bears, but keep it pointed toward the ground. Now pick up the other two and give them both to Alison."

"I'm not a chief. How many times do I have to tell people that? I'm just the elected chairman." He picked up the .30-.30, holding it by the barrel, and then gathered up the assault rifle and pistol, one after the other, and handed each to Alison.

"You take that rifle," Alison said. "I don't want it. My hands are full."

"How could I shoot with a rifle in each hand?" Sandrine asked.

"Like Rifleman," Jessie said. "Remember that one-handed rifle-toting hero? I can almost remember the theme song."

"I didn't think spirit helpers made fun of people." Sandrine made a face. "I never watched American television, anyway."

"You should have. That woman from a bottle, the genie with the incredible body and harem outfit, made fun of people all the time." Jessie winked.

"I liked that show. You can still see it on reruns. But what spirit helpers are you talking about?" Two-Bears asked. He looked at Alison. "Maybe your French friend shouldn't have a gun, or two guns."

"She's okay," Alison said. "And her name is Sandrine Le Bris, but maybe you should carry your own rifle. Can we trust you?"

"I don't think so," Jessie said.

"Of course." Two-Bears smiled and reached for the rifle. "But keep guns away from Sam for a while." He looked at Sam, shaking his head. "He's careless."

Sandrine tossed the .30-.30 back to Two-Bears, who dodged out of the way and then picked the rifle up from the pine needles.

"The way that gun's been handled it won't hit the broad side of a casino hall," Sam said.

"Amazing how quickly you get used to death, isn't it?" Jessie smiled at Alison and Two-Bears. "Remember what everyone always said about the dead, about ghosts whistling at night and making you sick?"

"You're not a ghost," Alison said.

"That's right," Two-Bears echoed. "You can't be. Not yet, at least, or you wouldn't find me around here."

"Who's not a ghost?" Sam looked at Alison and then at Two-Bears.

"Nobody." As he spoke, Two-Bears began to follow Sandrine along the trail, with Henry and Sam behind, and Alison last.

"Okay," Alison said from the back of the line. "We have to find my grandfather before those other men do. So we'll take this dentist back to the camp, tie him up, and leave Grandfather Two-Bears to guard him."

"Me?" Two-Bears turned around, swinging the rifle toward Henry's midsection.

"Hey, watch that gun," Henry said.

"Oh, sorry." Two-Bears pointed the .30-.30 at the ground.

"Someone has to," Alison replied. "We'll tape him up, so you'll be safe."

"All right, if he's taped up. Taped up? What about Sam?"

Alison looked at the back of Sam's head. "I don't know. Can we trust him?"

Two-Bears turned to look at Sam. "I don't know," he said.

"I don't know either," Sam responded. "I don't know a damned thing, and it's too late for that explanation you promised."

The river flowed in a long, gradual curve through the section of canyon they walked, cutting in and pooling deep against rough, black stone cliffs and then rippling into long whitened runnels that spread shallow from one pine-forested bank to another. Oak, chokecherry, locust, and other small brushy trees gathered close to the water, wound with wild grapevines that shone an intense green over the lightening gray white of the river stones along the far shore. The group kept to the higher bench fifty or sixty feet above the water, where walking was easy on the soft pine carpet. On the other side of the river the beach ended at a sharp corner, where the wall of the canyon rose straight from river to sky in columns of volcanic rock broken by brush-clogged cracks. Between these obstacles the canyon dropped hundreds of feet in first near-vertical and then more gradual benches of pine and oak.

37   Tali drove back to Black Mountain and walked into Mrs. Edwards's house without knocking. The old lady sat in the big soft chair reading a paperback book.

"I know how to get there," Mrs. Edwards said, lowering the novel and looking up through cheap, drugstore reading glasses. "But are you sure that's the right thing?"

"I don't know."

Mrs. Edwards set the paperback on the small, round table beside the chair and removed the glasses, laying them next to the book. She looked at the young woman for a long time. The white shell beads and turquoise caught light from the eastern window and shone against Tali's dark skin and hair.

"Jacob Nashoba was always lost, Tali," she said. "There was never anything we could do." The large old woman rose slowly from the chair and walked to a desk against the northern wall of the room. Opening a drawer, she brought out a sheet of blue paper and a felt-tip pen. Without turning around, she said, "Many of us are lost for some part of our lives, but if we are lucky and have help we can find our way back. Like Domingo."

She looked over her shoulder at Tali. "And you." She began to put words and lines on the paper. "But some people never have a chance. They're too far from where they began, too far from their homes, too far from their people. Strangers can't help them. They forget the stories they need. Jacob is one of those."

"Can you help me find him?" Tali walked close to the desk.

Mrs. Edwards turned around, holding the paper out and shaking her head faintly. "I've drawn a map. It's the old way. But think carefully."

Tali looked at the map and then turned toward the door.

"You are stronger than you know, Tali," the old woman said as the door closed behind her niece.

38 Jake awoke to a delicious aroma. He stretched and sat up, completely without pain. Beside him was a red bowl of sweet-smelling soup. He heard light, brittle laughter and looked around. The curved room was filled with young women in beautiful robes of bright and dark colors. They stood and sat in various positions, all watching him and whispering and laughing softly together. The old lady was gone.

He picked up the bowl and drank, the soup filling him with a warm strength. It was when he set the bowl down again that he realized the girls were dressed in the colors of his belt.

"Thank you for your belt," the old woman said.

He looked around to see a huge black spider crawling down the angled tunnel into the cave, its mandibles working actively.

"See what wonderful dresses I made of it," the spider said, waving two legs toward the girls.

Jake felt himself start to gag, but the feeling went away at once.

"You prefer the other one?" the spider said. Instantly she was the thin old woman again. "I went out to look around. Your father the sun is up. You can go now. Someone is waiting to have a talk with you."

Jake started to thank the old woman, but he found he couldn't speak. So he rose and began to crawl on hands and knees out of the tunnel.

She should have given him turquoise and a white shell bead, you know, and he should have gone over the four mountains.

39   Jake crawled on hands and knees out of the long tunnel into the fine, sweet light of dawn. Shorty Luke, looking very handsome, was waiting just beyond the tunnel entrance, sitting cross-legged by a small fire where a pot gave off the delicious smell of roasting meat.

"Eat, Cousin," Shorty said, handing Jake a long-bladed knife with a deer-antler handle.

Jake stabbed a cube of elk meat from the steaming broth and chewed it from the tip of the knife.

"Have some dried plums." Shorty pushed a finely woven basket toward Jake.

Jake swallowed the meat and felt contentment flow through him just as with the soup. He picked three or four dried plums from the basket and chewed the tartly sweet fruit slowly, watching Shorty all the while with great interest.

In place of Shorty's crewcut was long black hair braided on both sides, and his face bore slashes of paint in four colors on each cheek. Instead of his usual flannel shirt and loose jeans he wore a fringed deerskin shirt with the sun and moon and lightning bolts painted on it in four colors, deerskin pants, and beautifully beaded moccasins. Two eagle feathers dangled from the side of his ridiculously black hair.

"Iron Eyes loaned me his wig," Shorty said with a grin, "and the rest of this is a decorated version of what I wore in one of those movies, maybe *The Searchers*, I can't remember for sure. I was one of the only Indian actors in that one who wasn't Navajo, but we were all supposed to be Comanche. In Monument Valley, too. We all laughed ourselves about sick when the Mexican actor said 'Yatahey' to the white guy who was supposed to be Comanche. Boy those were the days. But on a more serious note, Jacob, I thought it would be good to dress up to hear your story, in your honor. Avrum is waiting for me back at the river, but we have as long as you like."

"What story?" Jacob ate more of the dried plums and felt increasingly contented.

"The whole story."

"Well," Jake began, but Shorty shook his head.

"It's best to begin a story with something like 'they say,' or 'it is said.' Okay?"

Jacob smiled at the little man with affection. He realized that he had never felt so well in his life since his momentary vision in Mississippi so many years before. All anger was gone. He had a feeling that something very good was approaching. "Shorty Luke, the story thief," he responded. "Well, it is said that everything began in a bar in Phoenix, but they say the next thing that happened . . ."

"Good," Shorty interjected. "You've learned how to begin a story. But maybe you should go backwards for a while. Maybe a long way back."

"I'll tell you everything, my friend. There are no gaps, and nothing is forgotten."

"I'll miss you, Jacob."

"But you'll have to finish the story for me, Shorty."

"I know." Shorty reached out and touched the tips of the fingers of both hands to Jake's closed eyes.

40   "You ever read any of those books Mrs. Edwards has around her house?"

As he spoke, Shorty looked up from where he'd bent to drink from the river. They'd struck the water just after day-break, walking directly down a side canyon from the west. As soon as they reached the river, Shorty had taken out four turquoise stones from a pouch and dropped them into the water with a few words.

Avrum stared impatiently. As soon as the prayer to the river had been offered, Shorty had disappeared. Avrum heard a hawk scream up above the tall pines and turned his head to see the bird. When he looked back, Shorty wasn't there. The anthropologist had walked about for what seemed like hours but might have been minutes, looking, not daring to shout, when just as abruptly Shorty strolled up behind him acting as if he'd never been gone.

"I don't read mystery novels," Avrum said, unable to keep the irritation out of his voice. "I tried a few, and it was always the same story, missing bodies, unsolved murders, found money. Why read the same story over and over, even if the names change? And where did you go?"

Shorty stood up, wiping his mouth on his sleeve. "You should drink," he said. "Keep you going." As the anthropologist knelt by the river, Shorty said, "I tried to read one of those, but I didn't get it. And that thing about it always being the same story isn't the problem. We tell the same stories all the time. My grandmother told me, and I tell my kids and grandkids. Always the same stories from the creation and the way things used to be. But nobody ever gets tired of hearing them. It's always like you're hearing each story for the first time. I don't know why. Now this present story I only know up to a point. It's going to take improvisation."

"Maybe because those your grandmother told you are true stories. They don't pretend to have heros."

"Sure they have heros. Monster Slayer, for example. Imagine him right now, down in this deep canyon. Just imagine. And that other one, the twin, all covered in black metal, walking the way a man covered in metal would walk. Noisy. Heavy."

"Okay, you win, Shorty. I know the stories you're referring to, which, by the way, shouldn't be told this time of day or this time of year, but nonetheless I don't understand a thing. And I won't ask again where you were for who knows how long, but we'd better get moving if we're going to find those plums." The anthropologist picked up his bow and the two arrows and readjusted the quiver.

"I think we head south now," Shorty said. He looked around him at the tall ponderosas and brushy oaks and then down at the river. "You know, it was just a few miles south of here that Josani and those others with Nana broke out of the reservation for the Sierra in Mexico. Just downstream a ways, at Turkey Creek. They went all the way to Mexico and then came back for their families who'd been captured. But the army had their families in prison somewhere else. It was very hard. We came up in the winter, with snow deep as the horses' bellies sometimes, fighting off to the west for a while so they'd think we were just raiding. We came up the Gila here to the Dark River and then up the mouth of Turkey Creek to the camp of our relatives. But the wives and children were gone, in prison. There were hard faces when we rode back, and we made the whites and Mexicans cry."

"Shorty, I know some of that history. I'm pretty sure your ancestors were scouting for the U.S. Army then, with Chato, against those that broke out. There were hundreds of Apache scouts helping find Geronimo, Nana, Chihuahua and the rest. I'm not sure about the *we* part of that story."

"We're all one. It's all one story," Shorty Luke replied. "We had no choice. We thought that we would never be left to live in our own country if those wild ones were allowed to be free. It was a hard decision to fight our own people. It was for the children."

"Well, I'm the one who knows where the wild plums are." Avrum looked south along the bank of the beautiful river.

"Do you think we should go south, then?"

Avrum nodded. "Yes. South on this side."

Shorty began to walk, looking back over his shoulder. "Looks like you made those arrows specially good. Is that lightning along the shaft?"

"We'd better not talk now," Avrum answered.

"Don't want to scare those plums." Shorty looked back over his shoulder and grinned.

41   Jake lay within the tangle of roots and considered his death. The dream had been so powerful that after crawling from the tunnel and meeting Shorty he had fully expected to awaken to warm sunlight, but instead he had awakened to his own stiff body and the dark root pit. He didn't feel anger any longer, but when he tried to move he found no response. His body seemed part the earth. He could, however, still see the world around him and hear and smell and taste that world. He could taste, for example, the tracks of the ant that walked across his lips, and smell the vinegar of the ant's passage. He could hear a hawk calling far off. He could see and smell the black earth and gray rocks all laced with silvery webs that made up the hole caused by the fallen tree, and he could see a lip of growing light just outside the hole and maybe, he wasn't sure, maybe the green of pines against what might be sky. High up on what appeared to be a huge pine the Plymouth Rock rooster perched, its magnificent breast shining and its red eyes staring through all of that space directly into Jake's.

As he tried to be certain of the rooster, Jake heard a woodpecker drumming nearby and then the same careful, metallic tread he had heard before. The steps of a man. And he could hear, see, smell, feel, and taste the decaying earth that tumbled down upon him as a man knelt at the edge of his hiding place and looked at him.

"Well, finally," Jensen said. "Jake Nashoba, and you appear to be somewhat alive. I don't know how in the world I overlooked you here before. You can move your eyes, correct? I guessed as much. One of my bullets probably smashed your spinal column, paralyzing you but leaving mental facilities intact. An ideal situation, I'd say. So you've had the pleasure of lying here for these hours contemplating your minimal future."

Jake looked up at the blond face. There had been so many times in Vietnam when a small, dark face might have watched his death, and he would have understood such a death perfectly. But this made no sense. He tried to piece together the elements that had lead to his being in this absurd situation, and he couldn't do it. There were gaps now where there never had been any before. Everything seemed to begin with a pair of brown feet that gripped the earth like talons. And then there was a confusion of times and faces, including the one speaking at him.

Jensen turned and looked at Walter crossing the side of the ridge fifty feet further up. He shouted, but as Walter began to respond, the large man suddenly straightened, lurching faintly backward and dropping his rifle. Jensen stared at what looked like an arrow sticking out of Walter's chest before Walter fell sideways down the slope. Jensen swung his gun back down toward Jake.

The Plymouth Rock rooster detached itself from a branch of the ponderosa and plummeted like a stone toward Jensen. Jake watched the great silver bird tumbling out of the sky. Lightning slid smoothly across the clouds above the bird, and thunder exploded behind him. *Ishkitini*, Jake realized. It wasn't the rooster at all, but a great horned owl hurling itself toward the man.

A few feet above Jensen's head, the enormous bird tilted its wings with a roar of wind and swung back into the sky, so close that the man crouched toward the earth, cursing. At the same instant Jensen screamed and clutched at his left shoulder where the feathered shaft of an arrow protruded. He rose and stumbled in a complete circle, and Jake saw the white stone arrowhead with perfect clarity where the arrow shaft stuck out the back of the shoulder. Then the man grabbed the rifle from the ground, raised it with one hand with the stock resting against his thigh, and fired a long burst toward the river and then fired again. He fired yet once more while running backward until Jake could no longer see him from where he lay in the hole.

For what seemed hours, Jake watched the slowly boiling thunderheads, trying to distinguish the spidery threads of lightning that played inside the clouds and thinking of the rooster that had come to his aid as he had known it would. An

Adams Irresistable, he thought, that was the fly that would urge the big browns up from their hovering depths with hackle given by his old friend. He imagined the still shadow of the trout, like a dark flame, finning down there in the current and then the shy, circling rise of the fish. A communication between worlds, a seduction of life from one realm into another. Finally he caught a partial silhouette of someone peering from above at him through the root wad tangle at one side of the hole. Shorty Luke moved around to the top and looked down at him.

"You hurt bad, Jake?" Shorty asked.

Jake stared back, blinking, refusing the lure.

"Pretty bad, huh?" Shorty held a bow and two arrows in his hands as he climbed down the side of the depression, pushing root tangles out of his way. He set the bow and the arrows down and knelt next to Jake's head.

"Can you move, Cousin?"

When Jake blinked, Shorty nodded. "That one killed Avrum," he said. "Avrum shot both of them with those arrows, and then he killed Avrum with his gun. That's a new part of the story."

Jake closed his eyes, trying to remember who this newly dead person might be. There were so many. Now the shadowy figure had killed someone else, but who? He couldn't remember anyone named Avrum, an odd name, but he experienced a welling sadness nonetheless flooding into the contentment he had felt earlier. Something was terribly familiar about the situation. The roots around Shorty's doubled body looked like snakes, like jungle vines, like spiders.

"I don't think I can move you, Jacob," Shorty said. "Might cause more damage."

"I'm dead," Jake said, but Shorty didn't seem to hear.

A wolf's head appeared above Shorty, the yellow eyes shrewd and concentrated. The wolf's right eye winked and the mouth grinned. Then the faces of two women showed beside that of the wolf.

Shorty looked up.

"Grandfather," Alison said. She dropped something onto the ground and slipped into the hole beside Shorty, the roots of the tree seeming to clutch and pull her in.

"That man must have shot him," Shorty said to Alison. "He killed Avrum, my brother."

Alison laid her palm on Jake's cheek and brushed his hair back. He could see water on her face, and he thought of someone else. Someone who had been with him recently. Tali?

"Your grandfather is dying," Shorty said.

Alison let the backs of her fingers lie against Jake's temple, and he felt a wonderful cooling sensation. He remembered Avrum Goldberg, and the sadness broadened. The faint, light singing returned, and he tried to see if the others could hear it, but they gave no sign.

"Alison," the woman up above said.

Alison looked up.

"We have to find that man. He'll come back to kill your grandfather and everyone."

"I can't leave," Alison replied.

The singing grew more high-pitched and obvious, and Jake saw Shorty casting furtive glances around. So Shorty Luke heard it. Of course Shorty would hear it, and in time it would become Shorty's story. Of course.

"Go," Shorty said. "You have those guns. I'll stay with your grandfather. If he comes back here, I'll shoot him with this." He picked up the bow.

Alison leaned over and kissed Jake's forehead. Her breath smelled like wild plums, and he tried to smile. "I'll come back soon, Grandfather," the girl said.

42   Tali left Mrs. Edwards's home and walked into the full light of the eastern sun. It spilled down the rim of the mountains, caught on the shake roof of her house, and flared around her.

She turned south and studied for a moment her husband's fragile-looking home and office, and then she glanced at her grandmother's little government house tucked against the forest that spread west of Black Mountain. The pines around the small community rose all the way to the cloud-scattered blue sky, so that the sky rested on their black points, and in clearings through the dark forest blue and yellow and white flowers bloomed both close to the earth and on tall stalks and shrubs. What they called Indian paintbrush grew beside the clearings in a steady line of orange and red.

Everywhere there was a feeling of water just beyond the dry air and earth's surface. She could feel the presence of the river and canyon, as though the whole place remembered the timeless, irresistible movement of earth like an offering to an ocean she had never seen. She could sense, now, the way the river must have attracted him. He would have been conscious of it even before he saw it or knew it was there. Perhaps the river had drawn him across so much space all the way from the war to find her and be taken by her. Perhaps she had merely been the river's helper.

She saw Jacob as she never had before. His strength was an illusion. Her husband, she understood now, was the most fragile, defenseless person she'd ever known. Like his displaced ancestors, he had gone wherever forces moved him, unconscious, connected to nothing. The river laid claim to all of the land and people, cutting deeper into the earth at every moment, ceaselessly changing and moving but remaining constant. She could see how it had captured and held Jake. He hadn't grown up with this river, didn't know the stories, didn't understand how to live with what the river meant. He had been vulnerable to everything. From his half-remembered childhood stories she knew that he had been born with different waters that couldn't have prepared him for the world she inhabited. Jacob Nashoba didn't belong. She walked slowly toward the log house.

43 Jensen ran for fifteen minutes, the pain in his shoulder ripping at him with each step. Finally, when he could detect no one following, he lunged behind a jumble of gray boulders and collapsed onto the ground.

He bent his head to look at the feathered shaft sticking out of him and his lips formed a bitter laugh. What would Nitske and those vets in the TRS camps think about this. You come to a fucking Indian reservation and you end up with an arrow in you. Not in, but through you. And not even a razor-tip, but a primitive stone fucker that shattered the hell out of bone. *Apocalypse Now.* Someone had been killed with an arrow. Scores of western movies came back to him. You had to get the arrow out, he remembered. For some reason it was essential to get the arrow out as soon as possible, and to do that you had to break the shaft. Then, he knew, the wound would bleed, but it was crucial to get the arrow out.

He shifted until the point of the arrow was lodged against the face of a boulder. The faintest touch of the shaft against stone sent barbs of pain through his chest and shoulders. Breathing steadily and deeply, he grasped the feathered part with his right hand and snapped the wood with surprising ease right at skin level. Amazingly, very little blood flowed down his chest.

When the flash of pain subsided, he looked at the thing he held in his hand. The arrow had broken so easily, he realized, because it had been made in two pieces. The long, feathered shaft in his hand seemed to be made of cane, and it had broken at what was clearly a splice. He rested for a moment, listening carefully. When he heard nothing, he breathed deeply again for several minutes and then reached his right hand over his left shoulder until he could feel the arrowhead. From its position, he guessed that it had shattered his clavicle, but at least it was slanted up and out enough for him to get a grip on it.

He jerked, and a searing light exploded behind his eyes. When he was conscious again, he felt with his hand. The arrow hadn't moved. Okay, he told himself, it's stuck in bone, so it stays in. He tried to move his left arm but found it useless. So much for that.

Using the rifle, he pushed himself to his feet. The thing to do was to kill the two women, then go back and finish off Jake Nashoba and the old man with the bow. This was even better than the TRS camps. He'd have the additional challenge of getting back to the vehicles with an arrow in him. First he'd have to get rid of Henry too, after the others. He'd have to do everything himself, rely only on himself, which was even better. Driving four hours wouldn't be such a kick in the pants, leaning forward to keep the fucking arrowhead off the back of the seat, but he knew a doctor in Phoenix who'd take care of him off the record.

He'd gotten one of the old pair, the one who'd shot him with an arrow. The old man had looked like an Indian from two hundred years ago, with his ancestors now. The women would undoubtedly be trying to help Nashoba, who was beyond help. As long as the girl's grandfather was alive they surely wouldn't leave him, so he had to hope Nashoba didn't die too quickly. And they probably wouldn't expect him to come back now that he had an arrow through him. Meanwhile, he'd have to go back to camp and get a compress on the hole in his shoulder before he went hunting again.

He walked clumsily to a big tree and leaned there until the dizzyness subsided, then he moved to another tree and rested for a moment.

He saw the women as soon as he appoached the river opposite the camp, and was somewhat surprised that they had beaten him back there. They were in front of the tents, the rifles held so awkwardly that he almost laughed. Henry was standing, apparently talking with the women, and someone he didn't recognize was tied up, or taped up, sitting on the log.

44　Mrs. Edwards listened to the pulse of Domingo's sleeping breath. The air in the room thickened with the healing fragrance of cedar and mesquite. Finally, she thought, after all this time I am old, an elder. She smiled at the idea. But it had taken so long to arrive. She remembered back along the meandering path of her life. Her own mother, so young then with deep black eyes and white teeth, smiled at her and braided her hair on a day when they had not suspected she would come to be kept behind barbed wire and whipped for speaking her language in the old brick school. For one entire month she had crept about the school with a metal ball chained to her ankle, her tongue swollen with words she couldn't say in daylight. At night on the narrow, cold bed in the long room with other crying students, she learned to speak her words to shadows that gathered. She had begun to feel them coming down from the mountains during the first days, even, but by the end of a month they had come each night from the farthest peaks to gather her lost words and keep them safe. Later, she knew, they would return all of those words to her and that way she would never forget. The other children whose beds were close heard her, she knew, but they must have understood, for they pretended not to notice, or perhaps they spoke their own words silently for safekeeping.

Words were powerful, her mother and grandmother had warned her, and couldn't be allowed to drift aimlessly. The white teachers were surprisingly smart about that, she reluctantly admitted to herself; they knew that if they could kill the children's words and give them new, strange ones those children could never go home. Many of the students had fooled the teachers with one trick or another, though some, she remembered, truly had never come back. Young people today wouldn't have believed such stories, so she never told them. Her own mother and father had been carried to school in chains.

She remembered her father taking two days to walk home from the coal mine in Globe, blackened and coughing, with ninety-five cents for each day worked in the mine. Her father had been fired, she learned, because the white union miners didn't like Indians working for almost nothing. And always there had been her grandmother, whose cousins still lived wild in the Mexican Sierra even then, and who would take her aside to teach her. Word came that a child of those wild ones, a young girl, had been tied to a tree by the Mexicans and left to die, and then words ceased to travel northward altogether. When even those holdouts were silenced, the grandmother had elected to die also. But by then she had taught her granddaughter a great deal. Through the women everything was remembered, the massacres and treachery of the Mexicans and white Americans, the poisonings and hangings of Apaches, the people taken far away to die in prisons, and the stories of clans and origins, of Changing Woman and her sons, of medicines, dreams. The survival of the people through everything, so that now, despite all that had been had done, despite all that was lost, they still lived in their own land and knew who they were. Because of the parents and grandparents many generations back.

For a time she had feared the line would be broken when Tali's second no-good husband, a Ute that one, had taken Tali to Phoenix to live. He'd fled the reservation and taken the girl with him because of her, Mrs. Edwards. He had enough sense to be afraid, but not enough to care for a woman and children. And the stories had come back immediately. The man was no good and wouldn't work, so Tali had become a dancer, one who gave her body to men's eyes. Tali had thrown the Ute away, the voices said, but she was ashamed to come home, so she danced.

Mrs. Edwards had gone to the town called Show Low and boarded a Greyhound bus for Phoenix, a place she'd never been. When the huge bus wound its way down the twisting road of the Mogollon Rim, she had stared through the window, knowing that this was all her people's country, from the great pines up above to the stunted piñons and junipers and oak of the steep canyons and brittle cottonwoods of the lower creeks and finally the desert with its dry mesas and tall, branched cactus. They had known all of this and moved about freely through these incredibly different lands before the Spanish and Americans came. She knew her ancestors had walked and ridden through every canyon and dry streambed of that country, all the way to Mexico and beyond, and she could still see their shadows in dark angles of stone and bright desert.

She couldn't see any shadows at all in the city, however, only the glare of a flaming sun on white concrete and thousands of moving cars and black roads that sparkled painfully. She had walked out of the bus station and watched for a few minutes and then retreated under the protecting shade of an awning. A driver leaned out his window and shouted a question, calling her grandmother and asking if she needed a ride, and she had gone into his yellow car at once. The driver was Diné and understood her situation. He had waited in his cab while she turned the knob of Tali's motel room door, without knocking, and walked into a small space containing three children, empty cereal boxes, soiled clothes, two beds and a television. The children had run to hug her, and she had been relieved to find that each was clean and well fed, even if fed on sugar cereal.

Mrs. Edwards had known better than to argue with her shamed niece, grown into a woman as strong-headed as the sister who had given birth in the act of dying. Instead, she had written a note in the clean, smooth hand learned in the brick school, and taken the crying children into the cab and back onto one of the gray buses for home. The Diné cousin would not accept money, and Mrs. Edwards knew that he had been provided for her. Tali would follow, she reasoned, and she would have them all home again. The youngest, Trini, reminded her of her own grandmother, and she knew that the lines of power ranged freely across generations. These could be saved.

It had been only a week later when Tali called for her brothers to come to Phoenix. The next day they had arrived at Black Mountain in Angel's pickup, Norbert and Jimmy with Angel in the front and Tali sitting wrapped in a gray blanket in the bed of the truck, a man lying with his bandaged head in her lap. From that moment on, the old lady swore she would not let Tali escape again, and she began to watch the half-Indian outsider with the eyes of an eagle. Eagle, Mrs. Edwards told the awestruck children who gathered around her on winter evenings, had created owls everywhere, and Owl, she explained, took babies and children whenever she could. Time wasn't the way whites like John Edwards understood it to be. Human beings did not move from birth to death in a long line of forgetting for two thousand years. Human beings bore an insubstantial form that might shift and change as what white people called time turned and crawled back inside its own coils like a red snake. Jacob Nashoba had come many times to Black Mountain, and time and again the old lady had worried his story within her hands like a wet clay pot.

She confided in two persons. Shorty Luke knew every story and therefore understood how almost everything began and ended. And Shorty took every story into himself and made it new each time. She had watched him take Jake Nashoba's story from her and begin to knead and work it as he came to know the stranger, recognizing the shadows and forms of old stories in this one. And when she felt Shorty had worked his strong hands deeply into the story she invited him to coffee, where they tried to comprehend how the story might conclude this time.

Avrum Goldberg became the other one she spoke with, though she did not tell him everything. The anthropologist had come, after a long struggle and much of it in her bed, to understand a great deal. He had ceased very early to be what he had been taught to be and had become what he had always been. You are now what you always were, she told him. Outside, he would remain a strange clay fired in Black Mountain soil, but his bones remembered a tribal, nomadic people of mountain, desert, and mesa. Therefore, he understood.

When spiders began crowding the corners of Mrs. Edwards's home, spinning webs across drywall angles and folding themselves beneath old *People* magazines and undusted end tables, crawling and weaving and singing all night, she had called her visitors' attention to this fact. Of course, Shorty had said. And Avrum had nodded. She's weaving a new one, Shorty added, and the anthropologist nodded again. Tali gave him the belt last week, Shorty murmured as though to himself. So now it begins in earnest.

"I learned that line in Hollywood," Shorty said. "I forget which film, but it was the hero's line, and I was an extra hired only to ride and die like always. But I listened to the lines while standing offstage with Indians who spoke Italian and Armenian, and I took the hero's words for myself. So now it begins in earnest. So. Now. It begins. In earnest. *Ciao*, cowboy." He grinned at Avrum and Mrs. Edwards.

Avrum had clutched a medicine pouch, his high moccasins and breechcloth damp with the summer air and his long hair limp behind his headband. "Shorty doesn't understand that Hollywood stops fifteen hundred miles away," he said.

"Hollywood never stops," Shorty replied.

"Words never stop," Mrs. Edward declared, glaring at both men. "So this mixedblood outsider knows that one?" She nodded toward a high corner of the room.

"But doesn't know he knows. Yet," Shorty said. "I've come to that part of the story, but now that part has drifted beyond this moment like one of those leaves you see in a stream that overtakes another and moves on while the other moves around and around. Sometimes stories do that. She has the words now." He nodded in turn at the high corner where a shiny black spider sat contentedly in the center of her web.

"She works in mysterious ways," Avrum added, and the other two looked at him in surprise.

"Stories giveth and taketh away," Shorty replied.

"Go home," Mrs. Edwards had finished, tired of the pair's constant serious play. But the three had come together many times after that to discuss the story and decide who needed an elk hindquarter that week. Shorty always seemed to know something he held back, and Avrum always seemed surprised by the little he himself learned.

Now, alone with the surviving twin, the old lady took a deep, exhausted breath. A storm had moved in to hover over the Black Mountains and threaten the people, but little rain had fallen. The rain seemed to be holding back. "You," she said to Domingo, "are the surviving twin. You have great responsibility. Do you hear the thunder, Domingo? One of the brothers has won. We are the survivors."

45 "Yes," Shorty said. "I hear the singing, and, like you, I saw the wolf. You aren't alone, Cousin." He began to sing softly.

"What am I doing?" Shorty added. "I'm slaying monsters, of course."

Jake closed his eyes and found himself in the room of soft earth. He was sitting up with his back straight, a wonderful feeling of life coursing through his body. A great black spider crouched close by. "Welcome home," the spider said.

"Where is Tali?" Jake asked.

"I'm right here, Jacob." The spider had become his wife, tall and dark and beautiful in her black skirt and blue velveteen blouse. White shell beads hung around her neck, and turquoise dangled from each ear. "You knew this all the time, didn't you?"

"Welcome back, Grandson. *Halito.* It's been a long time."

Halito. Jacob turned toward the smiling old Choctaw man, the flow of a big, dark river in his brown eyes.

46 Jensen stepped from behind the tent and raised his rifle. "Throw down the weapons," he said, "or you're dead. Sorry that sounds so trite." He staggered and then braced himself, keeping the AR-15 aimed at them.

Alison and Sandrine let the rifles fall at the same time. Jensen walked toward them with his gun held in his right hand. The left arm hung straight at his side. His face was drawn and gray.

Sandrine raised her hands above her head, and Alison imitated her. Henry raised his arms beside them.

"Put your arms down, Henry. Good grief." Jensen looked from Henry to the women. "I'm kind of sorry you dropped your guns like that, because if you hadn't I would have had an excuse to kill you both and everything would be simpler." He seemed very tired, and the front of his camouflage shirt was stained black. "You can let your arms down now, too."

"I came here looking for Henry, but I guess I got lucky. However, I have a little problem to deal with before I go back to kill that old man and finish off Ranger Nashoba." He took deep breaths as though to steady himself and glanced at Sam Baca where he sat taped motionless on the log. "Who's this?"

"A guy they don't trust," Henry said. "From their own tribe."

"No shit?" Jensen looked closely at Sam. "Looks like an Indian cop of some kind. We'll just keep him taped up for now. I told you to put your arms down, you stupid fuck. Where's Stroud?"

Henry lowered his arms and nodded toward one of the tents, his round face, with its beard stubble and big eyes behind the wire-rimmed glasses, pale and frightened looking. "We put the bodies in there. It seemed like the decent thing to do."

"The decent thing to do?" Jensen half-staggered to the log and sat down, keeping his face toward them and the gun pointed at the group all the while. He looked at a large nylon stuff sack lying next to the log. "You came back here and ate after you surrendered to these two great warriors, didn't you, Henry?"

"We didn't have time." Henry looked guiltily at the bag. "We just got here. You look like you're bleeding."

"You were a fucking supply clerk in Nam, weren't you, Henry?" Jensen kicked the stuff sack so that it flew against Henry's leg and draped over his boot.

Henry nodded, watching the rifle.

"So I guess you probably sat on your fat ass over there in Nam snacking while the grunts were out in the boonies getting their heads blown off, didn't you? You're an old hand at stuffing your gut while there's a war going on. You eat while other men die."

"At least I was there," Henry said, and everyone looked at him with surprise. "I may have been a supply clerk, but at least I was in a real war, not just some bullshit game-playing for assholes who can afford it."

Jensen jerked his head at Alison and Sandrine and half-turned toward them, keeping his eyes all the while on the two men. "You two come around where I can see you more easily. Isn't it wonderful when a spineless piece of shit like Henry here suddenly finds his backbone? Doesn't it give you hope for humankind?"

When the two women were more directly in front of him, he looked at Sandrine. "Did you notice I didn't say 'mankind'? A little political correctness is important, don't you think?"

Sandrine glanced toward the trees upstream from the camp, where Two-Bears had suddenly thrown himself flat on the ground. She was hoping Jensen wouldn't look in that direction, because the roll of toilet paper in Two-Bears's hand stood out glaringly.

"What's wrong with your back?" Henry asked, craning his neck to see Jensen's shoulder.

"Oh, that." Jensen smiled. "Just part of a real, authentic Indian arrow."

Henry took a step to the side to see the arrowhead more clearly. "Good God," he said. "That must hurt like hell."

"Pretty accurate, Henry, except the benevolent God part," Jensen replied, his voice wavering. "It hurts like hell," he added in a near whisper.

"What happened to the rest of it?"

"I managed to break it off just about skin level. But unfortunately that foreshaft seems to be lodged in bone, and I can't get quite the right angle on it myself. I'm afraid I'll need some help getting it out before we finish our little search-and-destroy mission. So here's what we'll do. Ladies, you step further over there where I can see more easily."

273

When the three of them were together in clear view, Jensen stood up. "Now, Henry, I want you to pull this arrow out."

Henry stared, unmoving.

"Henry," Jensen said through terse lips. "Let me be precise, because I'm in some pain right now. You are going to grasp that point and shaft in two hands and jerk it free in one motion. While you're doing that, I'm going to have this rifle on full auto and pointed right at these two women, my finger on the trigger. Now I can imagine three possible scenarios. One, you'll try to disarm or disable me in some way, in which case I'm sure I'll have time to at least kill both women, an event I suspect you want to avoid. Two, you'll be clumsy and cause me to involuntarily squeeze the trigger, in which case the results will be the same. Three, you'll extract the arrow with one quick pull, allowing me to retain both full consciousness and motor reflex control and no one will be hurt at all. Now, let's be careful."

Henry walked around Jensen until he stood immediately behind, a foot taller than the other man. With slow deliberation, he grasped the hardwood shaft with his right hand where it protruded from the shoulder and placed his left around the arrowhead. Jensen winced and sucked in a deep breath, and Henry said, "Wait a second."

Pulling a bandanna out of a pants pocket, Henry wrapped it around the arrowhead and then replaced his hands. "Ready?" he asked. "Now, don't accidentally squeeze that trigger."

"Do it," Jensen replied.

With a sudden pull, Henry had the arrow out and was holding it in amazement. Jensen lurched backward and caught himself against Henry's chest, then staggered a half-step forward, his jaw clenched.

"It's not bleeding half as much as I thought it would," Henry said.

"That's nice. Now one of you ladies go to that small red pack over there and find a large gauze pad and tape and bring it to Henry. Be careful or someone will certainly get shot."

"Get the disinfectant out, too," Henry said, "that brown stuff in the bottle. And the arm sling in that front pocket. Now, Lee, I'm going to cut your shirt open with my knife. I'm not going to stab you in the back or anything, so don't go psycho and accidentally pull that trigger."

"Have I ever doubted you, Henry?" Jensen said.

In two minutes, Henry had the shirt open, the large compress taped tightly to Jensen's shoulder, and the left arm in a sling across the chest.

"The bleeding has already stopped," Henry said as he finished adjusting the sling. His voice had taken on a professional tone, the kind of voice he had learned to use with patients. "Now, I'd like to wash this blood off. Miss Le Bris, if you wouldn't mind pouring a little water over my hands, I'd greatly appreciate it. And Alison, perhaps you could get the soap out of that first aid pack." He handed a container of treated water to Sandrine.

"Not necessary," Jensen said. He fired a burst into the side of Henry's chest, causing the big man to fly over the log and jerk spasmodically for a second before becoming still.

Sam squirmed wildly away from the direction Henry had fallen, and Sandrine screamed as Jensen swung the rifle toward the women.

Alison was doubled over, retching and crying at the same time, and Sandrine now had both hands over her face and was shaking her head, saying , "No, no, no, no."

"Yes," Jensen said. "A big, fucking yes. What did you expect? You think I could trust him for a second? I saw how the three of you had worked things out. But now it's just you two, one paralyzed grandfather, an old man with a bow and a few arrows, and whatever this taped-up thing here is." His face had become grayer and more creased, the lines around his eyes forming dark webs.

Jensen stooped so that he could look closely at the portion of Sam's face not covered by duct tape. Sam's eyes widened, and he shook his head. Jensen reached a hand out and fingered the tibal badge on Sam's shirt.

"Tribal cop, huh? Well, the sensible thing would be to shoot you right now." He stood back and seemed to study Sam.

"But I just might need some kind of official trade goods to go along with these ladies." He motioned at Sandrine and Alison with the rifle. "I'm sure you didn't think I would just kill women, or girls? You behave and I'll let you both go. I promise. Honest Injun. Now our next step is to return to the spot where I collected that impressive arrow, and the two of you will walk in front of me for insurance. Back across the river."

Alison lead the way to the water and began to wade across with Sandrine beside her. The two women held hands on the slippery stones, and Jensen walked a few feet behind, the rifle held outward in his right hand.

When the three were on the other side and climbing up the bank, the face of Xavier Two-Bears appeared from behind one of the tents. When the others were out of sight, he stepped around the tent, dropping the roll of toilet paper onto the ground and staring across the river. Sam began squirming and kicking, and Two-Bears walked close to him, grasped a corner of the tape over his mouth, and ripped it free, clapping a hand instantly across Sam's lips to silence his scream.

When Sam seemed quiet, Two-Bears removed his hand and stepped back. "Can I trust you, Sam?" he asked.

"Untape me, goddammit. Trust me for what?"

"Not to shoot anybody except maybe that one bastard."

"You've known me all my life. You think I go around killing people? You lost your mind, too? Who are these people and why was somebody supposed to pay you?"

"You shot at Jake."

"Not at him. I just tried to scare Jake."

"All right, but we don't have much time. I sort of rented out the canyon to this militia group for private training. Nobody was supposed to know about it."

"That's why you wanted Jake out of here. How much?"

Two-Bears picked up Jake's folding Buck knife, opened it, and cut the tape off Sam. "Five thousand for five days." He turned and looked at the AR-15s on the ground, picked one up and held it awkwardly, examining it closely, and then shook his head. Leaning the rifle gently against the log, he grabbed the .30-.30.

"You bastard. We were partners on the elk deal, but you didn't even tell me about this."

"They were different deals, Sam. You take that fancy assault weapon. I'd just shoot my nuts off or yours with something like that. I didn't go to Harvard to be no hero, but I guess we don't have much choice."

"I guess the hell not," Sam said. "Given the fact that you invited a bunch of lunatic murderers onto the reservation. That motherfucker is a psychopathic killer. But if I was you I wouldn't use a .30-.30 that's been smashed all to hell. Better take one of those." He nodded toward the AR-15s.

Xavier turned with the .30-.30 and headed for the river, with Sam following, muttering, "Your ass."

The two men began to wade across, Xavier once again holding the rifle out like a Hollywood warrior dressed for dinner. Water squished inside his expensive boots, and his narrow heels caught and wedged between river stones. He felt huge blisters on the toes and heels of both feet. When he reached the far side, he fell to his knees and grasped roots to pull himself up the crumbling bank, pushing the rifle ahead of himself. Sam climbed up effortlessly beside him.

47   Avrum Goldberg lay curled between two granite boulders the size of pickup trucks, each of which had tumbled some millennia before from the cliffs hundreds of feet above the river's western shore. For thousands of years the boulders had stood where their parallel trajectories had deposited them, just at the edge of the low August river, so that the water swept out of a deep eddy a few hundred yards

upstream, spread smoothly along a gravel bar, picked up its pace across a rocky riffle, and then straightened to collide with the lower buttress of the first boulder, lap upward with a faint white froth, and curl into the second boulder before slip-streaming southward into a shadowy cutbank.

At flood stage, during the wild spring snowmelt, the river threw great logs and even large rocks against the granite, scarring and polishing it. Debris piled up on the shoreward side, beaver-gnawed sticks, moldering pine needles, decaying branches, in a dark brown drift. Death had fitted Avrum Goldberg, in his pale brown elk and deerskin, his long graying black hair, and dark flesh, to the current-bent debris, so that he seemed to belong comfortably. The osprey lifting a trout from the riffles and swinging toward its upstream nest didn't notice the anthropologist, and the pair of bald eagles, still accompanied in their high circling by last year's nestling, saw nothing out of the ordinary. Just inches from one submerged moccasin tip, a twelve-inch rainbow trout rose to a mayfly and sank again to lie in the shadow of the stone.

Shorty Luke looked long at his friend before lifting the body with a hand under each arm and pulling Avrum upward to the dry pine needles of the forest floor. Taking off his green nylon rain shell, Shorty laid the jacket over Avrum's bloody arms and chest, leaving the open eyes to watch the circling eagles. Shorty spoke a few quiet words and poured a thin line of pollen between himself and Avrum. Then Shorty returned to Jake Nashoba, who lay in a similar position in the root wad hole, his eyes alert to the bit of sky, twisted roots, and fragments of trees in his vision.

"Our brother was sure good with that bow," Shorty said to the unresponsive ranger. "I guess he must've practiced a lot." He picked up the bow and fitted an arrow to the string, sighting upward toward the treetops. "We used to have to ride around on horses aiming bows and arrows in movies, but I got to admit, Jacob, that I don't have the slightest damn idea how to use one of these things."

"He's coming back right now," Jake tried to say, but only his eyes moved. He could feel the shifting pressure of the earth that measured the approach of the white man. But the man wasn't alone.

"It's not so different from before, is it?" Jessie appeared at the edge of the root wad hole, peering down at the ranger. Shorty gave no sign of noticing.

"You weren't really much more alive then, were you, Grandfather?" Jessie went on. "Sure, you walked around, read those books, came down here to fish, and stuff like that. But all that time you were just watching, not really doing anything. August is a cruel month, isn't it? Everything is ripe and ready to become seed. The big clouds come and that one throws lightning all over the place. The fish are probably hungry and getting fat for winter just like the bears and everything else. You feel the snow just over there somewhere, and you want to plant seeds, too, seeds that will lie there all winter and then go yelling and laughing in the spring."

Jessie sat with his feet over the edge of the hole. "Pretty weak philosophizing, isn't it? Well, I was a history major and didn't go to class much anyway. But my point, Grandfather, is that you and I are now changed, we don't know for how long, and we just have to look at the world from this new vantage point for a while. I, for example, am fulfilling somebody's vision quest now, in actuality. And though I'm not what she expected, I think I'm pretty good."

Shorty stood and lifted the bow. He notched an arrow on the gut string and flexed the recurve of the powerful, sinew-backed bow, looking intently toward the trees.

"Shorty Luke finally knows they're coming," Jessie said to Jake. "I'm afraid there isn't much I can do. It's Shorty's story now, with lots of potential for clichéd violence, retribution, and so on like those movies he was in."

"Shush," Shorty said, looking at Jessie. "For a dead person you talk a heck of a lot. In fact, Nephew, you ain't any different than when you was alive."

279

Jessie stared at Shorty in surprise. "I didn't know," he began, but Shorty cut him off.

"Course I heard all of that yammering. Just didn't want to encourage you. It reminded me of a couple of movies where the hero talked everybody's ears off before kicking the bucket. The difference is, you're doing it after."

"Well, Uncle, I hope you can hear those ones as well as Jake and I can."

Shorty looked down at Jake. "That true, Jacob? You hear them, too?"

Jake replied in the affirmative with his eyes.

"He should, since that one is already pointing his gun at you." Jessie nodded toward the trees where Jensen stood in the clearing with the assault rifle resting against his shoulder and his hand on the trigger. The left arm was in a sling across his chest. In front and to the side of Jensen stood Alison and Sandrine. Up the slope twenty feet lay the body of Walter, with an arrow sticking out of the chest.

"Don't try the cowboys-and-Indians stuff," Jensen yelled weakly. "I'll bet you don't even know how to use that bow now that I killed the real Indian."

Shorty pulled the bow back as hard as he could and let an arrow fly. The arrow angled awkwardly away to his right, and he shook his hand in pain. Before he could fit another arrow, Jensen was laughing and urging the women before him. They crossed the space to stand a few feet from Shorty.

"I'm going to shoot you, old man," Jensen said, "but the way I feel it seems anticlimactic to just do it. There should be some kind of meaningful dialogue first."

Shorty shrugged. "A guy could fill that in afterwards. That part's easy. Cut and retake stuff."

Jensen smiled, the smile curving into a grimace. "But it would be more dramatic to shoot these two young women first. So many options. Maybe I should finish off the ranger while you're all forced to watch. I see the brightness of your eyes, Nashoba, so I know you're still with us. Your friend who put the arrow in me made the whole episode much more interesting, but I wasn't trained by SEAL and SpecOps vets to kill paralyzed rangers, helpless old men, and unarmed women. Although it may well be that my teachers did a lot of that themselves." Jensen's shoulders sagged, the rifle tilting slightly toward the earth.

Sandrine suddenly pirouetted on the heel of her left foot, throwing her arms out for balance, and hurled herself through the air, striking Jensen directly on the bandaged wound. Jensen screamed in pain and fell forward into the pit, landing across Jake. At once, however, he was on his knees, the rifle still in his hand and now aimed at Jake's head.

"You fucking bitch!" he yelled at the rim of the hole. "Do you realize how goddamned much that hurt? I ought to blow Nashoba's brains out and smear them all over your fucking face. Now if you don't show yourself up there in ten seconds this ranger's head is going to be compost."

Alison looked over the edge. "Please don't," she said. "Don't kill him."

Sandrine appeared beside Alison. "Kill me, not Alison's grandfather."

Jensen climbed awkwardly out of the hole, using his feet and knees so he could keep the rifle pointed at Jake, his face knotted grimly. Once on top he turned the gun toward the women and Shorty, who stood in line.

"That's stupid. I mean, he's ninety-nine percent dead and you're one hundred percent alive. Does it make sense that I should spare him and kill you? Jesus. I'm tired. You're all dead." He pointed the gun at Shorty, and there was a single shot. Jensen looked down at his own stomach, where a splotch of blood had appeared. "How'd you do that?" he said to Shorty. There was another shot, and Jensen spun around, losing his grip on the rifle and falling to one knee. Blood began to spread across his shirt on his stomach and right shoulder. "I'll be damned," he muttered.

"Don't make any facile jokes," Jessie said. "Violent scenes shouldn't be tempered with wit or jokes, or they lose their force, right, Uncle Luke?"

Xavier Two-Bears approached the group, holding the little lever-action .30-.30 in front of him. Sam walked behind, peering around the chairman.

"I hit him, didn't I?" Two-Bears said in amazement.

"I can't believe you hit anything with that gun," Sam said, stepping up beside Two-Bears.

"Too predictable," Shorty Luke said. "The minute Two-Bears showed up back there at camp with that rifle and started following you, everybody knew this would happen. Let's try it different. Eighty-six that and do a retake."

Shorty gestured toward Sandrine with his chin. "And way back when Jessie told Jake about you studying some kind of fighting in China or somewhere, it was like the camera focusing on a gun over the fireplace. I saw all this stuff when I was out there in Hollywood, and it used to drive me crazy that they didn't think of new ways to do it. So we've got to think of something else."

"You mean I'm not supposed to be shot again?" Jensen said, getting to his feet. "That's a fucking relief." The blood had disappeared from his camouflage shirt except for that around the arrow wound.

"Maybe," Shorty said. "But you shouldn't swear so much, white man."

"What about Jake?" Jessie put in.

"Well, Jake's not predictable, or hackneyed, as they say. Seems pretty original to have him down in a hole like that. He's the hero, right?"

"Maybe the wolf should tear out Jensen's throat," Jessie offered, becoming the wolf as he spoke.

"Spirit wolves don't do that," Shorty said.

"How about if I just shoot all of you?" Jensen looked at Shorty hopefully. "Nobody would expect that, I mean, the bad guy just killing everybody and going home, back to his rich grandfather, beautiful women, fast cars, paramilitary hobby, and so on. The good guys all dead as hell and the bad guy unpunished. You've never seen that on television."

"Too postmodern," Sandrine said. "Or too *noir*."

"Don't you know a story, Uncle Shorty?" Alison asked.

Shorty looked at the girl appreciatively. "Maybe. This worthy opponent of Jake's has already lost the use of one arm. If somebody cut off his leg, we could imagine that he went up to the sky and sent lightning down. But Mrs. Edwards wouldn't like me messing with that story."

"Back to the old plot?" Jessie asked. "Nobody would expect the same thing again."

"Could be," Shorty said.

"Now wait a goddamned minute." Jensen had picked up the rifle again. "I vote for total annihilation, bad guy victorious, and all that. Okay, the chief comes blazing away out of the woods just as we knew he would, but he can't hit the broad side of a barn because he's never shot a gun before and that's not much of a gun anyway. His retarded friend there is too frightened to do anything."

"Retarded?" Sam lifted the pistol.

"So I blast the chief and the tribal cop, much to everyone's shock. See, they expect the chief to be a kind of surprise hero, but he's ineffectual and just gets blown away. Then I kill everybody, finishing with a dramatic speech to the helpless ranger and a bullet between his eyes. Camera pans back to take in the whole scene, pine trees, river, clouds overhead, slight wind ruffling clothes. Very peaceful and ironic. Last frame is me walking away through all this beautiful nature."

"That's good," Jessie said. "I like that."

"Cut," Shorty added. "Mrs. Edwards wouldn't like it."

"Maybe Mr. Jensen should just surrender," Alison interjected. "That would surprise everyone. Then we could all walk out, carrying my grandfather on a stretcher, and turn Mr. Jensen over to the police." She looked at Xavier. "I don't know if you would have to be turned in, too, Grandfather. But you didn't really do anything bad anyway."

"Grandfather, schmandfather, I'm surrendering to nobody," Jensen said. "Holy shit," he added, staring down at Jake.

The earth had opened up, and two enormous mandibles framed by spider legs reached out and seized Jake. In a moment he was gone, dragged into a hole that closed at once.

"My idea," Shorty said.

"Good one," Jessie replied admiringly.

Shorty turned to Alison. "Don't worry, your grandfather has gone home."

Sandrine, pirouetting on the ball of her left foot, moved in a full circle until the heel of her right boot struck Jensen hard on the temple. Jensen collapsed, the rifle sliding away from him and into the root wad hole.

Jensen lay on the ground, his eyes closed in pain and his good right hand holding the side of his head. "I've had about enough of this," he said, keeping his eyes shut. "Damn, that hurts."

"Tie his hands," Shorty said to Sandrine and Alison.

"With what?"

"There's always something," Shorty said. "There was always something to do it with."

Alison looked around and then walked fifty feet toward the river, returning with an armful of wild grapevines.

"See," Shorty said. "There's always something."

"Careful with that shoulder." Jensen tilted his head to the left as the women began tying his hands behind him. "Hurts like a sonofabitch."

"Maybe we should have lightning hit him while he's tied," Jessie said.

"Maybe you should go away now, Jessie," Shorty replied. "I think it's time for a poignant scene in which you have to go to the land of the dead, leaving your loved ones behind."

"No," Alison yelled. "Not yet."

"What will I do without my animal helper?" Sandrine added.

"He's no animal helper," Two-Bears said. "He's properly a ghost."

"If not now, when?" Shorty asked. "New role." He nodded at Jessie. "Ghost now, just like Xavier says. Whistling in the dark, bringing bad dreams, all that."

Jessie drew himself up to full height, crossed his arms, and peered down at the group with great dignity. Lightning flashed behind him, and they all saw its flare through his transluscence. In a moment he was gone.

"Jessie!" Alison wailed.

"Well done. To every thing there is a season," Shorty said. "I wonder how Mrs. Edwards is getting along with Domingo."

"Someone will have to come back down for Professor Goldberg." Sandrine looked toward the river.

"Not to mention the other bodies all over the place. This is going to be great for tourism. Anyone know how to get out of here?" Xavier asked.

"Sure. Right over that ridge there, not very far." Shorty nodded. "Avrum would have wanted it this way."

"Avrum would have wanted not to get shot, I'll bet," Jensen replied morosely from where he stood with his hands tied behind him.

"You didn't get shot again, at least," Jessie said, materializing abruptly and then vanishing.

Jensen shivered. "I hope he doesn't keep doing that."

"Last cameo, I think," Shorty said.

"Now what?" Xavier held the rifle by its barrel and leaned on it like a cane.

"Now you shoot yourself if you keep doing that," Shorty answered. "Surprise ending."

Two-Bears irritably lifted the rifle. A rooster crowed from the cliffs across the river. "You know that story about Vulva Woman?" Two-Bears asked, looking at Shorty.

"Now we go home," Alison said. "No more stories. We'll follow you, Grandfather."

Shorty looked at her carefully for a moment. "No, Granddaughter, it's your turn. You lead."

Alison began walking, with the others following in a single line. Behind the surviving twin, Sam Baca said, "Does somebody want to explain what the hell's gone on here?"

"Well," Shorty Luke glanced over his shouder at Sam. "It is said . . ." He looked back toward the treeline above them and was silent for a moment as he kept walking.

"It is said that Jacob Nashoba went home."